Thunder crashed and t̶͟͞ ̶l̶i̶g̶h̶t̶n̶i̶n̶g̶ strobed again and the banjo broke into a Mexican-sounding tune.

Juli turned to see a black-clad woman wringing her hands and wafting straight at her.

The banjo grew louder and the woman's specter grew more agitated.

"All of those ghosts were warning spirits," Anna Mae said. "But everything I've read about ghosts says they're not supposed to be able to cross running water."

The ghost was halfway across and from about midknee up she was a deeper blackness against the shining black water.

"Around here in the summer, the Rio Grande don't usually run so deep you'd drown, less you laid down in it," Willie said.

The ghost glided further out and was covered about to the hips when she let out a long banshee wail. Willie shone his flashlight into the water.

The light bounced off wriggling, snapping forms clinging to the black robes and dripping from the sleeves and mantilla like fat whipping fringe.

Willie whistled low, the flashlight jiggling. Juli saw that his hands were shaking.

"Shee-ee-ee-it," Brose said. "Lookit them cottonmouths. We ain't crossin' here tonight or no time soon. . . ."

Praise for *The Songkiller Saga, Volume 1, Phantom Banjo*:

"This book is fantasy, fun, and must reading—not because it's fun, but because Ms. Scarborough is a highly skilled storyteller."

—DIRTY LINEN

Also by Elizabeth Scarborough

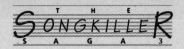

THE SONGKILLER SAGA 3

STRUM AGAIN?

ELIZABETH SCARBOROUGH

SPECTRA ™

BANTAM BOOKS

NEW YORK · TORONTO · LONDON · SYDNEY · AUCKLAND

STRUM AGAIN? (Songkiller Saga #3)
A Bantam Spectra Book/May 1992

SPECTRA and the portrayal of a boxed "s" are trademarks of Bantam Books, a division of Bantam Doubleday Dell Publishing Group, Inc.

Song "I Will Go" composed by Roddy McMillan
copyright Jean McMillan.

ISBN 0-553-29705-8

Published simultaneously in the United States and Canada

Bantam Books are published by Bantam Books, a division of Bantam Doubleday Dell Publishing Group, Inc. Its trademark, consisting of the words "Bantam Books" and the portrayal of a rooster, is Registered in U.S. Patent and Trademark Office and in other countries. Marca Registrada. Bantam Books, 666 Fifth Avenue, New York, New York 10103.

PRINTED IN THE UNITED STATES OF AMERICA

OPM   0 9 8 7 6 5 4 3 2 1

For Bob and Kay Zentz, friends of the work and folk music torch-bearers. Thanks.

ACKNOWLEDGMENTS

Thanks to Victory Music Cooperative and Chris Lunn for information, inspiration, entertainment and friends. Thanks to Michael Smith—for permission to print the lyrics to "This Here Mandolin," (words and music copyright 1975 by Michael Peter Smith, Bird Avenue Publishing [BMI]). Thanks to Tim and Marian Henderson—for permission to quote "Dust" (copyright 1977 Snake Hollow Publishing [BMI] from *Sandspurs* cassette). Thanks to Andrew Calhoun —for permission to quote "Long-Legged Lover," which is a great song I used in a not-so-great scene I've since cut. Thanks to Jim Page—for "Anna Mae," (from *Visions in My View* copyright 1986 Flying Fish Records Inc., Jim Page Whid-Isle Music [BMI]) and to Larry Long—for writing *his* song "Anna Mae," available on RUN FOR FREEDOM, copyright © 1985 Larry Long, Flying Fish Records Inc. [BMI]

Thanks to Tania Opland—for general support, advice, criticism and willingness to strain her eyes reading the manuscript. Thanks to William Pint, Felicia Dale, and Tom Lewis—research assistance. Thanks to Allen Wayne Damron for so many magical performances and good road adventures. Thanks to Charles de Lint and characters for keeping faerie, fantasy, and folk music thriving north of the border. Thanks to Suzette Haden Elgin, C.J. Cherryh, Jane Fancher, Robin Bailey, Warren and Gigi Norwood, Mercedes Lackey, Mark Simmons, Emma Bull and Will Shetterley for agreeing to make a fictional journey to ConTingent. Thanks to Okon, especially Tom and Mary Wallbank, Marilyn and Curtis Berry, Randy and Lisa Farran, Richard and Lyn Morgan, for hospitality and inspiration, and to filkers everywhere both in and out of tune and on and off key. Thanks to McShane Glover for liaison, expediting, and general support. Thanks to Janice Endresen and Bob Crowley for books, walks, talks, music and saving the forests. Thanks to Bennie and Danna Garcia for information, inspiration, and wonderful tapes and records to keep me going and to Rittie Ward, Annette Mercier and

Barb the bartender from the Ruston Inn for inspiration. Thanks also to Tom Paxton for getting me through Vietnam with *his* music and John McCutcheon for the wisdom to use his time, energy, and clout to work within the system to make sure that The Songkiller Saga remains mere fantasy.

STRUM
AGAIN?

RETURN OF THE
WAYFARING STRANGERS
▲▲▲

Seven long years had passed and gone since a herd of devils drove the old songs, the power songs, the charm songs, from these United States of America. Most people didn't even notice when it happened, because people hadn't been singing the songs themselves for years. But in fact, getting rid of the songs and their singers was as good a plan for bad as ever there was, because from ancient times the songs have contained spells to ward off the worst of the evils the devils want to work upon humankind.

I was with a certain small group of musicians when they first discovered the songs were going missing, I mourned with them as their friends and colleagues were crippled, diseased, or murdered by the devils and their minions. And I was with them when the magic banjo Lazarus told my friends to take the songs to their roots. I traveled with the singers to England and Scotland, where, in spite of great dangers of both the bodily and the spiritual kind (and I mean spiritual as in spirits, ghosts, ha'ants), they began retrieving the songs from the depths of the past. I myself was personally possessed by the very gentlemanly ghost of the great ballad collector, author, and lawman Sir Walter Scott, and he even took me back through the curtain that veils this world from the next to meet his relatives.

As soon as I was pretty sure my friends were safe, however, I said good-bye to Sir Walter, dropping him off at his tomb, and made my way back to this country, where for the past six years or so I've been tellin' what happened to the songs, what happened to my friends, and how the singers are returning to bring the songs back again. Every time I tell this story somebody among the folks I'm telling it to, somebody with a good ear and eyes inside their mind that can see the pictures I'm telling them about, spreads the stories a little farther. Oh, they forget parts sometimes and make up something that sounds good to fill in the holes, but that's okay. That's what my friends call the folk process. It doesn't hurt a thing and sometimes makes the story more interesting like.

Also, sometimes, as in this case, when I got too busy with the practical matters of meeting, greeting, transporting, and arranging for the safe housing of my friends when they came back, I got too blamed busy to see the whole story. In that case I find it best to mostly let it be told by someone else, an heir to my other stories. Probably by now, like other interested parties, you've heard how it all began either from one of us or from one of the people who's heard us, in person, in letters, by computer network, telephone, legend, report, rumor, or just plain gossip. If you haven't, it doesn't matter a great deal, you'll catch on.

Anyway, like I started to say, I was busy as a cranberry merchant at Christmas during the time this story is talking about, and more than usual I was part of the story rather than the teller, so a lot of this part is told about me not by me, in the interests of modesty.

CHAPTER I
▲▲▲

The cowboy they called Ute didn't look Native American, Shayla St. Michael thought, but then you never could tell. As Shayla and the rest of the small band of Californian ecofeminists gathered around the camp fire, Ute fixed them with a sardonic glance and continued sharpening his blue pencil with his pocket knife. He'd already cooked the women a nice vegetarian meal with a few edible nonendangered native plants and onions from the Valley, piñon nuts imported from New Mexico, and a little tofu imported from the soy fields of Kansas.

The smoke that rose, some might say fragrantly, to the sky, was authentically coming from a fire of dried unspecified animal dung. He used to tell the tour groups which animals, but that had proved unwise. Unspecified was safest.

Now, sated with their politically correct meal, the women sat around the camp fire and watched the smoke spiral toward the moon.

"I think this is lovely. No television, no radio, no computers—" began Barbara Harrington-Smith, a corporate tax lawyer.

"I disagree," said Shayla, who was a graphic artist for a large publisher. "I'm bored. We walked a great deal, true, but I miss my evening jog even though I do understand that we might trample indigenous wildlife of the fanged serpentine variety and be immediately chastised for our thoughtlessness. And I did as instructed and didn't bring any work."

"Also," added Heather-Jon Argulijan, "this fire stinks."

"I could tell you a mite more about the interestin' things that have happened on this ranch," Ute said in his quaint western twang. He was not offensively macho. Though the ecofeminist group had requested that their guide be a cowgirl, the tour director explained that the cowgirls were all attending management seminars that week or competing for top prize money in the rodeos and wouldn't be available but assured them that Ute, while absolutely an authentic member of his profession, was also extremely progressive in his attitudes and in fact was the one who

insisted on bumper stickers that proclaimed "ERA Will Rise
Again" for all of the ranch's Jeeps and pickups.

"Oh, God, not another environmental impact statement,"
Heather-Jon moaned. "I'm sorry, Barbara, but I just can't take
any more."

Barbara sometimes thought of Heather-Jon as the weakest
link, but she was also usually a lot of fun, and fun seemed to be
what was missing.

Ute grinned at Heather-Jon in a noncondescending, brotherly,
and respectful way. "Why, ma'am, as important as such a thing
is to all of us, I don't reckon I'd undertake to tell you women
about it orally like. That's somethin' that it's only fittin' should
be read carefully in big old folios of recycled hard copy. No'm,
what I had in mind was to tell you the story of how an old hand
on this here ranch and some compadres of his, includin' yours
truly—"

"All men?" asked Shayla in a still-bored tone that indicated
she was just sure they all would be. She inched a little farther
from the fire and slipped on her wool socks and pulled on a
poncho her roommate had woven for her from the wool of or-
ganically grown sheep.

"Hell no! Why, there was Sister Julianne Martin and Sister
Anna Mae Gunn, Sister Terry Pruitt and Sister Ellie Randolph,
not to mention Sister Gussie Turner, who did the advance work
and told me most of what I'm about to tell you."

"Isn't this a little—you know, out in the sticks, as a place to
start a movement?" Heather-Jon asked.

"Good as any, better'n most," he said. "There's songs in this
story too, and as I sing 'em while I'm tellin' you about how they
was used, I'd appreciate it if y'all would join in, especially if you
can do some nice harmony or play a mouth harp or anything."

"Comb and tissue okay?" asked Mary Armstrong.

Ute's eyes, pale as prairie skies and framed by wrinkles only a
little leathery since he was careful to use plenty of sunscreen, lit
up. "That's fine, Ms. Mary. Fact is, I always have wished I could
get the hang of a comb and tissue and never have. I'd be much
obliged if you could maybe give me some pointers? I'd be glad to
show you a thing or two about ropin' in exchange."

"That would be acceptable," Mary said gruffly, but she
squirmed around a little, clearly pleased.

"Well, then, for your information, ladies—and I use the term
'ladies' as one of respect and admiration and in no sense as a

restrictive or class-conscious kinda thing—I happen to be by profession a cowboy poet."

"What the devil is a cowboy poet?" asked Heather-Jon.

"I couldn't have put that question better myself, ma'am, but if you'll bear with me, I believe I'd rather not say right now. In line with the amended Code of the West, I aim to show and not tell you all about it. First off, I want you to imagine a little woman about sixty, sixty-five years old, but quick on her feet and strong from lots of dancin' and a good judge of people and a way with 'em from years of bartendin'. She had thick curly hair that she just plain let go gray, as if there was nothin' wrong in the world with that."

"And do you think there is?" demanded Barbara, whose well-styled bob was salt and pepper.

"No, ma'am. Just shows she wasn't one to put all them chemicals into the water system. Besides, lotsa people pay to make their hair lighter. What's wrong with just lettin' nature change it, is what I always say. Anyway, this woman had gone through some tremendous changes in her life because she happened to enjoy a certain type of entertainment with which we cowboy poets are also in sympathy, which is how I came to hear this story. You see, there were a bunch of devils, and I don't mean only of the strictly Judeo-Christian brand, mind you, more what the Indians might call the evil spirits. These folks decided to eliminate this particular type of entertainment—oh, hell, call a spade a spade. They used to call it folk music, though strictly speakin' that's not always an accurate term. Anyhow, these devils, who were rich and sophisticated and behind all the troubles in this world that people didn't dream up all by themselves, decided to take away the music that sometimes makes people feel a little better about themselves and their work. Gives 'em a kind of what we cowboy poets would call an eagle's-eye view of their situation, helps 'em get their lives back in control."

"Like a therapist?" Heather-Jon asked.

"Yeah, but you don't have to make appointments, and most folks could do it themselves even though sometimes they hired other people to do it for them—which is not as good but better than a poke in the eye with a sharp stick (which was all the devils had for them). Anyhow, for a space there—and y'all may not be too well aware of it, but me and my compadres were—these devils by killin' and connivin' managed to get rid of most of the most important singers of the songs and make everybody forget the words to songs people had been singin' for hundreds of years.

After a while, they even made people forget the melodies, so the songs were gone from memory in this country. Everybody forgot every song sung by every dead singer. When the great Sam Hawthorne died on the very day the Library of Congress folk-music collection got blowed up, almost all the songs in the country were wiped from people's minds. You notice I said people's minds. Sam had this magic banjo which he passed on before he died, and it remembered the songs, though nobody knew how come. Now, this magical banjo eventually passed into the hands of a very small group of people. One of them was this woman I'm tellin' you about, Ms. Gussie Turner. Others were the women I mentioned previously, Julianne Martin, Anna Mae Gunn, Ellie Randolph, and Terry Pruitt. All fine musicians except for Gussie and Ms. Randolph, who was a more academic kind of lady. Then there was Mr. Brose Fairchild, a gentleman of more than one color who was a crackerjack blues man and purveyor of Baltic ethnic tunes. And last but by no means least Mr. Willie MacKai, who used to work right here on this ranch where we are now working—though that's another story. These were the people who came together and ended up as the guardians of Lazarus, Sam's magic banjo.

"Well, Lazarus knew good and well that Gussie and Willie and their friends couldn't get back all those forgotten songs as long as they stayed in these United States, so the banjo helped them write a song in which it told them to go overseas to the British Isles, where the roots of much of American folk music were still dug in deep and sendin' out shoots. They went over there and with some help from a bunch of ghosts, includin' that of the famous writer Sir Walter Scott, his ancestor the Wizard Michael Scott, and a bunch of their kinfolk, they got back the songs. Then they went after songs from other places than Scotland, such as Ireland, France, Spain, and the like.

"In the meantime Ms. Gussie, who had become a hell of a storyteller by virtue of bein' possessed—though mind you in a very respectable and respectful way—by the ghost of Sir Walter, came back here to do a little low-profile advance publicity.

"Now there was one of these devils, a redheaded user of many aliases, who was a little more complicated than the rest of them and tougher to figure out. She was the chief devil in charge of debauchery. Among other things the musicians learned in Scotland, one was that she used to be the Queen of Fairyland and had come down in the world since then. So she was the one who both helped them and hindered them when the musicians

wanted to go into the ballad world to reclaim the old songs that would help them release the rest of 'em. Of course, as a devil she was bound to uphold what the rest of the devils wanted, which was to try to keep the musicians from living through the songs, making them their own, and bringing them back to this country to revive all the other songs with the powerful magic contained in the oldest and strongest ballads.

"However—as she told the other devils—as the official De-bauchery Devil she was in charge of wine, women, and song. Musicians were some of her best people, and she was always a little ambivalent about the whole devilish operation to kill them off along with the music. Also, she was always a little wild, as if she was high on some of her own stuff. It seemed to Gussie that the redheaded devil's unpredictableness made her the worst devil of them all—she was like the old mule who'd be nice to you for two weeks just to get a chance to kick you.

"So Gussie was wary when this carrot-topped character plucked her off a nice reliable bus to give her a wild ride in a fast red sports car."

▲▲▲

At least there was nothin' dull about this new life of hers, Gussie Turner thought as she held onto the dashboard for dear life. Beside her the redheaded woman held a quart-size Sipeez cup full of alcoholic beverage and gunned the red sports car down the mountain.

The redheaded woman—who wasn't a real woman at all, as Gussie knew, but the Debauchery Devil herself, formerly Her Majesty the Queen of Faerie—turned red eyes and sharp teeth in Gussie's direction and grinned. "So. Long time no see, ducks. It took a bit of doing to catch up with you. What-ever have you been up to?"

"Oh, a little of this and a little of that," Gussie said. "I might ask you the same thing. Last time I saw you, it looked like you were going to have some explaining to do to all your buddies in the Department of Bad Works. Then you tell me you've been rehabilitated, and I'm afraid I don't quite under-stand what that means. Habilitated back into what? A better devil, a fairy queen or—dare I hope—maybe a relatively rea-sonable human being?"

"There's no need to get *lewd,* dear. Actually, I suppose you could say I've been pursuing both the first and the last of those choices—in a way. Once one is in the Company, you

know, one is well and truly in, and there's nowhere to go but
down. Naturally they weren't very pleased with me for letting
your lot out of my spell, but as I told them, you cheated fair
and square and I had no choice in the matter at all. I did hold
out hope that you'd been the teeniest little bit corrupted, however. So now I'm on probation, more or less, under the direction of the Shame and Guilt Department and am also
answerable to the Corruption and Repression people. I'm still
pretty much in the same line of work, I just feel deliciously
naughty about it now."

"Serious drugs are a little more than naughty," Gussie said.

"Spare me. You sound just like my supervisor. Of course
they are, but I'm not allowed to use them nearly as much now.
The boss has withdrawn support for them in favor of something a bit less gauche, he says. But I shouldn't talk about such
things with a civilian. Look at you! You look—well, excuse
me, but you look old. What have you been doing with yourself
while all of your little friends have been tootling away in exile?"

"Part of the time I've been in exile too," Gussie said. "But
you knew that. You know everything that's been going on,
don't you? I've had reports of you followin' me around."

"Don't flatter yourself, lovey. If you could see my schedule,
you'd know how ridiculous that sounds. And what I have to do
these days—and do straight most of the time, mind you—is
just too sordid for words. Besides, a lot of it's boring. Spiking
the punch at AA picnics, hooking business people on prescrip-
tion drugs, convincing housepersons of the joys of clandestine
tippling and visiting neighbor housepersons of the opposite
gender."

"Serves you right," Gussie said. "But I'm afraid I wouldn't
worry about bein' bored for too long, if I was you. People are
a lot like cats—lock 'em out of one place where they can make
trouble, and they'll wriggle into another."

"Well, sure, and they already have. All that humanitarian
nonsense left over from the lefties who dominated the sixties
—and everybody knows, thanks to my colleagues, that all of
that sort were very immoral and did a lot of drugs—all their
ideas are out the window in favor of the old-fashioned American values. Equally deadly, of course, and every bit as destruc-
tive in their own way, but the problem is that they're not *my*
way. I can't even persuade a lot of these uptight asses to relax
a little, let up the tension. Guilt, shame, and psychological

pressure twisted tighter than thumbscrews—that's what's driving people bonkers now. Absolutely nothing in it for me."

"Don't you worry, honey. These things come in cycles. People can only take so much tension, and then they find some kinda outlet again."

"Do you really think so? That's what I'm hoping, of course. Why do you think I've come to meet you? I'm very very glad to see those friends of yours returning here, if you want the truth. The boss is smug about the progress he's made with his programs here and in the Middle East, Russia, and the People's Republic of China. Backed off on the British Isles, of course, though he doesn't put it that way. Still too many amateurs doing the music there."

"We know," Gussie smiled.

"And he thought it would be so easy in Canada, but there's an unforeseen complication that crept in while his attention was elsewhere." She sounded rather pleased as she cleared her throat and said, "Some of my former subjects, it seems, migrated up there after my downfall and somehow or other have bonded with the native bogies and sprites and whatnot. And of course, my people have always been very involved with the sort of thing *your* people do—"

"Music, Torchy," Gussie Turner said, not unkindly, using the name by which she had known the Debauchery Devil in Britain. "Folk music. Can't you even say it anymore?"

"I suppose I could," Torchy said. "But I was trying to give you a break and not call attention to this little conversation. If I were to start tossing such terms about, someone might turn out to be listening, you know."

"You were saying about Canada?"

"Well, anyway, with my former subjects so lively in the cities and countryside, all sorts of people are still actively singing and playing you-know-what. Even though there are a lot of paid performers and festivals and such happening, the power is still coming from a wide population base, and the boss hasn't been able to do more than seal the borders so the—er—perpetrators can't cross from one border to the other."

"I knew that," Gussie said. "So would your boss if he weren't such an illiterate sonofabitch. What's happened to music and the Faerie in Canada is in all of Caitlin Midhir's books. A couple of Lettie's musicians, Charles De Lint and Eileen McGann, turned us on to them."

"They're out of print in *this* country," the Debauchery Devil sighed. "Chairdevil used the Accounting Department to see to that. So Canada will have a bit of a reprieve, but ultimately we'll achieve our aim. You must know that."

"And just what is that aim?" Gussie asked, accepting the proffered Sipeez cup from Torchy as the redhead drove into a highway tunnel clinging to the mountainside. Gussie took a long swig from the cup, which held a mixture of her own invention called a tequila sun*set*.

"Why, honey," Torchy said, switching accents and personas so that she was no longer Torchy-Burns-the-English-pub-singer or the slightly more upscale former Queen of Faerie, but her American, Texican self, Lulubelle Baker of Lulubelle Baker's Petroleum Puncher's Paradise. "I thought you'd never ask. In some ways I'm just real excited about it because, as you may know, one of my former titles was Queen of the Air. If I'm not queen, at least I'm veep in charge of certain aspects of what goes *into* the air. Now we control all that, you see. What's on the air, what's in the news, what people read and hear and see. With that power, it's just a matter of time until we get at what we eventually mean to do.

"I am not givin' away a thing when I tell you this. We mean to corner us the market on myth. When we do, we'll have it all changed around and remade to suit us. You mortals will follow along like little ol' baa-lambs. Hell, honey, all you gotta do is take off your blinkers and look around you right now. It's happenin', sugar. It's happenin' already."

Gussie, who was from Amarillo herself, was a little more comfortable with Lulubelle—the persona the redhead had adopted in South Texas when she first attempted to seduce the late Sam Hawthorne's magic banjo, Lazarus, away from Willie MacKai. At least Lulubelle talked like a regular person and didn't pretend to be better than she ought to be.

Lulubelle was given more to smirks than upper-crust smugness and continued: "The songs are just a start—but they've been a pretty big obstacle. Don't think it's going to be easy for your little buddies to get back into the good old U.S. of A. and bring back them foreign songs we done lost in these parts. Americans want 'merican things now—and no whiny songs about people that ain't good enough or don't have the gumption to have a nice house, three cars, and all the other necessities of life."

"Those would be truly dull songs," Gussie said.

"You bet your cash box, sugar. That's why there ain't no more songs *a*-tall," Torchy-Lulubelle said.

"You're overdoing it, *sugar,"* Gussie said. "You sound more like a John Wayne movie now than a South Texas hooker."

"That don't make no nevermind. Give me another swig of that, will you? Bless me if it ain't dry as a desert out here." Then she cackled at her own wit because, as they emerged from the tunnel, the headlights no longer picked up snow and deep valleys but sand and cactus. "Welcome to Nevada," a sign said.

"What happened to the mountains?" Gussie asked Torchy-Lulubelle.

Her cackle faded to a silly giggle. "I thought I mentioned I'm not s'posed to get high anymore."

▲▲▲

Julianne Martin, Anna Mae Gunn, Brose Fairchild, Willie MacKai, Faron and Ellie Randolph, Terry Pruitt and her boyfriend Daniel Borg crouched beside the muddy bed of the Rio Grande. Julianne had become even more psychic in the last seven years, ever since she had spent a lot of time living in the bodies of long-dead ballad heroes. "Shush, Lazarus," she said to the magic banjo, which lay across Willie MacKai's back. Even muffled up in rags, it was still trying to noodle out "The Rivers of Texas." "I'm listening."

She heard a land full of silence and noise. Dogies, now scientifically slaughtered on the premises of their host ranches, no longer bawled, since they were pumped full of tranquilizers as well as other additives to make them as hefty and tasty as Brazilian beef. Since the cattle were stoned, cowboys no longer sang to them and could devote their spare time to reading Bible tracts, survivalist catalogs, and cleaning their weapons in anticipation of a chance to use them on something other than rattlesnakes and prairie dogs. Off to the west and up north in Oklahoma, on the Indian lands, drums were silent, voices stilled, powwows all commerce and no dancing, the night air full of the thud of fists, the roar of truck engines, the howls and screams of the injured. On the Mexican side of the river, behind her, the guitars were silent and the borders devoted to murder. No songs told the tales of the slain, or the exploits of the runners while big companies from the U.S. poured filth into the waters of the Rio Grande and

unsafe machinery chugged away, pumping poison into the
fragile desert air with the blessings of both governments.

Willie MacKai, who was a little more psychic himself these
days, put his arm around Juli and said, looking across the river
at the ranch land he used to patrol, "Ooo, déjà vu, huh?"

"I just don't see why we couldn't come back the normal
way," Terry Pruitt complained. She was tired, had been too
hot all day and now was too cold.

Willie MacKai said, "Because if we did, darlin', all our
troubles would have been for nothin'. They had to slack off on
us back in England where you live and the music is so strong,
but the sooner them music-hatin' devils figure out that we're
back and we got the goods with us, the sooner we're going to
have to think about what they're gonna do as well as what we
need to be doin'. I don't reckon they'll be foolin' around with
cute tricks this time, not if they can just get us outright." Not
that the devils ever had been fooling around exactly, except
for the Debauchery Devil, who had a sense of humor that was
way beyond warped.

In the time preceding the flight of Willie and his friends
and the banjo to the British Isles, musicians had been dying—
murdered, really, though it never appeared that way—not just
by ones and twos but in groups. Killed in fiery car and plane
crashes or dropping dead of diseases that were custom-made
to silence makers of music.

Willie had been more of a foolin'-around kind of guy back
then. He'd changed some and he knew it. Back in Scotland,
under a spell engineered by the long-dead Wizard Michael
Scott, ancestor of Sir Walter Scott, and the Debauchery Devil,
Willie and three others in the group had put in considerable
time living the lives depicted in ballads. The songs that it fell
to Willie to live in were not the rough-and-tumble kick-ass
adventure ballads he had always loved, not the cut-bait-and-
keep-moving kind. He'd seen the old times through the eyes
of young girls tossed around on those stormy years like pieces
of driftwood—used, abused, impregnated, murdered—and
he'd come to understand and care for those poor lost little
girls. Not only could he sing their songs now with conviction,
but something else inside him changed. He had started thinking of women a little differently. Not that he didn't still han-
ker after them. He felt more tenderhearted now and sort of,
well, not even brotherly was the right word. Sisterly, really. He
was having a hard time coming to terms with that and mostly

chose to ignore it and concentrate on what Anna Mae called their primary mission.

Once he and the others were freed of the spell, they spent the rest of their time learning songs and music as Willie had never learned them before—and he was someone who had already learned and forgotten maybe a thousand songs, maybe two thousand, though until the trip he had retained only a couple hundred of them.

He and his friends had gone to bring the songs back alive and they by-God had done it, Willie thought. He had amazed even himself. After he, Julianne Martin, Brose Fairchild, and Anna Mae Gunn had returned from ballad times with the help of counterenchantments their friends had conjured up, they had set about learning old and new music with a vengeance. All the music Willie had learned in his whole life before was like a drop in the bucket to the way he learned then. He had already known how to play five or six instruments, more or less. He learned to play a dozen others, learned to read music, from the necessity of helping Faron Randolph and the others revive songs that hadn't been sung in years, but *had* once had a little tune written down by some school-trained musician. He spent most of his days talking to and playing with musicians of all ages, all levels of skill, people who could play music and people who could just remember a few odd lyrics here and there. He learned the songs he himself had lived in dozens of variations, though sometimes there was only a line or two of difference. He learned the songs the others had lived and more besides. Not all the songs were good songs, or powerful, or funny, but sometimes even the bad ones had the power to evoke a piece of someone's life, or at least somebody else's opinion of it.

He learned to do something else he had never done much before too. That was to sit around and just play the music with other musicians—though he was a word man himself, with stories and scraps of poetry in his head all the time. He silently heard the words to the tunes he played with, or made some up as he went along. Faron Randolph did this constantly too. It used to be common, back in the old days before SWALLOW, when everybody felt fine about plundering everybody else's material, stealing a pinch of this and a handful of that and coming up with a new recipe that fit the current situation.

He had begun to feel a new way about the music and his

role in it at this time too. Always before he had been a performer. Although he was inclined to be generous with his spotlight and promote new talent, when he was performing he liked—as did most entertainers—to be the sole center of attention. For the past few years he had felt almost impatient during the times when it was his turn to share a new song with a new group of musicians, even though he knew that teaching songs was a big part of what he would be doing when he got home to the States. But he knew what he knew, and he didn't know what the others knew. The desire to know more and more songs, to sift and sort through them, investigating them as if they were a brothel full of beautiful women, developed into as much of a thirst as the one he had once had for booze and, while it fortunately didn't replace the lust he had for the ladies, it calmed it down considerably.

So here he was now, a changed man, focused and ready. Of course, just at the moment his new skills weren't as much use as those he had learned as a boy—skills learned at the same time he first began to love music, but having very little to do with it, except that those skills, like all others, were fodder for song. He remembered the lay of the land, when to move and when to be still, what was edible or provided water in a pinch, what to do if someone got heat stroke during the day.

"Once we're across, then what?" Brose asked.

"We'll call a cab," Dan said hopefully.

" 'Fraid not," Willie said. "We're in for a long walk to the road. If Gussie made it to the rendezvous point okay and didn't get stopped along the way, we'll have a ride."

"You should have let me call my folks," Ellie complained. "After all, they just live in Tulsa, and Gussie had to come from Washington state."

Willie didn't say anything, but Brose told her, "Your folks are good people, Ellie, but they ain't been smack in the middle of this like Gussie has. She knows enough to expect damn near anything to happen and be ready for it. You gotta admit some of the shit we been through would be a little startlin' to most individuals. While your mama and daddy was tryin' to sort it all out, they could be taken suddenly dead. They don't have Lazarus to help 'em the way we do, remember."

"Neither does Gussie," Faron said grimly.

CHAPTER II

▲▲▲

Now fully in Lulubelle Baker persona, the Debauchery Devil drove her red sports car across Nevada so fast even radar couldn't detect it. She screeched to a halt in Las Vegas.

"What are we stopping for?" Gussie asked.

"I'm sorry, sweetie, this is work," Lulubelle apologized. "This is one of my other responsibilities, one I kind of enjoy now that all my other pet projects have been modified to such a borin' extent. Come on in if you want to."

"I thought all your debaucheries had been done away with," Gussie said. "Surely gambling counts as one."

"Well, it's sort of an exception since it deals directly with money, and the boss feels that the connection to greed is a redeeming factor."

"Uh-huh," Gussie said, gawking at the neon like any rubberneck tourist. Well, what the hell. She figured that she was at least three days ahead of time already, since she had originally planned to take the glacially slow *Silver Snail* bus all the way from Seattle to San Francisco and switch there to a pickup truck belonging to a friend before driving for another day or so to get close to where she was now.

Night had fallen as they drove toward Las Vegas, but now, on the street, it was bright as day from the brilliantly flashing signs. Gussie lost Lulubelle in the crowd of people—some of them in jeans and sweats, some of them in fancy evening dress —milling around the one-armed bandits in one room, waiting for a show to begin in a hallway that looked as if it could hold a grand ball. In another direction, Gussie saw roulette wheels and heard the voices of the dealers, the exclamations of winners, and the swearing of losers. She also glimpsed a snatch of red hair. There were, of course, a lot of people with red hair there, many of them women, but that particular shade was the one she had been looking at for the last several hundred miles. Sure enough, there was the Debauchery Devil, who, having made a lightning change of clothing into a red-sequined strapless number, was all snuggled up to some boy who didn't look old enough to drink, much less gamble. The boy grinned as he raked in his winnings.

"I didn't think you ever did anything *nice* for anybody," Gussie said to the redhead.

"Why, sure, honey. In this place they call me Lady Luck. Now that I've encouraged that sweet young thing, he's going to be a true love of mine the rest of his life. Doubt if he'll ever get over me."

"I see."

"Oh, don't be so prim and schoolmarmish. Honestly, for a bartender you are the awfulest old prude."

"I'm just not sure I believe this," Gussie said. "You seem to be a whole passel of people."

The redhead deserted the young man with a peck on the cheek. "Okay, I'll show you," she told Gussie. "What's your pleasure?"

"I don't even play Lotto."

"Well, not *here* you don't, but if you wanted to I could fix it for you. To tell you the truth, I'm partial to poker myself, and the horses. The boss says I'm reactionary—still kinda like tradition. The cards and I go a long way back, what with tarot and all. You play poker?"

"I don't reckon I have enough to get in a game around here," Gussie said.

"Sure you do, sugar. Whatcha got on you?"

"About twenty-five dollars."

"Get you some quarters and try the one-armed bandits."

"No. I need that money."

"Don't be such a spoilsport. Come on. *One* quarter."

"Okay. Just one," Gussie said grimly, and she dropped her quarter into a slot and waited. Torchy-Lulubelle didn't wait, however. With a bored look on her face she thumped the machine with the heel of her hand, and the pictures all came up dollar signs while the coins came pouring out. "Now there's your stake. Let's go play us some poker."

As they passed the line of people dressed in splashy sequined and beaded dresses and tuxedos, Gussie couldn't help craning her neck to see who was in the floor show. "What is it?"

"Just another damn lecture."

"But I can see there's chorus girls or something on the sign even though I can't see what it says."

"Yeah. Well, it's about how to use sex in advertising."

"No singers or dancers or comedians?"

"Shoot, no. Nobody wants that stuff anymore. Where's the profit? Although they do have some snappy advertising jingles during the lecture, and the chorus girls do lots of high kicks to keep the audience interested. It's all the rage these days to have meaningful, profitable entertainment. Part of what my boss is promotin'. Now how 'bout that game of poker?"

"I feel more like another tequila sunset. A *lecture*? *Really*? What have things come to? That's the most boring damned excuse for a show I ever heard."

"Yeah, they don't pass out programs anymore, just informational pamphlets. Barrel of laughs."

Gussie bought her chips and felt totally intimidated sitting down in her smelly and soiled pink sweats among all the well-heeled high rollers at the table the redhead indicated. The other players looked at her like they could smell her too. But when the dealing commenced, Lulubelle blew a kiss at the deck. Gussie won without trying and kept winning. It wasn't even fun it was so effortless, and evidently Lulubelle felt the same way, because before long she leaned over and gave Gussie a hot buss on the cheek and wandered off.

Gussie cashed in her chips right afterward, much to the disgust of the opposing players. There were two men at the cashier's window. One of them handed her one hundred thousand dollars and asked if she wouldn't like more chips. She stared at the money and asked if he had traveler's checks instead. At that point, the other one stuck out *his* hand, said he was from the IRS and she had to give him back 30,000 of what she had just won. After she'd done that and signed the appropriate paper, he very kindly directed her to an all-night bank in the lobby. All the way to the bank she kept wondering when her winnings were going to turn into dried leaves or dust as fairy gold is supposed to. Then she thought, well, it might disappear for other reasons. The IRS could find reasons to take it even out of her account without her knowing about it. If she bought traveler's checks, anybody looking for her could trace her. If she kept it in cash, she'd probably get mugged. Oh, well, easy come easy go.

She stepped back into the night and found an all-night auto dealership. One brown minivan later she was on the road again, leaving Torchy-Lulubelle to wield her power. It did cross her mind to wonder why the Debauchery Devil in her Lady Luck guise decided to favor somebody who was supposed to be her opponent. But then, that was one thing about the redhead, you never could tell what was on her alleged mind.

Gussie felt pleased about the van as she zoomed out of town. Nobody knew where she'd gone or what she'd bought, and that would make it hard finding her again. As soon as she was safely down the highway, she pulled off at a truck stop and climbed into the back on the nice soft, new-smelling cushions to sleep off the tequila sunsets. Wouldn't do to be picked up for DWI now that she'd come so far.

Before she drifted off, she wondered again about the red-headed devil. The woman had blabbed everything she knew about the meetings where the devils had conspired, had even described the other devils. All this presumably while under the influence, but though she had talked drunk, she didn't act any drunker than usual once they got to the casino. And why had she just let Gussie win like that? The devil-woman's feck-lessness and unpredictability were oddly familiar to Gussie, putting her in mind of the way certain musicians used to act. She wondered if Torchy was really as crazy as she seemed or if she was up to something.

▲▲▲

"Dereliction of duty, DD," the boss said, leaning back in his swivel chair.

"O Contrary, Chair. I have a lot of duties," the Debauch-ery Devil said, shrugging. "Couldn't pass through Vegas without making a few converts, now, could I?"

"DD, you have the right attitude, but you're such a flake," the Expediency Devil said. He was a new improved model over the slightly old-maidish-looking previous one. This one had crisp dark curly hair and a lean, mean form that if he had been mortal would have been the result of meticulous, but efficient, exercise.

"I just think there are more pressing problems these days than a lot of broke-down warblers nobody listened to even before we wiped out their particular kind of—er—act," she said (in deference to the sensibilities of the others). "We have the people pretty well reconditioned now. Nobody's going to listen to a few jerks who haven't been heard from in years and can't even reenter the country legally." She blew a disdainful smoke ring from her Brimstone Light cigarette.

"She does have a point, Chair," the Expediency Devil

agreed. "And we have other agendas. Mustn't let this little prejudice of yours stand in the way of—"

"Don't you be telling me my job, XP," the Chairdevil snarled. "Fortunately, I have learned never to rely on DD and have arranged a reception committee at the border."

"Who's handling it?" XP asked.

"Minions who cannot be deterred by the spells in the cursed instrument carried by Mr. Willie MacKai."

"Minions have failed before."

"Ah, but these minions are cottonmouth water moccasins and a flash flood as well as some very nasty wetback muggers. I don't think a banjo, even a magic one, is going to be much protection."

▲▲▲

The water moccasin nest lay in wait, just under the surface of the water. These cottonmouths were no smarter than average, but they had supernatural instructions to lay in wait and kill the humans who would enter their domain. To the west, red lightning, heat lightning usually, flashed in the night, making Julianne Martin nervous as she remembered the night in Maryland at the folk festival when lightning had burned away her hearing. Now she heard better than any of them, since the Wizard Michael Scott had magically mended her ears. During her deafness she had learned to listen with her inner ears as well as her external ones. Right now she heard trouble, and sure enough, as Willie rose and headed to the banks of the river, starting to wade across, the red lightning, usually the sign of continued drought and even a harbinger of prairie fires, turned white, to sheet lightning, and storm clouds clumped like a pack of mad dogs, clashing in the skies of the west, blotting out the moon and stars. Thunder crashed and the lightning strobed again and the banjo broke into a Mexican-sounding tune.

"What's that one, Willie?" Julianne asked, her voice coming out thin and nervous. The rocks, the water, the molecules of sand, all seemed alive with warning. The world beyond the physical one was fairly howling with agitation, and Juli's inner ears, the ones that heard that kind of thing, were ringing with alarm bells and sirens. So when Lazarus started the tune, the first one in a while, she paid close attention.

Willie paused in the act of starting to wade, whistled to himself for a moment, and said, " 'La Lloróna.' I used to sing it. There's different stories about it. Some say she was one of Pancho Villa's wives, some say she was widowed in the revolution, others say she was a grandee's daughter, but most agree that for some reason or other she drowned her own child, and for that reason she haunts the riverbanks—although naturally there's a lot of disagreement about *which* riverbanks—sobbing and moaning and—"

The banjo thumped itself with a dramatic chord and quieted to a soft trickle. Above its notes Juli clearly heard the sound, a wailing and moaning. The others heard it too. They were all staring over her shoulder. She turned to see a black-clad woman wringing her hands and wafting straight at her. Juli jumped aside or the ghost would have gone straight through her.

"Is that her?" Ellie whispered.

"I'd say so, yeah," Brose whispered back. "Ain't shy, is she?" He rolled his eyes and shook his head. "I got a feelin' about this."

The ghost glided up to a fascinated Willie, who mumbled, "Excuse me, ma'am," as if he was about to tip his Stetson, which he wasn't wearing. He took a step back toward the river, but she stopped him when she suddenly raised her arms, the sleeves of her mourning weeds fanning out like raven's wings. A tattered black lace mantilla covered her face, which shone through white as the moon through cloud cover, except for where the eyes belonged, where two black holes glistened as if with tears. Juli leaned forward to see into her face, but the other musicians shrank back slightly. They'd all had lots of dealings with ghosts in the last few years, but none quite so—ghostly—as this one. The banjo grew louder, and the woman's specter grew more agitated.

Juli was pleased at the way Willie handled it. He began to sing softly in Spanish.

> "Ay de mi, lloróna, lloróna,
> Lloróna de ayer y hoy;
> Ayer maravilla fui, lloróna,
> Y ahora ni la sombra soy."

The winged arms swooped back down to the apparition's sides and clasped at her chest before one hand made the sign of the cross. Juli felt a sense of satisfaction from the ghost, a melancholy pleasure at being acknowledged. Whatever La

Lloróna's reasons for drowning her child, Juli couldn't help but feel that if she had known the circumstances back in those days when life could so easily be pure hell for a lone woman, much less one with an unsanctioned infant, she would have found the ghost more pitiable than fearsome.

The two glistening black eyeholes turned toward her for a split second as if in response; then in a tornado of black tattered dress and lace, the specter whirled and melted into the river.

"Oh, yeah," Brose said. "I seen 'em do that before. That time after Anna Mae's festival when we was chasin' Willie and y'all in Gussie's station wagon cross-country? The rest of us was in Faron's van, and I was drivin' while everybody slept? The highway flooded out, and damned if one of those ghosts we saw on that trip didn't warn us all by goin' into the water and drownin' hisself again just so I'd know it was deep out there."

"All of those ghosts were warning spirits," Anna Mae said. "But everything I've read about ghosts says they're not supposed to be able to cross running water."

But the ghost was halfway across, and from about midknee up she was still deeper blackness against the shining black water.

"Around here in the summer the Rio Grande don't usually run so deep you'd drown, less you laid down in it," Willie said.

The ghost glided farther out and was covered to the hips when she let out a long banshee wail. Willie shone his flashlight into the water.

The light bounced off wriggling, snapping forms clinging to the black robes and dripping from the sleeves and mantilla.

Willie whistled low, the flashlight jiggling. Juli saw that his hands were shaking.

"Shee-ee-ee-it," Brose said. "Lookit them cottonmouths. We ain't crossin' here tonight or no time soon."

The specter, still squirming with snakes, turned, stared at them as if dripping snakes was the most natural thing in the world, and ponderously began wading back.

Juli and the others stumbled away from the riverbanks as the ghost emerged from the water. *La llorona* began crying again, moaning and twisting her hands, coils of snake twining around her bone white fingers like grave worms. Thunder cracked in the west. Llorona strained toward them, the snakes slithering away from the bottom of her gown in all directions.

She was still trying to warn them, but Juli wondered if the ghost knew that coming any closer with all those snakes was apt to do more harm than good. She supposed ghosts got out of touch with such mortal considerations, having been dead themselves for so long. As the ghost advanced a step, Juli and the others retreated farther from the banks, trying to stay ahead of not only the ghost but the hissing snakes.

The hissing was suddenly augmented by another hiss—that of rain washing down on the desert. The hiss grew rapidly louder and harder until it turned into a roar. The ghost and her snakes had chased the musicians perhaps twenty yards back from the riverbank when all of a sudden the roar got very personal, very close, and the air grew suddenly wet.

Like an attacking army, an enormous wall of gleaming water swept down the riverbed from the west, driving a mist of dust before it while lightning lit the way.

"Flash flood!" Willie cried, as if she hadn't noticed.

Juli turned and ran, as did the rest, scrambling across the sand and up the nearest high spot while the water rolled like a locomotive past their backs and instantly dispatched waves to nip at their heels.

When at last she stopped, panting, at the top of a bluff which was now pretty much an island, she saw that everyone else had made it to safety as well. In fact, they were all but standing on top of each other as they watched the water eat up the dry land. The former bank was obliterated, water surging for what seemed like miles of flat land.

The ghost, the snakes, and every vestige of the landscape they'd just been looking at had utterly vanished.

▲▲▲

By morning the sky to the west was so clear it looked as if rain had never even crossed its mind. While the musicians slept, the flood waters raced out to the Gulf of Mexico. Just before dawn the river—while still full of water—was no deeper or wider than it had been before the flood. The sun even baked the ground dry again before everybody was fully awake.

"That's amazing," Terry said. "It's like it never happened— one moment the river's a torrent—"

"And the next minute it's going like, 'What, me? Flood?' " Dan said. "Weird."

"That's why they call 'em flash floods," Willie said. "At least it washed the snakes away."

"If it hadn't been for the ghost, we'd have been snakebit *and* drowned," Brose said, shuddering. "I guess if folk music is dead, ghosts must figure dead stuff gotta stick together. Spooks sure have saved our bacon more than once."

"Maybe the other side is overcrowded," Juli said, smiling wanly.

"It'd be crowded with *our* asses if that redheaded devil's buddies had anything to say about it," Brose growled.

"Well, it looks calm enough now, and there'll be federales sniffin' around to see what washed up pretty soon. Anybody want to go wadin'?" And before anyone could answer, he waded into the river, jeans, boots, and all—just in case there were some snakes left—carrying the banjo high over his head the way a soldier carries his gun when similarly fording. The banjo accommodatingly played "Wade in the Water," and Willie, who was trying awfully hard *not* to think about the snakes from the night before, sang in breathy snatches, "Wade in the water, children, / Wade in the water. / God's gonna trouble the water."

Julianne plowed into the water behind him, her long batik skirt kilted to the waist, her running shoes tied together by their laces around her neck, and a knapsack slung across her shoulders.

She took up the verse, "Look at those children / Dressed in red—" and Willie and the others sang, "Wade in the water."

"They must have been the children Lazarus led," she continued, improvising on the biblical figure, substituting the name of the banjo for Moses.

As Brose followed, he sang, "Look at those children dressed in black," and the others sang, "Wade in the water."

"They flew away, now they wadin' back."

Willie felt like a kid sneakin' back home after a night out that he didn't particularly want his folks to know about. On the other side of the river was home—the ranch he had visited throughout his childhood and youth, where his father had once worked as foreman, where he himself had worked after he tried to quit music. Seven years ago he would never have imagined *he'd* be a wetback making a clandestine crossing. Hell's bells, he was an American citizen—they all were except Terry Pruitt. They were all beginning to realize what fragile protection their citizenship was when the right people had been bought and paid for.

Now here he was, here they all were, singing any old song

that came into their heads while trying to evade the authorities at a remote spot along the Rio Grande. Participating in whatever music the banjo suggested was better protection than silence, or weapons, or arguments. The banjo's power was their best shield and early warning system, since it always started playing songs pertinent to whatever danger or problem was about to jump on them. Sometimes it just didn't play soon enough.

On the other side of the river, Willie stopped to dry himself off with the part of his T-shirt that hadn't dragged in the river, pulled off his jeans, socks, and boots, wrung out the jeans and socks, and dumped water out of his boots. Juli wrung out her skirt, and behind her Brose, Faron, Ellie, Terry, and Dan also dripped out of the water and rearranged their clothing.

The banjo was still tinkling with "Wade in the Water." Julianne Martin took another handful of skirt and wrung it between her hands. Suddenly she stood still and stared back at the river, feeling a rushing inside herself as great as the flood of the night before. "Hey, you guys! It works! Did you notice how we seem to be remembering these songs, even though we're home? I mean, we relearned the European ones, right? But then there was 'Wade in the Water'—"

"We were in Mexico when Willie remembered La Lloróna," Faron reminded her. "Maybe they're respecting borders. Besides, Mexicans still use their folk music a lot, and it's probably harder for the devils to get at them with all of their songs still being sung so often and by so many people. And we weren't exactly *in* the U.S. yet when we remembered 'Wade in the Water,' besides which, we didn't sing the original words."

"Could be it worked on account of it was a black gospel song and I'm here," Brose said. "But that didn't work the last time. Maybe just because it's religious."

"They do seem a little more responsive to hymns than you'd expect strictly nonpartisan devils to be," Faron replied. "But we haven't had occasion to try out many Buddhist gospel songs on them. Next time let's see if 'Om Mani Padme Om' works."

"There's always the 'Zen Gospel Song,' Bryan Bowers used to sing," Dan reminded him. "Although in our present position, 'Om on the Range' would probably be more appropriate."

"No, really," Julianne said, her voice sounding far off. Willie looked at her sharply. She was staring into the distance as if she were listening. "Do you feel it? I feel as if all the songs that I lost before just came flooding back into me. I never realized it, but they left an empty space inside me somewhere. We've learned lots of things I didn't know already, of course, but this is like—well, weird. Maybe we should try to remember a song from this country that we used to know before."

Anna Mae grunted. "How about that Mark Graham Zen Gospel tune, 'I Have Seen Your Aura and It's Ugly.' "

That was about as close as Willie had ever heard Anna Mae come to kidding somebody, but Juli was so set on what she was feeling, she didn't seem to notice. "Sorry," she said. "I can't remember that one because I never knew it, but you could do it."

Willie remembered the song, however, and he started singing it. Brose countered with an a cappella of "House of the Rising Sun," after which he nodded vigorously. "Yeah. Great. It's workin' okay."

"Super," Willie said. "So now we know we've got access to at least our own old songs as well as the ones we brought back. I guess the banjo told us straight when it said that by taking the music back to its roots we could retrieve it."

"Let me try one," Dan said, but Willie shook his head.

"We're still sitting ducks, and we've got a long walk ahead of us to where we're supposed to rendezvous with Gussie. Keep hummin' to yourself, though, and try to remember as much as you can. We'll need all the ammo we can get against these critters once they realize we made it over here."

Tickled pink to have their repertoires reinstated, even though they were rusty from lack of practice and Lazarus was the only instrument available, the musicians spent the rest of their traveling time that predawn morning singing snatches of songs to each other.

▲▲▲

Gussie awoke at dawn and drove to the first truck stop for three cups of coffee, which she knew good and well would make her pee clear across Arizona and New Mexico. She looked for some kind of music to play in the San's fancy sound system had but didn't see anything displayed at the truck stop. She asked about it, and the cashier directed her to a bank of instructional tapes on various languages, how to interpret the stock market, how to improve her presentation, and a lot of other topics that were of no particular interest to her. "I was looking for music tapes," she said.

The bored-looking cashier pointed to another rack, which held a single row of tapes and a single row of CDs by nobody she had ever heard of with one exception, "Soul-less" by Duck Soul. Remembering that the van's system contained a CD player, she selected a square disk box and paid for it.

Back on the road she popped it in, but the first cut was the god-awfulest collection of noise she had ever heard, not at all like the hypnotic hard rock she remembered Soul playing when he barged into the private folk festival at Anna Mae Gunn's house, just before everything started getting totally out of hand.

She turned off the tape player and tried the radio. No music channels anywhere. Nothing but boring, depressing newscasts and financial and farm reports—the latter all bad.

She listened to hog prices, which were down, as were pork bellies and alfalfa, just to hear about something familiar. She tuned up and down the dial twice before she realized her problem was that she was lonely. She had started this journey with a sense of anticipation, knowing she would see the friends from whom she had been separated for the last year or so, while she did her storytelling as sort of advance preparation for their arrival. For the best part of seven years she had been surrounded by people—and not just family, friends, and co-workers as she used to be. Shoot, in Scotland she'd not only been with the musicians and with Faron and Ellie most of the time, she'd also been sharing her body with Sir Walter's spirit, and having once made room for him, she now felt as if part of her was vacant—it was a little like grieving for a man dead years and years before she was born. Since returning to the States she had been alone only for little snatches between storytelling audiences.

She missed her cats, most of them still at her old house in Tacoma where her kids Lettie and Mic now lived. Pretty soon she wouldn't be able to keep up the mortgage payments, wandering like this, and unless Mic found a better job, the kids wouldn't be able to buy it. Her favorite cat, Satana, had died while she was in Scotland. She missed her kids, her cats, her friends—and she badly missed Sir Walter too. She wished he could have come with her, but he'd had to return to his rest when the time came for her to go. She still had the copy of *Lay of the Last Minstrel* she'd bought at Abbotsford, and in a way it was like having Wat still with her. But not quite. Right now she was so lonesome she even missed that redheaded hussy of a Debauchery Devil, whatever the critter called herself.

She would be glad to get off this long highway and be among friends again. But she didn't speed or even pull out into the fast lane, or in any way, shape, or form draw attention to herself. Bad enough that the van was obviously new, with dealer's plates instead of conventional ones. The devils had connections in law enforcement, and she didn't want to attract the wrong kind of Smokey . . . or even the right kind.

▲▲▲

The devils also had connections among automobile dealerships, especially in Las Vegas, and once they had checked the jet flights and the buses, they found the dealer who had sold Gussie the van. But they got a late start. They didn't discover what the old lady was up to until Torchy showed up drunk around noon mortal-time after a night of gaming, drinking, and turning tricks, which was her favorite way of relaxing, and gave them a garbled version of her activities and handed over the money she'd made from prostitution to the Chairdevil.

"What do I want with this?" he asked.

"Aw, c'mon, boss, keep it. It's just not traditional for me to keep it all," she'd said, and told them a long-drawn-out version of how she had picked up and lost Gussie. After that they called the meeting to decide what to do.

The Chairdevil didn't exactly take the whole thing seriously anyway, since he had his preparations in place in Texas already to meet the weary travelers as they attempted the border crossing. Even desultory investigation turned up Gussie Turner's connection with the minivan, and the Chairdevil put out an all-points on her, until her van was finally spotted outside of Albuquerque.

CHAPTER III

▲▲▲

The man who had once been Willie MacKai's boss looked over the latest applicant for the remaining position as ranch hand. "This is a very impressive résumé, son," he said, slapping the folder down on the desk beside his kangaroo-skin booted heels. "Yes, sir, very impressive. B.A. in English, M.A. in creative writing and a minor in folklore from UT, and M.B.A. from Baylor. Manager of a small-press publishin' house in Houston. Mighty impressive if I was lookin' for a schoolteacher. Lord, son, whatever made you think of applyin' for a job as a ranch hand?"

"Well, sir, as you can see by my résumé"—Spencer Guttenberg indicated the folio on the desk with a soft and well-cared-for hand sullied only by dishwashing jobs to help pay for extracurricular activities while he'd been doing all that schooling—"I am already qualified and am, in fact, a poet. I'm a member of PEN and have had several works published in *Harper's* and *The New Yorker* as well as the small presses before I acquired my M.B.A.—"

"Is that a fact?"

"Yes, sir, but you see, when I take stock of my life, I realize that writing poetry is only half of what I wish to do. Actually, I was inspired in college by the works of J. Frank Dobie, Curley Fletcher, and S. Omar Barker. You see, sir, it's—uh—actually my ambition to be a cowboy poet, and so far I've only had the time to do the latter half. So I thought I would like to apply for a job—oh, not as a foreman or anything, just as an apprentice ranch hand, you might say—and then I would learn the cowboy side of things."

"You don't say?"

"Yes, sir."

"A cowboy poet?"

"That's right, sir."

"Well, now, son, I know all about J. Frank Dobie. Used to have a hand who was quite an authority on him, though this fella was more in the line of a guitar player and singer than he was a poet—still, he knew a lot about it. I never heard of them other fellas though."

"Haven't you heard the song taken from the Curley Fletcher poem, 'The Strawberry Roan'?" Guttenberg asked.

"Oh, *that* song. I ain't heard that in years. Do you know it?"

"A little," Guttenberg said, adjusting his spectacles. "I forgot it for a while, and then I found it in a collection of poems."

"You'll have a lot to learn if I give you this job, son. Cowboyin' is different than schoolboyin'."

"I know that, sir," Guttenberg said with the beginning of a gleam in his eye. "And I will endeavor to remember Fletcher's immortal words in order to maintain proper perspective and humility. 'I know there are ponies that I cannot ride. / There's some of them left, / They haven't all died. / But I'll bet all my money the man ain't alive / That'll stay with old Strawberry when he makes his high dive.' "

He recited the last in as deep a Texas drawl as the boss and grinned at him.

The boss threw his hat at him and said, "Okay. I don't know who told you about the likin' I've took to singin' cowboys and cowboy poets since Willie MacKai took off, but you go take your bedroll and guitar out to the bunkhouse with the rest of 'em, and Dally Morales will take you on the grand guided tour."

"Much obliged, sir," said Guttenberg, hitching up his spectacles, slinging his bedroll over his shoulder, and picking up his guitar case by the binder's twine that held it together. He walked from the office with such a bowlegged swagger he almost fell off his boots. He had played his part shrewdly. He'd heard about all the cowboy poets hiring on here at this spread and figured by now that most of them, who had got their start in cowboyin', might need a dude to break in who didn't know squat about brandin' cows or bustin' horses but who could sure as hell clean up their syntax and scansion.

▲▲▲

"It's about twenty miles to the road where Gus is supposed to meet us," Willie told the others. "Now, that's not all that far by car or horseback, and I don't imagine it's all that bad a jog on a paved path for a couple of us, but this ain't no paved path. You don't run far around here if you know what's good for you. Heat stroke happens, even to seasoned hands, even to Mexicans if they don't use good sense. There's rattlers too, and you don't want to jog right into one. So we'll stay together and take it easy."

"Does this make us wetbacks?" Dan asked jokingly.

"Yeah, I guess it does. And we're likely to meet some of the other kind too. Used to be they were all just working people looking for better pay so they can take care of their families. But when I was working here, that kind of wetbacks were getting scared off by the other kind—the kind who come up carrying fancy sports bags and high-powered weapons and good running shoes. Drug runners, gunrunners, other kinds of smugglers and worse."

He didn't say what was worse, and nobody wanted to ask. Recent experience had made them all leery of what Gussie would have called "borrowing trouble." There was no need to borrow it. They found their own share soon enough.

▲▲▲

The Doom and Destruction Devil usually dealt in large-scale belligerency—small wars, police actions, low-intensity conflicts, invasions—but his department did contain more personalized services, and it was these the Chairdevil decided to deploy when the first line of offense failed.

"Time for minions again, Threedee," Chair told him, having asked him to remain while the others went to supervise their worldwide divisions.

"I have a lot going on just now, Chair," Threedee said. "I don't think I have a war-mad politician, ganglord, or anybody of that caliber to spare."

"How about your serial killers?" he asked. "Any of them in the Albuquerque area?"

"Well, nobody right now of your Speck or Bundy caliber, but I have a few crazies and some talented amateurs who eliminate a few individuals on a regular basis—Indians, Mexicans, blacks, prostitutes, sometimes coeds, sometimes homosexuals, often little old ladies. These people aren't professional, you understand, but they do love their work."

"How about in the vicinity of the MacKai party?"

"Piece of cake. Got a group coming into position right now on another job. Shouldn't even have to redeploy them. I think your MacKai party is probably going to stumble over them in the middle of another operation."

"Fine. Then get your New Mexico people on the job and pop down to supervise the business in Texas, will you?"

"Boss, I've got a million irons in the fire. How about the business in Africa? How about that Chinese-Mongolian deal I've been working on for years? And I'm afraid that if I don't keep stirring the Middle Eastern situation, a peace accord may break out at any time."

"This will only take a minute. Attention to detail is important, Threedee. You should know that by now. Now get on the horn to Albuquerque."

Threedee picked up a special handset, punched a button, and spoke into it. "Now hear this. This is your voices speaking, aka the master, aka the devil who makes you do it. Be it known to you that little old women driving brown minivans are an abomination in my sight and should be slaughtered like sheep. This kind of sow frequents Highway Sixty-six, heading east. She will be laughing at your stupidity if you let her live as far as the Texas border. Find her and scourge the earth of her presence. That is all."

"They believe that crap?" Chair asked wonderingly.

"Some people are so eager to come to us, they'll believe anything as long as it tells them to do what they want to already, boss."

▲▲▲

James Francis Farnham heard the call and was for the first time in two years (following a conviction and imprisonment for the robbery, beating, rape, and mutilation of two elderly sisters) able to answer. He had been a model prisoner, everybody agreed, in the prison facility where he had been living and working with other men. He had no problem with other men, guards or prisoners. Other men did not remind him of his grandmother, who had raised him and deprived him of all of the things he was entitled to, of his mother, who deserted him to work at a job where she did not earn enough to buy those things, or of his ex-wife. He had seen to it that she, at least, wouldn't screw anybody else around. He had never known his father and so had no particular grudge against men.

He couldn't easily get a gun without waiting so long that the trail would get cold, but a gun was not his weapon of choice anyway, and you didn't need a license for a hunting bow or a butcher knife. He stole a car easily enough within a block of the probation office and cruised out Route 66, while visions of body parts danced in his head.

Before the old girl reached the Texas border, the voices had said. Now, what was important about that? She was running away, that was what. Bitch. Who had she screwed so that she had to run away now? He'd bring her back from the border okay. He had just the hardware to do it and enough butcher paper to conceal the evidence.

He spotted the van at a truck stop outside Roswell. The voices were wrong. She wasn't heading east. She was heading southeast. She was trying to confuse him. Lying to the voices. Trying to throw him off her track.

She climbed back into the van. She looked just like the voices said. Small, gray-haired, deceptively sweet looking in her little pink jogging suit. Too bad he'd arrived after she stopped or he could have taken her there, when she got out to go to the ladies' room. Never mind. She would no doubt stop again in Carlsbad, and he'd catch up with her there. Darkness was coming soon too, and he could always wait for an opportunity to run her off the road.

▲▲▲

Gussie would never have noticed the dark blue truck with the camper shell if it hadn't been for the personalized license plates that said SHONUF. She wondered what kind of a person put something like that on license plates. Some kind of a business, maybe? She also noticed that although the truck had pulled into the truck stop outside Roswell as she emerged from the station, the driver didn't get out and buy gas but exited right behind her. A few years ago she wouldn't have made much of that, but she was more cautious now.

She was still ahead of schedule. Though she could have driven through Amarillo, where she used to live, to visit friends, she decided that she would rather swing down through the Big Bend to see Remie Collins and her husband, Don, who ran a white-water rafting business through Santa Elena Canyon. They were old folk-music cronies, and their raft trips were perfect for musicians or storytellers. The laws and tastes of people changed often while they were in the city, but stories and old songs around camp fires went back to cavemen, so deep in racial memory that not even devils could wipe them out.

Unfortunately, scouting organizations didn't seem to do

camp out anymore, or that would have been the perfect place to spread the music. The organizations had sold off most of the old camps for timber. Nowadays kids raised on slasher movies that were set in such camps weren't all that eager to go away for the summer. And the timber made money for other programs, such as urban scouting centers, where the scouts in the cities could go to swim, start jogging contests through city parks, or take off for trips to other cities. "We do have a few units devoted to survivalist skills," the lady at scouting headquarters in Tacoma had told Gussie, "but they don't use camps. Timber sales bring in too much money for us to maintain camps for a few weeks' use when there are national parks whose facilities cost so little. And camp fires are restricted in most areas now. Forest fires, you know."

So Gussie figured maybe raft trips chartered by tired city folks who wanted to float down desert canyons would be a good alternative venue for telling her tales in a wilderness setting and later, for reintroducing music.

The blue pickup had dropped back for several miles, but once more she saw it in her rearview mirror. Maybe she should stop in Carlsbad. The person in the pickup could be one of the messengers in the little underground she and the rest of the network had established. With phones easy to tap, mail easy to tamper with, and computer networks a cinch to break into, she, Lettie and Mic, the Curtises, and a few of the others still remaining from the clumps of small-time folk musicians and fans from years ago sent news to each other mostly by the grapevine—messages given to relatives and friends along with identifying lines and code words that could be answered. Of course, that could easily be intercepted too, if anyone cared to, but it wasn't quite the cinch electronic surveillance was. Besides, most of them sort of enjoyed the intrigue, and more than one wiseass had asked how long you had to be in the network before you were issued your secret decoder ring.

But SHONUF was not any code she remembered, and her memory was excellent. Besides, nobody, not even friends, knew about the new van yet. The truck had not followed her from Las Vegas, she was sure. She decided against Carlsbad and honked on toward El Paso, glad she had picked a minivan with good gas mileage instead of the larger, less efficient RV or standard-size van. She wanted to keep within the speed limit to avoid attracting the attention of the police, so she

hoped she wasn't also going to have to find out how fast the
sucker was.

▲▲▲

Julianne heard the scream first. They had been walking slowly,
through the hottest part of the day, too busy sweating to talk,
following Willie's instructions and keeping their eyes on their
feet so they didn't step on a snake that hadn't had time to
rattle. Juli's canteen, not the round metallic kind but a light-
weight insulated thermos, sloshed against her hip, half-empty.
She had stopped to extract a handful of trail mix from her
knapsack, so she wasn't as busy as the others with the sound
of her own feet moving. The scream was strangled, broken off.
"Shhh," she said to the others. "Hear it?"

There was another short, chopping noise, a thunk of some
sort, and a groan, a babble of voices.

Willie started sweating a little more than he had been.
"Good thing you heard it, darlin'," he told her. "Comin' from
that way, would you say?" he asked, pointing northeast.

She nodded.

"Then we'll go this way for a while," he said, pointing due
north. "There's still a line shack around here someplace."

Another scream, this time long and shrill. Julianne, who
had through the spell of the Wizard Michael Scott inhabited
the bodies of Scottish ballad heroes for most of a year, shook
her head and gave Willie a long considering look. It was not a
look of derision or accusations of cowardice. She knew he was
afraid, and she thought it was a more sensible response than
her own. But how would his dreams be, how would his life be,
how could he fulfill the mission he had to fulfill if he turned
away? She knew the person she had become wouldn't be able
to handle it.

Brose touched Willie's arm. "Come on, buddy, let's have a
look-see," he said.

Willie shrugged. "Just tryin' to protect the rest of y'all. It's
fine with me." He told himself he wasn't so much afraid for
his own skin as for the women. Having inhabited, in spirit
anyway, the bodies of countless victimized sweet young ballad
ladies, he probably had a better sense of the odds than they
did. Whoever was screaming was probably beyond help, and
whoever caused the screaming was probably armed, which
Willie and his friends were not.

Anna Mae Gunn was already ahead of them, striding off in

the direction Julianne pointed. When Willie caught up to her, she gave him a fierce grin and a thumbs-up sign. Once she would have snarled at him for his initial reluctance, but she'd spent her ballad time being the sought-after dandy, the choice ladies' man who was always pursued by crowds of women who wanted him to be absolutely fearless as well as good in bed. The same kind of man was resented, and often punished, by men who were threatened by his attractiveness. Such a man was apt to be on the defensive, trying to keep his hide in one piece, instead of looking for ways to dispense with it voluntarily.

Dan caught up in two long lopes with Willie, Brose, and Anna Mae. Meanwhile Terry walked with Julianne, who, if she had been a dog, would have had her ears cocked.

The noises were coming from an arroyo, beside which was parked a Jeep.

Willie held out his arms to the others to stop and crept to the lip of the arroyo. His lips formed a silent "shit" as he saw the three men with assault rifles, guns and a machete among them looting the prostrate bodies of two other men and a woman. A baby with a bloody head lay in the crook of the arm of one of the women.

Willie swept his arm backward, signaling the others to retreat. He'd hit the bull's-eye in his prediction of the odds. Six unarmed adults weren't apt to do a hell of a lot better than five.

Anna Mae looked as if she were about to protest when he rejoined them, but he shook his head and started away at a trot that encouraged the others, so that, fortunately, they were out of range when the first shots were fired after them.

CHAPTER IV
▲▲▲

Dally Morales was in a mean mood. He hated training tin-horns, and besides, he had gotten another rejection slip in the morning's mail. Obviously he'd gotten another New York editor who didn't know his cinch from his Stetson. Said the piece was too dissonant for him! Dissonance, hell! Dally thought. Sucker wouldn't know an internal rhyme if it walked up and bit him in the assonance.

Dally had learned quite a bit about all that poetic stuff from Swede Swensen, a former logger poet who had hired on about five years ago when the last of the big-time timber companies bit the dust. What with that and a night-school course at the extension college the boss had arranged for the benefit of the hands and their families just inside the property line up toward Del Rio, Dally had gotten the hang of cowboy-poeting. He'd kept the textbook, though, and it was more thumbed through than a mail-order catalog.

Now he had a college boy from Houston to break in as well as three other fellas. The other three at least were experienced ranch hands, though one of them was bad for punning, and the Japanese fellow who went by the handle of Nobby (short phonetic for Watanabe), and who was the most seasoned cow hand, did not, in Dally's opinion, quite have the hang of being a cowboy poet—he kept trying to do cowboy haiku and had presented as an example of his work:

> "Steamin' shit
> Upon the land
> I pluck rapier cactus spines from my ass."

Kinda missed the point, as the punner said, havin' cowboy poetry that didn't rhyme *all the damn way* at the ends of the lines.

But Dally rounded up the whole crew and herded 'em out to the Jeeps, taking along plenty of jerky and cheese and crackers, as well as a six-pack of Evian water (the water at the ranch was so hard it would coat your teeth after one swallow).

They set out on the trail, along the fences, visiting every water trough and line shack on the spread.

He showed them how many miles it took to feed a steer, how far they had to walk for water. He showed them the pens and the trucks and the shacks. He showed them where wetbacks crossed the Rio Grande and the holes from which cactusnappers had stolen fine specimens of aloe vera and other choice dry-climate greenery, the candelleria, the saguaro.

Darkness was falling as they swept around the scrub back to the road and the ranch. The sound of gunfire split the air like a bad headache, riding heavy on the heat waves.

Dally hadn't shown his protégés any rope tricks or much about shooting yet, but he soon had the opportunity.

Just ahead of them three men with guns and machetes were piling into a Jeep, and while Dally and the trainees watched, the Jeep peeled off after a larger group of men and women who were fleeing on foot.

Dally handed the wheel over to the Japanese, took a loop in his riata, and swung, casting his loop over the back bumper of the other Jeep so that it towed them behind it. While the gun-toting trio were figuring out what was going on, Dally took his hunting rifle from the console between the seats and shot first one then the other assault rifle clean out of the hands of the men wielding them. Shots spit in all directions, and the six fugitives fled before the Jeeps bit the dust.

Spencer Guttenberg and the third trainee followed Dally to retrieve the automatic rifles where they lay on the dirt outside the Jeep. While Dally was bending over the fender to loosen his riata, the man with the machete took a hack at him, but the Japanese separated the hand from the machete with a karate chop he'd learned at a very young age from old Bruce Lee movies.

The six people in front of them lifted their heads when they realized they weren't dead, and a big mocha-colored man said from between white teeth, "Goddamn, we was saved once by La Lloróna. *Tell* me you guys ain't the ghost-fuckin'-riders in the sky."

The youngest of the rescuers tilted his spectacles in a gesture that was worthy of Clint Eastwood and said, "No, sir. But you might call us poetic justice."

▲▲▲

Gussie figured out when she didn't lose the blue truck in El Paso that she was definitely being tailed. She tried everything she knew to shake him, because by now she had abandoned any idea that he was friendly. She was hungry and thirsty and wanted to go to the bathroom. The candy bar she'd picked up in Roswell was just supposed to tide her over until lunch. She thought about stopping someplace and going in where there were a lot of people, but she didn't like to leave the protection of the car. She could not call the police for help. Experience had already shown that the law cared nothing about helping her or people like her, though some completely strange officer who didn't know who she was might plunge in and save her momentarily—always assuming that it was not a policeman in the car behind her. But more and more she knew it wasn't. She caught a glimpse of the face in the rearview mirror from time to time. Like the musicians, she had shared a body with a person long dead, had been ensorcelled and had danced with the dead, and from this she had gained a sense of pitch where life and death were concerned. The person behind her was among the living okay, only not exactly. The five-hundred-year-old ghosts she'd known in Scotland were more alive than the driver of that truck.

So she kept driving, though the tank was nearing empty and her bladder was full, her mouth dry, her heart pounding, and her palms sweating. Darkness fell, and she recognized the double rectangle of the blue truck's lights just behind, about four cars back. More and more, though, as they drove out of the city and dipped down into the country at the heel of the boot formed by the map of Texas, the blue truck was right behind her, trying to gain on her. Now she cursed herself for a damn fool for not trying to attract a cop. She sped up in hopes of getting a speeding ticket. The blue truck sped up too, of course, and pulled alongside, just like in the movies, and side-swiped her. Her brand-new van.

"Bastard!" she shouted, and waved her fist at him, but all she could see were his headlights as he fell back, sprang forward, and crashed into her again. Well, at least this was Texas instead of California. Not much chance he was going to send her flying over a steep mountain pass in the middle of the desert. She just kept driving, even though according to the fuel indicator she had to be running on fumes.

And then, as he pulled up to ram her again, the van sputtered, bucked, and died. The truck made an impact and Gussie locked the driver's-side door, and as she leaned over to lock the passenger's-side door, she saw headlights coming from a side road and changed her mind and slid over to the passenger's side, banged open the door, and jumped out, running for the lights.

▲▲▲

Now why was the goddamn thing backing up? Gussie wondered, as she ran for the lights. When she tripped, she realized that she was not on a side road at all, but out in the open. The door of the blue truck was open, light spilling from it glinting off a blade in the hand of a smooth-faced man in a tractor cap. She caught only a glimpse. He hadn't realized yet that she was out of the truck, but it wouldn't take another second. She felt that if she could just get to those lights, even if they weren't car lights, surely there'd be other people, surely she could get help.

She didn't look back, and the roar of her own breath in her ears and the thud of her feet, the thump of her heart, let her hear little else for what seemed like hours. And then she heard an engine start and distinctly heard wheels behind her.

Go to ground. She had to go to ground. Run. Hide. Hunker down and blend in with the darkness. She veered left, so that she wasn't running in a straight path, and from the corner of her eye saw the truck's high beams splitting the dry desert ground and scrub brush. The truck had left the road and was bumping across the uneven ground, lights bouncing up to pierce the indigo sky, then dropping back onto cracked and open ground.

Gussie's legs were lead, her heart an anchor in her chest when she needed to be light enough to just blow away. Oh, lord, why had she gotten out of the van? She could have held him off awhile at least.

She saw a bush right in front of her and thought she'd drop down behind it, so maybe if the pickup's headlamps didn't shine directly on her he wouldn't find her. The space was vast. On the other hand, nobody else was around except whoever was behind those green lights—please God don't let them belong to some lonely aircraft beacon or radio tower—and the night was long. She could hide for a little while, but sooner or later she'd have to run again.

The brush was full of thorns and stickers, naturally, and tore at her face and arms as she bent down. Fortunately, she hadn't yet had time to change out of her sweats and running shoes into more comfortable shorts and sandals, but she was sweating gallons and was sure her pursuer could hear her breath over the engine of his truck.

There it was, a dark blue truck driving through a field on a dark blue night, headlights bobbing up and down, "Don't mind me, I'm just some kids out spoonin'. Don't mind me I'm just some drunk good old boys out tastin' a little freedom, drinkin' a little beer, raisin' a little innocent cain." Like hell.

She closed her eyes and clenched her fists. Childlike: "you can't see me. I'm not here." Why couldn't she have brought the basket bag with her cuticle scissors or Swiss army knife or even just the heavy bag itself to use for a shield, to hit him with?

She'd forgotten the money. A big wad of it was in her bra, more in the basket bag, more under the floorboards. At least I got a little mad money this time, Mama, she thought to herself and felt like giggling. Clean underwear probably wouldn't matter a hell of a lot if he caught her with that big old knife of his. Oh, lord. He *can't* see me. I'm *not* here.

And then she felt a little warmth, and light pierced her closed eyelids. Oh, shit. He'd found her. For a moment she thought, Don't open your eyes or the light will bounce off them and the shine will give you away. But the roar of the engine was still distant, somewhere to the right of her, and she risked slitting her eyelids ever so slightly.

The light wasn't shining directly into her eyes, but it restored the brown gold color to the bush in front of her, though it washed it a little with pale green, as it did the pink of her sweatsuit. All around the little circle in which she squatted the ground looked black. The light poured down from a green globe bobbing over her head like a goddamn "follow the bouncing ball." Over across the field were two more lights, still paired like headlights, but this third one was directly over her. It bobbed away and bounced back toward her, bobbed away and bounced back, just like Lassie had done on TV when Timmie was lying hurt somewhere and Lassie wanted the father to follow and come to the rescue.

The light wasn't bobbing in the direction of the truck, so, still hunkered down, she followed it. As long as it was away from that truck, one direction was as good as another.

▲▲▲

Buddy Lamprey stopped at the Marfa cafe for his usual donut and coffee and a little flirtation with the waitress Janey Lynn, with whom he had gone to high school. She'd been one of the brightest girls there, and Buddy had had a crush on her, but in their senior year she married some college boy from Lubbock, and three kids later she was back home taking care of both the kids and her widowed daddy here in Marfa. He had to hand it to her, though. She wasn't singin' the blues. She seemed happy to be home and she was a damn good waitress. She could have made good tips at some fancy place—hell, he thought, she could have made good money as a civil engineer or a geologist or something, she had always been at the top of her science classes—but Marfa didn't have anyplace fancier than the cafe. It was, as Janey Lynn liked to say, the crème de la nondairy creamer of northern Presidio County.

And he, of course, was, except for the Bears, the law west of the Pecos—one of ten law-enforcement officers serving the entire county. The crime was mostly drunk or domestic or both, and there wasn't much of anywhere to run once you blocked one of about two roads. The distances were long and lonely, though. He enjoyed his coffee and Janey Lynn's company when she wasn't too busy. They'd jaw a little and swap science fiction books, and she'd always give him a report on the famous Marfa lights.

"They're out tonight, Buddy," she hollered from the kitchen. "The usual three, green and real active tonight, from what I hear."

"Wish you'd get off night shift so we could go watch together, sweet thang," he teased.

"Yeah, they're long gone by the time I get off at eight," she said. "I used to see them all the time before I left home, though. I think that's what always interested me in science so much. The experts claimed it was swamp gas, but any fool can see there's no swamp out there. Still, it's gotta be caused by somethin' natchrul, don't you 'magine?"

Lamprey felt uncomfortable. He had run into a thing or two before he left the Texas Rangers that wasn't exactly natural. He didn't want Janey Lynn to think he was weird or anything, though, so he kept his mouth shut and stared out the window while he waited for the next morning's sweet rolls to come out of the oven.

▲▲▲

There was something sane in conspiracy theories that all the
shrinks had overlooked, Gussie thought, as she ran three steps
behind the bouncing green light. At least if that knife-wielding
bastard got her, she wouldn't waste a lot of time while she was
dying wondering "Why me?" Nope, she had a pretty fair idea,
and it would be illogical and ludicrous besides to imagine that
somehow or other she had managed to attract a totally independent and unaffiliated butchering maniac.

And if he did get her, that would make her a martyr to the
cause, wouldn't it? Not that she couldn't wait indefinitely for
such an honor, but at least it would make sense of her death
and give it some kind of purpose. They'd probably write a real
powerful song about her. They'd damn well *better*. And if the
cause failed and they couldn't get anybody over here to listen
to the moving ballad about how heroic she was, they could
just take the song back over to Britain where people *would*
listen, or she'd come back and haunt them. Come to think of
it, another ghost among all they'd seen lately wouldn't be any
more impressive than her living self, so she thought if it was
all the same to everybody else, she'd prefer to get out of this
with a whole skin.

Behind her the truck tires screamed and the engine roared,
and she glanced back to see the headlamps sweeping crazily
around the field as the truck turned in circles, the taillights as
red as some crazy wild animal's eyes. As if they were indeed
eyes, they found her, and when the truck spun around again,
she felt the glow of the headlamps hot as sunlight on her face
and arms. For a moment she stood frozen as the maniac behind the wheel jerked his tires into a straight line to head for
her, then the green light bobbed back overhead so that she
was momentarily caught in a cross-spot like some kind of opera star. Realizing what a good target she was making, she
jumped sideways, away from the light, heedless of cactus and
stones, and as she jumped, something long and skinny
whizzed through the light to land in the glow of the green with
a thunk and stand there quivering. An arrow—long steel
sucker. Not the play-acting Indian kind, but a serious, bear-
hunting type arrow, the kind sportsmen used when they
wanted an extra challenge.

Jesus, hadn't the bastard ever heard of guns? But if he had,
she'd have been a goner already.

Her eyes had been fixed on the truck, and it bore down on
her, targeting the green light. Then, abruptly, there were three

green lights, and two of them charged toward the truck, swooping toward the windshield. The brakes shrieked and the headlights twisted sideways.

But the wheelbase was too short for that, and the truck must have struck a boulder, because all of a sudden the headlights were on top of each other instead of side by side, and Gussie heard an awful grinding sound as the wheels still in contact with the ground dug into it. Had he survived? She wasn't about to go look. She ran instead toward the remaining light and now noticed, beyond all the extraneous illumination, other lights, small and distant but stable. She could just make out the neon sign that said "Cafe." The green globe fell behind as she stumbled toward the new beacon.

▲▲▲

James Francis Farnham was awakened by the smell of gasoline and burning rubber, the sound of grinding, spinning tires, and realized without surprise as he turned off the ignition that he was going nowhere fast. He had failed the voices, after all. He had not kept the old bitch from crossing the border. He became aware of a sharp, burning pain in his left leg as he pulled himself out of the driver's seat, toward the passenger door. He must have damaged the leg when his weight slid over against the driver's side and a boulder dented the door. On top of the passenger's side of the truck, he took just an extra moment to claim a flashlight from the glove box. Reluctantly he decided to leave the butcher knife behind. Something that would work just as well was easy to find. The same wasn't true of the crossbow, of course, but he was out of practice anyway, or the bitch would have been skewered by now. Besides, it was too incriminating.

Limping away from the ruined truck, he saw the green lights jigging up and down, as if they were laughing at him.

CHAPTER V

▲▲▲

Hugh Graham, the man from SWALLOW, was everything a SWALLOW agent was expected to be. He was possessed of a good memory, a firm grasp of mission, a knowledge of the law, a knowledge of music, and the self-assurance that would help him convince others of his arguments and would allow him to intimidate them when necessary. Just an edge of self-righteousness was also required, and this particular agent had more than his share of that. Since he was English by birth, he also possessed a touch of international glamor that impressed a lot of the small-town operators he had dealt with in the course of his career.

Lately, however, despite the fact that he traveled constantly, his work held less thrill for him than before. He couldn't think why that was. He had been effective—that was clear by how seldom he had to talk sternly to radio stations and restaurant and bar managers to impress upon them the gravity of hiring entertainers who performed songs protected by—or even worse, *not* protected by—SWALLOW.

Protected songs, of course, could not be performed, except by the licensed artist, without royalties being owed to the artist through SWALLOW. The royalties were paid as a flat fee by the clubs and radio stations on a monthly basis. Then SWALLOW distributed them on a proportionate basis, with the top artists, like Duck Soul, taking the lion's share of the acquired "dues." The money was a fairly hefty amount for people like Soul. Well, back when there *were* people like Soul, it had been a hefty amount. It never had amounted to much, if anything, for the lower-echelon artist. There were no longer any of those either. In fact, Graham supposed that mostly the dues were pretty much split between SWALLOW and Soul these days.

In case anyone else *tried* to play unauthorized music, however, Graham knew the rules: (1) Unprotected songs were not supposed to be played in clubs that paid the fees. (2) Any artist who wished to perform had to likewise pay a fee to SWALLOW (a) to protect his or her interests with the clubs,

(b) to license the material, and (c) to collect the fees. (3) Under the new laws each artist was also supposed to pay royalties every time he or she performed songs by other licensed artists. The only way to escape this clause was by singing only one's own licensed material. Even material that had previously been considered in the public domain was subject to licensing laws since an individual artist's arrangements were considered the work of that artist. So unless substantially altered—and the alterations had to be authorized by SWALLOW—an arrangement of a traditional tune that was not an authorized, much-altered version fell into the same category as an entirely new song.

Furthermore, there were now the obscenity laws SWALLOW enforced. Those laws were why Hugh Graham ultimately decided that a posting in America would be a better career move than remaining in Britain or on the Continent. The laws were difficult to enforce in Britain. Itinerant folk clubs, often composed of amateur musicians or mere fans, drifted like floating crap games (to use an American idiom) from pub to restaurant to private home, providing entertainment for the evenings often without benefit of money or contracts changing hands. People played pirated music and unlicensed songs at parties that SWALLOW was sure involved some sort of fee, but since SWALLOW representatives were not invited to the parties, they had not been able to find out where and when such violations occurred.

Graham was flying back to the home office listening to a Duck Soul tape—after all, he had gotten into the business because he loved listening to music. Since he was a top SWALLOW agent, and his salary was supplemented by commissions that were bounty on the fees and fines he collected, he sat in first class, drinking the fashionable beer he favored. He was a short man, but trim from afternoon workouts in hotel and motel rooms, or sometimes at a gym, track, or park when the neighborhood looked safe. He'd started working out in the afternoons when he realized that the late nights, irregular meals, and frequent intake of alcohol were wearing down his body. He used to arise no earlier than eleven o'clock in time to shower and shave after a night checking for violations. That part was pleasant. The unpleasant part was informing the performers and the management of their wrongdoing. He used to admire musicians before he got into this business. If he hadn't learned to divorce his appreciation for the music from the bloody-mindedness of its performers long ago, he wouldn't have been able to continue his work.

Listening to the steady thump of the drum machine, the lyrics being bawled into his ear, he began to feel that perhaps the time had come when he no longer did appreciate the music. Certainly he didn't care any more for Duck Soul and his lot than he had for others he'd dealt with—although he had never been called upon to chastise Soul yet.

Soul had managed to override the obscenity laws due to a cross-generational language barrier, and Graham could *almost* understand both sides of the conflict now. The law said that records containing obscene lyrics couldn't be sold to minors, and stores went out of business all over the country as SWALLOW agents helped police crack down. They confiscated lots of old English and Scottish murder ballads and, for a time, rap and rock records, but then the producers of the music got smart and garbled the lyrics so badly no one but the targeted teenage audience could understand them. When the lyrics were printed for publication, of course, they were perfectly innocuous. When the rap records *were* intelligible, they were encoded. He wondered how the kids deciphered the messages in the songs.

But though for a time his job had been increasingly interesting as he enforced regulation after regulation, it had, now that most people were used to the regulations, finally become grindingly dull. Because except for Soul, and until recently the few of his brethren who could afford to pay the licensing fees, taxes, and union dues, and to bypass the laws, there was now very little music for the man from SWALLOW to listen to, never mind regulate. He was wondering what he ought to do about that—request assignment in England or Europe and search out new frontier, regulation-wise? Even though the music scene was still so wild and untamed over there as to be impossible, it would be a challenge.

Or perhaps he might quit altogether. Because, since he was not an unintelligent man, he began to see that there just might be some sort of cause and effect between the zeal with which he had done his job because he was such a music lover and the fact that music of most species was now, in the States, extinct or endangered.

▲▲▲

Gussie didn't plan what she was going to tell the police when she half fell through the cafe door. She just wanted to put the door between her and the nut who was after her. When she saw the brown uniform sitting at the stool in front of the counter, she thought she had hit a snag, and she was too tired and too plain scared to deal with it.

"Help me," she panted. "Lock—the—door. There's a crazy guy out there. Got a knife. Blue pickup. Chased me. Lights—green lights—God, do you mind if I sit down?"

She fell into one of the booths along the side of the room, and the cop, standing cop-style with his hands on his hips and his feet spread, said, "Take it a little slower now—this guy *what*?"

She looked up but couldn't see him for the sweat that was pouring into her eyes. She grabbed a handful of napkins from the rectangular metal dispenser and mopped her face, then did her best to look like an innocent little ol' soul who just had the pee-waddin' scared out of her. "This *nut* followed me, officer. I—" She took a better look at his face, which was very familiar. She hadn't seen it for seven years, but they had spent an intense week together in a traffic jam along the Oregon Trail when the devils were trying to kill them. "You're that ranger, aren't you? Bud—?"

"Buddy Lamprey," he said in a guarded voice and then, looking more closely at her, asked, "Gussie? You back? Why didn't any of you write and tell me what happened?"

"It's a long story, Buddy. But they're after me again. Would you take me back to my van? Have your gun out."

"What happened?"

"Buddy?" Janey Lynn said from the counter. "Look!" She pointed at the three lights that hovered just across the street, on the edge of the field, as if they were looking in the cafe window wondering if they could afford something. "What do you suppose they want?"

"What the hell *are* they?" Gussie asked.

"The ghost lights," he said, as if she should have known.

"Ghost what?"

"The ghost lights. You're in Marfa. Those are our famous ghost lights."

She sighed. "It figures," she said, and leaned toward the

front window and waved, calling, "It's okay, boys! I'm fine now! I'm with friends! Thanks! Y'all can go back to hauntin' that field again!"

They bobbed a few times up and down, split up, circled each other, and receded.

CHAPTER VI
▲▲▲

"It seems to me," Barbara said, "that there are a lot of coincidences in your story, Ute. That woman seems to know a lot of people."

"She'd been movin' around some, and runnin' with people who moved around for a livin'. Also, ma'am—"

"Barbara—" the woman said, looking a little pained, as if it were a wearisome task always to have to be educating people— even women—to the politically correct etiquette of the moment. She also looked as if she saw a certain amount of humor in the need to do so, however, and added by way of explanation, "We're to call you Ute, so as far as I'm concerned, you may call me Barbara. But I draw the line at Babs or Barbie."

"Fair enough, Barbara. Anyhow, as I was tellin' you before, Gussie had been a part of a pretty small group—what you might call a subculture—for some time. Folk musicians, and what later were called acoustic or alternative musicians, traveled around like Gypsies or Indian tribes, swappin' songs, swappin' venues. Some of 'em stayed put, but even those got to know fellow musicians from a different place when they came to visit, and they tended to put each other up or recommend one another to supporters who would offer a spare bed to a traveling minstrel. Sometimes, after the music lost its broader popularity and the number of fans dropped, supporters got to know each other too, fans, agents, reviewers, record distributers, journalists, prose writers, poets—even cowboy poets, logger poets, and maritime poets. Union organizers too—people with causes."

"Well, of course I've heard that music has been used in conjunction with causes," Barbara said. "One or two members have suggested that we employ it, but on the whole using something so frivolous seems to me to undermine the seriousness of the message we're attempting to communicate."

"I'm sure you know best about that, ma'am—'scuse me, Barbara, but it seems to me that if you're tryin' to send your message to a lot of people, you need to communicate on a lot of different levels. Talkin' is going to reach some people with a tin ear to whom the emotions behind a topic are irrelevant ways to manip-

ulate people. They'd prefer to manipulate statistics and let them manipulate people. But for a lot of folks, if you can tell them what you're talking about and make it into a story that shows how it could affect people like themselves and put it to a tune they can whistle if they're so inclined, they're going to remember that a lot longer than a statistic or a speech."

"Perhaps," she said. "But I believe most people approach the important issues in a more rational manner."

Ute nodded sadly and stirred the camp fire with a stick, adding some sage and broken-off bits of tumbleweed. "I expect you're right about that. Which in a way is my point. The people who understood and appreciated the kind of music I'm referrin' to were not a large majority of the population anymore, and so, in order to find the kind of thing they enjoyed, they corresponded with each other and talked on the telephone and went to visit one another at festivals. When someone they particularly wanted to hear was playin' in a town where another supporter they knew happened to live they'd visit one another's homes. That's how the subculture got started. 'Course, like any other small group of opinionated people, they fought a lot among themselves over little stuff that a lot of times didn't amount to much more than ego and hurt feelings."

"Now that I can understand," Heather-Jon said. "The way some of the New York ecofeminist group carry on, you'd think every one of us out in the west had personally cut down all the trees, slaughtered the wolves, and poured oil and paint thinner into the rivers and ocean on a regular basis. And done it because we were trying to get dates with loggers and industrialists."

"You did notice that we don't cut down a lot of rain forest here in order to feed our cows, didn't you?" Ute asked.

"But aren't you aware that irresponsible ranching has extended the desert lands?" Barbara asked.

"At one time, yes," he said. "But we've abandoned those practices. That's one reason the boss has started hirin' himself what he likes to think of as the creative cowhand. Managin' any kind of resources today and takin' the kind of pride in your work it takes to do a good job, the boss feels, involves havin' a sense of your own tradition, of where that tradition's brought us in terms of how it affects people. It takes brains to think up ways to save wear and tear on everybody. For instance, you talk about the problems with the desert and the drought down here. Can you think of any better way to explain this country to, say, one of your* *friends in New York, than with lines like the ones Tim Henderson wrote back in the eighties?*

> *"Dust in the living room blown from the yard,*
> *You sweep and you mop and you dust the place hard;*
> *Red light'nin' at night, ain't no sign of rain,*
> *So you oil up your dust rag and you dust once again."*

"We-ell," Barbara said. "I think I see what you mean, but that song could be taken as somewhat reactionary, speaking only to traditional homemakers."

"For Christ's sake, Barbara," Shayla said. "Who is it that we're always having trouble communicating with if it's not the traditional homemakers who got so turned off by the movement's radical roots that they'd poison their petunias just to spite us? He's right. This sort of thing might reach them."

"What were those lines about the wife telling her employee to dust more slowly?" Heather-Jon asked.

Ute sang,

> *"And the ranch wife calls out,*
> *Joselita go slow;*
> *You're sweepin' up dreams*
> *From the Edwards Plateau."*

"Yes," Heather-Jon said. "It's beautiful. Don't you see, Barbara, how those lines address the solidarity of the ranch wife with the women of the other region and her attempt to involve her minority employee, increasing awareness of the environmental problems besetting the lives of other women?"

"Yeah," Shayla said. "No other reason to ask your house-cleaner to go slow. God knows their hourly wage is enough that it seems to take them forever to clean most houses as it is."

They debated about it for a while until pretty soon Heather-Jon got bored and began to think this was not feeling much like a vacation, even a working holiday. When she looked across the fire, she caught Ute's eye and said, "Yes, I can see how being a part of both this country and that sort of music might create a bond between the policeman and Gussie. It just seems fortunate for her that it was he who was in the cafe."

"Yes, it was. But then, there was just as much that was unfortunate happening, so I guess it all evened out, you might say. Anyway, strictly in the line of duty, Buddy drove Gussie back to *her vehicle, and though her battery was run down from her leaving the lights on, neither her purse nor her other money was touched. He took her back to his house until he got off duty and arranged it so he could drive with her over to the ranch three counties away in case the crazy man came after her again. He filled out his report of what happened to her and fudged it a little so that he could ride shotgun for Gussie. Both of them figured from past experience that the crazy knifer was probably looking for her specifically rather than mature women in brown minivans in general. He just couldn't go into his plan in any detail with the department, because of Gussie being the quasi-desperado that she was."*

▲▲▲

The hands were on the lookout for Gussie along the rendezvous point, and when Gussie in her minivan and Buddy in his own truck showed up, Nobby and Swede pointed them toward the big house, where the boss and Willie were in deep discussion with Dally Morales over a six-pack of near-beer. The boss had a heart attack the year Willie left, which was when he decided that maybe his liquor and his cigars didn't matter to him so much as doing something a little different in his life, and that was about the time he looked into taking on cowboy poets and a few cowgirls as well, tradin' one kind of stimulation for another, you might say.

The big house was Spanish style, cottonwood and adobe. The housekeeper was Dally's sister, Carmencita, and she really did do her best to keep the house more or less clean, but the boss was the kind of man who believed that the way to know where everything is was to always have it out in plain sight or at least have some idea of which layer it was under. Tack was of course supposed to stay out with the tack, and there were plenty of people to oil leather and to doctor stock and so forth; nevertheless, there were oily rags and bits and saddles, flea-bitten blankets and a stretched-out rattlesnake hide, deer skulls waiting to be discovered by Georgia O'Keefe imitators or Dallas interior decorators, and all kinds of books, mostly history and poetry, and papers all over the house.

Carmencita kept laundering the rugs and the Mexican blankets that hung on the wall because the boss's two mongrel dogs and six cats kept bringing in bugs of one kind or another.

Willie and the boss were the only ones still up by the time Gussie and Buddy drove up to the big house. Willie pounded them both on the back, hugged them, and made introductions. The house still smelled like the chili Carmencita served for dinner, and Gussie's eyes watered almost as much as her mouth from the fragrance.

"Glad to see you finally made it, darlin'," Willie told Gussie. "Damn, it's good to see you."

"I almost didn't get here at all," she said. "I've got a lot to tell you. Where are the others?"

"Turned in already." He ran his hands through his thinning hair. "We've got a lot to tell you too, but everybody else was so worn-out they hit the hay early. We didn't get us a whole lot of sleep last night. But you know me, Gus. I'm a nocturnal critter, and bein' shot at does wonders for gettin' my adrenaline pumping, even at my age."

"I know what you mean," she said.

He turned to Buddy. "We can use your advice too, my friend. We seem to have a law-and-order type problem on our hands."

Buddy asked what it was, and Willie told him about the murdered Mexican family and the murderers still tied up and locked in the root cellar. "I hope there's a family of rattlers down there to do them in," he said, "but I'm afraid the snakes would extend professional courtesy."

Buddy began guiding them through the channels of authority he thought were most likely to be realistic and flexible, and the boss called a couple of favors in from old friends. Gussie listened for a while, feeling more and more hungry, more and more sleepy, and more and more out of her depth in the conversation. She had no good idea what they ought to do, and even if she had, she couldn't have gotten a word in edgewise. Finally she cut in to ask if there was someplace she could sleep, and the boss left the others talking long enough to show her the two guest rooms at the head of the stairs, where the other women were sleeping. The men were bunking with the hands. "I'm sorry there's only two beds in each room, ma'am," the boss told her. "You could actually have my bed if you liked, but—"

"It's okay," she said. "You got a couch?"

"That's no place for a lady."

"Mister, I appreciate the courtesy, but this lady couldn't possibly climb all those stairs in the shape I'm in. I'll just bunk down out there."

"Fine," he said. "Feel free to turn on the television. We got a nice satellite dish, so reception's pretty good."

The evenings were too cool for air-conditioning, but the front door was left open, the screen door latched, so a slow swell of lukewarm air moved through the front room. The cats had their own flap and came and went all night, bringing more things that tickled and itched. The dogs scratched and in their dreams growled almost as loud as Gussie's stomach. She was so tired she had thought she would sleep a week, and she would have sworn that when Willie wandered into the living room about the time the sun made her toss off her blanket that she hadn't slept a wink.

Willie looked down at her. She knew he was no early riser. He had never been to bed. He was chewing a peanut butter sandwich and drinking a cup of coffee.

"What I wouldn't give for an Egg McMuffin," she groaned, sitting up.

"Carmencita's fixin' us up sack lunches and some breakfast," Willie said. "Meanwhile, why don't you fill me in? Buddy said somethin' about you gettin' chased around by some asshole who thought he was Geronimo or somethin', shootin' at you with a bow and arrow."

As she began telling him about meeting Torchy, the gambling winnings, and the trip from Las Vegas culminating with meeting the maniac outside of Marfa, the others sleepily filed into the room, rubbing their eyes, dry-brushing their teeth, or chewing on a prebreakfast munchie. Halfway through Gussie's story, Carmencita called them into the kitchen and they downed coffee, *huevos rancheros,* homemade tortillas, steaks, and hash browns, with cinnamon buns added for good measure.

As Gussie finished, the banjo, which was sitting in the corner, began twanging loudly. Gussie laughed. "Reminds me of Lettie when she was little. Always wantin' to be picked up. I sort of recognize that tune, though I can't quite put my finger on what it is. Must be one of the ones that's been forgotten."

Juli had scooped it up, even saying, "Shh," to it as she cradled it in her lap and put her hands on frets and strings. She closed her eyes, as she had before when the banjo was trying to communicate with them through her. It was haunted by Sam Hawthorne's spirit, of course, and only once or twice when it had had something vital to tell them had it played such unfamiliar tunes. Sure enough, Juli opened her eyes, said

"Somebody get a pencil and take this down. Or better yet a tape recorder."

Dally Morales, who had come into the kitchen for fresh coffee, dashed back out to the bunkhouse for the brand-new tape recorder he'd bought himself in San Antonio. Meanwhile, Faron Randolph was jotting down which notes Juli's fingers were drawn to as the banjo taught her the tune, which chords she struck as she became familiar with the melody.

When Dally returned with the tape recorder, Juli began singing,

> "Gussie Turner told her tales
> Across this land all over,
> And everyone who heard her stories
> Knew her for a rover.
>
> Oh, she told of an outlaw band
> Who sang forbidden songs,
> And the evil things who hate to sing
> Swore she wouldn't live too long.
>
> One day her band, they came back home
> And Gussie rode to meet them;
> The Queen of Elves, a red-haired gal,
> Said she'd go with Gus to greet them.
>
> The red-haired gal, ol' Lady Luck,
> She gave our Gus a fortune.
> But the redhead's friends had other plans
> To be poor Gussie's portion.
>
> For she told of an outlaw band
> Who sang forbidden songs;
> And the evil things who hate to sing
> Swore she wouldn't last too long.
>
> They sent a lowly murder man,
> He sought with bow and arrow.
> He searched for her both high and low,
> His search was wide and narrow.
>
> Oh she run here and she run there,
> She run left and right-o,

Till the very desert pitied her
And sent forth three ghostly lights-o.

For she told of an outlaw band
Who sang forbidden songs,
But the evil things who hate to sing
Swore she wouldn't live too long.

Now the lights attacked the murder man,
And him they did lay low-o.
Gus followed them to the lights of town,
And then she had to go-o.

She met her band and they met her,
They travel far and near-o
To bring to people songs the devils
Don't want them to hear-o.

So go sing with the outlaw band
Go sing forbidden songs;
And the evil things who hate to sing
Ain't likely to last long."

Willie leaned over and kissed Gussie on her sleep-creased face. "And that, darlin', is 'The Ballad of Gussie Turner' written for you personally by Lazarus."

Gussie nodded sagely. "And very fittin' and proper it is too. I think we got us a theme song."

"I got it!" Faron Randolph said. "The verse tune is from 'Jack O'Ryan,' and the chorus is 'The Bonnie Ship the Diamond.' "

Then they had to sing those songs, and the words came back as if they'd never been wiped from memory. Everybody looked kind of thoughtful for a moment after that, relieved that the magic they'd brought back with them was working to unlock songs, but a little uncertain just how it would continue to work.

Gussie broke the silence. "Now I'm ready to hear the ballad of 'Seven Years Toiling in the Song Mines,' " she said, "with emphasis on the last twenty-four hours."

"We can tell you on the way, darlin'," Willie said. "Right now we got to get movin'."

"What's the rush?" she asked with a mouth full of cinnamon bun.

"The border cops are on their way. Buddy's going to stay here to help the boss and his boys. There'll be much less explainin' to do if we're off the property."

"That's okay," Brose said. "We can go hole up at my place."

▲▲▲

But seven years had passed, and Brose, at least, couldn't go home again. He couldn't even *find* home again.

He was driving while Willie slept and the others, who hadn't gotten enough sleep between the long night and the short morning, nodded blearily in their seats. The banjo was plunking away to itself like a muttering chicken, another tune Brose knew he knew and associated with Oklahoma, somehow or other, but couldn't quite put his finger on.

He turned off the highway at the exit to the access road leading to his property. He wondered which of the animals he had saved from the humane society would still be there and which gone; the cats, the chickens, the old dog, the lame horses, and the dried-up cows. The boys from Austin had been taking care of the place for him when he left. There was no mortgage to pay—the place was an inheritance, and he had sure as hell never increased the property value. The buildings had been barely standing, the yard grown into weeds where the animals hadn't gnawed it down, and even the refrigerator had to be shut by means of four belts linked together that had to be buckled and unbuckled every time he wanted a beer. But it was home. From Scotland he had called his friend Burt Sherry and asked him to help the street kids from Austin with the animals now and then and to contact him if there were any problems. He hadn't heard from Burt in about six years, so everything must be okay.

Of course, it wasn't. Brose was an amazing musician, a talented amateur veterinarian, and possessed a number of other hidden skills. Business management was not among them.

He was so sleepy he was almost on automatic pilot as he turned the van onto the road that used to lead to his house. It took him a moment to realize that something was wrong—it wasn't bumpy enough. He had never improved the road—

it was nothing more than a corduroy dirt track leading to his house. Now it was a broad paved street.

The dirt corduroy road should have led through nothing except fields where once the sick, crippled, and rehabilitated animals had grazed. Instead he found himself driving through a housing development gridded with other broad paved streets with hundreds of houses that each looked like Mexican haciendas and all looked like each other lined up on each side of each street, row upon row, as far as he could see. He drove down the road, thinking there was some mistake, until he came to a little cul de sac, where he turned around and drove back. Some of the houses weren't quite finished yet. Some had only half their sod, the rest of the yard bare dirt with the little bitty trees still in burlap waiting to be planted. His cotton-woods were gone. He drove up and down the streets but didn't see anything familiar, so he drove back out to the access road and kept looking for his place. All he found was another road into the seemingly endless development and a sign that said, "Future sight of Plaza Grande Shopping Mall by the Cairncross Developing Corp., builders of Sola Vista Subdivision."

Brose drove the van back onto the highway until he came to an exit with a convenience store. He went in to use the phone, remembered he had no American money, and gently dislodged Gussie's basket bag, which she was using for a pillow. She grunted, but resettled herself without waking up. He was a little surprised to find the wad of big bills inside, but she also had a couple of ones, and these he took inside with him and changed. He called the listing for the developer, but nobody answered. Then he called the home in Austin where the boys had been staying, and the number was out of service, so finally he called Burt Sherry. A woman's voice answered.

"Evvy Ann? That you?"

"Who's this?"

"Brose Fairchild. Burt around?"

"Burt hasn't been around for quite some time, Brose. Neither have you, for that matter. Can I help you with something?"

Her voice still had the same cute Lubbock accent, but she sounded cold and defensive.

Brose was beginning to feel pretty cold himself. "I just got back from my trip, Evvy Ann. My place is gone. You know what happened to it?"

"Well, of course, I do. It was seized for back taxes by the government. Those kids who were living out there were put in foster homes, and Burt went out from the humane society and had to put down your animals—all but three of the cats and the puppies. We found homes for them."

"Well, I appreciate your not mincing words, Evvy Ann," he said, the air going out of him.

"Dammit, Brose, you've been gone more than seven years. What do you expect? You know what the government is like. Your taxes gotta be paid. You never sent any money, and Burt and me sure didn't have any extra. I'm sorry, but that's just how it is. We'd all like to be able to have nice trips, but people have responsibilities. Speakin' of which, the kids just got home from school." She sounded as if she were about to hang up.

"Thanks, Evvy Ann," he said, but as he pulled the receiver away from his ear, she spoke again.

"Brose?"

"Yeah?"

"We kept one of the bitch pups and she just had a litter. If you want one of the puppies, maybe—if you're here for good and could find a place to take care of her—you could maybe stop by. We—I—the kids might like to see you again."

"Uh-huh. Thanks," he said, and hung up.

As he climbed back into the truck he felt for a moment blind, numb, and deaf except for hearing the plaintive notes the banjo was still plunking. Through a haze of solidifying pain and anger, he recognized the song as the Woody Guthrie dust-bowl ballad, "I Ain't Got No Home."

CHAPTER VII

▲▲▲

Anna Mae Gunn had been dreaming of a bleak day in Scotland when Brose climbed back into the van and started the engine. His face was full of dismay, anger, shame, sadness, and weariness. Lazarus, leaning against the driver's side of the backseat, was softly playing a tune. She realized it had been playing the same tune for some time.

Brose slumped over the steering wheel. As Anna Mae sat up, the banjo changed its tune abruptly to a Scottish one she recognized from a hundred house concerts and parties, and she began to sing the words, at first softly and to herself, but somehow, she knew, she was singing them for Brose:

> "I will go, I will go, when the fighting is over
> To the land that I love where I left to be a soldier,
> I will go, I will go."

The song was the story of a band of soldiers from a certain glen who followed a prince into war:

> "When the King's son came along
> He called us all together
> Saying brave highland men
> Will you fight for my father?
> I will go, I will go."

But the song was about the price of war, even when after surviving the battles:

> "When we came back to the glen
> The winter was turning,
> Our goods lay in the snow
> And our houses were burning.
> I will go, I will go."

Brose hunched over the steering wheel, his shoulders shaking, his crazy bristle of red gray hair nodding with the force of his grief. Anna Mae picked up Lazarus, which was continuing the tune, and stepped forward, dropping her arm around Brose's shoulders, leaning her cheek into his hair. His hands on the wheel were wet.

She found she was crying with him. She'd left her home too, a farm somewhat neater than his, leaving her stock to her neighbors and her favorite cat to find his own way while she joined the others to try to retrieve the music that had always meant so much to her. No prince had called her to battle, though the ghost of Sam Hawthorne had called her on the telephone the night he died and explained to her about the plot to eradicate the music to which he had given his life. She had organized a gathering as he'd asked her, and as a result lost both her best friend and her home. But she had known it was lost when she left. Maybe Brose had known all along too, but he hadn't had to admit it to himself until now.

The tune played over and over as she hunkered down beside Brose until her legs ached. Toward the end the ghostly presence that played Lazarus rapped out a drum roll on the banjo's head, and the tune, after a pause, continued.

> "I will go, I will go
> When the fighting is over
> I will go, I will *go.*"

▲▲▲

Willie liked the back roads sometimes, and since he was driving at night between Austin and Tulsa, he suited himself and drove along, following the white lines, watching the half-moon cruise along at the upper edge of his window. He had slept until nearly one while Anna Mae relieved Brose, and Gussie curled into a defensive ball in the space behind the backseat, mumbling something out loud every once in a while. Terry and Dan spread their sleeping bags under the hatchback, while Ellie dozed sitting up with her head against Faron's shoulder.

Julianne took the passenger seat. She told him the jist of what had happened with Brose, which she had learned from Anna Mae, but then he held up his hand for her to stop talking. He didn't want to know. He couldn't do anything about it, and he couldn't bear to think that he had somehow brought the destruction of Brose's life down on him when his old friend had rescued him the first time the devils got ahold of him. He looked in the rearview mirror at the bodies sprawled and sleeping all around him. With so much company, he wondered why he suddenly felt so lonesome.

He had felt so full of purpose in Britain, as if he could take those songs and all the new skills and all the new knowledge he was gathering into him and come home and transmit his feelings to everybody else. Now that he was here, that confidence was leaking out of the cracked vessel he knew himself to be.

Whether it was the sign advertising gas or the sign advertising the tavern that attracted him most, he couldn't have said, but he pulled up and filled the tank and walked into the tavern, leaving Lazarus behind. The first thing he noticed about the tavern was that, except for the noise of the pool table, the voices of the customers, and the wrestling match on television, it was quiet. No music—country, rock, or otherwise. Nobody even singing drunk and off-key.

The customers consisted of three men bent over a card table, a woman flirting with two men simultaneously at the bar, and three more fellows, two old and a young one, farther down the bar. They all looked bored out of their minds and way too serious for a Saturday night.

The bar had a few pretensions, including a mirror behind it, and in the mirror Willie saw the bartender, an older woman with black penciled eyebrows etched onto her forehead and hard eyes underneath, skin that even in that dim light looked as if it might repel armor-piercing rockets, and a long improbably blond ponytail curling out from one of those slug-shaped hair combs women wore lengthwise on the backs of their heads. Her bangs were the same blond, dingy at the roots, and had that too-short curly look like Mamie Eisenhower's used to.

Her lipstick made him think of the line from *The Shooting of Dan McGrew*. "My God, how ghastly she looked in her paint, the lady that's known as Lou." But she turned and set a drink down in front of him.

He shook his head. "I didn't order anything."

She jerked her thumb to the end of the bar, where one of the older men held up a shot glass. "It's on me, Willie. Haven't seen you around in a coon's age." Willie was too tired to do anything but give the man a blank stare, and pretty soon the fellow said, "You are Willie MacKai, ain't you?"

"I'm not sure if it's safe to admit it or not, but yes, I am."

The man laughed. "What a kidder. Fellas, you never heard

nothin' till you've heard this guy perform. You playin' around here, Willie? I used to go hear you all the time, but you probably don't remember me. Bob Beezle? You were mostly surrounded by females back then."

The man's question reminded Willie that while he knew and his small group of friends knew and their network of supporters knew that there had been a conspiracy to keep them from performing, the general public didn't know. If Torchy had been telling Gussie the truth, first folk music in particular and then most kinds of music in general were just gradually withdrawn without anybody particularly missing it. That was a depressing thought. But at least the man who bought him a drink remembered him, and that seemed like a good sign.

"I been on a European tour," Willie told him. "Learned lots of new material."

"Well, how about playin' us something?" the man asked, and to the bartender he said, "That's okay, right, Simone?"

"I don't have a guitar with me, friend, but thanks for askin'," Willie told him.

"I can fix that," he said. "But first, a toast to the greatest performer that ever lived. Simone, it's on me. To you, Willie!" and Willie couldn't very well not drink his whiskey, after which Simone poured him another one.

While the man next to him was telling Willie the story of his life, a guitar appeared from somewhere in the vicinity of Bob Beezle, and someone slid it down the bar toward Willie, much to the disgust of Simone, since there had been drinks on the bar before the guitar knocked them off.

He picked up the guitar confidently. It was an old Ovation, curved plastic back. Good sound. The strings didn't seem too old as he ran down them with his thumb. "What do you want to hear?" he asked.

"I don't know. You're the singer. Play something," the man said. "Simone, another drink for my friend Willie."

Willie tuned and began to play one of his old standards, a Mexican song he had learned as a youngster. As he sang the words and strummed the familiar rhythms, he couldn't help seeing the bodies of the family lying in that ravine, a whole family, maybe more than one, wiped out as if they were coyotes or cockroaches. The tune he was singing was a happy one, but the pain of the memory lent it the death-edge common to so many songs in Spanish, what the poets called

duende. He closed his eyes as he sang and was a little surprised to suddenly hear the announcer of the wrestling match
talking over him. He opened his eyes.

All of the patrons of the bar had turned back to the television, including Bob Beezle, who had just reached up to turn
up the volume so it drowned out Willie's song. The tune died
away under his fingers.

"That'll be twenty-two fifty," Simone told him.

"Beg your pardon?"

"For the gas. Twenty-two fifty."

Numb and disoriented again, Willie dug for money and
discovered he didn't have any American money. "Excuse me,
ma'am, I need to go back out to the car. I just got back from a
trip and only have foreign money on me."

"No tricks, buddy. I can see your license number from
here," she said.

Willie first wanted to kill Beezle, or at least yell at him, and
then wanted to die himself. He half expected the van not to be
there when he got outside, for the whole trip and everybody
who'd been on it with him seemed to be a dream. The people
in the bar didn't appear to be aware of anything strange but
continued with their pastimes as if he weren't there. He didn't
think Beezle would hear him if he called him names, didn't
think his fist would connect with anything solid if he tried to
punch the man. He felt dizzy, disoriented, and had the queer-
est feeling, as if he hadn't played at all.

Then he told himself maybe he'd just played badly, even
though he knew he had improved as a musician about seven-
hundredfold in the seven years he'd spent abroad. But to
these people his music simply made no difference. Those jerks
just preferred the television. If there was magic in his music,
they were immune. Funny, when Beezle had claimed to be a
fan.

Puzzled and pissed off, Willie wove his way out to the van,
noticing that maybe abstention hadn't been so good for him—
he couldn't seem to hold his liquor like he used to.

The half-moon was high and the stars were bright as he
crunched across the gravel parking lot, away from the neon
signs. A woman was leaning up against the van, looking up at
the moon. She was wearing boots, jeans, a tank top, and a
Stetson and turned to smile at him as he walked up.

"Hi there, sugar. How was your glorious comeback?"

"I remembered the goddamn song, which was more than I did when I left this country," he growled at her.

"Hush now, sweetie, you'll wake all the good people in the van. Come on back inside and I'll buy you another drink."

"I don't need a drink, but if you could scare up twenty-two fifty, and I know you're just the gal to ask to scare things up, I'd be much obliged, and I wouldn't have to wake anybody." He didn't mind in the least taking advantage of the Debauchery Devil.

"Why, Willie, you've gotten considerate in your old age!"

"Look, lady, can we just drop the crap? What are you doing here?"

"I came to warn you, Willie. You know what a soft spot I have for you."

"Yeah, baby, I know. You're all heart."

"No, but really. You saw how those people acted in there. You're just going to be beating your head against a wall if you try to play that some old stuff. Nobody wants to hear it. You sing about Mexican bandits and cowboys and lonesome pickers, and most people have never even seen anybody like that in the media, much less for real. People watch game shows and talk shows and soap operas now. They like real-life stories about serial killers and the latest war. They're just not interested in all that rehashed crap you people sing about."

"It doesn't seem like it, does it?"

"No, and you've been away for a long time. Look at what happened to poor old Brose. Lost everything, even that beat-up old stock of his. The kids he was trying to help are all working for me now. All the last part of his life was wasted because of this kick you've been on. You've still got some of your charisma, Willie. The people who remember you will follow you—well, except for that guy in there. Don't let them waste the rest of their lives. I'm sure Gussie Turner mentioned that she came into some money before she met you—"

"Yes, ma'am, she surely did."

"I guess you realize that if the tax people should decide she owed them a bigger cut than what they took out at the casino —and I guess you also realize that it could be arranged that they *do* decide such a thing—she could lose the rest of it and her house and all, whereas if they don't come to such a mean, unfair decision, well, she could use it as a stake for all of you to get started again in new lives. Am I makin' any sense to you, honey?"

"You going to give me the twenty-two fifty or not?"

She dug into the bosom of the tank top and pulled forth a warm twenty and a warm five. "Think it over, tiger," she said, and sauntered off, hips switching.

He walked back into the bar. The bartender's unshapely rear was to him, and he saw her hard face reflected in the mirror as he put down his money. Another old, hard, disillusioned face was right beside it, looking straight back at him.

Back in the van Lazarus was gently thrumming, a vaguely familiar melody.

Julianne was awake and asked, "Well, did you and Torchy or whoever she is this week have a nice talk?"

"Yeah, she said if we'd go home, all is forgiven, and we can take up new careers." To avoid going into it any further, he asked, "What *is* that tune? I used to know it pretty well."

"You know, it's the Stan Rogers song about the ranch wife who's afraid she's getting old, and every time she looks in her mirror, she sees all these lines and can't quite decide if the mirror is lying to her or not."

"Would you drive for a while? I'll pick somethin' on Lazarus and keep you company."

That was the most companionable Willie had been since they'd crossed the border, so Julianne slid over and Willie took up Lazarus, running quietly through all the American banjo and fiddle tunes and songs he could think of as they crossed the Oklahoma border and drove toward Tulsa. Lazarus finally insisted on playing, "Nobody Knows You When You're Down and Out."

▲▲▲

As the van drove away, the man who had called himself Bob Beezle, followed by the rest of the occupants of the bar, danced out the door and into the parking lot, threw his tractor cap in the air, grabbed the Debauchery Devil, and whirled her around, exulting, "I've still got it, DD! Still the Great Deceiver! Did you see his face? No, of course you didn't, but it was priceless, wasn't it, gang?"

The mixed group of devils and minions absolutely agreed, all but the Stupidity and Ignorance Devil, who said, "Yeah, The music was real purty, but he wasn't talkin' very clear."

"He was singing in Spanish, Stu," another devil informed him.

"Oh."

The Chairdevil hugged the cowgirlified Debauchery Devil to him and said, "I think this is the trick! This is how to handle 'em! We've been giving them too much big-time attention, making them feel too important. I believe this sort of thing—indifference, I mean, negative reinforcement, will be even better. You'll have MacKai in the bottle quicker than Aladdin's genie, DD. If there's anything this show-offy type of person can't stand, it's having nobody pay any attention to him."

"You're going to call off the murderer then?" she asked cautiously.

"I wouldn't go that far," he said.

CHAPTER VIII

▲▲▲

Ellie wasn't quite as worried as the others about having a home to go to. Her dad had tracked her all over the British Isles, Scandinavia, and parts of France and Germany, and if she forgot to send postcards, he sent cards from Tulsa. Whenever possible, she phoned home—collect—and whenever possible left her parents a number they could call. So she was looking out the window, drinking in the familiar sights she remembered from her girlhood. ("There, look there, y'all! That park over there is where Faron and I got married.")

She'd phoned ahead from the last gas station and took the wheel for the last leg of the trip. Her folks' house was just the way she remembered it—almost.

Faron jiggled her elbow and pointed to the old maple on the front lawn. It was gift wrapped with a big yellow ribbon and a huge yellow cluster bow.

She didn't have much time to admire the effect, however, because the screen door banged open and her daddy waved at her from the front porch and started trotting down the cracked cement toward the car. Her mama, who was a jogger, outstripped her dad and reached her first, enveloping her in a big hug.

"Ellie, for Christ sakes!" Faron yelled, grabbing the wheel and stomping the brake as the abandoned van started to roll off unattended.

"Good to see you, son, come on in the house," Barry Curtis, Ellie's dad said, giving him a one-armed embrace around the neck through the open window of the van. "You folks too, come on in. Molly just went to the store and picked up some frozen yogurt, and I baked some chocolate-chip cookies."

They sat on the floor or in the big, cat-scarred chairs, their hands full of ice cream and fresh cookies, their laps full of cats. Juli dozed and Willie paced. Gussie set down her empty ice cream bowl and folded her hands in her lap, saying, "Now I think it's about time Ellie's folks and I heard more about your trip and what you learned after I left Scotland."

"I'd like to hear about that," Barry said. "Even with the

size of our overseas phone bill, I don't feel like we got the whole story."

"I know good and well we didn't," Molly said. "Come on, you guys. Give."

Ellie began, "Well, at first we had a little trouble making connections since we ended up going on the road with the Gypsy circus. But Rosa—she was the new Phurai Dai after her husband disappeared—she and her uncle knew a lot of really neat Gypsy songs. Her uncle tried to give Faron his violin, but, Mama, you wouldn't believe how *beautifully* that man could play. He even played a Gypsy lament for that horrible Giorgio. He told us that at one point Giorgio tried to break his hands—a wonderful talent like that, and Rosa's *uncle* to boot, and Giorgio was going to maim him. But this song he played was *so*—so—" She sniffled, and her father handed her a Kleenex.

Faron also reached for a Kleenex and blew his nose heartily. He wiped his eyes and continued. "It was really something," he told them. "It makes both of us cry just thinking about it."

Brose's face spasmed with pain, and he walked hurriedly out the front door mumbling, "Gonna walk."

"Giorgio was in a Nazi prison camp when he was just a kid," Dan put in. "It sort of snapped him, and he was breaking all kinds of Gypsy law and putting his people at risk, mistreating Rosa and the old man and the kids when they tried to interfere. But the old man had been in the camps too before he managed to escape, and he knew what it was like. The song was his own composition."

"Besides"—Terry made a face—"the poor guy fell under the influence of that damned redhead. She had him peddling drugs."

"Anyway, he tried to give me his violin," Faron said, "because he'd given it to me once before when he thought Giorgio was going to break it. I told him to leave it to me in his will."

"There's somethin' I got to tell you kids when you're done," Molly said, worry darkening the bright expression that had livened her Indian-dark features since her daughter arrived. "Somethin' important. About that bill. Remind me, Barry."

"Okay," her husband said. "But now then, y'all were traveling with the Gypsies. Then what?"

"Well, they took us to all these little islands, and guess what? They had great libraries the devils' minions hadn't even thought of touching. I stayed on Iona while the others toured the Orkneys."

"Ellie was in hog heaven," Faron said.

"So were we," Willie said, pausing in midpace. "In little old places like that where there ain't much to do, it's a lot like the town I grew up in—people make music all the time. Hell, we was playin' one party after another with some of the best damn musicians you ever saw in your life. Lots of them couldn't *sing* worth shit, but then, a lot of 'em could, and they could all play rings around any of us on any instrument they took a mind to play."

"We stayed there the first year," Terry said. "And another in the Shetlands and the Hebrides. The music was wonderful, but I thought I was going to mildew."

"Well, then Ellie got a card for us forwarded from Hy Mac-Donald sayin' he was back from the oil fields and did we still need help. So we wrote back that we'd admire to do that very much and asked him to meet our ferry the next month."

"He introduced us to some great people who knew people in Cornwall, Wales, and Ireland. We spent a year in Cornwall and another in Wales. One of the people we met knew someone whose granddad had been a private collector of broadside ballads, so we combed London and the surrounding area for music while Ellie researched those for a year. She knows the words to—what—five or six hundred of them?"

"*And* I learned Gaelic," Ellie said. "A little anyway."

"Enough to make fun of us when we try to sing in it," Faron said.

"Anyhow, after that we got a ride with this chantey singer who was skipper of a fishing boat, and he took us over to Ireland. God, I have never seen somebody's personality change so drastically between land and sea!" Ellie said. "He was a doll and so entertaining you couldn't believe it when we met him at the party, but once we were away from shore, it was like Captain Bligh time."

"Ah, Ireland," Willie sighed. "Picker's paradise."

"Especially if the picker happens to lean hard into country and western like you," Anna Mae said. "Have you folks ever heard Irish country and western? It's like 'How I miss the old homestead with Mama and Daddy sittin' by the fire smellin' the peat smoke.' "

"The Irish are just very emotional," Dan told her. "That's why they like that kind of music. Willie was a huge hit, and we learned lots of great Irish stuff when we could get them to stop egging Lazarus on to playing 'Foggy Mountain Breakdown.'"

"How come you had to come through Mexico, though?" Gussie asked. "I couldn't believe your message."

"The Canadian border is closed tighter'n a drum, darlin'," Willie told her. "We heard that from Liam, our skipper buddy. They were deporting all U.S. musicians from Canada, and the U.S. was deporting all the Canadians too. Some new trade agreement. Not wanting the arts to contaminate each other or something dumb like that. Just when we were tryin' to decide what to do, who shows up in port but Jim Hawkins."

"That chanteyman from the festival? The one who got us out of the traffic jam from hell?"

"Live and in color," Willie said. "He was sailing a yacht back to Mazatlan for some wealthy folk and decided to take a little detour to drop us off."

"We learned some cool songs in Mexico too," Dan said. "But we were ready to come home. The buses were crowded and hot and smelled bad, but the people were pretty great, and it wasn't too hard to get a place to stay and some food as long as we had Lazarus."

"We caught a ride to the border," Willie said, "and were about to cross when all that business with the snakes and the ghost and the flood and stuff happened—"

"Whoa, whoa, wait up a minute," Gussie said. "Go over that part a little slower." He did.

"I think that's more than I *wanted* to know," Molly said, shuddering. "Those snakes sound *awful.*"

"Well, I'd still like to hear more details," Barry said. "But I guess they'll come out when you've been home a little longer."

Ellie threw her arms around her father's neck. "You don't know how good it is to talk to you again. I just missed y'all so much. It's just so good to hear people talk—well, normal."

Terry's boyfriend Dan grinned at her. "But you don't talk normal—*I* talk normal. You guys have an Okie twang."

Molly Curtis stuck out her tongue at him, but Ellie said, "No, it was so funny. But here we were, jamming with all of these people, with these *beautiful* singing voices who talked in these gorgeous Irish brogues and Scottish burrs and all these fascinating English dialects and accents and stuff, and I was just so lonesome to hear people who sounded like home."

"You used to *hate* how people talked here," Molly reminded her. "You tried to talk like the people on TV so you wouldn't sound so pig-ignorant."

Ellie twiddled an end of her hair and grinned. "Well, yeah. Maybe I just thought we sounded pig-ignorant because *I* was if I *said* a thing like that."

"You should have seen her," Faron put in. "She'd go up to anybody who sounded like they were from west of the Mississippi or south of the Mason-Dixon Line. She's got a whole address book full of phone numbers she's supposed to call to let people know she got home all right. And I kept having to pull her away from homesick soldiers who got the wrong idea."

Ellie hit him with one of her stuffed animals, which her parents had arranged on the sofa to greet her. "Yeah, but we learned some great filk songs from some of those guys, and the marching chants were funny. What did they call them? Judy calls? Mom, Dad, if a Major Chuck Hamilton phones, you'll let him know where we are, won't you? He's been stationed overseas ever since this started, so he still knows lots of folk songs. He was supposed to be coming back to Fort Sill. He put us on to some really good informants. Not everybody I met was as nice as he was, but I still met some great people, including some older folks. When they heard that Faron and I were going to do music someplace, sometimes they'd come along. We met three people who'd learned Appalachian versions and Ozark versions of the British ballads from their folks and had completely forgotten about them until they came to the jam session."

"Seems to me like that might be a place to start looking people up if you want to reintroduce the music," Barry Curtis told her. "Because I'll tell you for sure, honey, there aren't any more radio shows or folk festivals or even bars or restaurants where you could get your foot in the door anymore."

Ellie nodded. "Maybe not, but some of the people I've met are pretty rich too, and maybe they could help us."

Gussie, who'd been listening drowsily, looked up. "Speaking of rich."

Willie, pacing from one room to the other and back again, apparently absorbed in his own thoughts, said, "Tell 'em about comin' into all that money, Gus."

"I surely will. You want some by the way?" She dived into the basket bag and pulled out a wad of bills. "Its our seed money to get us rollin' here. We need at least one other vehicle, for starters."

"Oh?"

"Well, I assumed we'd split up and I'd keep doin' what I'm doin' to get people worked up about hearing the rest of you. Except that I'd just as soon I wasn't entirely by myself after what happened outside of Marfa."

"Uhhuh," Barry said. "Which ghost saved you that time?"

"Actually, it was a bunch of lights—them and Buddy Lamprey—"

"The Texas Ranger who was going to arrest me last time you saw him," Willie explained. To Gussie he said, "Well, to tell the truth, darlin', we're home now. We got the songs, and I think Ellie's experience with the people she met while we were over in Britain show that once we help people remember these old ballads, the rest will start coming back to them. I think you could probably just go on back home and spend time with Lettie and Mic if you want to. Relax and let the rest of us take over."

"But you'll need to know where I've been, who I've talked to, what I've found out, won't you?" she asked in a surprisingly small voice.

"Of course, we will," Julianne told her. "It's just that since you're not actually a musician, there's no need for you to keep sticking your neck out anymore."

"I see."

"She doesn't," Anna Mae said. "And I don't either. Only eight of us are musicians, counting Hawkins, who's still at sea, of all the people involved in this. We have every bureaucracy and power structure in the country pitted against us, plus the supernatural stuff. We're going to be on the road a lot and singing a lot and hiding a lot. We need someone who can make calls and write letters and talk to people and—"

"And organize," Molly Curtis said. "I hate to break the news to you guys, but they're tryin' to pass a bill in Congress that you have to license musical instruments. Especially banjos."

"What? How can they do that?"

"Some guy beat his wife to death with two banjos. The gun lobbies got together, no doubt inspired by you-know-who with the little horns and pointy tails, and started petitioning the congressmen to pass laws against instruments that could be used for murder, in an effort to pressure them into repealing gun laws. Instead, Congress seems to be takin' it all seriously."

"That's *terrible*," Anna Mae said. "We need to—"

"Organize," Molly said. "That's what I mean. So, if y'all are going to run off Gussie, leave her here to work with us, will you?"

The banjo, resting against the arm of the sofa, began tinkling a tune.

"That's familiar," Willie said. "What is that?"

Gussie smiled smugly. "Lazarus is on my side. Even I know that one. *My* mama told it to me as a rhyme, and later in school we learned it as a round."

"Sure," Molly said. "I know it too." She sang in a light, warbly voice, but entirely on pitch. "Make new friends but keep the old; / One is silver and the other gold."

Willie lifted a brow at the banjo and gave it an ironic half salute. "Okay. So Gussie comes with us. But where? Where do any of us go and what do we do now? I still think the fastest way to get the songs spread out is to travel separately."

"Fine," Anna Mae said. "But who takes Lazarus? The banjo was our protection before, and if one of us takes it, that leaves the others vulnerable to attack."

"Not if you're careful," Willie said. Part of him had been aching for some time to be back on his own again, to have some time to himself, to choose whom he would be with, to not have to account to anybody else.

"How careful do you have to be?" Gussie asked. "Just to let folks know you were comin', just to tell this story, I've been prowlin' school yards and kids' parties like some kind of pervert, riskin' jobs to talk to customers in bars and at conventions where I work, and I certainly have not been getting paid or invited special to tell my stories—and still that redheaded devil has tracked me down. And I wasn't even performing music. So I'd say offhand you have to be *real* careful."

Willie was pacing back and forth in front of the sofa in a tight little line, so fast he made Ellie dizzy. She wanted to grab him by the belt and make him sit down and be still.

Instead she bopped him with a stuffed bear and grinned up at him, thinking he'd take it as a joke and get the hint. He didn't say anything and didn't smile, just headed for the door.

"Where are you going, Willie?" Julianne asked. "We have to decide about some important issues—"

"You just go ahead and decide then, darlin'. I'll be fascinated to know what it is you come up with. I need me a little
space right now."

"Willie, come on back here. We've got things to discuss—
oh, of all the adolescent, unproductive—" Anna Mae growled,
but she was talking to his back.

▲▲▲

*"What a sad way to end," Shayla sighed. "After all that running
around, collecting songs, and so on, to just fall apart like that.
But that's been my experience with movements too—internal dis-
sension, politics . . ."*

*"Well," Barbara said, "they were dealing with a very minor
issue after all. I'm assuming, Ute, that the devils in your story,
and the ghosts for that matter, are metaphorical devices. I mean,
it truly doesn't matter if anyone remembers little jingles or not,
does it? Except to advertising people. I'm sure at one time in the
distant past such entertainments were very important, but that
sort of music is a relatively simplistic comfort in an astonishingly
complex world. When you say that all music was gone, you don't,
for instance, mean to imply that all of this has anything to do
with the reason one never hears classical music anymore, or why
it is impossible any longer to attend symphony performances or
the opera?"*

*He cleared his throat. "Actually, ma'am, some of the great
classical pieces derived their basic inspirational melodies from
little folksongs, and most of the operas and ballets are celebra-
tions of common myth and folktales so I'm afraid that yes, in the
United States, just in the seven years that Willie and his pals have
been away, all music except that specifically permitted to filter
through, has become kaput. The symphony halls and opera
houses have closed down—even music schools went out of business. Country music, which had its origins with the people as
much as with Nashville, and rock and roll, and jazz, which origi-
nated in black slave music—so did swing and big band music to
some extent—everything except the stuff put out by Duck Soul
and other devil-sanctioned acts disseminating the kind of messages the devils had in mind has simply ceased to function as
part of our culture. Even rap has gone out of business, because it
was folk music too, although it came from its very own roots.
The roots behind it though were jump-rope chants and hunting
chants in Africa, for Caucasians, Gregorian chants and further
back, the magic chants of European tribes—the magic chants of*

Indians. When the folksongs were killed, the root songs, the rest of it all dried up like a South Texas river during a dry spell. With every song that died, you see, it's been easier for the devils to erase ten more. Just as when Willie and his friends recovered one song, they retrieved it with seven more as interest. As soon as they, and the songs they learned and Lazarus came back in the country, the songs that have been lost became available to memory again, but meanwhile institutions had been destroyed.

"Really," Barbara said. "Someone should have organized those people. And you aren't seriously trying to tell us that all of this happened supernaturally?"

"Not all of it, no ma'am. A lot of it was just purely the cussedness of human nature."

CHAPTER IX

▲▲▲

"Oh, now I've gone and depressed poor Willie. Or was my singing really that bad?" Molly asked when Willie had left. She was partly teasing to relieve the tension but partly serious. She was uncharacteristically shy and a little sensitive about her singing, especially in front of all these professional musicians. Even when all she was singing was a long-forgotten childhood singsong.

Julianne shook her head. "Of course not. Something happened in a bar on the way here that upset Willie, and he's been acting like an asshole ever since."

"Well, I know my voice isn't the greatest, but—"

Dan unfolded his long body and stretched. "I bet he just needed to walk. I'm pretty tired of being folded up myself. I think I'll go walk too."

"Me too," Terry said.

"You kids be careful now," Barry told them. "This end of town can get pretty rough. It seems to have gotten rougher since they recruited the Neighborhood Militia to patrol for drug traffic. It's like martial law around here sometimes. Reminds me of the sixties with the National Guard called in to control the looting during the race riots, except that everybody was pretty much minding their own business."

"We'll watch ourselves," Dan promised breezily as they left.

Julianne returned to the topic at hand, saying earnestly, "No, really, Molly. Look, the whole point of our trip was to bring back old songs so everybody could remember them— not just so we would be, like, musical anthropologists or something. Where we've been, people have been singing and playing everywhere just because they can, just because they know songs, just for the fun of it. You're embarrassed now because people don't do that very much here. It's like everybody's a specialist. We were the song specialists, and if anybody else tried to sing or make music who wasn't a bona fide musician, it was somehow or other wrong. Like you were invading our territory. I've certainly talked to musicians who got all pissy because somebody was singing along and spoiling their act—not necessarily because it sounded bad. They could just be mouthing the words."

Barry nodded. "Well, everybody likes to have something that makes them special, and a lot of people tend to see anyone else who does the same thing as competition to be squashed—not just people in show business either. And if the person horning isn't as good, it can kinda devalue the whole effort for insecure performers who've put a lot of sweat into developing the one thing about themselves they consider to be worthwhile." Barry and Molly were social workers and sometimes it showed.

"On the other hand," Juli said, "the person who's devoted so much energy can't know everything about it, and the person who's just chiming in might know something useful. Like just now, with you, Molly."

"You know what I think?" Anna Mae asked in a tone that said she was fixing to tell them. "I think this hang-up about being embarrassed to sing unless you've got a license or something is just another way for *them* to get at us. You notice they didn't have that kind of attitude in Scotland and Ireland. The best singers lead, but everyone is *expected* to contribute— though I'll admit it was kind of hard to sit through a bad voice singing fifty partially remembered verses of some ballad."

Faron, Ellie, and the Curtises exchanged amused looks. "Sounds like a filk-sing," Faron said.

"A what?"

"A filk-sing. *Kind* of like making up new verses to old songs, only the new songs are all about the stuff you find in science fiction and fantasy stories and shows. But some people used to write their own whole new songs, and some of them were great."

"That's how I met Faron," Ellie said with a sigh and a smile at her husband. "At a filk-sing. He was the cleverest one there."

"Hmph," Brose said. "Never heard of it. Where'd all this happen?"

"At science fiction–fantasy conventions," Barry answered. "We used to be real involved in one here in Tulsa every year in late summer."

"Used to, Dad?" Ellie asked, sounding stricken.

"Oh, everybody lost interest about the time you kids left. You know, we couldn't get the books anymore except at used bookstores when all the major publishers shifted to strictly nonfiction. And filking got ridiculous—everybody started thinking they were some kind of star and bein' snotty to everybody else, and there were big feuds going on. It just wasn't any fun anymore. We still have our meeting once a year to sort of reminisce and see if anybody's interested in starting it up again, but so far it seems like too much trouble."

"Umm," Molly said. "Lots of things that used to be fun seem to be too much trouble anymore. Nobody's interested. Seems like no matter what kind of stuff is on TV, people'd rather watch that than do anything they could do themselves. Listen to me. Do I sound like I'm getting old or what?"

"I feel like I'm gettin' older by the minute," Brose said, heaving himself out of a man-eating armchair with a great sigh. "I think I need me a little exercise. Gonna go jog. Find me some of that rough company y'all was talkin' 'bout." He didn't want to hear about anybody else's problems. He had plenty of his own just then.

"Maybe we're all just tired and overwhelmed by what's ahead of us. I know Willie's pretty discouraged right now too," Juli said. "He was doing so much better, and then, I don't know—I think if I had any money, I'd be tempted to go back to Britain."

"Hmph," Gussie said. "I don't think they'd let you in again, money or not. Now I think we ought to do somethin' about collectin' some more instruments. Even though you can all sing perfectly well a cappella, you look a little naked with nothin' in your hands. I reckon if those damned devils are tryin' to license all instruments, we'd better get ours before they succeed. If nobody's played music in a long time, the pawnshops should be real glad to see us."

"Can you bring back six more banjos just like Lazarus?" Faron asked.

"That would solve a few things, wouldn't it? You'd better come with me. No matter how liberal anyone chooses to be about who sings and who doesn't, I'm still, if not tone deaf, tone impaired when it comes to choosing instruments."

"We'll tune them to Lazarus," Faron said, picking up the banjo, which was jingling a refrain to "There's a Meetin' Here Tonight." "The most magical thing about this banjo really is that it's always in tune."

▲▲▲

The devils were all gathered around their big table at the board meeting. The Chairdevil looked sharp in his black suit with the narrow red pinstripes, his black silk shirt and red tie, his black hair slicked back like a gangster's. Actually, of course, it was gangsters who had originally slicked back their hair in imitation of the Chairdevil, but most people didn't know that.

The Debauchery Devil wore big black sunglasses and drummed her long red fingernails on the table.

The Chairdevil grinned. "Fellow devils, I want to thank you all for your enthusiasm and cooperation. We are well on our way to establishing our own rule here, and our various strategies are proceeding brilliantly. Our control of the television stations, computer networks, and radio stations is well established. They broadcast news of our triumphs constantly.

"Sports are pretty much tied up with litigation and corruption, so people can't enjoy their favorite stars anymore.

"By cleverly playing on people's fears of the hereafter, we have managed in a very short time to elevate health to godhood on its own. Ill health is, if not actually more sinful than screwing your neighbor's wife, at least socially less acceptable. I think we've pretty much managed to convince people that if they follow the correct regimen, they will not become diseased or die, and that if they do, they have somehow fallen from grace. *Then,* once we have them convinced that they have to follow the straight and narrow, we change what that *is.*

"They are only supposed to read about real things and real people, and we keep only enough fiction in these accounts to keep them always feeling like they're fairly scruffy by comparison and somehow or other not doing something right. Can't have the unwashed masses getting all cocky and uppity on us now, can we?

"Schools have cut out their music programs, thanks to our campaign to eliminate first the old music and then other kinds from the consciousness of the livestock out there. Our censorship programs have been very successful in cutting out any but the dullest and wimpiest kind of pap that bears no resemblance to what the kids learn from each other in school, never mind in the real world.

"And of course, the Debauchery Department, led by our own DD"—he waved acknowledgment to the redhead, who bobbed her foot in acknowledgment so that her high-heeled shoe fell away from her sole and snapped back again—"has chemically created a generation liberally sprinkled with children who can't think, can't concentrate, and are easily irritated. They should be malleable tools when it comes to our other plans.

"We have put our drug programs on the back burner and elevated health at the expense of our other addiction programs to bring as many people as possible back to the reality we have lying in wait for them—and if you think it's good now, wait a few years.

"By the time these irritable children and their little friends grow up to a world full of disillusioned elderly people living in the literal, brutal reality we intend to keep rubbing their noses in every single day, they won't know who they are, where they came from, and what it all means, *or* have a clue why they ought to continue. There will be nothing for them to do but to give us our ultimate dream and blow the whole damned thing up! And we don't even have to create a button-pushing minion. They'll do it themselves, just for something to do."

The devils, except for one, were on their feet applauding. The Debauchery Devil was glad she had on sunglasses now, because her red eyes were blazing. They were trying to do her out of a job! Bombarding people with reality, smothering them with virtue, left her with no organized power base. Just all the little stuff that went on underground. Of course, that would get bigger and bigger ordinarily, due to human nature. Still the Company had always organized the chemical and fleshly escapes people indulged in. There was no whisper of that at this meeting. Slowly, slowly, she slipped her red high heel back onto her foot and swayed to her feet. She clapped one short staccato clap followed after a few deliberate seconds by another.

The Doom and Destruction Devil glowed, however, as the boss extended a hand toward him and said, "I'd like to thank Threedee here for the inspiration for this program."

Threedee waved his palms in modest disclaimer. "Hell, boys, we've been using this tactic for a long time. Take a bunch of people and put 'em under pressure, fill 'em with self-righteous baloney about how good they are versus how bad somebody else is, bore the shit out of 'em long enough, and they'll start takin' bites out of each other if you don't give 'em somebody to kill soon enough. It's not original or anything."

"I'm ashamed it's taken me so long to see the modern applications," the boss apologized. "But one day when

Threedee and I were doing a hot tub together and he was talking about his latest operations, it just came to me. I'd like that kind of input from all of you others from time to time."

Right, thought the Debauchery Devil. She felt ready to blow something up then and there. If only she had never signed that treaty with hell. Had never agreed to the tribute each year, especially to that clause that said if she didn't come up with a sacrifice, she herself was forfeit—not just for the standard seven-year contract she had with mortals, but for so long as her services were required. After which—if there was an after—they could dispose of her as they liked.

Of course, back when she signed the contract—so long ago she almost couldn't remember—she had been a wild, free creature, full of starlight and harp music and the smell of rain in the nighttime woodlands. All sensation and magic and no logic. And hell, of course, had then, as now, all the wiliest, craftiest lawyers. But then she had believed if she didn't compromise, her kingdom would be annexed anyway. The treaty had bought her and her people a few centuries more of song and laughter, until that cursed Janet had ambushed the Ride and stolen away the sacrifice. That was her own damned fault too—her and her weakness for sexy mortal males who undoubtedly had a fairy in the woodpile somewhere. Their charm and winning ways worked as compellingly on mortal women as it did on fairy queens—and on debauchery devils, for that matter. The Janets of the world had their own kind of ruthless powers.

She'd gotten used to trading starlight for neon lights, the smell of rain in the woods for the smell of floral room freshener superimposed on vomit. And the songs—well, the songs were just about to go too.

The boss interrupted her reverie with a severe look from his slitted red eyes. "DD, have you got something to say?"

She shrugged. "I was just wondering what—uh—contribution my department is going to have to make in all of this now."

He looked her straight in the eye, and she saw all the grimiest, ugliest, noisiest, smelliest, itchiest, hottest parts of hell opening up before her. "I've been wondering that myself."

"It doesn't sound like you've got much for me to do in this new scheme."

"No. Your problem, DD, is that you're not just an escapist, you're escape itself. There's not going to be any room for you in the new order. Not in this country anyway. And the rest of our staff is taking things pretty well in hand in other countries —our minions there can't afford your fancy ways anymore anyhow."

"Fancy ways?" The boss sounded like he'd been talking to the TV evangelists.

"So I guess we're sort of temporarily overstaffed. Of course, there is the little problem of that gang of loudmouths who got back in here. If they were by themselves, we wouldn't worry. Sooner or later the pressure of the rest of the society we're molding will grind them into submission or force them to self-destruct. But there is that magic noisemaker. For eight years your assignment has been to retrieve that thing, and you haven't done it yet. What do you do on company time anyway?"

"Oh, I'll get it boss. . . ."

"Your problem, DD, is that you're unpredictable. Not reliable. That was always your problem. If you had delivered the agreed tribute way back when you had your own kingdom, we wouldn't be having this discussion now. I gave you this chance to redeem yourself, to prove yourself of some value, but I must say that unless you bring the profit to the company that we contracted for, well . . ." He clucked his tongue and flicked his nails together as if he were flicking a cigarette lighter, with the same result that a little tongue of flame licked up between them.

"Boss, you're a slimeball," she said.

"Don't try to brownnose your way out of this," he warned.

"And don't think I take your threats lightly, but pardon me if they seem to me to be a little—inevitable anyway, the way you have things planned now. In other words, if I do bring you all that you want, the banjo, a sacrifice, what have you—what's in it for me?"

The boss beamed at her, doused the flame, and held his arms open as if about to embrace her. "Now *that's* the spirit."

CHAPTER X
▲▲▲

"Oh, come now," Barbara said to Ute. "Don't try to tell us there was anything diabolical about the success of the campaign against addictive substances. Surely if anything supernatural was behind it, it was a blessed miracle, not some devilish scheme."

"She's got you there, Ute," Heather-Jon said. "Maybe you've been isolated out here on this ranch instead of on the streets in the cities. You have no idea how scary it was getting for a while there, and then suddenly everything that was being done against the drug dealers started working and the detox programs became big business and people began recovering and leading productive lives—"

"If they survived the recovery," Shayla said.

"What?"

"I had several friends who committed suicide about that time. They recovered from alcohol and drugs, but they weren't able to reenter normal life without them. If you were a lousy businessperson before you became a drunk, recovering from alcoholism doesn't suddenly make you a better businessperson. There's still the IRS and bill collectors and ex-husbands and all of the other things that make life difficult to face that, if you had the need to escape from it in the first place, are still harder for you to face maybe than they are for most people. Some of the people recovered and found someplace. A lot didn't. A lot died or went crazy. Or something."

"Well, yes, but society at large benefited and so did most of those people individually."

"Yes, ma'am," Ute agreed. "It sure seemed that way mostly. But you recall, only seven years have passed by this time, and the devils were thinkin' long range. You know, when I studied comparative religion up in Austin, the professor told us that the Hindus have this wheel of life where something that happens on the upturn of the wheel and is a good thing there becomes a bad thing on the downstroke. That's kind of what the devil corporation had in mind in this case, I think. A salvation that brought the seeds of its own damnation because it didn't go—as most solutions don't—quite far enough.

*"But Willie and his buddies were only just discovering some
of the ways things had changed. They were discovering some
changes in themselves too, and the way they were ready to ride
back out of the chute and into the arena. Furthermore, with a
little nudge from a two-timin' redheaded supernatural entity, a
certain six-year-old boy was deciding that he was more than
ready for a few changes.*

▲▲▲

Nothin' but nothin' was happenin' in the neighborhood anymore, Jaydee Endicott thought disgustedly, as he sat on the
dilapidated front stoop of his apartment building, watching
the street. Schools were so crowded he went only a half day,
even though his mama had to work until three at the hospital.
Used to be, his big brothers were home to boss him around
and take care of him, and *used* to be Harold, his eighteen-
year-old brother who was the youngest next to him, used to
play with him sometimes. Now Harold was in the m'lisha and
didn't have no time for babies, he told Jaydee.

Used to be the playground over back of the church was
open, but the m'lisha bosses, they said playgrounds was used
too much for drug deals and doin' bad stuff to kids, so you
couldn't play there no more.

Used to be summer and at least you could go outside and
play kick the can, till the projects manager said you wasn't
allowed to play with no litter an' be a litterbug.

Used to be the other kids would play with him in the vacant lot, tossing the ball and such, but now the vacant lot was
being excavated for a new building that also took up the lot
where Grandma and Grandpa's house used to stand before
they had to move away because the building men wanted to
tear down their house. Used to be Grandma and Grandpa
would give him cookies and let him watch television, but now
television was no fun anymore. All it had on it he could even
watch was *Roadkill Rabbit, Diego the Death Squad Commando,*
and the *Junior G-person* call-in show, where you could report
your folks for using drugs if you wanted to. Jaydee didn't
much want to, and he got tired of shows where nothin' happened except somebody chased somebody else or blew somethin' or somebody up. That's where all the other kids were,
watchin' them things, but Jaydee didn't like to, not all the
time. He liked it better when Grandma took him out in the
vacant lot and helped him name the stars. But that was when

he was little. He never got to see Grandma anymore since Grandpa died.

So he sat on the stoop and watched the people do things. Miz Persimmon Simmons, the stripper, hung her wash out her window, a line of tiny little strings with spangles and fringe on them and a whole rainbow of the tie-dyed T-shirts her ponytailed boyfriend Juan always wore. Jaydee liked those T-shirts, specially the one with yellow, red, orange, turquoise, and purple in it. Maybe if it got old or somethin' and Juan didn't want it no more, he'd fetch it out of the trash for himself sometime. Use it for somethin'. Had to be good for somethin', pretty cloth like that. Maybe make him a sweatband like the m'lisha wore, only prettier, or somethin' for Mama.

Across the street in the little rectangle of grass the streets ran around, Old Man Bulk sat with his cane. He had on a clear plastic raincoat over a sweater. The m'lisha didn't bother him none because he used to be an important man—a fighter. Now he was a little crazy, punch-drunk, and Mama always told Jaydee not to get too close to him.

Most people walked alone or in ones and twos. You couldn't even have a club anymore cause the m'lisha said that's what led to drug gangs. Only people allowed to have a club was the m'lisha, and Jaydee watched them every afternoon strut past or lounge, casual like, against the power poles, scratchin' itchy trigger fingers. He wondered if he'd see somebody shoot somebody with one of those big assault guns they carried, like them mob guys shot ol' Siffy Bascomb last week. Siffy was a friend of Harold's, and Harold was real mad about it. Man oh man, Jaydee would sure like to see somethin' like that. Maybe it would be Harold sometime. Jaydee tried on how it would be with Harold gone—he'd probably get all his stuff. Even that didn't seem very exciting or interesting, though it made him shift his position back and forth from one side of the stoop to the other, looking for Harold to see if he might be on his way home.

Horns bleating, people yelling, cars braking, the jackhammers that sounded like the m'lisha target-practice range on Saturday nights, the beepers and the roar of the big yellow cranes and earth-moving machines next door, the smell of dust and cold rain, fast food and backed-up sewage, sweat and dirty diapers—even the gray brown haze in the air—nothing in his world was friendly until Mama got home unless Harold seemed to be feeling like less of an asshole than usual.

A warm soft weight bumped against the back of his arm, and he twisted to see what it was and caught only the glimpse of an orange plumey tail-tip. The other arm got the same bump as the soft weight rubbed against his back, and this time when he turned, an alley cat stared up at him and meowed hello, just like she knew him. Her ear was kinda torn up, and there was a ridge over her nose where she bumped the garbage cans, but otherwise she was a fine-lookin' cat. Her coat was real nice, like she took good care of herself. Didn't have no diseases, he bet, no matter what Mama would say.

And right away he knew there was somethin' special about her. She reached up and patted his cheek with her little paw, making a low rumbly sound inside her chest that sounded good—must be a purr. He'd never seen a real cat do it. Real cats mostly disappeared quick around here. He stroked her back and felt the purr coming up out of her, like it was going into his hand and up his arm and through his whole self, making him feel happy all over.

He petted her some more, and she looked up and gave him a lazy cat grin and blinked at him. "Hey, cat, you some fine cat. You stay cool so somebody don't eat you, hear?" She purred and he was sure she understood him. She was a smart cat. She'd found him, hadn't she?

He was still playin' with her when Mama came home, loaded down with grocery bags. "Where'd that thing come from?" Mama demanded. "You know they don't allow animals around here."

The cat ran off with a last longing look at Jaydee, and he followed Mama into the house. He argued his case all during the late lunch Mama always fixed when she got home, so's she and Harold and Jaydee could all eat together. She and Jaydee would have snacks in front of the TV later on.

"Aw, Mama, she wouldn't hurt nothin' and she's real smart. I'd take good care of her. I could feed her outdoors and leave my window open for her so she could come and sleep with me. Please, Mama?"

"I said no," Mama said.

"I'll take care of her for you, Jaydee. We can use her for a moving target."

Jaydee was on top of Harold before he knew it, madder than he had ever been, screaming things and crying so loud even he didn't know what he was saying. In the next minute Harold was holding him at arm's length giving him a shake.

"Harold Endicott, you stop teasin' your little brother like that. You'll do no such thing."

"Oh, Mama, 'course I wouldn't. Jest jivin' you, little brother," he said, but Jaydee didn't know if he meant it or not. Harold caught his eye. "Really," he said.

After dinner Harold slung his rifle back on and went out to patrol, and Jaydee went back out to the stoop to find his cat.

She was gone. He called and called, but there was no sign of her. He sat down on the stoop to wait. That was when he saw the stranger walking up the street. Funny-looking fellow. His hair was red and gray, and he had a big gut. His skin was all mottled, dark brown on light, like there was somethin' wrong with it. But Jaydee didn't think at first that there was anything wrong with the man. Just from the way he walked, even though he seemed kind of sad, Jaydee thought maybe this man was the second wonder of his day. And he kept on thinking so until the man stopped at the fence across the street and Jaydee's cat jumped out from behind it and began making up to the man like she was his.

▲▲▲

The sidewalk felt good under Brose's shoes after all those miles riding. It felt solid and hard and real, and nothing else did right now. Too many ghosts. Too much intangible bullshit. Too much now-you-see-it-now-you-don't. Like his life, for instance, his home that disappeared when he wasn't right there looking at it. All the good he had once thought he was doing for critters as unwanted as he had always been himself. He walked for miles, and pretty soon he noticed that the faces on the street were all as dark or darker than his and not too friendly. Lotta noise on the street, Brose noticed, construction noise, voices, traffic from the highway. No radios blaring, though, no ghetto blasters blasting, and for sure no good wholesome all-American kids break-dancin' to combat drugs or making rap music about how good life could be with just a little hard work and drive. So much for stereotypes and stereos both.

Nope, and furthermore, kids wearing red sweatbands and carrying assault rifles stalked the streets. Must be the militia Barry had mentioned. Brose had seen them coming twice and crossed the street and started looking for a way to turn around and go home, feeling the sweat break out on his forehead despite the coolness of the day. This was beginning to look less like Tulsa and more like Beirut all the time.

The neighborhood he'd come from had been before civil rights, and it had still been a big improvement on this. The people he saw moved around like extras in a zombie movie. Maybe they were stoned, but the eyes were clear and the mouths had an angry, dissatisfied twist to them. A woman with a full grocery cart and a kid riding the bottom of it glared at him. A young man in a business suit said, "We don't allow loitering, you know. If you have no place to go, move on downtown with the other street people. Just a friendly reminder. You wouldn't want the militia to take you in."

Brose held up both hands, palms open. "Just out for my evenin' jog, man."

"You aren't jogging."

"No. It may have escaped your notice, but I'm on the fat side and I just started, so it's still at the some-jog-and-most-the-time-stand-around stage."

The man gave him a dirty look and moved on. Brose walked quickly away and had started to turn around when he saw the orange cat. She darted down a side street and he followed her. She looked like the cat they had had in Scotland, and Brose had a funny feeling he couldn't quite put his finger on about that cat. He lost her when he turned the corner and finally stopped to get his bearings, leaning up against one of the kind of huge fiberboard fences construction companies put up to block off a project.

Suddenly he felt a soft bump against the back of his neck. He turned his face into the plushy side and tickling whiskers of the orange cat.

"Hey, there, kitty-cat, what's happ'nin'?"

The cat slitted big green eyes at him. He reached up and stroked it. "You any kin to our Scotch cat, huh?"

The cat mewed and stepped onto his shoulder. Its paws weren't even dirty or wet, and it gave him a throaty purr. A little boy came tearing across the street from an apartment building entryway flanked by two rows of trash cans.

"Hey, mister, where you goin' wit' that cat? Das *my* cat!"

Three of the vigilante sweatbanded kids appeared and ran up the street, brandishing weapons. "What's happenin', Jaydee? Who's this guy?"

"Catnapper, das who," the little boy said.

Brose very carefully plucked the cat from his shoulder with

one hand, but its claws stayed attached to his shirt. "Come on, kitty-cat. You're gonna get me killed," he told it.

The cat squalled.

"You're hurting it!"

"Don't you go hurtin' my baby brother's cat," the middle militiakid said. The little kid's brother and his two friends made a little half circle around Brose. He was sweating as he pulled the cat's paws forward a little to dislodge the claw and set the animal back on the fence. Again he held his hands up, palms out.

"I can't help it, guys, I'm irresistible to animals is all."

"Yeah, who you think you are? Come around tryin' to run off with people's cats. He try anything with you, Jaydee? Try to give you anything?"

"No, but he tryin' to take my cat."

Brose had taken in stray kids as well as stray animals, street kids, runaways, as unofficial foster kids. But initially he'd met most of them when they were in jail. On the street, when *he* was the suspected criminal faced by three self-righteous, armed, and nervous teenagers, he was less sure of himself than he had been at home. But the little kid was reaching for his cat, and the older boys stood around glaring. Like everybody else, they looked pissed off and unhappy, but they also looked arrogant and a little power drunk. Brose had the kind of curiosity that all of a sudden stopped him wondering what they might do to him and started him wondering why they looked that way to begin with.

"Catnappin'. Thas a capital offense, ain't it, Harold?" One of the boys asked, leveling his rifle at Brose.

▲▲▲

Jaydee thought maybe he was going to see somebody get shot after all. The big man was sweating a lot and he looked scared.

"Jesus, fellas, I'm a musician, okay? I'm just in town for a gig and I thought I'd take a walk. Really, I'm just a musician, and yeah, I like cats, but I sure as hell don't steal 'em when there's so many for free."

"You a *whut*?" Jaydee asked. "Whut did you say you was?"

"A musician. Here. I'll show you."

The big man sat down on the curb, and with only a little nervous glance once in a while at the guns and angry faces of Harold and the others, he talked to Jaydee as if he were the most important person there. "A musician. You know. I make music."

"I remember that," Savoy Jones, Harold's best buddy, said. "Used to be that stuff all the time, but nobody do it no more."

"Why not?"

"Dunno. Just never hears it no more. Cos' too much, maybe?"

"Naw. How much it cost to do somethin' like this?" the man asked, and beat a tricky little pat-a-pat with his hands on his thighs, like rain falling or footsteps coming home. It sounded simple except for an odd beat here and there that gave it a little laugh in the middle, and the man's big blotchy hands looked like they were dancing.

Jaydee had known it all along. This was a special man, the same way the cat was special. He set the cat down and plopped down beside the man. "Sounds funny. Don't it hurt?"

"Try it and see what you think."

Jaydee watched him and tried to do what he did, his mouth hanging open as he concentrated. "Thas good," the man said. "Now try this," and he patted himself faster, his slaps coming fast as the jackhammer on himself for about thirty seconds, tops and sides of thighs, forearms, and cheeks, then said, "Any of you fellas know about rap?"

"Yeah—still some of that on video when I was little," Mo Jones, Savoy's brother, the third militiaman, said.

"Well, people used to do it on the streets a few years ago," the man said. "Kids like you. Lots of them used a drum machine, but when I was a kid, we did it like this, whatcha call hambones. You just chant to it, really, make up a poem, like in the army, y'know?"

"Soon's I rack up enough points in the m'lisha, I'm joinin' the army," Harold said. That was news to Jaydee.

"If you do," the man said, continuing to beat out a rhythm, "you'd do this to a march instead of hambones, and your sergeant would call out the chant. Makes the march go faster. Goes: 'Hambone / Hambone where you been? Round the world and back again. Whatcha gon' do when you come back? Take a walk by the railroad track. Left / right. Left / right. Leftright. Left*right.*'"

Jaydee watched closer this time, his hands trying to follow the man's but not quite catching up, so that he ended up patting air part of the time. He got the first part pretty good, though. "Do that business with your cheeks again, mister."

"Come on, y'all, sit down and you try it. You have to pooch your cheeks out with your tongue to get that popping sound. Sounds a lot like some of our kin in Africa talk."

Jaydee wanted to learn African talk. He saw some of the neighbors at their windows. Even Maurice Chisholm, who was his age, had pried himself loose from the TV long enough to look out the window. Five more m'lishamen and a whole crowd of other kids of various ages crowded around in back of Harold, Savoy, and Mo to watch the man.

"Hey, Maurice! Come over here! I bet you can't play hambones like African talk!"

Maurice came running. Jaydee followed the man as he chanted soldier songs one after another, and pretty soon Jaydee could follow most of it. Harold was almost as good as the man himself.

Sweat poured down the man's face and arms and soaked his shirt, and his hands left tracks on his clothing and smacked where they hit his skin as he played. He was laughin' now, showin' Mo and Savoy how to beat on each other and play "duets." The rifles lay at their feet in the gutter.

"Whoa, men, I am just about out of marching chants," he said.

That's when Jaydee noticed that Mama had come to stand on the edge of the crowd. He expected her to tell him to come home or tell them to stop that, but instead she smiled at the man and said, "Shoot, that's nothin' but old jump-rope songs," and chanted to the slaps, clapping her own hands in time. "Miss Susie called the doctor, / Miss Susie called the nurse. / The nurse called the lady with the alligator purse. / In went the doctor, / In went the nurse. / In went the lady with the alligator purse." And "Apples, peaches, pears, and plums / Tell me the name of your true love. A-B-C-D—and then you see, you have to guess which letters spell my true love's name, and then I sing 'Johnny, do you love me? Yes, maybe so. How many children will you have? One-two-three-four'—and then you have to guess that too." She stopped, grinning wider than Jaydee had seen in a long time. "You know, I had clean forgotten those old things till I saw you sitting there. Why, I can remember a lot of them now—let's see."

Jaydee looked at the man, who grinned back at him and mouthed, "Women," with a shrug.

When Mama ran out of jump-rope songs, the man said, "Well, now, if we put a little melody to it, we could do another kind of music our people used to do when they felt bad. By singin' about how bad they felt, it kind of cheered 'em up, see. Usually they used guitars or somethin', but you can hambone it. It's a real simple kinda thing—only got eight parts to it, and we call it eight-bar blues. Try this now." And he started teaching them songs that sounded very grown up to Jaydee. The m'lisha forgot to go patrolling with their guns, they got so busy making up new parts. Now Jaydee could do several simple rhythms and was beginning to pick up on the special complicated ones that went with the songs.

Finally it was getting dark, and Mama said he had to go in. His skin and palms stung all over, but it was a good sting, and Maurice practiced duets with him all the way to the door. The man walked back down the street, Harold and his m'lisha buddies walking along with him, drumming on themselves or on him as he went, making up new lines and laughing.

Across the street the orange cat sat on the fence and switched her tail until the man was out of sight, then calmly began licking her paw in a satisfied fashion.

CHAPTER XI

▲▲▲

Terry Pruitt and Dan were on the way back to the Curtises' house when they saw Willie stalking furiously toward them.

As Terry turned up the walk to the house, Dan turned off and fell into stride with Willie, who acted as if he weren't there. Dan didn't say anything, just walked along beside him. Since he was taller and his stride was longer, he was able to walk with the appearance of someone calmly strolling while Willie stomped in giant steps. After a while Willie said, "This isn't gonna work, you know."

"What?"

"All our noble efforts to return folk music to the land of the chronically disinterested. It just ain't gonna work, buddy. They'd rather watch TV. Hell, most of the time, *I'd* rather watch TV. It's okay over there where there are all those people with all that history to talk about how powerful it all is, but here nobody gives a good fart."

"I thought that's why we were here. To convince them that they should. I guess a person gets used to having a magic banjo around, huh?"

"You get used to anything, buddy."

"So far I haven't. You can't really blame people for not caring about the music when those whatchacallems wiped everybody's memory, Willie."

"Well, sure, but I played for somebody earlier today who remembered me—they *asked* me to. After all we've been through and all the trouble and danger and pure hell it's taken to get back here, they didn't even listen, just turned back to the TV."

"Yeah, well, some audiences are hell. I don't have to tell you that."

"Maybe not. But now it's like because I have the banjo it's up to me to organize all this, and frankly, buddy"—he turned a bewildered face to Dan—"I got all I can do to organize myself most days."

Dan shrugged. "We're all good at different things, Willie. I'm not much of an organizer or a businessperson myself, but

Terry's great at it. She's shy, though, and I love talking to people, so usually I find all the neat things to do and the people to play with, and she tries to make sure we show up."

Willie said, "Seems like I've got two speeds. Full tilt and flat on my back. More and more I feel like as soon as I slow down, I'll slip up, and there'll be Lulubelle and her gang to get me and the rest of you with me."

"They might, except that if you fall asleep on the job, probably one of the rest of us will be awake then. And there's this about traveling together, if we get caught by the short hairs, at least we'll all have lots of company."

"I guess that's what's been getting to me. So much company all the time and havin' to consult everybody else. I play a lone hand usually."

Dan shrugged again. "Sometimes I do too. I need to get away from everybody else to listen to my own inner voices. But I don't always have anything important to say to myself. So most of the time it's okay to be with people."

Willie sighed, and the storm wind that had puffed him up died down. He hadn't known what to make of Dan before. Hadn't especially thought about it much except to note that Dan wasn't all that bad for one of those "sensitive" guys. As far as figuring out what somebody else was about, Willie generally had his hands full trying to figure out Willie. He mistrusted guys like Dan generally, though.

Willie, on the shady side of middle age, had been brought up in hard country and taught that a man was supposed to be hard and tough and the more you hurt him the tougher he got. That was one reason why when he hurt he wanted to get away from people or get drunk. Because the truth was that he wasn't very hard or tough at all. He hurt like hell all the way through and sometimes not over anything that ought to be important.

Any one of those young girls he had shared a body with during his ensorcellment in Scottish ballads had been through harder things than he was going through now, though it occurred to him that if he had been in his own flesh instead of just in the minds of those girls, he would never have taken their problems so seriously, would never have known how deeply they hurt, would never have been able to offer the comfort and advice that, as the disembodied spirit who was a caring part of themselves, he was able to give.

He would have told them that they needed to be hard and

tough and maybe hugged them while they cried but secretly thought less of them for doing it. Or helped them get drunk. As long as you were drunk, it was okay to cry or say just about anything.

He wondered a little about Torchy, and her current role as the Debauchery Devil. She'd let it slip that being a devil was her punishment for failing in her tithe to hell the year Bird Janet saved Tam Lin from being the sacrifice himself. Since the Queen of Faerie, who at the time was Torchy, had had nothing with which to pay the yearly tribute, she'd had to go to hell herself. What did a nice fairy queen like her do in a place like that? She'd become the worst kind of whore, using her glamorie not just to hide her magic realm from men or to help them see it, but to tempt them to drugs and drink and all other manner of things that would waste their lives in far less wondrous ways.

He wondered if her buddies assigned her that role or if it had just sort of come to her, when she lost everything and needed the anesthetic of some kind of chemical fairyland to make it from second to second. Unlike him, the poor bitch was immortal and didn't even have the possibility of drinking herself to death.

But then there was Dan, who didn't drink and wasn't hard and tough, at least not in the way Willie had learned to be. Dan had more in common with those medieval ballad girls than he did with Willie. Usually he was as happy to see you and as friendly as a big old hound dog, but sometimes he did get quiet and withdraw from the group. Then afterward, something which had always irritated the hell out of Willie, he'd want to talk over whatever had made him withdraw to begin with.

Maybe Dan wasn't withdrawing to hide his feelings. Maybe he was withdrawing to keep from having to act like an asshole when he got pissed off and negative. Which was to some extent what Willie was doing now, though once he'd started talking to Dan, he'd figured out that he wasn't pissed off at the rest of the group so much as he was by the incident in the bar. It had discouraged him, and he had basically been trying to pass the discouragement around. He also realized he didn't actually need all that much time alone. He was used to being by himself in crowds, used to having crowds of people around him from back when he was on the road. In fact, if there weren't a bunch of people around him, he did his best to go find some.

He didn't feel like he had to explain any of that to Dan. He had the feeling that Dan knew all of it to begin with or he wouldn't have started walking with him. Dan might seem wet behind the ears, but in fact he had spent years working as a photojournalist for big-city newspapers before discovering that the music he had played with his Norwegian grandfather was his true love.

Willie said, "I appreciate you tryin' to help, buddy. I need to walk a while more by myself, though, if it's all the same to you."

"No problem," Dan said, and turned back toward the house.

▲▲▲

When Willie, Terry, Dan, and Brose returned later from their walks, they had to be careful where they stepped. Instruments littered the living room.

Gussie beamed proudly and said, "Take your pick, ladies and gentlemen. There's plenty for everybody."

"This is like Christmas!" Terry said.

Willie resisted the pull of a beautiful old Martin guitar long enough to chide, "Gussie, I told you to hang onto that money."

"Oh, Willie, what a lousy time for you to suddenly become grown-up enough to worry about things like that," she said. "If I lose it all, I do. Lettie and Mic will give my cats a home, and I don't even care about my collections anymore. *This* is my collection. Now stop fussin' and spoilin' everything and play something pretty, will you?"

CHAPTER XII

▲▲▲

Early November in Oklahoma is unpredictable. Usually it's still pretty warm, but sometimes it gets cold at nights and the wind strips the trees of their big yellow and red leaves, which fly at the windshields of cars and sail down gutters on fresh gushes of heavy rain.

Inside the Curtis house the furnace rumbled for the first time that season, filling the house with the pleasant smell of warm dust. Everybody convened in the living room, sitting in chairs and on the arms of chairs, except for Willie, of course, who paced. They weren't many to accomplish the overwhelming task before them but they formed quite a mob for such a small room.

Molly sat in the old rocker with the stuffing poking out between long clawed places in the faded flowered upholstery. "I still can't make sense of what you say happened to you. But while you've been havin' all those adventures, Barry and I haven't heard anything we would properly call music for over five years. Play us something you learned, please. Anything. It's been a long time."

Julianne sang a cappella while the others were tuning the song of King Henry, whose courtesy to a monster won him not only his life but a bride who was the making of his kingdom and the love of his life. Brose, taking his cue from her, took up the twelve-string guitar he had just tuned and sang a low-down bluesy version Molly was sure she never before had heard of "The Brown Girl," and segued into "Black Girl" or "In the Pines" and back to the ending of "The Brown Girl." Not to be outdone, Willie picked up Lazarus and stood in the center of the room, his eyes closed, the banjo crying in a minor key, as he sang "The Dowie Dens of Yarrow." And Anna Mae played a concertina and sang "Kempie Owen," her voice droning away into a tense vibrato at the end.

Dan also played the concertina as he sang a tune from the Shetland Isles, and Terry sang in the Northern Scots, which was so close to the Scandinavian tongues.

Then Gussie brushed off her skirts and said, "I believe I

have one to sing too." Gussie generally couldn't carry a tune in a bucket, but what she performed wasn't exactly a song. It was a border-gathering song, the battle cry of a wronged woman whose goods had been stolen and her friend murdered, "The Fray of Suport," and it was that song that had led her and Sir Walter Scott to the stronghold of his robber-baron ancestors and told her more than all the history books about life on the Borders in Scotland. As she sang and her voice faltered, Willie and Anna Mae, then Terry, Faron, Brose, and Julianne joined her. Finally, even Ellie and her parents added their voices to the long cry of "Fy lads! A' a' a' a' a' / My gears a' ta'en."

The cry expressed very well what they all felt at having their tapes, records, songbooks, and folklore books stolen or destroyed, their memories looted of words and music by unseen forces.

But about that time one of the forces decided to allow itself to be seen.

"Okay, okay," said the redhead who was suddenly and without prior notice or approval sitting with her short-shortsed bottom on Barry Curtis's knee, swinging the flip-flopped foot of a long bare leg back and forth impatiently. "I get the picture. No, no, don't quit playing. You—tall, gray and handsome," she said to Dan. "Keep sawing away on that thing, will you? I need a little cover here."

"Torchy, what in the hell are you doin' here?" Willie asked.

"I'm gettin' to that," she said, pulling an extra-tars-and-nicotine Brimstone Light cigarette out from between her bright-red-lipsticked lips with bright-red-nail-polished, tobacco-yellowed fingers. She took two deep drags, exhaled the fumes upward to encircle the light fixture in the ceiling, and said, "Okay, so here's the deal. I want in."

"In what?" Gussie asked.

The Debauchery Devil waved her cigarette in a negligent circle, setting fire to Barry's T-shirt before she put him out with an absent sweep of her other hand.

"You know, in with you guys. I want to help you."

"How touching," Anna Mae said, scratching a sour chord on the fiddle she had picked up just before Torchy made her appearance.

"Yeah, well. I been thinkin' about a career change for some time, y'know? Low job satisfaction lately. I don't get no respect. My—uh—co-workers in the Company work their wiles on humans with all their subtle suggestions and magicks and stuff and don't respect me because most of my spells need outside potions and chemicals to work. I mean, even when I started showin' them how you can use a person's *own* chemicals to hook 'em, on each other or sports or somethin', they still treat me like the town drunk, the community chest, you know. That little chitchat I had with Ma Turner there when I gave her a lift to Vegas"—she nodded to Gussie—"got me to feelin' down, and I remembered how sweet that old Sir Wattikins' ghost was when he saw me back in Scotland and didn't realize how things had changed for me. People I used to be queen of are still around just north of here, where what you guys do is still going strong—why them and not me? I want a little respect too. I want to be a bloody queen again."

"You shoulda thought of that before you fell in with evil companions, darlin'," Willie told her.

With a steely look in her eye, Molly patted the floor beside her and crooked her finger at the redhead. "Until your coronation, missy, if you want respect, I'd say you better start actin' respectable and remove your butt from the knees of other people's husbands."

"I wasn't bothering him, was I, luv?" Torchy asked Barry, who wisely kept quiet and pretended to be thinking of something else entirely. Molly patted the floor beside her again, and with a deep put-upon sigh the Debauchery Devil sank to sit cross-legged on the indicated spot. Then, as if nothing had happened, she continued to Willie in particular and the others at large, "Naturally I expect to compensate you for your assistance."

"Lady, we already got our hands full as it is without becoming soldiers in your rebellion," Willie said.

"I knew you'd say that, but you see, it's the same rebellion, actually. So that's all right, isn't it? I need you to do what you want to do anyway if I'm to have a chance at being—well, if not queen of anything, at least an independent agent again. Magic doesn't work awfully well where it's overcrowded and so awfully—I don't know, industrial I suppose you could say. I used to think it was the iron, but I've grown quite used to that. I suppose it's because no matter what clever little trick you do to keep people thinking about you, there's always some bloody rational explanation. For instance, in the old days, on the isolated farms and in small villages in Britain, people used to set out milk and bread for us. Nobody'd touch it because they knew it was for us, you see. In the morning, still cold and a bit foggy from the sea and all that peat smoke, here's your farmer or his wife pulling pants or skirt on over nightdress, sliding into clogs or boots, opening the door, and out of the corner of the eye seeing that the full cup of milk and the bit of bread they'd laid out just the night before had vanished, leaving only crumbs and a nasty clabbering ring.

"It never occurred to them to say, 'Oh, the dogs did it,' or to think that some homeless person helped himself, though those things might easily have happened. But they didn't *want* to think so because we were their luck, and if we accepted the offer it probably meant we'd agreed to stay friendly, and if not, well, they were in big trouble, even if it only meant that the milk had gone bad."

"Kinda like a protection racket then?" Brose asked.

"Not really. More like an alliance. If they thought we were on their side, then they felt a little safer. The world may have been emptier back then, dearies, but was just as full of danger, if not more so. Having supernatural friends was about all you *could* do before some killjoy dreamed up public assistance. Actually, we were prob'ly as reliable."

"More so, I'd say," said Molly, who worked for the State Department of Health and Social Services.

"And, well, of course, today people don't believe in anything except that Dobermans go mad because their brains grow too large for their skulls, fast-food restaurants snatch up the odd rat when the price of poultry is too high, and using a certain brand of dish soap leads to longer and happier marriages *and* nice hands. Not to mention clean dishes, I suppose."

"*I* thought you said you had to become a devil because you didn't pay your own protection money to hell," Brose said. "How's anything we do going to change that? Are they just going to let you go?"

"No, but I know the ropes now. I don't know why I was such a fool as to think I needed to keep my bargain with them when they never keep their bargains with anyone else. They're trying to co-opt even the limited bit of power I have left into other branches now—pestilence has been edging over my way so that boozing and doping are now known as the quite respectable-sounding 'substance abuse' and are supposed to be diseases. I can't manage to suffuse them with glamor and daring anymore—no more than I can smoking. I've tried. I've really tried, but it's no good. Besides, the others now think that they can crack people just as effectively from the pressures of daily life combined with a simple, frail human nervous system. They even made *me* sober up, and I suppose that's why I've thought of this plan."

"We don't have any reason to trust you," Anna Mae pointed out.

"No, but you can bet your braids, ducky, that you won't get very far without my help, and with it you might stand a chance of surviving, even if you don't set the world afire with songs."

"Oh, you have some help to offer?" Willie asked a little sarcastically. "You didn't mention that."

"Really, sweetie, I'm way past expecting anyone to do anything for me from the goodness of their own hearts. Now, as I see it, one of your biggest problems is that other than that thing"—she indicated Lazarus, which was for once not playing anything but was strangely silent, as if it were listening too— "you've no protection at all. You have long distances to go on roads or in airplanes all within the jurisdiction of my employers. I needn't remind you of the little traffic jam you got into before you left this country, nor the *unfortunate* string of air crashes that not only killed your friends but cost millions in lawsuits and layoffs and put large companies out of business. If they wish, my employers could make sure that as soon as you set tires onto the next highway exit, you'll be in limbo forever, especially if the banjo isn't with you. Now it is true that knowing the songs gives you a certain amount of protection, but you can't always be singing them. Meanwhile, our people are tracking you—not always in the same sort of concentrated way they did before, but more casually. So I think that I have something that just might help here."

She pulled out a Ziploc bag full of something sparkling and clear and tried to hand it to Willie, who eyed it suspiciously.

"What is it?"

"Something I had the lab make up from an old family formula especially for you. Go *on*. It's not illegal or anything, not just yet, but you must understand that I have to exercise the power I do have along the lines of my occupational specialty. I still have the labs at my disposal, so I had them make this up. You've heard of angel dust and devil dust? This is fairy dust. And you don't need to smoke it, ingest it, or shoot it up. You just sprinkle it on."

"Watch it, Willie. She's setting us up," Anna Mae said.

"I am *not*," Torchy said, wounded. "It's very nice really. It helps you be aware of us without our people—except for me, of course, since it's my formula—being aware of you. It also imparts just a soupçon of glamor, which ought to be helpful with the public, as inundated with charisma as they are these days. If you use a bit daily after bathing and before bedtime, you ought to be able to flit about the country by normal means without the Company tracking you. Then, of course, all you have to do is convince a large portion of the population that they should stop doing all of the other things they have to do and sing folk songs instead. I wish you the very best of British luck on that one, and I'm not being facetious, because unless they do, I don't see how we'll ever get them to believe in me again either."

"I think," Juli said gently, "that you'll find that you first have to believe in yourself before others can believe in you."

The Debauchery Devil gave her a quick and brittle smile. "Thank you for that bit of trite conventional wisdom, sweetie. And do keep in mind that your best audience may not always be college-educated liberal Democrats. I might be able to come up with a few lists of names that Fear and Loathing and some of the others have in their grip who are very solidly conservative, simply because they're scared to death to be otherwise. Of course, we don't want to lose *ground* with those who are already inclined to believe in us, but on the other hand, if they were enough, we wouldn't be in this fix, now would we?"

"I think we've been infiltrated," Anna Mae said.

"She did arrange for the money," Gussie said. "I was wondering why she did that."

"The cowboy poets were my idea too," Torchy said.

"The who?" Brose asked.

"The cowboy poets. *You* know. Back at the ranch. I arranged it all as a sort of tribute to you, Willie dear. Your poor old boss missed you so much he was getting terribly depressed after the little heart attack the Plague and Pestilence Department zapped him with. No booze or cigarettes, tsk tsk. But in my own inimitable divine way I figured that what he really was most addicted to about his way of life was the bullshit, which was in short supply without you, Willie. So I—er—dusted up on my muse skills and seduced the foreman into poetry. Quite easy, actually, with that Mexican romance-language folk heritage pumping through his hot little veins. At that point the Chairdevil hadn't actually come out against poetry anyway."

"Found a loophole, did you?" Barry asked.

"Well, yes, and a good thing I did too. Since the Company has withdrawn its backing from alcohol, nicotine, and other drugs, I have never seen such disgustingly clean-cut cowboys in all my born days. The rodeos encourage them to think of themselves as athletes these days, so what was left for them to get high on but poetry? Now, I admit I *did* send a young fellow in to provide a big dose of academic despair to all that naive enthusiasm, but who knows who will convert whom? So see, that leaves you a bit of a toehold."

Willie cocked a sardonic eyebrow at her.

"Oh, come *on*," she said. "I've gone to all this trouble for you, really stuck my neck out. I'll tell you what. I'll throw in a little luck spell so that your songs fall on the right ears, how's that? But you can't go galloping around in a great big bloody herd forever. You need to cover as much area as possible."

"Divide and conquer, huh?" Anna Mae asked.

Torchy ignored her. "Now, ideally each of you should go back to your home ground to vector this music, where you're most in touch with the culture and where the songs you sing will have the most meaning for the people's lives. Except that you"—she pointed to Anna Mae—"have such a nasty personality you should probably *not* go back where you're known and instead go back to the reservations or something and let Willie, who can charm anyone, take care of the east. After all, Brose is from Texas too and—"

"Wait just a damn minute," Gussie said. "We haven't agreed to anything just yet, so you can stop telling these people their business."

"Some people are sure touchy! I'm only trying to help," Torchy said in a wounded tone, her scarlet fingertips fluttering to her throbbing overripe breast.

"What I'd like to know," Willie said quietly, stopping in midpace to stand stone still, which had the same effect as if all of a sudden the traffic on the highway outside had come to a complete and silent halt. "What I'd really like to know, darlin', not to sound ungrateful or nothin', but what, exactly, do you get out of this deal besides the joy in your heart of knowin' you have done the right thing?"

"Oh, well, power, of course, and adoration. But I can wait for the end results. If you're still alive by the time I come into my rightful throne again, you'll naturally have first pick of the *best* flunky positions, since by accepting my terms you will, in some ways, be swearing fealty to me now."

"Well, damn," Brose said sarcastically, "do dat be all yo' want from yo' po' slaves, missy?"

"That and one other little insignificant thing. I'll need the banjo, of course, properly handed over to me so that I can show my bosses what a good girl I've been and throw them off the track."

"Aha!" the rest of the people in the room crowed in chorus and in eleven-part harmony.

"You bitch," Anna Mae said from between clenched teeth.

"We can't give you Lazarus," Julianne said. "It's our protection."

"Oh, *really,*" Torchy said. "Haven't you been listening? I'm offering you other protections. Besides, that thing does you as much harm as good. Wherever it is, it focuses my Company on the lot of you and starts them thinking up ways to destroy you. If I have it, they'll feel that you're powerless and, if they don't sense your presence, will forget all about you. Short attention span, y'know. Goes with the territory, when you're a devil. Besides, if you keep it, *which* of you will keep it? You *will* all have to travel around like a football team trying to shelter under one umbrella, and how much song spreading do you think you'll get done that way? As it is, you know, even *with* the banjo and *with* all of my protections, the moment you start singing, you've blown your cover and signaled my people that you're there again. You will have to move along almost instantly."

"Oh, great," Juli said. "A life of one-night stands."

"Don't be such a baby," the Debauchery Devil said. "Do you think it's been a picnic going from being a magical queen of sylvan glades to hanging out in bars and opium dens for the last four hundred years? I'm only doing this because while I was hanging out in b-bars, p-p-people like W-Willie were the only ones who reminded m-me of what I used to buh-buh-buh-*be!*" And she burst into unexpected and greatly suspect tears, each one dropping to the worn linoleum of the Curtises' floor, where it bounced and clattered and lay shining, reflecting rainbows of color.

Brose scooped up a handful of the crystallized tears. "Don't nobody give her a hanky until we get these appraised," he said, holding one up to look at in the glow of the inverted-fishbowl-shaped light fixture in the center of the room. "They might be diamonds."

That stopped Torchy's crying, and she looked down at the glittering tears with a brave smile of sharp white gore-red-lipstick-smudged teeth. "Well, I'll be blessed," she said, scooping up some of the gems herself. "I haven't been able to do that in centuries. What comes of fallin' in with decent companions, I suppose. What more proof of my sincerity can you possibly want than these? Here, you can each have one and conjure me up whenever you get in a bind or need a bit of a win at bingo to keep body and soul together. I really must have the banjo, though."

Lazarus began to play a sad song in a very minor key.

" 'MacPherson's Lament,' " Willie said.

"Yeah," Faron said. "I was able to play it on Uncle Theo's violin, but I didn't remember the words until Anna Mae sent the song back through Lazarus. What was that story again, Anna Mae?" he asked. "I know the song, but what was behind it?"

Anna Mae bit her lip and sleeked her black hair back behind her ears. "If everybody will be quiet for a moment so I can hear, I'll get back into it." She sat still for a moment while the banjo played the same refrain over and over, and when she opened her eyes, she was gazing at Willie, except that she wasn't looking so much at him as through him, and into the past. Her voice came out strong and her alto could have been a tenor, with a Scottish burr thickening her words. She was back in the song, recalling the part of her that had once been one with MacPherson. "I was born the son of the MacPherson and a Gypsy, brought up as a MacPherson and taught fiddling in my father's house until I learned of my Gypsy blood from the taunting of other boys. I found my mother's people, Gypsies and Jacobites, and with them became a freebooter. The Laird o' Grant wanted me deid, and caused my own clansmen to go against me—shepherds it was who caught me sleeping in a field and captured me. I was not betrayed by a woman, as some say. The woman was a lass I sometimes saw in the village, and she cared for me and sent o're the Bridge o' Banff for a reprieve to free me. But meanwhile I was marched up the scaffold to hang a quarter of an hour before the pronounced time. It was a grand day. Folk came from all over to hear me play my fiddle one last time and to bid for it when I was deid. I offered it to any of my clan who would play the lament I wrote for myself at my funeral, but there were no takers. . . ."

Her voice trailed off and she sang, in her own voice to the accompaniment of Lazarus playing all alone,

> "There's some come here tae see me hang
> And some tae buy my fiddle,
> But before that I do pairt wi' her
> I'll brak' her through the middle.
>
> He took the fiddle into baith his hands
> And he brak' it o're a stane—"

Her voice stopped in midnote, and Lazarus stopped too with a sudden thunk: one string popped off. Four more thunks, like corn popping in a kettle, as the other strings broke and sprang up, coiling toward the tuning pegs, which fell out. The banjo's head filled like a balloon until the skin tore loose from its moorings and the bone ring that held it to the wood popped free. Then the neck caved toward the ruined head until it snapped, dangling by the metal rod that held it together.

Eleven pairs of eyes turned toward Torchy angrily, and with fear and fascinated curiosity. She held up both palms. "Hey. I never touched it. Don't you think if I could have, I would have taken it before now?"

Ellie's eyes welled up with tears, and she left the sofa to crawl around on her hands and knees, picking up strings and pegs and pieces of the ring, wiping her eyes on her wrist as she searched like a dog who'd lost its ball. Faron started crawling with her and picked up a peg and handed it to her, putting his arm around her.

Anna Mae looked to Brose, and to Juli, and finally at Willie. "I guess Sam's spirit was telling us one more thing."

Willie nodded and picked up the broken construct of wood and metal and shoved it into Torchy's outstretched hands. "I reckon so. I guess you got yourself a deal, devil."

▲ ▲ ▲

The Debauchery Devil flourished the vanquished banjo before her boss.

"How'd it get broken?" he asked.

"MacKai did it," she said. "He got pissed off when one of

the others accused him of hiding behind it and slammed it against the door. But here it is, and it will never cause us any trouble again. You want to do the honors, or shall I?"

"Ugh," the Chairdevil shivered with distaste. "Be my guest. You've earned the right."

She smiled at the mutilated instrument, and it burst into flames in her hands and disintegrated.

The Chairdevil had no objection to looking at the ashes. "So much for the magic of Wizard Hawthorne," he said.

CHAPTER XIII

▲▲▲

Ute stopped talking, picked up a bundle of sage he had brought tucked in his shirt pocket, and lit it from the camp fire. He waved it around, fanning its sweet pungency toward each of the women in turn, then propped it up between two rocks. He started to overturn the coffeepot on the fire when Shayla St. Michael shielded the fire with her hands.

"Hey, wait, stop. What are you doing?"

"Turnin' in," he said.

"But you haven't said what happened next. What did they do without the banjo?"

"About what you'd expect. They left. Some of 'em split off and some went together."

"Well, yes, but just like that? I mean, how could they just leave after all of that?"

"Ma'am, I can see where up and movin' 'just like that' as you say might be a little hard for you or me, involvin' big decisions and considerable separation anxiety and trauma and like that. However, these folks were essentially movin'-type people. Why, Willie MacKai back in his heyday used to log a couple thousand miles a week sometimes. He'd say he sang and played for free— the part of his gig he got paid for was getting there. And they were all like that, even Gussie, now that she'd become a storyteller. And remember too, the reason they had gone away and the reason they had come back where they knew it wasn't gonna be real healthy for them was that they had some songs to spread, and they couldn't do it, even if they wanted to, from the comfort of the Curtis living room. They had to take those songs all across the nation and they had a lot of ground to cover. Also, with Lazarus gone, the decision of where to go, where to start, and who with was up to each individual."

"Yeah, but it must have been hard, after being together so long, for them to split up like that," Heather-Jon mused.

"Well, as that Torchy-devil pointed out, they couldn't exactly get maximum range for song spreading as an ensemble. Gussie was the only one who'd planned much of anything. Musicians are the people who coined the phrase 'play it by ear,' you under-

stand. When a lot of what you do depends on what everybody else does, too much organization can get in the way of your flexibility and be a pain in the ass."

"I suppose so," Barbara said. "And they did have all that protection. Yes, I can see where moving along and splitting up was the most sensible thing for them to do."

"I'd have been lonely," Mary said softly. "Even the Gypsies take their families with them."

Ute sat back down on his rock, set the coffeepot back down, and stared into the flames. "Yeah, though I guess when you're movin' and you've got somethin' new to do and see, it's a lot easier than it is to be left behind."

▲▲▲

Ellie sat on the divan, her dad's old cardigan wrapped around her, her hands thrust deep in the pockets where she fingered Lazarus's strings and pegs as if they were rosary beads left to her by a friend who had recently died. She'd known all along the others would be leaving. She'd thought she and Faron would be going too, but her whole family ganged up on her.

"Seven years is long enough," her dad said. "Besides, we want you and Faron at the convention this year to tell the others what happened. Nobody plays or sings much filk anymore, but the most musical people in our group still come. I'm sure they're gonna want to hear what you and Faron have to say."

"We sort of planned on using Tulsa as a control base," Gussie told her. Ellie knew she was just trying to make her feel as if she were doing something important too, and she also knew that she and Faron and her parents *would* be making a vital contribution to the mission, but even though she was glad to be home, part of her was just used to going, and it wanted to leave when her friends left.

"It's easiest for you and Faron to cover this area," Anna Mae said briskly. "If you don't, then one of us will have to, and we don't have the contacts you do."

"Oh, I *know*," Ellie said. "I'm just going to miss you all so much."

Terry gave her a hug. "We won't be able to stay together either, so you'd have to miss us anyway."

"We'd better figure out who's going where," Gussie said, "so I can give you each a list of contacts and code phrases. My feeling is that we need to fan out from this area and stick to the Midwest and south central area right now, since we only have my vehicle for transportation."

"I think that's wise," Anna Mae agreed. "We don't know how well Torchy's protections work, or even if they do, and we should be within reach of each other in case one of us runs into more trouble than he or she can handle."

"We'll be damned lucky if it's only one at a time," Willie said.

"I've got a list of our contact people in the South Central & Southwest areas that Morgan Richards put together with help from Lettie and Mic, Gussie and some of the other music network who've kept in touch," Barry told them, pulling out a sheaf of paper and dealing the pages like cards to each person. "Y'all realize that as soon as you memorize these, you'll need to eat them."

"What? No self-destruct?" Dan asked.

"Most of these folks will know Willie and maybe Juli or Brose already," Barry continued. "But for the rest of you, we've set up a code that will help you identify them and vice versa. Just in case there are any phony cops or IRS people or SWALLOW agents lurkin' around. Morgan also sweeps our phones every week so you should be able to call in safely from pay phones or cellular lines."

"Maybe we should just all concentrate on one area at a time and then have Gussie round us up when we think we've got things started there and head on out to another area," Juli suggested.

"I don't know about that," Willie said. "I move faster alone and I reach more people."

"We're talking big cities here, Willie, and not being able to use any kind of publicity. I really think the territory's going to be plenty big for all of us," Anna Mae said.

"Nope," Willie said stubbornly. "Torchy's idea of each of us taking home ground is better. If I can't find an audience in Texas, I can't find one anywhere. Y'all can do whatever you want, but I'm headin' back south. Anyhow, I'm not sure cities are where we're gonna get listened to. People in small towns are lots of times more interested in having someone entertain them than people in cities who're up to their asses in entertainment already."

Anna Mae nodded cautiously. "Well, yes. That's a good point. But on the other hand, if someone wants to trap you, a small town has fewer places to hide. Still, much as I hate to admit it, I think you may be right. I'd like to try my luck first in Anadarko, where I was brought up. I don't have any relatives still there that I know of, but I feel like I understand where people there are coming from. Besides, my people had their own songs that weren't dependent on the big-name folk musicians. Maybe they've still retained them and would be willing to help us."

"I'm sure Lucien Santos, my teacher in Joplin, could help us," Julianne said eagerly. "And he's very influential. Besides, I want to see if I can still contact George."

Brose shrugged. "I got no preference. I'll go along with Gussie, I guess. I got no home now at all. I sure as hell don't want to go back to Texas, but it seems to me from what I've seen around here that people are going to need us just as bad in cities as in little towns. Only rich people have access to a lot of the entertainment in the cities. Folk music always was mostly intended for poor folks anyhow."

"That's true," Terry said. "And Dan and I don't know anyone over here. I don't think we'd be overloading an area if the two of us went with Brose and Gussie to some major city. I still don't think it's wise to spread ourselves too thin. Remember, we still don't know if that stuff Torchy gave us in the plastic bag is any good or not. Perhaps once we figure that out, it will be safe to spread farther."

"I guess if y'all are splitting up, though, you'll need it in separate bags," Molly said practically, and brought out more Ziploc bags. They divided the fairy dust and the crystallized tears among them, though no matter how much dust Willie shook from the original bag, there always seemed to be about the same amount left.

Julianne was the first one to notice that and mention it, and Gussie nodded, saying, "Good. Seems to be the real thing then, or if it's not, at least we won't get busted for having some illegal designer drug we never even heard about. So far ol' Torchy seems to be on the level."

Willie said nothing but seemed to recover his spirits, solemnly intoning "Twinkle Twinkle Little Star" as he sprinkled a pinch of the alleged fairy dust over his head and did a little pirouette, then repeated the nursery rhyme as he sprinkled first Julie, then Anna Mae, Terry, and Brose. Gussie couldn't help giggling as he sprinkled her, and Dan ducked out of the way, but Terry held him by the ribs and Willie sprinkled both of them. He sprinkled Faron, who pretended to flutter around the room, which normally Ellie would have found amusing. When he sprinkled her, he kissed her on the nose, then announced, "Each of us havin' been duly sprinkled, I now pronounce us all Methodists."

Ellie roused herself enough to help pack the van with all the instruments Gussie had bought, sleeping bags and pillows for the trip and the bag of groceries with plenty of bags of chips and Oreos, plus the trail food Willie had picked up at the store and the diet drinks everybody wanted. Bear hugs were exchanged all around, and then Willie, Brose, Anna Mae, Juli, Terry, Dan, and Gussie piled into the van and drove off, Juli waving through the back window until the van turned a corner.

"Well," Ellie's mom said with a deep sigh, "I sure hope they'll be all right, and I'm gonna miss 'em, but we have some heavy planning to do if we're going to get this meetin' together. Honey, Daddy and I are going to go over to the Richardses this evenin', and I think you kids ought to come with us and tell Morgan and Leeann more about what's been goin' on."

She shrugged, not trusting herself to talk. She knew she was going to cry. Faron said, "I'll go over there with you. You comin', hon, or are you too tired?" Ellie shook her head and turned away as her eyes started filling.

The inside of the house looked so empty, as familiar as it always had, and at the same time as alien and barren as the face of the moon. She threw herself down on the bed she'd had when she was a little girl, in the room where she, Juli, Anna Mae, Gussie, and Terry had all took turns using the bed and sleeping on the floor while the guys slept on foam pads on the living room and kitchen floor. She'd miss tripping over bodies in the morning. She waited until she heard the front door close, and the car start, to have her cry and let it all out. When it had dwindled down to exhausted sniffles, her hands again went to her pockets for comfort, and she drew out the banjo strings and pegs as if they were jewels and took the piece of torn vellum that had been the banjo's head and smoothed it lovingly, reading the words inscribed on it in blocky, childish printing, "May the Circle Be Unbroken," repeating it aloud like a mantra.

She straightened the kinks at the ends of the strings with her fingers and noted with surprise that the strings weren't wiry or plastic at all. They were like long curling hair, silkily wound around a central core. She'd never seen any strings like them. Back in Scotland, the tiny ends of these same strings, strings that always stayed in tune no matter what the banjo played, were a magic charm to bring her friends back from the lives of the ballad characters they inhabited. Surely they still had some magic in them. She braided them into a bracelet and twisted it around her wrist. It felt soft and light, like a curl of her own hair. The pegs were fragile looking as china or ivory, but appeared to be some kind of bone. Funny, no one had ever mentioned that before.

She fell asleep and dreamed, instantly recognizing the turn her dream was taking and saying to herself inside the dream, "Oh, yeah, this must be the ballad of 'The Cruel Sister.' " In the dream a woman who looked like Anna Mae, wearing a long old-fashioned dress, and an expression that would have done any one of Torchy's co-workers credit, was pushing a woman who looked like Juli into a stream. The clothes of the woman who looked like Juli were also old-fashioned, heavy, with long skirts that bubbled and belled out in the water, and slowly sank with the weight as the Anna Mae–woman pried loose her clinging hands from the bank, taking a fistful of water-sleeked fair hair and plunging the disbelieving, begging face under the water before releasing her. Ellie knew with perfect dream logic that it was because both of them were in love with Willie. Juli flailed and cried and went down three times as her clothing dragged her under, and Ellie tried to wake up and reach her, but no matter how often she thought she was awake, when she tried to move, she found it was as if she had no body. Juli's body tumbled in the current, spinning around and around until she reached a big waterwheel and an old daub-and-wattle building that looked like something out of Shakespeare. "She floated till she came to the miller's mill-pond," a voice sang in Ellie's head.

And then a shadow fell over the water, and a big man who looked like Brose hauled Juli's dripping body from the stream. Ellie saw him pull out a knife, but somehow she wasn't grossed out even though she knew when he laid the body on the bank and raised his knife, then lowered it, that he was carving into the drowned woman's body. He held up a curved bone, as smooth and white as if it had never been part of a flesh-and-blood body, and the line, "He made a harp of her breastbone. / Each note could melt a heart of stone," sang through her head. Like an Indian in a western movie, he held up a sheaf of her hair, which was thicker, longer, and more golden blond than the real Juli's was, and the words came, "He made the strings of her long golden hair." And finally, "He made the pegs from her little finger bones" sang through her head as Brose began attaching small objects to the top of the harp.

The dream got fuzzy then, and she seemed to doze until she heard the tune of the song again and realized she was looking at a man in a room full of dismembered and partially assembled instruments hung like meat in a freeze locker all over what looked like the inside of a garage. The man stood over a workbench that held a broken white harp. Ellie knew it was the harp from her last dream—she could see the golden gleam of the dangling strings and the bone white gleam of the instrument's body. She didn't know the man, but he was not young, even though his hair was mostly black. He had a hawk-ish nose and a lean, gnarled body in baggy-seated jeans and a plaid shirt with the elbows out. Around his neck a leather bag hung, bobbing in time with his movements. He was whistling The Cruel Sister song as he bent over a piece of what looked like white cloth, carefully lettering words, "May the—" in an awkward, childish block printing.

"Ellie, honey?" Faron's voice was soft in her ear, and his fingers kneaded her back.

She woke and turned over to face him, feeling the imprint of the banjo pegs on her cheek and chest, the softness of the bracelet around her wrist.

"I just had a dream," she told him, "and I reread the message on Lazarus's head again 'May the Circle Be Unbroken'—see? I think I dreamed about the luthier who made Lazarus, Faron. Sam had the banjo made from an older instrument, I'm just sure of it, and I think it's up to us to have these pieces made into something else. It's not just that Lazarus protected us all that time, it's like having it remade is part of bringing the songs back."

Faron touched the pegs thoughtfully. "If your folks will loan us their car for a day or two, I think we should drive up to Arkansas and see some old friends of mine. Did I ever tell you about Callie and Aldin? They left good jobs as scientists to become luthiers. I wonder if they're still building instru-ments. Maybe they couldn't make another banjo out of these, but they might be able to make something."

▲▲▲

A cold rain was falling by the time the van pulled into the tribal center at Anadarko, Oklahoma, and the sky outside the van's steamy windows was dark, though it was barely four in the afternoon.

"Maybe we should wait here with you tonight," Brose said. "Might be nobody you know is around, and—"

Anna Mae gave him an impatient look and shouldered her knapsack.

Juli had been drawing hearts with eighth-note flags on them in the fog on the window, and now she said quietly, "I wish we didn't have to split up too, Anna Mae."

"Well, we do," Anna Mae said through tight lips, and swung the door open. She wore a beat-up pair of Faron's old blue jeans and one of Barry's T-shirts with Molly's zip-front hooded sweatshirt over it. The rain pelted her lank dark hair, which was braided on either side of her face and tied with rubber bands. Rivulets ran down her face, and Brose, catching her eye, disregarded her surly attitude and grinned at her, giving her a thumbs-up sign of encouragement. She'd do fine. She was the most organized and determined of all of them, and the most driven. During their travels she had always been the one to arrange the harmony parts, to urge the others to learn new skills, to ask questions of the musicians they were learning from, and to arrange the practical details—not because she was bossy but because it occurred to her that sooner or later those problems would have to be faced, and she was a problem-facin' kind of woman. She reminded him of all of the witches, wise women, ladies, queens, and clever peasant girls he'd been a part of during his sojourn in the ballad times, and he had expressed concern for her only because he knew that even the most together lady likes to have somebody give a damn once in a while. After she jumped from the van, she gave him a twist of a smile and a roll of her eyes and hiked her pack up farther onto her back.

Gussie parked and hopped out to join her, Julianne right behind her. Even Willie, who Brose suspected had a sneaking admiration for her, climbed out to say good-bye.

"I see you got your extra clothes," Gussie said, and rummaged in her purse. "Now, here's some money from the gambling winnings. Let me know through the Curtises if you need more, and I'll get it to you."

Anna Mae tucked one wad into her jeans pocket and an-other into the hastily sewn pouch she wore around her neck like a medicine pouch. Brose had seen her tuck her devil's tear and the tightly rolled baggie of fairy dust into the same pouch earlier. When she finished tucking, she looked up, a little embarrassed to see them all still standing there. "Well, so long," she said finally, her mouth tight, her eyes full of excitement—and reluctance. Kinda like a paratrooper must look before the first jump, Brose thought.

"Wait a minute," Julianne said, "I want a hug." The two women embraced, then Gussie hugged Anna Mae too, fol-lowed by Terry and, more enthusiastically, by Dan, who was a hugging sort of guy on general principle.

Willie held her lightly, kissed her on the cheek, and said, "You be careful, now, darlin'."

Then it was Brose's turn, and he enveloped her in the big-gest bear hug he could muster and kissed her on the mouth while her hard skinny arms threatened to cut him in half, they were so full of both warmth and tension.

Then without another word she turned on her heel and strode up the sidewalk to the main building. She hadn't taken a guitar with her. She wouldn't need it for Indian songs, and if there were no more drums, she could pound on almost any-thing.

As they piled back in the van, Willie said to Terry, who had been holding the map for Gussie as she drove, "I'll ride shot-gun this time, darlin'. I'm gettin' out next."

The next leg of the trip the van echoed with silence as if it were one of the abandoned castles they'd visited in Britain, and it took Brose a while to figure out what was the matter. The banjo wasn't twanging away in the background, as it had almost every day since he'd met Willie out in the middle of the desert right after the banjo came into Willie's possession. First the banjo, then Anna Mae—their absence left a hole big enough for a storm to blow through.

"Just drop me off anywhere and I'll hitch to the Texas border, darlin'. No need for you to go out of your way none. I can find my way around," Willie told Gussie. He sounded so itchy to be gone you'd have thought he was covered with fleas.

Brose leaned forward between the two front seats of the van. "Long as we're not goin' out of our way for you, why don't you forget hitchin' to the Texas border and we'll let you off at Oklahoma City so you can catch a bus, MacKai.

Hitchin' may be even more hazardous to your health than it was when we was kids."

"That's right, Willie," Gussie said. "Stay with us awhile, hon. It won't seem quite right without you."

"Okay, darlin', but I think I'll take a nap now. Reckon you can find your way into the city okay?"

She could and did. The rain continued to fall, and traffic was comparatively light as they pulled into the parking lot across the street from the bus station. Gussie gave Willie a wad of money before he left the van.

"Where you buyin' the ticket for, buddy?" Brose asked.

"I don't know. Wichita Falls, maybe. I just gotta be home for a while. I feel like a battery that's been out of its charger a little too long. Probably I'll end up back at the ranch eventually."

He leaned over and gave Gussie a kiss on the cheek, but before any of the rest of them could scramble from the van, he grabbed a guitar and strode off toward the lights of the bus station, looking as alone and disconnected from them as any stranger.

They swung back east and drove steadily into the night. By midnight they reached the Southeast corner of Missouri. Since there were only five of them left, they pulled into a campground, almost empty now that winter was coming on, and put down the backseats and spread out sleeping bags Barry had insisted they bring along. The lodgepole pines, bare fifty or sixty feet up the trunks before branching out into foliage, sighed and heaved above the roof of the van, and a little creek gabbed and gossiped on its way to the Weosha River.

"There used to be a lot of music in and around the Ozarks," Julianne said, biting into one of the Oreo cookies Barry had packed so they wouldn't starve to death, as he always seemed to be afraid they might do. "Vance Randolph made a career out of the music and lore from the people there. Now most of them are retired city people I guess, but I ought to be able to find an audience. Lucien will know where to find one, even if he doesn't approve, and maybe George will have a better sense of who needs us, now that he has a— broader view of things."

"Well, if you do get in touch with George, you give him our love, you hear?" Gussie said. After all the ghosts they'd met in the last few years, Juli hearing from her late husband seemed as normal as any of them trying to contact a living relative.

The next day the rain let up and they drove into Joplin, Missouri, without incident. The consulting rooms of Lucien Santos were just where Julianne remembered them to be. A light shone from within, sparking rainbows off various-colored crystals in the window. Gussie wouldn't let Juli go until she checked and made sure she had everything. Julianne carried her spoons, money, the tear, and fairy dust in a purse slung around the narrow waist of her flowing Indian print skirt and a banjo over the shoulder of an ancient navy blue fisherman's sweater that belonged to Barry. It covered her T-shirt. To compensate for the cold, she wore socks under her sandals and a pair of Molly's long johns under her skirt, and for extra warmth wore around her neck a wool tartan scarf she'd bought at a gift shop in Scotland. With a last hug and a wave, she walked up to the door of the shop and knocked. The door swung open, and a man with a black beard and hair peeked out briefly as Juli shot them an "okay" sign.

"I'm gonna miss that girl," Gussie said. "I hope that crackpot doesn't fill her head up again with any of the foolish notions he gave her before."

"Supernatural stuff, you mean?" Brose asked.

"Oh, no. I guess we all know *that's* all right. I mean all that garbage he tried to tell her about how people always deserve the luck they get. Why, I know for a fact that isn't true, and so do you. Torchy told us herself that *she* is responsible for luck, and I pity the poor soul she decides to withhold it from."

"Well, I hope she is on the level when she says she's given luck to us, because I'm here to tell you, I'm havin' second thoughts about going back to Kansas City," Brose said. "Nobody in their right mind would stand on the corner of Twelfth Street and Vine, with or without a bottle of wine. Good way to get mugged. But one of the names on that list of Barry's is a friend I used to play Balkan music with back at the humane society, so I figure he can help me circulate again."

Strawberry Hill in Kansas City, Kansas, across the river from Kansas City, Missouri, was full of older houses with big porches and oaks, elms, and maples crowding tiny yards. The names on the mailboxes tended to end with "ski" or be uniformly unpronounceable.

Brose walked up to the door of the house and knocked. The lady who answered it gasped a little to see a gentleman of color—and such an odd color, with his bristly red hair and mottled skin—standing on her porch. But then Brose asked, "What size shoes did Clementine wear?"

And the woman, who always liked to have the right answers, added, "Number nine. Boxes without topses, special made for Clementine. And you are?"

"Brose Fairchild, Mrs. Kaminsky. Is Hank home?"

"No, but he will be in a minute. Who are your friends in the car? Do you suppose they'd like some of my fresh potato soup with homemade sausage? Hank always says I make enough for an army."

"That's mighty kind," he said, and waved the others in.

Terry and Dan were the only ones in the group with no ties in the area, so later that night they accompanied Gussie to one of the addresses Barry had given her. No lights were on when Gussie drove up to the big house in Westport, the oldest portion of Kansas City, Kansas, from back when it was a point of departure for covered wagons. The night was turning cold, and an icy wind knifed down the street as she walked up to the door and knocked. A middle-aged woman Gussie had never seen before answered the door, and Gussie felt like a damn fool as she asked the code question from "The Arkansas Traveler." "Say, farmer, can you tell me where this road goes to?"

The woman blinked twice and rubbed her eyes, and Gussie thought she was for sure about to call the cops, but then she said, "It's never gone anywhere since I lived here; it's always right there when I get up in the morning."

Gussie smiled and stuck out her hand. "Dr. Callahan, I presume. There's three of us. Have you got room?"

Dr. Callahan opened the door wider, and the overhead light in the van broke through the night as Terry and Dan grabbed their instruments and bundled them out into the night.

▲▲▲

"This is all very romantic, Ute," Mary Armstrong said in a practical tone, "but I don't see how they were going to manage to go live with a few strangers and teach them songs. Wouldn't their adversaries track them down that way? Besides, it seems to me that that would be a very slow way to spread the music."

"That's a real good point. You're right on both counts. They figured it the same way you do, but they planned to keep movin' so that by the time the devils found one safe house, they'd be on their way to another. As for the hosts, they were courageous

*people and that's a fact. Bad things could and did happen not
only to the singers, but to the hosts, but not before the music had
been spread a little farther."*

▲ ▲ ▲

The Randolphs didn't end up taking their trip to Arkansas
after all.

"You can't go *now*," Molly told them. "We need you to do
about three thousand things to help us get ready for ConTingent."

"We could do it in a day," Ellie said.

"But ConTingent's only two days away," Barry said.
"This'll be the biggest one since TuCon died. We're expecting
a hundred and fifty hardcore book-and-music people, and we
were able to get our old hotel."

"That funny old pink castle?" Ellie asked. "That's great,
but, Dad, what's the big deal? That's a really small crowd.
There used to be a couple thousand at TuCon. What happened?"

Barry shrugged and scratched the ears of the cat, who had
deposited herself on top of a pile of paperwork on the kitchen
table. "After you left and the music kept disappearing, the
books began to go. I guess your redheaded friend's pals must
have had minions in the publishing business too. Or maybe it
was just that folk songs and folk stories and myth have always
been the basis for books, and with the songs gone, the stories
sort of followed."

"Uncle Vance Randolph used to say people never knew
whether folk songs were stories made into songs, or the songs
were written first and the stories told to expand on them,"
Faron said. "I wonder what he'd make of that."

"Hmph," Molly said, taking a hard chomp from a stick of
celery she was nibbling while she worked at the computer
across the kitchen table from Barry. "If he wasn't already
dead, those devil things would have killed him by now anyway,
so I guess he wouldn't have said much. But anyway, you see
why we need you to stay here."

"Sure, Mom," Ellie said. "Except that I think Lazarus
wants us to do this. You haven't been with us through everything, and even though we've tried to tell you, it's a little hard
to make anybody else understand; when I have dreams or
funny feelings of *any* kind, I pay attention nowadays. When
Faron suggested Callie and Aldin might be able to rebuild

Lazarus, I just knew it was the right thing to do. If we wait too long, I'm afraid somebody or some*thing* might try to steal or destroy these little pieces I was able to save."

"Why don't you just invite your friends to come down here too, then?" Barry said. "You can give them the pieces when they get here."

"I should have thought of that," Faron said. "They'll love it. They read science fiction and fantasy all the time—or at least they used to. I'll call them up now."

"Tell them Emma Bull and Will Shetterly are coming to be our guests of honor from Minnesota," Mollie said. "Also"— she adjusted her reading glasses and peered into the list on her screen—"C. J. Cherryh, Jane Fancher, and Misty Lackey from Oklahoma, of course. And Suzette Haden Elgin is going to interrupt her linguistics workshops to come down from Arkansas. Robin and Diane Bailey are picking up Mark Simmons in Emporia on their way down from Kansas City. And there's several people coming up from Texas, but nobody whose name would mean anything to them. Anyway, it ought to be a good crowd. We invited Charles de Lint and Caitlin Midhir to be joint guests of honor originally, but they said it's impossible to get across the border now. The customs people have somehow or other compiled a list of anyone who's ever been a musician, and when IDs are checked, anybody on the list gets turned back unless they have the proper papers, which they can only get down here. Spider and Jeannie Robinson couldn't come last year for the same reason. But Nina Kiriki Hoffman still remembers where her banjo is and is coming down all the way from Eugene, Oregon. And Warren Norwood is bringing his dulcimer and Gigi has a new harp. Jane Yolen would have shown up too, except that she's come down with something. We've let these folks know over the years what's been going on, and they all want to be here, now that you're back, and hear what you have to say."

"Okay, I guess it would probably be better if Callie and Aldin could meet them too," Faron said. "But we need to keep it all very quiet, make sure any room more than one of us is in at a time has plenty of exits in case of fire or a raid."

"Or lightning or some other disaster." Ellie shuddered. "I wouldn't want to see a repeat of what happened at Anna Mae's memorial festival."

▲▲▲

Faron called Mountain Home information for the number and then got an ambiguous and anonymous message on an answering machine, but the voice sounded like Aldin's. "For anyone who's calling because you heard we were dead, we're not, in spite of everything. Please leave your message at the tone."

Faron felt a little edgy as he left the message and tried to make it as cryptic as possible for the benefit of spies while letting them know where and when to come. He didn't like giving out so much information to an impersonal device, but on the other hand, an event with one hundred and fifty attendees in a public hotel was hardly a state secret. At least they had only Saturday to get through. Saturday nights used to be the busiest time at TuCon and other science fiction conventions. There were masquerades and dances, maybe a skit spoofing some popular TV show or movie, and filk-singing all night long, concerts sometimes by the writers and fans who were the best musicians. But this whole event would be squeezed into Saturday.

▲▲▲

"I can't understand why anyone would travel as far as some of these people were traveling to go to Tulsa, Oklahoma, for heaven's sakes, to attend such a small affair," Barbara Harrington-Smith said, leaning back on her bedroll and watching the stars twinkle overhead as she, a city-bred environmentalist, watched the firelight flicker across Ute's face.

"Well, ma'am, you're a busy person, that's real plain, and so were these people, but maybe reading and writing and singing songs has just never been that big a part of your life. To these folks, it had been their livelihood, and when many of them had to quit it to make a living doing the kind of things you do maybe, it was like they had to cut down on their breathing. They were more than anxious to find an excuse to sit around together in a restaurant, talking about old times, books and stories they still remembered, or old shows, or old jokes, or where somebody had found a cache of books or magazines and how the others could get ahold of some of them. In the old days book dealers and craftspeople would bring things to the convention and fill a room with their wares like a medieval market place. Now maybe each attendee might bring one treasured possession to share, or a few less treasured ones to sell off or barter for something else. Videotapes of the old television shows or movies were highly prized, as

was equipment to play them on, since the newfangled stuff they have now doesn't play the old tapes and only what's currently popular is reproduced, as you ladies probably know."

"And that's as it should be," Barbara said. "After all, those tapes are synthetic products that require dangerous and toxic chemical processes to produce—only that which time has shown to be valuable to society should be preserved by such expensive means."

"You surely don't mean the game shows and talk shows they still have along with all the documentaries and specials?" Shayla asked, looking up from the tack she was polishing the way Ute had shown them earlier that day.

"Game shows are intellectually challenging to an otherwise comatose public and have been known to ask politically relevant riddles. Talk shows are excellent forums for social and environmental issues," Barbara said, as if reciting a lesson.

"Well, ma'am, some of the people at this function I'm talkin' about could argue that Star Trek *in all three generations did the same thing, only in an entertaining kind of way that let you know not only that there were important things to think about, but let you think, now if this or that catastrophe happened, how would it affect regular people, people like me? So I want you to imagine— they've held this convention special this year, later than usual, when other people are havin' Thanksgivin' dinner, here's this gathering at a hotel, hardly enough people to fill one little meeting room. A storm's come up outdoors, and the lights have flickered a couple of times. The wind is rattlin' the glass doors, and there's a rumor that it might snow. . . .*

CHAPTER XIV

▲▲▲

Ute stretched out by the fire and leaned on his elbow, his fingers twiddling with a small bundle of smoking sage, his eyes fixed on the camp-fire flames as if he were remembering something that happened to him. Except, Mary Armstrong thought, his memories seemed to be those of other people, as if he had been a psychic fly on the wall, buzzing from thought to thought.

Saturday evening rolled around at ConTingent with no fanfare, drum rolls, or very many musical instruments of the regular kind in evidence. With so many songs forgotten during the last seven years, people had tended to find themselves with instruments and no repertoires, which was discouraging. There'd be the old guitar or fiddle sulking at you from some corner, looking neglected, and even if you remembered how to play, you didn't know *what* to play. The instruments soon got packed away.

People who made up their own songs or for some other reason were still able to play discovered that when they tried to fly or take buses or trains with musical instruments, their instruments were lost, destroyed, or badly damaged in transit. Of course, the musicians who lost their instruments this way were angry, but they only *knew* that they had encountered an unusually malicious baggage handler. Most of them didn't even suspect that the offending handlers were, actually, carefully placed minions of Torchy's Company who had been replacing the regular kind of handlers gradually over the years with other minions. The Accounting Devil had seen to it too that the inevitable damage to the instruments made them uninsurable, so that the musician lost out all the way around.

In short, any musicians still brave enough, inventive enough, and unimportant enough (otherwise, they would have been destroyed along with their instruments) to still be traveling by public transportation of any kind had learned a long time ago that traveling with an instrument was no longer worth the trouble. Still, those in the science fiction–fantasy community who had once been musical—or still were in a discreet fashion that no longer extended to bringing their in-

struments out in public—were curious to see what Faron and
Ellie would have to say—or sing. Faron brought a guitar because it was the best accompaniment for some songs, but he
also brought his favorite instrument, his old mandolin, even
though the neck had badly warped during the time he'd been
gone.

In the northern half of the hotel's ballroom, which was
divided by a plastic folding wall, people sprawled against the
walls or sat on one uncomfortable straight chair with their feet
propped up on another. Some of them sat hunched over
chairs with ring-binder notebooks spread open on the seats.
These notebooks, once crammed with songs, were for the
most part sadly blank, but pens were poised expectantly.
Other chairs contained tape recorders. Suzette Haden Elgin
sat crocheting a castle, and Caroline Cherryh had her brand-
new portable compact disk laser recorder set to pick up every
word Faron said.

Faron had changed. Everybody said so. When he left, he
had been a skinny, gawky kid who didn't open his mouth
often, but when he did, it was to say something unusually witty
or unusually enlightening. Otherwise, you wouldn't have
looked at him twice. Now it was as though all of the witty,
enlightening stuff that he had kept stored inside him was
seeping out through his pores, making him look more filled
out, kind of—taller, stronger, more authoritative, *shinier*
somehow. He didn't even have to clear his throat and bob his
Adam's apple up and down for people to pay attention.
Suzette thought he must have been practicing the linguist
tricks for gaining charisma she knew about from her work as a
doctor of linguistics, but even she couldn't detect exactly what
he was doing, and they had always been close friends. Ellie
was different too—still young looking and plumply pretty, but
in a way that somehow made it look as if soon all the actresses
were going to start wanting the Ellie Randolph look—naive
and yet with a sophistication that spanned time, vulnerable in
her babyish roundness but strong and sturdy too, girlish and
yet somehow womanly. Of course, what nobody knew was that
while Ellie and Faron had changed inside—as anybody worth
their salt will over seven years of growing and learning and
living through new experiences—it wasn't the inner growth
that was making them so attractive at all. Sad to say, most
people, even very smart people like science fiction writers, just

aren't perceptive enough to find inner growth necessarily all that rivetingly gorgeous.

No, what was making everybody hang on to their words was the fairy dust. It not only protected those who used it from the devils, but it also gave those who wore it a little of the old-time glamorie that the fairies had once used to confound mortals. Of course, since Torchy hadn't mentioned that particular property when she was making the deal, neither Faron nor Ellie were aware of it. They just thought everybody sure seemed glad to see them.

Faron and Ellie sat in chairs near the front of the room, and the talk ebbed and flowed around them—it did, that is, until Faron simply picked up his mandolin and began to sing the ballad about the Gypsy rover. Now, even back when he had been one of the Midwest's star filkers, he had never had a particularly beautiful voice, and Ellie's harmonies had always been tentative, though they were always right on pitch. But now! The nasal quality in his voice sounded like the bagpipes, and Ellie's sweet tones had the ring of the sheep bells coming through the dells.

Listening to the song, however, Mark Simmons wasn't thinking about Gypsies in the English countryside so much as he was about the first time he had heard any version of that song—long ago, on a sweet spring day with winter blowing away on a breeze scented with early crab-apple blossoms in his mom's backyard, and he thought about Cindy Smithers and her lavender cashmere sweater set and how she always looked a little lonely going with the captain of the football team and right then and there he had decided to take up the guitar. He didn't learn *D, F,* and *G* fast enough to win Cindy away from organized sports, but he had learned the whistling Gypsy song, and that night he relearned it, along with about a hundred others.

Ellie and Barry watched closely to make sure everybody sang along on the choruses. Actually, as soon as Faron started singing some of the songs, the verses came back too. Caroline Cherryh's new technotoy not only recorded the voices on tape, but printed out the words and musical notation as soon as it was sung, and she promised everybody copies.

One song flowed into another and night into day, and by morning everyone was hoarse, exhausted, and very high. The harmonies had been ragged at first, but as the night wore on, even the most annoying voices found their own range and their own best strengths and the people drank in the songs as if they were hot strong coffee zinging with caffeine.

By morning each person felt as if the other people in the room were dearer than family, closer than any friends—even though filk-singers had always been a fairly competitive lot in the past, as full of ego trips and hurt feelings and delusions of grandeur as any performers, amateur or professional.

At noon Barry brought in a cart full of pizzas, and people lit into them eagerly. After scarfing down a couple of pieces, Faron gave Ellie a high sign, and she brought out the old beaded purse she'd stuck the banjo's popped-off parts into.

They told the rest of the people about the banjo in as few words as possible, because by now they were so hoarse they had to talk in whispers. Dally Morales listened carefully and said, "Might be I could do somethin' with it. I'm pretty good with my hands, and I've seen that old banjo. I made a ukulele out of an armadilla shell once. Don't know as there's enough left of that skin for another banjo head, but I reckon I could come up with somethin'."

"We had some friends who were supposed to be here who might be able to fix it," Faron said, glancing at his watch. "Looks like they didn't make it."

"I hate to let it go very far away," Ellie told Dally, her fingers clutching at her purse.

"Well, that's up to you, ma'am," the cowboy shrugged. "To change the subject, you playin' that song about the 'Trooper Cut Down in His Prime' brings to mind again an old cowboy song."

And he played "The Streets of Laredo," after which someone else played a spoof. Pretty soon everybody was either inventing spoofs of the songs they'd just learned, or they were off in corners of the hotel scribbling away at new songs.

Toward evening a couple of wet, tired people—the woman small and plump with long blond braids, looking as if she'd just stepped out of a German folk painting long enough to change into dripping jeans and T-shirt, the man tall with an aristocratic goatee and long dark hair that would have looked good under a cavalier's plumed hat—slumped wearily into the ballroom. Faron and Ellie hurried over to them. "Callie, Aldin, boy am I glad to see you," Faron said.

"We were beginning to think you'd decided not to come after all," Ellie said.

"No," Callie said, wringing out her sopping braids with

both hands. "But you wouldn't believe all the car trouble we had. We started out at seven A.M. yesterday morning. At the border we lost a fan belt. Fortunately, we always carry an extra. Then we had a flat, and when we went to change it, our spare was flat too."

"Then there was that asshole who ran us off the road," Aldin reminded her. "That was after I hitched to the nearest town with the bad tire for the first time."

"The first time?" Ellie asked.

"All five tires went flat on the way."

"And when we finally got them all changed and started rolling, the headlights went out in the middle of the worst thunderstorm you ever saw," Callie added. "But we're here. So show us what you want done and let's talk."

Ellie pulled the banjo remains from her beaded bag. Callie and Aldin examined them, Callie uncurling the strings to marvel at their fine and hairlike texture.

When she replaced them in the bag, they slipped out of her hands and sprung to the floor every which way.

Ellie swooped down to scoop them up. "I hate to let these out of my sight. Somehow I feel like Lazarus could be—I don't know—resurrected, I guess, if you just put these pieces back together."

Faron stooped down to help her, his sneaker brushing one string to the side and against the wall, where it hid in a crack. "With all the bad luck you folks had coming down here," he said to Callie and Aldin, "it seems to me as if they may be onto you."

"They who?" Callie asked, and then Faron and Ellie had to go through the whole story again of how the devils came to wipe out the songs and how their little group had traveled across the Atlantic to retrieve those same songs. The songs themselves were proof enough for Callie and Aldin, who sang along as eagerly as a desert rat drinks water. Meanwhile, other convention-goers packed up their notebooks and returned to their hotel rooms to pick up their suitcases, knapsacks, and garment bags and take them to their cars before checking out of the hotel.

Ellie handed Callie a handful of pieces and the beaded bag, too upset at relinquishing Lazarus's remains to look at them very closely. Callie, for her part, was so tired she was trembling with fatigue and the excess adrenaline that had kept her moving for the last thirty-six hours or so. She didn't think to count the strings either. And just then Faron came up with the idea that maybe he and Ellie should share one devil's tear and should give one, and some of the fairy dust, to Callie and Aldin to protect them and the banjo parts. They got off on that subject, and then Aldin asked if he could get some help starting the car, which had died just as they got to the parking lot, and the upshot was, nobody ever did check the beaded bag to make sure all the strings were there.

Dally Morales packed his car, checked out of his room, and returned to the ballroom to say good-bye and renew his offer to help in any way he could. By that time, Faron, Ellie, Callie, and Aldin had already adjourned to the parking lot.

The ballroom looked sadly abandoned and empty in a way that made Dally hang his head a little in sadness. *As* he hung his head, he caught a glimpse of something shining in the corner and absently bent to pick it up and stuff it in his pocket. He was like that, always finding bits and pieces of stuff he'd try to make something out of later on. It didn't occur to him at the time to give the string a closer look. Like everybody else, he thought Ellie had given all the banjo fragments to the luthier couple.

But later on, as he drove home, he felt the string poking through the pocket on his plaid shirt, which he'd always kept buttoned ever since he gave up smoking and started chewing instead. He pulled it out and only then did he notice that what he'd taken for just any old discarded guitar string was in fact a golden-colored banjo string made of something that was springy, though not made of gut or wire, but looked almost like an especially strong strand of human hair.

CHAPTER XV

▲▲▲

Willie bought his ticket for Wichita Falls and boarded the bus, knapsack on his back and guitar case in hand. He felt like he was just a little too goddamn old to be takin' up hippy ways at his age and wished Gussie had decided to spend some of her money on another vehicle. He started to hump his guitar onto his shoulder and up into the overhead rack when the driver boarded and saw him.

"Can't do that, mister," the driver said. She was a woman of about thirty with what Willie always thought of as country-and-western hair—peroxide blond teased high into lots of little curls, and so hard you could crack eggs on it. "That thing belongs down below with the rest of the luggage."

Willie gave her his most winning grin, having to dodge around other boarding passengers to meet her eye. "Can't do that, darlin'. This thing's my livelihood."

"It gets off or you do, mister. Company rules," she said. Her eyes, under black penciled brows, were not only hard enough to crack eggs, they could have splintered diamonds.

"How about if I was to buy it a seat?" he asked.

"Sorry. We got human bein's as needs all the seats."

Willie looked around. There were many seats containing no people, and most of the rows of seats had only one or two occupants. He picked up the guitar and headed back toward the driver. "Okay, then. Guess I've always wanted to see more of Oklahoma City anyway."

▲▲▲

"Hmph," said Barbara Harrington-Smith. "I expected you to tell us next that just because the bus driver was a woman, this Willie person charmed his way out of the situation and made her break her company's rules."

Ute looked like he'd been caught with his hand in the cookie jar. "He didn't mean to, exactly, ma'am. It was the fairy dust, see. Once he got her in range, you might say, she was pretty much a goner as far as bein' charmed goes. Of course, bein' charmed only went so far, as I'm sure you'll be glad to know. She was, after all, a company woman and as the driver AND BAGGAGE HANDLER, *she had very definite notions about guitars and such. For instance, that since they weren't allowed on board and almost always ended up causing trouble—like when some irate musician who had been foolish enough to bring his or her instrument on board found it smashed by the end of the journey—she decided that such instruments and such people were automatically trashy troublemakers beneath her contempt. Only she had trouble reconciling that image with fairy-dust-enhanced Willie as he stood there, guitar case in hand, eyes glowing with indignation, looking to her every inch the sort of man she had always hoped to meet in bars before she stopped going to such places because nobody who valued their job did that sort of thing anymore. She was havin' herself a major conflict, you see, between what she thought of guitar pickers and their instruments in general—which is that they at the very least did not belong in public—and what she found herself thinkin' about Willie MacKai in particular—which was he had somehow blundered into evil companions, namely the guitar, and maybe a good woman could lead him to better ways. And she couldn't do that if she let him leave the bus. So she looked up at him, batting her eyes not so much because she was flirting because, like most people, she'd just about forgotten how to do that—"*

"Well, of course. That's a very frivolous and basically deceptive activity which has nothing to do with real interest in a meaningful relationship," Shayla said, as if reciting a lesson, though she was in fact reciting something she'd read in a magazine. (The article, in fact, had been penned by a protégé of the Chairdevil, a rather sour man who didn't care for sex at all or for women in particular and felt all of a lot of other people's power was sexual and they ought to be prevented from using it on defenseless people such as himself, who were nevertheless clever enough to write manipulative articles.)

"Yeah, well, she knew that, so she wasn't really flirtin', she was just blinkin' kinda rapidly on accounta, you know, biochemical and hormonal reactions."

"Oh, well, that's different," said Mary Armstrong, who was carefully focusing on the fire so nobody would notice that she blinked quite a bit from biochemical and hormonal reactions when she looked at Ute, who always seemed to have camp-fire smoke in his eyes when he looked at her too.

▲▲▲

Willie was surprised, when he got up close to the guitar-hating bus driver, to find her batting her eyes at him and smiling in what tried to be a cold, official kind of way but actually betrayed the hard hair and the hard eyebrows and showed that she was, after all, only about thirty.

"No need for that, sir. I don't know how you can claim that no-count thing is your livelihood since nobody makes a *livin'* with stuff like that 'cept maybe Duck Soul, but you *did* buy your ticket, and I can see the bus ain't all that full. I think if you take this here seat up by me, you can lay it out on that seat behind me and it won't bother nobody."

Even then Willie thought maybe getting off the bus was still the best idea, but he figured he was going to have some kind of trouble wherever he went, and since this particular trouble seemed to have unexpectedly blown over, thanks to his personal charm and way with the ladies and *maybe,* he grudgingly admitted, the pinch of fairy dust he'd sprinkled on back in Tulsa, he decided to proceed. One thing about the bus driver. There was *no way* he could identify her with any of the mistreated sweet young things he'd occupied in ballads. Oh, sure, maybe she'd had a rough childhood or a bad marriage or something, but so had he. No, he felt the proper attitude around such a woman was to be cautious.

Only problem was, it's hard to be cautious while you're asleep. With the guitar in plain sight, the shushing sound of the bus's tires on the highway, the rumble of its engine, the yellow lights of the city flashing on the drops of water beaded on the windows, and a general lack of sleeping in real beds, which had developed in him a tendency to nap whenever he was sitting still, Willie dozed off. He'd change buses in Wichita Falls, he thought as he drifted into sleep. Maybe head for Dallas or Fort Worth, where he had friends he might talk out of a vehicle. He didn't want to stick around where he knew people, mind you, just get himself some wheels and be on his own for a while. He always performed best alone. Maybe he should take the music he had learned to some nice select girls' school with lots of *intelligent* young women who could learn a lot from the ballads he knew. He fell asleep dreaming about it.

▲▲▲

Anna Mae walked past the block-long shuttered fireworks stand, past the boarded-up windows of the building painted with faded thunderbirds. The broken neon lights had once spelled out the words "Chief Cwana's Casino." At the far end of the compound, a tall wooden fence with broken slats guarded what looked like a patch of weeds. The only thing open was a dimly lit convenience store advertising cut-rate cigarettes. Its screen door banged back and forth in the wind. She wondered how the people inside could stand it. She fought the wind for control of the screen door and opened the unpainted wooden inner door. The wind avenged itself by whipping both doors from her hand and slamming the inner door open and the screen door back against the building. She stepped inside.

▲▲▲

Thomas George was ringing out the register when the bedraggled woman came in. The register wasn't hard to ring out. No sales all day. Same as usual. Sometimes tourists came in the summer to see what was left of the museum, but now with the new supermarket just off the reservation, the only customers he had were usually lost. Nobody came for the canned stuff, the tractor caps, the painted toy drums with the Naugahyde heads, and the bumper stickers that said "Oklahoma is Indian Country!" He'd marked his seed beads and German silver down fifty percent, but nobody came to buy it. No place to wear that stuff anymore without looking like a white tourist. They were the only people who had been able to afford anything since the casino closed and the fireworks stand was now limited to operation the week before the fourth.

He already had quite a bit of beadwork and silver jewelry people had given him in trade for counseling. He didn't take it from somebody who was still drinking, if he thought the piece might belong to the wife or the family. Old Mrs. Spotted Horse had given him a matching belt and hatband that back east art museums would at one time have paid quite a bit of money for. That was when he tried to get her pension with the phone company straightened out. He'd saved a few more pieces for his kids, but he wanted to wait until they were grown to give the jewelry to them so his ex-wife didn't just throw it away. Old ladies had gone blind doing that stuff. Occasionally some artsy tourist would buy some, but mostly the beads hung from their hooks till the thread rotted and the strands fell apart.

The woman strode over to him, her jeans squishing as she

walked, dripping water, but there was a way about her. She was definitely someone with an agenda.

"I want to talk to the elders," she said, as if he were the bartender and she was ordering a beer.

He looked to the right, the left, and made an exaggerated show of looking behind him and under the counter, in the empty till, then shrugged, smiling, and said, "Sorry. There don't seem to be any around." If she wasn't so wet, she might be kind of a pretty woman.

Didn't have a sense of humor, though, or if she did, it had washed away in the rain. "Shit," she said, then sighed and asked, "Does anybody who knows how to get ahold of any of them come around here, say, tomorrow?"

He looked her over more carefully. She had a city briskness about her and could have been a dressed-down corporate lawyer or one of the firewater fuzz, but he didn't think so. Her haircut wasn't very good, and her nails were cut funny—long on the right hand, to the quick on the left. He'd never seen a corporate woman with those flaws, however old their jeans might be, and if she were a fed or the fuzz, would she have come right out and asked like that?

"Maybe," he said after a moment. "That would depend on who's asking. You an anthropology student, maybe? We haven't had any of them around here in a long time."

"No," she said. "My name's Anna Mae Gunn, but maybe one of the older ones will remember me as Mabel, the name given me by my real mother—Betty Charley? I was adopted when I was about three."

"You lookin' for your roots or somethin' then?" he asked, giving nothing away.

"Not the way you're thinking," she said, not telling him anything either. "But I need to talk with some of the elders. It's important."

"Huh. Heap big medicine, huh? Maybe you could tell me, then. I'm the tribal shrink." He stuck out his hand. "Thomas George."

She shook it and suddenly flashed him a white smile that temporarily lit the gloom of the store. "I've been out of the country for a while. I didn't know things had gotten so crazy back here that whole tribes needed shrinks."

"Well, I was the twelve-step leader until recently. Then the government decided to crack down on substance abuse—especially on the reservations. It's a federal offense to be drunk or stoned here now, though, of course, it's not such a big deal elsewhere. So nobody much wants to see me anymore, since I'm supposed to report them to the feds. I see a few cases of domestic violence, rape, incest, that kind of stuff. Mostly now, since old man Parker died, I just—" He spread his hands encompassing the shop to show her he was lord of all he surveyed.

"You think I'm an undercover cop, don't you?" she asked. When he didn't say anything, she said, "That's what I'd think if I were you. But I'm not. I'm one of the People—Chickasaw, and I'm a musician. I want to talk to the elders about songs they may remember."

"You make it sound like an emergency," he said, closing the cash drawer. He wanted time to check this out before he committed himself, to find out about Betty Charley and if she had a daughter Mabel and if the only two old folks who weren't dead or addled with Alzheimer's would be willing to talk to this daughter. Besides, he had other obligations. "Look, I got to get back to my sister's place—I'm lookin' after her kids evenings while she works at the hospital. But I'll send up a smoke signal and let you know what I find out if you come back tomorrow, okay?"

"Yeah, sure," she said. He ushered her to the front door and locked it from the inside behind her, going out the back to his truck. He didn't realize until he was halfway to his sister's that he had never told her where to find a motel, and he hadn't seen another car in the parking lot when he left her standing there.

CHAPTER XVI

▲▲▲

Lucien, being a master psychic, was not, of course, surprised to see Julianne. "What kept you so long?" he asked, ushering her inside and allowing his hand to linger on her shoulder longer than was strictly necessary. "I was expecting you two hours ago."

"Oh, we made a detour to—" She started to tell him about Willie. Seven years ago she trusted this man with her secrets from beyond the grave, but a lot had gone down in seven years, and now she looked at him with fresh eyes.

His eyes were still as piercing as ever, but she noticed dark circles under them. "Lucien, you look tired," she said. "Have you been eating red meat?" It was her kindest guess. Actually, the crystals that studded his house, many of them still yellow-tinged from the ground, fairly throbbed with disapproval. *They* had been trying to clear the vibes, they seemed to insist, but with *some* people around, even the most awesome stone was overtaxed. Unfortunately, she couldn't quite tell whether their reaction was to her or to Lucien.

He ignored her question, taking her hands in his own and sitting down with her on a futon couch covered with a home-made crazy quilt. His eyes searched hers with that same old compelling intensity that made her want to give up her will entirely and put her soul into his hands—almost.

"Dear Julianna," he said, enlisting the broad *a*'s that would have made a person think he'd never been *near* Arkansas. Where was that accent from anyway? It wasn't exactly Germanic, or French, or Spanish—nor was it Gypsy, though perhaps it was supposed to sound that way. She'd never really asked him about his own life and past. How thoughtless of her. Who was he, she wondered, and remembered suddenly that her late husband George, who in death had used Lucien as a medium, hadn't cared for him at all while he was alive. "I heard about your loss," Lucien said, sounding somber, sympathetic—and seductive.

"Which loss?" she asked. There'd been so many of them. George, her career, her deafness, and then for a time her body, as her spirit went to inhabit ballad heros. She'd been burning through some major karmic debts in recent years.

He looked puzzled and sat back, cocking his head first to one side then the other, studying the sides of her face. "You *seem* to hear well enough now. I had heard that you were— that you had lost your hearing."

"Oh, yeah. I did. It was the most awful thing too, Lucien. But I just like kept my chakras clear and listened with my inner ears, and overall I think I've come out of it very well, really grew from it all, y'know? And I'm dying to tell you all about it, but I'm a little tired right now. Can I stay here?"

"In the shop? Dear girl, I wouldn't hear of it," he said. "You must come home with me. My house is much more comfortable."

"I always thought this was your house."

"Before you left it was. But the universe has been kind to me."

That was an understatement. He lived in a custom-built log mansion with enough stained glass in the windows, walls, and doors to provide windows for all the stone cottages and hotels in two whole villages in Scotland and a castle to boot. The downstairs was full of beautiful things—aura paintings, more crystals, chimes that sang in the breeze created by ceiling fans, Indian rugs and blankets on the floors, walls, and seating, African masks and ugly little dolls, brilliantly colored, patterned, and sequined flags he said were from Haiti for the celebration of Houdon ceremonies. One antique oak occasional table was filled with rare and beautiful tarot decks mingled with feathers and more crystals.

"Wow," she said. "The universe *has* been kind to you."

"Ah, yes," he said. "My teachings have been of some use, and I've been made comfortable by the gratitude of those I've helped."

As he led her to the guest room, she couldn't help thinking of the heroes she had inhabited, of how they expressed their humility in less . . . smug terms. Of course, that wasn't fair. Many of her heroes were already kings or princes or knights or something when their heroics took place and . . . It occurred to her again that she knew very little about Lucien. She found him as exciting and commanding as ever, but still, she didn't find herself nearly as anxious to tell him about what had happened to her and the others as she had imagined she would. "It's just because I'm so used to being with my friends, with other musicians," she told herself. "It just stands to reason that after being with one group of people for the last seven years, being alone with anyone else is bound to seem . . . strange. I probably just need to get to know Lucien again. This time I'll ask questions and really pay attention —not take him for granted so much—instead of just babbling my problems all the time." But she was a little disappointed anyway. After all she had been through, she had been able to reach into the hearts of so many people around her, both dead and alive, and Lucien and she had been so close. She was surprised she felt closed off from him now.

"Your room, of course, is haunted, but they won't intrude on you," Lucien was explaining with a smile. "This house is built on the traditional burial grounds of the Osage, but I received special clearance and had a cleansing ceremony and *feng shui* done when I started building, so all the spirits of the departed think of this as their home too."

She nodded. "You always know the right thing to do, and you have such a *feeling* for spirits from the other side. Speaking of which, have you heard anything from George since I left?"

"Only when he told me that you had been deafened and then that you were in some sort of—vehicular trouble. He was quite upset about it, and I was frantic. I feared it was a collision and you had been killed." He turned and put both hands on her shoulders and squeezed, smiling down at her. "You can't imagine how relieved I am to see you again after all these years. I couldn't find you, and George vanished shortly after that last contact. You must tell me all about your journeys, both spiritual and material, when you've rested. I have an encounter therapy group coming to my home in the morning, but we'll be out by the pool so you just sleep as long as you like."

"Fine," she said, and yawned, setting her bag down beside the water bed and stepping out of her sandals. " 'Night, Lucien."

"Good night, dear girl. Your bath contains a whirlpool— it's the little switch to the left of the faucet. Enjoy."

"Goody," she said. He hadn't mentioned that the bath was under a skylight, where she could look out and see the gibbous moon.

A shadow fell across her, between her and the moon. She felt goose bumps rise on her skin and turned on the hot tap again before settling back to watch the cloud glide across the moon. But when she looked up in the skylight, she saw no cloud and no moon, just a pale, bluish face surrounded by draggled, weed-tangled hair. The face stared down at her through empty eye sockets.

The tortured strands of green-slimed yellow hair dripped dirty droplets onto Julianne's naked shoulders and chest as she stared up into those endless eye sockets. Her mouth opened and closed, and finally her voice emerged, small and uncertain, "Y-you sure don't *look* Indian."

▲ ▲ ▲

Lazarus, the magic banjo, would have cried out, of course. Would have started loudly wailing away at some tune that let Willie know it was in trouble and he had to wake up and save it. But the guitar Willie had with him was just a plain old unmagical Martin guitar, great tone, nice action, plenty of bass, but dumb as a post.

So when, about halfway between Oklahoma City and Wichita Falls, the bus driver decided Willie was sleeping so sound he wouldn't notice, she reached back and hooked the cloth guitar case by the strap, opened the bus door, and heaved the guitar as hard as she could, one-handed like, what with having to hold onto the wheel and all.

The guitar strings jangled and whined as it flew—and landed in the outstretched arms of Willie MacKai, who had reared up from a sound sleep and intercepted it. Now the wonder of this wasn't so much that Willie knew in his sleep that a perfectly nonmagical guitar was in danger. He'd actually gotten kind of sensitive to anything concerning music during the last seven years. The *wonder* was that he functioned so well and was actually able to catch the guitar and not fall out the open door of the moving bus when he'd just woke up. Willie always claimed he didn't see color in the morning without four cups of strong coffee in him.

By that time the driver's hands were on the wheel, and she was staring forward as if the guitar had just slid out of the seat, opened the door on its own, and tried to fling it*self* out.

Willie MacKai was not fooled. He pointedly reached over and closed the door, then sat down with the guitar case on his lap, opened it, and extracted the instrument, which seemed oblivious to the near miss it had just had. He started tuning. The driver didn't say anything this time.

He then played all the verses and choruses of "Mama Don't Allow No Guitar Pickin' 'Round Here," all the time staring hard in the driver's rearview mirror just so she didn't miss the point. He woke up the entire bus, everyone proceeding, after a little initial grumbling, to sing along. They were responding to the novelty of the music during a long, boring trip, to an easy chorus, and to the fairy dust still lending Willie that air of bein' somebody special.

The bus driver fought it, but before long she found her lips moving against their will and the tune running over and over through her head and forcing its way out her mouth.

When the song was over, Willie grinned cockily into the mirror and said, "Well, now. That was pretty good. Any requests?"

▲▲▲

The rain came down harder after Tom George left the tribal center and Anna Mae cursed herself for failing to ask George for a lift somewhere where she could get a room. The highway was miles away. She looked around her and wondered how tight the boards on the casino were, but when she inspected them, they looked pretty tight. It wasn't as if she were carrying a crowbar with her. Same way with the fireworks stand. So then she thought, maybe there were houses somewhere close and she could use a phone. Again, she should have used the one at the trading post, but she hadn't gotten around to asking George before he kicked her out.

No light gleamed as far as she could see, but there could be something beyond that fence. Tom George had mentioned a museum, hadn't he? Judging from the state of the fence and the weeds she could see growing through the holes in it, she didn't have much hope, but she wanted to look around anyway, as long as she was there.

The only carpentry in the whole place that wasn't nailed down tight was that fence. She sloshed through the puddles in the parking lot to go over for a look-see and bent over to peer through where the bottom half of a plank was missing. Through the weeds and gloom she saw a tepee, a hogan, a longhouse, a hut. She remembered the place then. The museum of Native American dwellings had been built after she'd grown up and moved away, but she'd seen it once on a visit here.

The plank was about six inches wide, and the one next to it

was loose too. She pried it a little farther and squeezed through the fence. To her surprise the buildings were in fairly good repair, though the tepee had been covered with ripstop nylon to protect the hide coverings. It was pretty dry inside. She wouldn't really sleep here, just kind of wait until Tom George returned in the morning.

She started making noises to scare snakes, then wondered if that was a good idea, and finally decided to take refuge in a more traditional attitude. "I've come to join you, little brothers. I won't take much room." She felt as if she were being silly and sensible at the same time as she settled down close to one side of the entrance, where the ground was dry and the wind didn't blow.

She had nothing dry to put on or wrap herself in, so she hugged her knees to her chest and sat with her back against the side of the tepee, shivering. She thought of building a fire, but she was too tired and discouraged and too sapped by the cold wet wind to do it. How was she ever going to find anyone on foot? How would she get them to believe that a bunch of songs, not even Indian songs, would be of any benefit to them? For that matter, how would she or her friends get anyone at all to believe that the songs mattered? Tom George was suspicious of her—how much less suspicious would anyone else be? But those worries were only surface ones. Furrowing beneath them was the fear that she no longer belonged here. What had she done to help her people in the last fifteen years? Before that she had inadvertently betrayed fellow activists, tricked by her own naïveté. She and her white man's ballads no more belonged here than that casino over there, or Fourth of July fireworks.

With all of those worries and the cold biting her, she fell asleep slumped against the side of the tepee.

She dreamed of a fire in the firehole in the middle of the tepee. It warmed her and let her blood run free in her veins again and pried her eyelids from her cheeks with fingers of warmth. Coral and blue flames lit the center of the tepee with light that bounced off the eyes staring at her from across the fire. She sat up abruptly, jerking herself awake. The fire was really there. To make sure, she stretched her hand out to it and let the heat bite it, but not for long—she needed that hand.

The eyes were really there too, and now they moved nearer as a long muzzle came into view. A coyote. It settled back down on its haunches, still staring at her, then abruptly yawned and scratched behind its ear. Behind it, beside it, she became aware of other pairs of eyes. Beside her was a rabbit, on the other side a raccoon. As her eyes grew accustomed to the firelight, she made out a bobcat, a squirrel. But all of the animals weren't small. Eyes on a level higher than her own caught her, and she saw the club ears and massive shoulders of a bear, the shaggy mane and broad face of a buffalo. How had such a huge creature fit into the tepee? Must be a dream after all, she thought. Every totem animal in existence. A beaver and a mole away from her, a porcupine briefly bristled, rearranging itself, but nobody got stuck. She laughed suddenly, and the coyote looked at her inquiringly. She said, "It's nothing. You just remind me of an old Bill Staines song, 'All God's Critters Got a Place in the Choir.'" The coyote scratched contemplatively and gave her another questioning look.

"Oh, well, what the hell, it's just a dream anyway. I'll sing it for you." She did, singing the whimsical story Staines had written about meeting a porcupine on a camping trip, a song with a good chorus. They were a good audience. Nobody left. Coyote gave a short yip at the end and sat with his tongue hanging out. That had to do for applause.

The coyote barked again and the camp fire flared up, sending a blaze of fire and a puff of smoke up the smoke hole in the center of the tepee, into a sky that peered through the hole like an oxidized silver eye. Anna Mae stared up into that eye for a long moment, and when she looked down again, the animals were gone.

Where coyote had been sitting, a human shadow sat instead. The shadow's hands were outstretched to the fire, and they were not made of shadow, for the firelight shone through them as if they were made of clear plastic. On the wrist of one hand was a turquoise bracelet. Despite the fire's heat, the stone retained grains of frost across its surface.

Anna Mae recognized that bracelet, though she had never seen it before. Recognizing it, she recognized the shadow as her namesake, the woman whose name she had taken to shame herself for her own unwitting perfidy. This was the real Anna Mae. No reason she should be haunting Oklahoma, since she died up on the Rosebud Reservation from a bullet in the head. She must be haunting *me*, Anna Mae thought.

"Sister, forgive me for taking your name—" the musician told the shadow.

The shadow raised the hand with the turquoise in a dismissive motion. One song said when Anna Mae was found, her bracelet was frozen to the ground. The feds had cut off her hands at the wrist to be sent to D.C. for fingerprints. Only after a protest from the People had her body, which had been buried by the feds as that of a drunken Jane Doe, been returned for a proper burial. They had found the bullet wound in her head then. The song never said if the hands were returned too.

"What is it that you want?" the musician who had been Mabel Charley asked, but she suddenly knew. She remembered the songs, she remembered the stories, but if songs and stories were dead in this country, who else remembered Anna Mae but the woman who had taken her name? Forgotten, with only the official record in existence about her life and death, Anna Mae's spirit had sought out her namesake.

"I know two songs about you," the former Mabel Charley told the ghost. "Perhaps you have not heard them. Larry Long's song tells how you died and how the feds lied about it and the People reclaimed you. The other song belongs to an activist named Jim Page. It's to the tune of one of the ballads we brought back from Britain. It will show you how your myth has grown, how even the wind knows of you, how the lies of your murderers and their attempts to degrade you cannot withstand the truth of what you did and what it meant to people."

The ghost nodded, and the musician closed her eyes and began to sing, the story forming in her head and pouring through her, the melody flowing from her to the ghost and back. She had not sung this song for more than seven years, but she remembered it well, and with every word and every note the ghost grew more substantial, the Mic Mac auto-assembly-line worker who had left her children to work for the Native American cause grew less a ghost and more a real person, the song taking something of her namesake to flesh out the ghost. Then the realistic song was finished, and a real woman sat waiting on the other side of the fire.

The singer began the more mythic song written to one of the tunes of "The Cruel Sister," the one that went, "Oh, the wind and rain" except that the chorus to this one said, "Blow, Dakota blow, and the cold Dakota winds they blow." The other song was real, it told the story; this Dakota wind blowing through the second song blew it up to legendary proportions, made Anna Mae a universal symbol of brave, committed people fighting for their rights. The vibrato in the singer's voice increased as she tried to keep the tears from drowning the song. She closed her eyes and didn't open them until she finished.

The ghost rose and started toward her as she finished, but before the figure crossed the camp fire, the singer fell back into a deep sleep.

She awoke to birds singing, and the notes sounded a little like the first bar of "All God's Critters," an impression that faded as she grew more awake. Her eyes went to where the camp fire had been, but there was nothing there but a clean, bare patch of earth. It had all been a dream, of course, but an instructive one. She knew how she must reach Tom George now. She would sing him Anna Mae's song, sing him "The Ballad of Ira Hayes," sing every other song she could think of which celebrated their people until he understood. The dream clung to her.

She started to unwind. She should have been frozen, damp, and cramped, but she was warm and dry, with a hoarseness that did not feel like a cold coming on and the scent of wood smoke still haunting her nostrils. Her arms were crossed against her chest and she uncrossed them to rise and go try to find Tom George. An unfamiliar weight bound her right arm under the elastic of her sweatshirt. Curiously, she pulled back the sleeve. A turquoise bracelet enclosed her wrist. The stone no longer bore a hint of frost.

CHAPTER XVII

▲▲▲

The camp fire was down to embers. Heather-Jon shuddered a little, despite the warmth of the predawn air, and looked all around the perimeter of the campsite, as if expecting other eyes to be looking back at her.

"And that was how Anna Mae Gunn realized that she had had a true vision, in the tradition of her people, and had been accepted into the warrior clan by the woman warrior she'd named herself after," Ute said. He stuck something into the fire, and it belched a sudden bolus of sparks and smoke.

Barbara Harrington-Smith fanned herself, coughing. "Really, now, Ute, I've heard these musicians had groupies, but ghost groupies?"

"Why, ma'am, I'm surprised at you! Here I am tellin' you about genuine women heroes of two separate and interrelated causes, and you go usin' pejorative terms like 'ghost groupies.'" He sounded as if he were about to faint and added prissily, "The correct nomenclature, I believe, is 'visible spiritual remains of a formerly living individual who enjoyed, had reason to enjoy, and pursued the enjoyment of music of a certain type by a certain individual or groups of individuals and actively expressed their enjoyment thereof.'"

"I beg your pardon," Barbara said, chagrined.

"You got it," Ute said, grinning a big coyotelike grin.

Heather-Jon asked, "But what about all the things those other people are trying to do to prevent the music from spreading? That organization, SWALLOW, the immigration problems, and that murderer?"

"And I'd like to know how Brose Fairchild and Gussie Turner and the others fared in a more urban area," said Mary Armstrong, who was a sociologist and interested in how environment affected what people did and vice versa.

"Well, the man from SWALLOW was runnin' into a snag or two," Ute said. "Let's poke up the fire and fix us some breakfast, and I'll tell you about it before we saddle up."

▲▲▲

The man from SWALLOW had his orders and rallied to the cause. An outbreak of unauthorized, unlicensed song was festering in various parts of Oklahoma and spreading virulently to other parts of the country, and it was up to him to stop it—or at least to collect.

He'd had a fine time mopping up that south central area in the past. Some of the people had been under the impression that a few so-called traditional American folk songs were theirs to perform or share as they liked. He had quickly pointed out to them and to the proprietors of the establishments in which they sang that certain prominent collectors of folk music in the thirties had not only collected these songs from various sources, but had arranged and published them, copyrighting them in the process, so that they too were licensed. Naturally SWALLOW now held the license and the copyright.

He caught up with one perpetrator in Oklahoma City. The perp was a sixth-grade teacher who was singing licensed songs to his students. Hugh Graham barged into the classroom with his calculator clicking, interrupting the teacher in the middle of a folk ballad about the Donner Party.

"By the power vested in me by the Songwriters and Arrangers Legal Licensing Organization Worldwide, I hereby order you to cease and desist singing that song or to pay the sum of fifteen hundred dollars plus penalties for violating the license on said song."

"I beg your pardon, but you don't have the license on this song," the teacher said. "I learned this song from my great-grandmother and I'm only just now recalling it."

"Nonsense. That is the arrangement licensed by SWALLOW."

"Prove it," the teacher said. "Show me a copy of your version, and I can show you how mine is different."

Well, the upshot of the whole incident was, the SWALLOW man left the classroom in a huff and called into the home office, asking one of the secretaries to punch up the lead sheet for that particular song and fax it to him.

"I'm sorry, sir," the secretary replied. "But I don't show any lead sheet for that title. We have the title but no other data listed."

"That's not possible," Graham said. "You simply aren't trying hard enough."

"Well, excu-oo-ooze me," the secretary said. "I'm double-checking the files and it seems we have *no* data in terms of actual sheet music for any of the titles that I've found."

Now, Hugh Graham was greatly puzzled by that, because he, of course, was simply a zealous employee of SWALLOW and not one of the masterminds behind the plan to actually wipe out the music. In fact, nobody in SWALLOW except for one or two minions actually knew all about the plot—they thought they were making money with music, not obliterating it. But the fact was, when the devils finally succeeded in emptying the United States of the music, it wiped SWALLOW's own U.S. computers clean too. Which was kind of funny, because along about then, thanks to one of the people who'd been at the convention in Tulsa, computers all over the country were relearning and reloading the songs.

▲▲▲

Morgan Richards and his wife LeeAnn had been at the convention but they were not musicians. Though LeeAnn sang a little, there were back-fence courting cats who sang better than Morgan. But, lordy, did he like to listen! He soaked up that music like a sponge, and during the night when the Randolphs were telling their tale to the folks gathered at ConTingent, he helped C. J. Cherryh with her new technical gear and later used what she had gathered for a little scheme of his own.

Because even though he wasn't a musican, he was a real virtuoso on another kind of keyboard—he could make computers jump through hoops and sit up and beg.

When Faron and Ellie had explained that the main thing they needed to do to fight the devils was to get as many people as possible singing again, Dally Morales snorted. He'd been watching C.J. and Morgan program C.J.'s laser disk recorder, and now he said to Morgan, "Hell, there's more of this kind of stuff around than there are people anymore. Too bad we can't teach these damn machines to sing too."

"That wouldn't be too hard, actually," Morgan said. He just meant it by way of conversation at first, but later he got to thinking about it.

"I don't think it would be too hard to design a folk-music virus," he told Barry later.

"The devils have already done that," Barry told him. "Killed off a bunch of folks or rendered them voiceless for good."

Morgan looked patient and Molly punched Barry on the arm. She was the electronic genius in the family. "He means a computer virus, silly."

"Sure," Morgan said. "One that would invade the hard disk memories of the two major kinds of computers. I could infect a lot of machines by redesigning the communications software that's used by all the insurance agencies and real estate companies, TV, radio, and newspaper offices. I'll send it to them by modem. Several of the kids' games are also played on modem now, and I could do a version of the most popular one with the virus built in."

"You can do that? I think you're on to something," Barry said. "Of course, it's not really the same thing as having people sing the songs."

"I don't see why it wouldn't be almost as good," Molly said. "The kids said the important thing was that the songs be sung, be in the airwaves like, and this would help."

"But wouldn't people discover the virus and debug the programs?" Faron asked.

"I can arrange it so that they'll play the songs so fast that they fit between other functions, except in the case of the children's game, where the songs could be incorporated as part of the game."

He had been as good as his word and had spread the virus far and wide at very little expense to himself.

▲▲▲

So it was kind of funny that thanks to Morgan Richards's virus, the SWALLOW computer, the only computer in the U.S. that should have had all the songs listed, didn't seem to have any of them just at a time when practically every other computer in the nation was acquiring them. Of course, the secretary was just checking the main menus. If she'd known how to check for the computer virus in the communications program, she'd have found the songs easily enough.

But she didn't know how to check, and so Hugh Graham promised to use his influence to have her fired for incompetence when he couldn't get the proof he needed and ended up looking like a fool in front of that teacher and all those children.

The teacher, being a teacher and having heard every kind of lie and evasion there was, soon got it out of even an experienced sophisticated guy like Graham that the computer was down and out and not likely to be providing fodder for lawsuits any time soon.

"I'm sure we can work something out," the teacher said. "This really is my own version, and you can't prove otherwise —I'm teaching it to all of these children, and they have my blanket permission to teach it and perform it to whomsoever they please in perpetuity. But I wouldn't want to break the law. I would like to register this song with your agency in the name of the People of the United States of America with any possible royalties to be paid directly to the fund for rebuilding the Folk Archives at the Library of Congress."

Still steaming, Hugh Graham proceeded to enter the registration with his company on his portable computer linkup.

CHAPTER XVIII

▲▲▲

Gussie, Terry, and Dan picked up Brose the day after they arrived, and the four of them drove to Volker Fountain outside the Nelson Art Gallery to discuss strategy. The fountain was dry this time of year, the grass around it brown in patches. Dead leaves filled the basin where water splashed in the summer.

"Seems to me the obvious thing is to start busking," Terry said briskly. She sat on the edge of the fountain and shredded a leaf between her elvishly long fingers while a breeze bearing the scent of rotting leaves brushed her straight brown hair against her cheek. "That's what we do in the U.K."

"Busking?" Gussie asked.

"You know, street singing, playing for tips. It comes from an obsolete French word meaning"—her voice took on Oxford tones—"to shift, filch; prowl, catch by hook or crook. Later it referred to cruising as a pirate. I suppose we could be considered pirates of a sort. Anyway, if there are no legitimate venues, I suppose busking's what we need to do."

"We could ask Monte and Nancy to have a party," Dan suggested. He was lolling on the grass, his head supported by hands cupped behind his neck, his long legs propped up on the rim of the fountain. "We could sing for that, and their guests could spread the word." .

Gussie shook her head. "I been thinkin' about that. I don't think we ought to do any music at all in our safe houses. Might make it easy for the devils to find us and come after our friends. Better to keep movin'."

"Busking it is then. We can do it anywhere until we're thrown out," Terry said.

"I'd like to try the ethnic neighborhoods then," Dan said. "I'll bet some of the Thai and Cambodian refugees still know some of their music. And there's a big Greek and Middle Eastern population here. Maybe I could get some of those folks to teach me some tunes from the old country. Those devils might have overlooked that kind of music." Dan was always interested in singing anything he had to have translated and that would let him practice playing some weird ethnic instrument.

"They'd probably trade you for some of the Child Ballads," Terry said. "You know how people are—if they're Indian, they want to learn jazz, if they're English they want to learn Chinese—"

"If they're black," Brose said, "they might play in Balkan bands like me." He gave his button-box accordion a squeeze by way of illustration. "On the other hand, maybe not. But it seems like a good idea. 'Cept I got a mind to check out the places that take care of sick folks—hospices and hospitals and such. Bound to be somethin' happenin' there. Jails are good too. Lotsa bored people in jails, but I might wait for that. After all, while we're sizin' up the street scene and doin' a little buskin', we could end up gettin' our buskers busted."

▲▲▲

Joyce Kranz fled the classroom and the school with life, limb, and sanity barely intact, drove across Inner-city Viaduct and through downtown Kansas City, Kansas till she reached the State Avenue exit, drove past shopping malls and ugly one-story businesses until she found one ugly one-story building in particular and parked beside several other large American-made cars in the lot. A small sign beside the door said, "Loyal Order of the Siblings of the Tiger, Private club, Members only." With shaking hands Joyce pulled her keys out of the ignition, relocked the car behind her, and walked on jellied legs into the dimly lit club.

She wasn't doing anything wrong, though if it was found out she'd been going to a bar to imbibe alcohol, she'd be barred from the substitute-teaching rosters for good. Screw it. If she could find anything else to do for a living, she would tell the schools and their rules to shove it for good. Besides, who said she was only coming here to drink? She could drink at home, couldn't she? Except that if anyone saw her at the liquor store, it would be as bad as if they saw her going into one of the few, dangerous bars left on the Missouri side. But she had grown up here, among the Tigers. She was a Tiger and the daughter of Tigers, and she could come over here anytime she wanted to.

A stooped little man with a farmer's palsy greeted her at the door. "Hello, Joycee," he said. "Sorry to hear about your mother."

"Hello, Frank," she said, trying to smile. She could remember this man as an iron-haired fifty-year-old, before years of bouncing around on a tractor and eventually losing his farm to the bank anyway had drained him worse than a vampire.

"Come over here to get away from the Blue Laws, eh?" Frank said slyly. Of course, Kansas was and always had been technically dry except for the clubs, but Missouri had amended its Blue Laws regarding the sale of liquor to extend to weekdays as well as Sundays now. It wasn't like prohibition exactly—drinking wasn't outlawed, but it was socially and bureaucratically frowned upon, and health lobbyists had made liquor difficult to buy.

The bar at the far end of the linoleum-tiled floor looked like light at the end of a tunnel. Joyce sat down on a red vinyl stool and buried her head in her hands for a moment to compose herself.

"What's a nice girl like you doin' in a place like this?"

Joyce looked up, battle ready, to see a small woman with a mop of curly gray hair grinning at her from behind the bar.

Before Joyce could speak, however, the older woman spoke. "Stressed out, huh? Just want a drink to calm down a little?"

"That's right," Joyce said, and let her eyes say, "And what business is it of yours?"

"Well?" the older woman asked.

"Well, what?" Joyce's voice came out challenging, and she realized she was still very much on the defensive.

"Well, what can I get you? I'm the bartender. Relax, honey. No need to apologize. I know what it's like these days. You think it was easy to find this job? But look, the health nuts got a point, you know? Booze ain't particularly good for you— especially habitually or in large quantities. But now and then a person needs to relax, and you look like you do. So what'll it be?"

"Is it possible to mix whiskey with a little diet soda?" Joyce asked. She used to drink that years ago when she still went out for drinks with friends once in a while. It had a name, but she couldn't remember it.

"Oh, I can see right now you're a confirmed alcoholic," the woman said. "Just kiddin'. Don't mind my big mouth. I'm used to talkin' when I tell stories, and I just get carried away sometimes. Why don't you talk? Tell ol' Gussie what's got you so upset you're driven to drink."

"It's just life. Everybody has problems."

Gussie nodded to Joyce's hands trembling against the top of the bar and just gave her a look.

Joyce said, "Well, how would you feel if every time you went unarmed in front of a new class of somebody's cherubs you had to search their hands and laps for weapons before you could start?"

"You're a teacher then," the bartender said.

"A substitute."

"What's your subject?"

"English literature—supposedly. I don't get to teach that very often, though today I was supposed to."

"Must be real rewardin' in some ways, though, to get to stand up there and talk about Shakespeare and Dickens and all those great writers and their books all the time. Sir Walter Scott is a personal favorite of mine."

"Really? Well, you're a minority. You know what I teach when I am trying to teach those youngsters to read?"

"No."

"Advertisements. Classified ads. Occasionally, when something earthshaking is occurring and I am working for a particularly liberal school board, we are permitted to study current events. But no Shakespeare, no Dickens, and certainly no Scott."

The bartender handed her a glass of sparkling beverage. "Here. Hope that's not too strong for you. I suppose teachin' kids to read the newspaper could be useful to them, but you'd think their folks would want them to know about the great writers too."

"Think again," Joyce said bitterly. "Fiction breeds unrealistic expectations and does not properly prepare children for life in the real world."

"Is that so?"

"That's what the handbooks all say. We are to teach the kids that 'what you see is what you get unless, of course, you can increase your earning capacity, in which case you can see and get more.' Fiction is nothing but lies, blatant escapism that leads to a distorted sense of reality and despair. That part's not a direct quote, but you get the drift."

"I get it."

"But you know those weapons I told you about?"

"Yeah. What about them?"

Joyce leaned over the bar, the tails of her blouse's pussycat bow dragging through a puddle Gussie had not been quick enough to wipe up. "I'm not worried they're going to use them on me so much as on themselves. Poor little suckers are desperate—and I wouldn't be saying this except that you poured me this strong drink—desperate for some unrealistic fun. Even hopping hormones can't meet all of a kid's needs to explore beyond the boundaries of home and hearth and KC, Mo. Am I making myself clear?"

"Yes, ma'am. Loud and clear. Clearer than you can realize. I did mention, didn't I, that I am a storyteller?"

"Yes, but I didn't pursue it at the time, not knowing what you meant." Joyce downed her drink with a flourish and wiped her mouth on the back of her hand. "So pour me another and tell me what you mean."

"Sure. Better yet, the place is kinda empty, I'll give you a free story with your drink. Now one time there was another teacher, and—scuse me, ma'am, but you don't have any moral objections to stories with magic in them do you?"

"Not in the slightest," Joyce said, and crowded close to the bar with both hands around her drink, feeling as if she were having hot chocolate and cookies in her grandma's kitchen.

"One time there was this teacher, and he was a pretty talented fella in the ways of magic too. One of his old students had made it good and become king, but he was havin' a few problems. He fell in love—I guess you could call it love, anyway—got the hots, at least, for the wife of one of his vassal-lords, and nothing would do but that his old teacher had to help him hoodwink everyone so's he could get the beautiful Igraine in the sack. . . ."

Joyce only identified a little with the beautiful Igraine, tricked by the wizard's magic into thinking Uther Pendragon was her husband, suffering later when she learned her husband was killed by Uther's treachery, then pragmatically accepting the necessity of marrying Uther. Much more compelling to Joyce was the plight of Morgaine, Igraine's daughter, growing up under the thumb of her father's murderer, and of Merlin, whose sacred magic had been used to pimp for Uther. She understood full well why Merlin would undertake Arthur's teaching himself, to make sure Uther's son became a *good* king, instead of a tyrant like his father. Of course, it was all more complex than that. She hadn't thought about Camelot in years, but now it occurred to her that there were a lot of parallells between the intrigues of court and school politics. She felt a little better, thinking that in some ways she and Merlin were in the same boat.

"I had forgotten that those old stories *got* old precisely because they're so universal," she told the bartender. "It's a shame they're out of fashion now."

The bartender shrugged. "People make the fashion. I know some others, including how stories and songs got lost."

"Lost?" she asked. "Surely they're just not used anymore."

"It's one of those use-it-or-lose-it situations. And there's a reason we're losing it—the songs and stories I mean. But that's another story."

Joyce smiled at the bartender, feeling infinitely more relaxed than she had. Drinking *could* be therapeutic after all. "How much do I owe you then?" she asked, reaching into her purse for her credit card and daily-memo-calculator.

"It's on the house," Gussie said.

"No, really, you've been entertaining me as well as those two stiff drinks. I hope I'll be able to drive."

"Oh, I think you will . . ." the bartender said.

She was right. Joyce was able to drive home and even enjoy the drive. She thought maybe she could slip in a few stories after all, with tales of commerce and current events, draw comparisons—as long as she was talking about what the school board wanted her to, they couldn't object to her attempts to make the material more vivid, could they? She graded all of her test papers before she went to bed and was pleased to find the next morning that she suffered no ill effects from her night of sin. Midway through another awful day at school, when the discussion was supposed to be about economics and solving the national debt, she tried to remember the story of the king who turned everything he touched to gold, but could only come up with a vague allusion that baffled the students.

That night was Friday night, and she drove back to the Tiger club, where the bartender took advantage of a large clientele to launch into the story she had mentioned earlier. Joyce stayed over at her mother's house Saturday and drove to the club as soon as it opened, where the bartender resumed the story for her and two other people. When the bartender got to the part where she had been possessed by the ghost of Sir Walter Scott, she said, "Sorry. Last call. Hope y'all can come back Monday. Bar's closed tomorrow."

"I have a jewelry party tomorrow anyway," Joyce told her.

"Is that so?" the woman said.

"Yes, I promised my friend Margie I'd do it. She's a nurse. It's not so much the jewelry, you know, though some of it's nice." She held up the fake opal-and-diamond ring she wore on her left hand, where a married woman would wear a wedding band. "It's extra income for some people and then too it's a way to meet people. Margie works evening shift, so she doesn't know many people aside from work. You're probably familiar with how it works? I host a party and get free gifts in return according to the amount of sales Margie makes and whether or not we persuade someone else to have a party and so on. I—I don't suppose you'd like to come?"

"Oh, now, I do admire that ring of yours. Would there be one like that there? Could I bring a friend?"

Joyce felt herself go hot in the face and realized she had been hoping the woman would come. Over the last week she'd almost started to think of the bartender as *her* teacher. "Please do. Tell me, Gussie, have you always been a storyteller?"

"No, ma'am. I never used to do it at all except for tellin' a joke once in a while. I sort of started when I met up with Wat —Sir Walter Scott I mean. I swear that man knew all the stories that were told in legend and song."

"Song too? You've mentioned songs before. Do you sing then?"

"I have friends who do."

"Well, tell me, what are your fees? I think it would be great to have some entertainment for my friends so that the jewelry party doesn't seem quite so crass—as if I'm just peddling things. More gracious, don't you think?"

"Yes, I surely do agree. And I'm sure one of my friends would love to bring some songs. We'd appreciate gas money, and I know I wouldn't mind havin' a chance to get a pretty ring like yours, but maybe we could work somethin' else out too," she said mysteriously.

"Good," Joyce said, a little amazed at her own daring, and slightly worried too. She decided she may as well be clear with the bartender about her concern before things went any further. "I'd appreciate it if you didn't mention—well, I hate to sound like a snob, but my job's involved—if you just didn't tell anyone where you know me from or what you do. I wouldn't want them to know I drink."

Gussie smiled and her apple cheeks dimpled mischievously. "No problem, sugar. I'll just tell anybody who asks that you buy your diet sodas from me."

"You don't mind lying about it?"

"Nah, they don't need to know that I never charge you. I hope you won't think I've been above myself, but I never put nothin' in your drinks, honey. Tell me if I'm out of line, but I never did think you really wanted a drink—just a little company."

"I *thought* those must be awfully watered drinks. While I do admit that I find your presumption in changing my order condescending, Gussie, I've got to say that your perception was absolutely correct. And I'm pleased to learn that I haven't suddenly become an alcoholic after all. Let me draw you a map to my house."

Margie was explaining how the jewelry party plan worked to the women when Gussie and her friend arrived and shucked off their coats. Joyce was relieved to see them. The jewelry was okay, she supposed, but she was bored by the chirpy presentation and really didn't see anything she wanted for her free gift. She had already earmarked another of the fake opal rings for the bartender.

Tonight Gussie was not wearing her pink jogging suit, but a red tartan skirt and shawl with a white blouse. She looked the perfect picture of a nice older lady. Nobody would guess she was a bartender. Her friend looked like a model on her day off—tall and thin with shoulder-length brown hair, high cheekbones, large luminous eyes. Her fingers were the longest Joyce had ever seen, and she was clutching a guitar case. As soon as Joyce spotted them, everyone else turned their way too.

"Hi, y'all. My name's Gussie Turner. This here is my friend Terry Pruitt." Terry smiled a smile that was like a flower blossoming—her rather austere face suddenly was warm, human, and utterly lovely. Joyce had at first thought that Terry was wearing a nice outfit too, but up close she saw that it was just a white cotton T-shirt with the sleeves rolled up, a pair of new wide-legged jeans belted with a decent belt, and a vest in some colorful ethnic print. An earcuff sporting two silver feathers flashed through a sheaf of Terry's brown hair as she unpacked the guitar and tuned.

Gussie took command of the room easily, with a little inquiring nod at Joyce, and, sitting sideways in a chair in the middle of the group, proceeded to fill the room with her story and gestures in a way that somehow did not annoy the other women. Margie was plainly fascinated.

Gussie told them some of the first part of the story Joyce had already remembered, but somehow made it fresh for her as well. The difference was that every time she got to an incident where there was a song, Terry Pruitt sang the song, taught them the chorus, and encouraged them to learn the rest of the song. Gussie added, "Learning the songs, ladies, that's how you keep them going. That's how we keep the world turnin' and keep at bay all that bedevils folks and makes them want to give up and die."

"For every song you learn," Terry said in her melodic voice, "every *note* you learn, every *word* you rhyme with another, every time you sing it, you sing away one shaft of pain, one piece of misfortune, one disappointment. Try it."

The whole room tried it, tentatively at first, but gradually some of the women chimed in churchy harmonies, and then some did a little better. Some couldn't sing at all, but Terry encouraged them too.

Gussie stopped the story before she got to anything new and said, "If you want to hear the rest of it, somebody better give another party and invite us. There'll be more songs too, but for now I think I'll let Terry sing a couple more, then we'll be off."

Terry, grinning, dedicated "Health to the Company," to the audience but then turned to Joyce and said, "I'm going to play a tune now I composed just for you, for being kind enough to invite us and sponsor our music. It's called 'Planxty Joyce Kranz.'"

"'Planxty Joyce *Kranz*'?" Gussie asked, as if they hadn't rehearsed this part, which Joyce was sure they had from the comical bewilderment on Gussie's face. "Is that anything like 'Planxty George Barbizon' that O'Carolan wrote?"

"O'Carolan wrote lots of tunes with titles starting with the word 'planxty,'" Terry said, using Gussie's question as a cue to instruct the audience. "'Planxty' is an Irish word that means something like "in honor of" or "dedicated to." Back in the days of minstrels and harpers, and these days too, a musician was sponsored by a great house—given hospitality and a place to play his music and sometimes a salary. O'Carolan had lots of patrons, and they're the ones he dedicated his planxties too. Though mostly we do songs rather than tunes, I'd like to offer this planxty to Joyce for having us here tonight and promise to try to compose a different one for anyone else who'd like to have a party like this."

The notes poured out as liquid, sweet and tart as lemonade on a hot day, as soothing as a cat's purr, as magical as bird flight. Terry's long hands danced on her instrument, tripping out the notes of Joyce's own personal song. Joyce had a sudden longing to know it, learn it, keep it, and suddenly remembered something.

As soon as the tune ended, she darted down to her storage locker, where a former lover had dumped his stuff. Yes, there it was, the old guitar. She carried it by the neck back up the stairs and handed it to Terry.

"I used to play piano when I was a little girl. Can you help me learn my song on this?"

▲▲▲

"After that," Ute said to the mounted women riding with him across the hard-packed earth, "Terry ended up givin' a lot of guitar lessons, the ladies ended up givin' lots of parties, learnin' lots of songs, and eventually Joyce started usin' some of them with her classes—showin' 'em how the great advertising jingles sometimes had their origins in old, old songs or at least from ancient or historical themes. Margie, who worked in the nursery, began singin' lullabies to the babies and eventually started teachin' them to the mamas. After a time the mamas started havin' their own parties. Lots of songs got spread that way."

"Whew," said Heather-Jon, "that fairy dust must have been powerful stuff to affect all those women that way."

"Could be," Ute said, squinting into the sun, then taking his industrial-strength sunglasses out of his shirt pocket and saving his eyes from the rays. "And it could be that the songs and stories themselves were just that exciting, or that the women needed them just that much."

"Maybe," Shayla said, twisting on the designer pockets of her custom-made riding jeans with the built-in politically correct canvas chaps on the front of the legs. "Pardon me if I don't believe all sisters are created equally receptive to enrichment, however, and those were very boring, middle-class women."

"Not after Terry and Gus got through with 'em, they weren't," Ute told her.

CHAPTER XIX
▲▲▲

Willie left the bus feeling pretty cocky and got a ride with the family of one of the other passengers, a soldier, as far as the outskirts of Abilene. He had fixed the bus driver good, and the passengers had followed after him like puppy dogs, wanting to learn more songs. That fairy dust was great stuff.

The soldier and his family begged Willie to have dinner with them, to meet the rest of the clan, to play his music at the family reunion. But Willie was still sick of people then. He thought for the first several miles of walking along, guitar in hand, that he was so sick of human companionship that he never wanted to see another person in his life.

He didn't even try to thumb a ride for a couple of hours, then his feet got sore, his arm got tired, the wind picked up and cut through his jeans and jacket, numbed his fingers and nose with cold.

He cussed himself for not taking the soldier's family up on their offer. After all, he was here to play music, wasn't he, not play Greta Garbo? And there would have been free food, a bed for the night. This stretch of road was not exactly teeming with motels and restaurants.

A red sports car whizzed past him a whole lot faster than the law allowed, and he swore as it sprayed him with dust. A few minutes later he heard the motor roar again, then he saw it, way off down the long flat road, zooming backward toward him nearly as fast as it had gone by the first time.

A familiar female face topped by red hair poked out the window. "Want a lift?"

"What the hell are you doin' here, darlin'?" he asked her.

"What the hell do I ever do anywhere, darlin'?" she asked. "Get in."

He was surprised to find that he was glad to see her—gladder than he would have been, in fact, to see any of his more human and predictable companions. For one thing, she liked him for all his worst impulses, and that was pretty rare in a female of any kind. Of course, *her* impulses tended to be worse than his . . . but nobody was perfect. Now that he no longer had to guard the banjo from her, he could freely admit to himself that he sort of enjoyed her. You never knew what she was going to do next.

He piled his guitar and banjo into the backseat and then climbed in beside her. "Thought you'd never ask, you gorgeous thing."

"Where to? For someone who's been bustin' his ass to go out and spread all this sunshine and song around, you seem to be a little behind at seeking an audience."

He bridled at that. "Goddamn, darlin', I just finished playin' a gig on the Oklahoma City–Wichita Falls bus. A man has to have a little time to his own self. And I'll tell you somethin' else for sure, once I got 'em broke in good, the folks on the bus were a whole lot more appreciative than those jerks back at that bar where I met you."

She smiled and stroked his thigh with her right hand. The hand was exceptionally warm, as if she had been lying out getting a tan all day and the sun had soaked clear through to the bone. "Don't you worry yourself about that, sugarpants. That was just some of my compadres havin' a little joke at your expense. You haven't lost a thing, and all kinds of people will be delighted to hear you. Trust me."

"Yeah, sure, darlin'," he said in a tone that reminded her in case she'd forgot that he didn't trust her any farther than he could throw her. He liked that about her, though. He was getting awfully tired of being around reliable people who insisted that he be reliable too. It was plain enjoyable to be around somebody who made him feel like a deacon of the church by comparison. And one thing about her, being a devil she could never assume that morally superior tone women had a habit of taking with a man. He would never ever have to identify her with those mistreated girls he had become a part of in the ballads. He'd never have to feel guilty around someone who was so much guiltier from the get-go than he could ever think of being.

Very different than if he had made love to Juli—which would only happen, he was sure, when and if they were both absolutely straight and probably had just had a nice vegetarian low-cholesterol dinner. She was trying so hard not to be one of those unfortunate ballad women that she would hold him absolutely accountable for every little word and action, every little embroidery on the truth to make it a little easier for both of them. The thought of how difficult women like Juli were

was almost enough to undo all the missionary work the Debauchery Devil was presently doing in his lap. Part of her was
female. Hungry, lusty female.

And then almost against his own will he saw himself taking
her hand away from his lap and bringing it up to his mouth.
He kissed her hand and set it back on the steering wheel
without explanation. He'd just remembered that the thing
about a woman like Julianne was, she wouldn't give you some
deadly disease and then laugh about it afterward. The Debauchery Devil glanced over at him and made a rueful face.

"Your loss, sugar."

"Let's just be friends," he said. "I don't guess I'm up to the
thought of the kind of competition I'd have."

"Maybe not. You remind me of an old consort of mine,
though. But I can see you don't have any faith in me. I don't
suppose I can change your mind?"

"Not a chance in hell, darlin'," he said, sounding much
surer than he felt. She lit a Brimstone Light cigarette without
the benefit of a lighter. The glow from the cigarette cast orange light on the cleavage created by her neon pink tube top,
on her bare shoulders and thighs.

"Well, at least I'm on home turf there. Why not?"

"Lots of things. You'd probably all of a sudden have your
skin start meltin' off your skull or rot away to dust right in the
middle of everything or somethin', just for kicks."

She gave him a death's-head grin and blew a smoke ring in
his face. "Oh yeah? You consider that kicks, do you? Why
should I do that when I could melt the flesh from *your* bones
instead?"

They rode together for quite a ways, and on the way
they . . . negotiated. The main problem for Willie was that
he was as free, more or less, as he'd been since the night Mark
Mosby died and left him the magic banjo. He no longer carried the awesome responsibility as chief picker of Lazarus,
didn't have to protect the banjo or anybody else but himself
now. He had regained all the songs he had ever learned and
then some, knew more about music than he ever had in his
life, and he had a mission. What he needed, he explained to
Torchy, was an agent.

▲▲▲

Brose's approach to finding venues was simple. He *thought*
about going into hospitals and volunteering to sit with the

dying. He *thought* about meeting some of the people at the animal shelters and seeing if he could play for fund-raisers. He *thought* about playing a lot of places. What he did was, he went back to Grand Avenue, where a lot of fancy offices faced a lot of the wreck of what used to be downtown Kansas City, and he sat down on the curb and played the blues and figured he'd keep playing it until some cop came along and offered him a venue in the city jail. He was *sure* he'd find an audience there.

He played sweet and smooth and with lots of little pyrotechnical doodads that showed he was no amateur. A woman in a real nice outfit walked past him. Strong-lookin' woman, dark-skinned, black-haired, wide hips, and big bust makin' a female outfit out of a business suit. She walked on past him without lookin'. Without even thinkin' about it, he started playin' "Baby, Please Don't Go." She turned around, tryin' hard to make her smile settle down and not take control of her mouth like it wanted to, then she walked back, dug into her coat pocket, and threw two bucks into his guitar case. He sang after her as if he were casting a line with the words as bait, though his butt stayed right there on the curb and his fingers stayed on the strings. After she was out of sight, however, Brose sprinkled a little more of that ol' devil fairy dust all over himself and hoped the next time he could get his audience to stick around awhile and draw a few more.

▲▲▲

The last few years had changed Willie in a lot of important ways, but they hadn't overcome his dislike of using the telephone or of dealing with business details. Fortunately, nobody seemed to expect him to *be* in business.

"Don't you worry about a thing, sugar," Torchy said. "I've been in touch with the current scene while you've been overseas gallivantin' around. I know where it's happenin' these days." They had been sitting in her car looking at the power boats cruising the polluted Town Lake in Austin. Torchy reached into the glove box and pulled out a cellular phone and dialed a number. Willie, who hated phones, got out of the car and paced for a while.

Once she called out, "Willie, sugar, how would you describe what you do?"

"Strong heart songs, darlin'," he said without hesitation. "Strong heart songs."

"Great," she said, and talked into the phone some more. Finally she flung open the car door and wiggled over to him, all sorts of things bouncing around in her short-shorts and halter top as she teetered across the gravel on four-inch red spike heels. "It's all set, sugar. I got you the gig."

"Great. Where is it and when?"

"Well, it's as soon as you can get there at the newest Temple."

"What's that?"

"Why, only the latest, snazziest, expensivest health clubs in the state. There are Temples in Austin, Houston, San Antonio, Fort Worth, Dallas, Corpus Christi, *and* Galveston, and they're planning one for Amarillo. If they like you at this one, you can tour the others. This is only for tips, of course, since they've never tried live entertainment before, but—"

"You're a genius. How did you do it?"

"Oh, it wasn't too hard. Lulubelle Baker is a major stockholder."

"*Lulubelle* and a *health club*?" Willie asked, remembering the establishment where he had first met Torchy in her Lulubelle Baker guise, Lulubelle Baker's Petroleum Puncher's Paradise, which had to be *the* sleaziest, nastiest, kinkiest, most degenerate lowlife whorehouse, dope den, and bar he had ever been in—and he'd been in some doozies.

The Debauchery Devil patted his cheek. "Diversification, darlin'. I haven't spent all these centuries listenin' to that blessed accountin' devil maunder on about the treasury report for nothin'."

"Thanks a lot, darlin'."

"*De nada,* sweetie, but just remember, you owe me. I'll give you a lift, then you're on your own for a while. I have simultaneous appointments in Paris with the the wife of a third-world dictator for a shopping trip, and with the dictator and his mistresses for an orgy. Busy, busy, busy. I have to make sure vice and debauchery don't fall on such unprofitable times everywhere as they have here. I'm happy to help you, but I do have my own career, you know."

▲▲▲

James Francis Farnham wiped the knife on the skirt of one of his victims, stuck the knife back into its sheath, and casually abandoned the stolen van in the flea-market parking lot. The flea market was held in an old warehouse. The van and the bodies were unlikely to be discovered until he'd had a chance to obey his voices and generate some new corpses.

He caught a bus to downtown Kansas City, Missouri, though there was not much in the heart of downtown now except slick new buildings and loony street people. Fucking psychos. He hated that kind of scum. He noticed a mottled-looking mulatto talking earnestly to a bunch of them, and that disgusted him even more.

Not all of the street people were men. There was a skinny blond girl with bad skin who held a baby to her flat chest and a snotty-faced two-year-old by the hand. One old bag with a shopping cart sat beside the mulatto. Then James Francis Farnham noticed that there was a guitar case open on the other side of the mulatto and knew he'd come to the right place. The voices had told him about the others. He could take as many as he wanted, though he only wanted the women. Maybe he could kill off the women till the mulatto told him what he wanted to know. Then maybe he could kill some more. He hadn't killed a man before, but a mutt like that wouldn't hardly count.

His jeans were full of holes by now, and his shoes ragged and dirty, his coat, stolen from one of his victims, struck the right note—too big, not the right style, and obviously a castoff from a person of the wrong sex. He fit right in with the crowd in the street.

"Say," he said. "Any of you know where there's a likely dumpster? I haven't eaten in three days."

"Sorry, bro, but they been emptied for the day," another man said unexpectedly politely. "But we just ordered pizza, and you're welcome to share."

CHAPTER XX
▲▲▲

"I want to try working the streets with you, Brose," Dan said one day shortly after they arrived in Kansas City.

"I thought you was off learnin' Cambodian music or somesuch," Brose said.

Dan shook his head sadly. "I forgot that this has been going on for seven years. No matter which neighborhood you go into, you can't hear any music but Duck Soul—even translated Duck Soul. Maybe there's some of their real music at parties or something, but so far I haven't been able to wangle an invitation. I'm just another big Caucasian with funny ideas that may get them into trouble."

"And you think the streets will be easier, huh?" Brose asked.

Dan put his arm around Brose's shoulders. Since Dan stood about six foot four and had a reach like a gorilla, this was no problem for him, even though Brose's shoulders, like the rest of Brose, were pretty broad. "At least we'll be together," Dan told him.

Brose gave him a disgusted look, but Dan just hugged him tighter for a moment and said, "Brose, it's worse than just bad —it's dangerous. It's like Sir Walter told us about the English burning harps and harpers and hanging bagpipers—music from other cultures is being completely dominated by the prevailing attitudes of the mainstream. The worst thing is, these people are either too new to the country or too young to realize that's not the way it's supposed to be. So I think maybe if I help you get English-language music back to the people, it will encourage the people in the other cultures to revive their own music before they end up having to return to their old countries—and in some cases, that would mean getting killed —to retrieve it, the way you guys did with the ballads."

"Okay, kid, just let me tell you, though, that it ain't easy. I get a tip now and then, but mostly folks is in too big a hurry. Sure ain't gathered no huge following to pass music on to."

"That," said Dan, "is why you need me. And maybe a better spot."

Brose just grunted. He wasn't sure about the kind of notice Dan would attract. Brose thought of himself as old and fat and funny lookin' enough to draw attention, but at least he had the sense to be paranoid about it, and trouble would have a hard time sneaking up on him.

Dan was different, though. He was kind of like a big puppy dog who thought everybody, even the dogcatcher, was his friend.

However, Brose soon found that like a lot of people who simply assume that trouble will not bother them as long as they mean well, Dan had no problems at all—at least not with the street people. The police were another matter.

"That's where I've been hangin' out," Brose said, pointing to the corner of Fourth and Grand Avenue. "You get ahead on out and see if you can find someplace better. I'm gonna park. Don't get hit over the head."

Dan grinned and waved, then strolled nonchalantly up the icy street, hunching his shoulders against a knife-sharp wind cutting along the sidewalks and through the streets, straight as the lines between the patches of WPA-laid brick that broke through the cement here and there around the manholes. "Damn fool," Brose said, drove a hundred yards or so farther, then pulled into a parking place, put money into the meter, and pulled his guitar and Dan's hammered dulcimer from the back of the van.

He found Dan talking to a bag lady, helping her pick up her shopping cart full of trash while she smacked at his hands, afraid he was going to steal her loot. As Brose watched, two younger people, a raggedy-bearded man with long unkempt hair and a skinny blond girl with a baby in her arms and a toddler clinging to her leg, closed in on Dan, joining the woman in her shouts. Dan was speaking soothingly. "It's okay. Really. Just a bit of an accident."

He towered over them all, his prematurely gray head bobbing earnestly. Two rat-faced teenagers, one Hispanic looking, the other with greasy sandy hair and volcanic-looking eruptions all over his face, joined the pack.

Brose came to the rescue, whether of Dan or the street people he wasn't sure, shouting, "Hey, buddy, here's your instrument! You gon' do a street concert for these folks, you gon' need your instrument!"

Dan beamed calmly and stepped away from the group, shedding the more menacing members with an "Excuse me" as he reached for his dulcimer. Brose was glad that musical instruments didn't have much monetary value anymore.

He set down his own guitar case and left the lid open, not bothering to tune beforehand but warming up his fingers with a quick jig while he distracted the others and waited for Dan to set up. Dan, of course, carefully tuned beforehand while Brose was winding tuners back so strings contracted with the cold didn't snap like icicles before he could get any music out. When Dan finally joined in, a satisfied look on his face as he bonged and chimed another jig on the dulcimer, Brose belatedly remembered the fairy dust and sprinkled himself and Dan, then looking at the scruffy lot around them, flung a pinch or two in their direction while pretending to limber up his picking hand. The bag lady blinked once, and the baby at the blond girl's breast laughed. Nobody else seemed to notice.

At least, nobody seemed to notice until the next clot of pedestrians walked by, and then six of them stopped to listen while Dan sang a funny song about the "Darby Ram" and Brose sang the "Brown Girl Blues," followed by "In the Pines." The pedestrians had seemed as harried and hell-bent for commerce as usual when they strode up, but as they walked away, Brose noticed that their faces had smoothed out a little. They walked with a little more of a beat to their feet, a little swing to their hips.

There was also an amazing thirty bucks in the guitar case. Fortunately Brose noticed it before the street people, who were holding out hands and hats to the next group of pedestrians.

Dan, however, scooped up the money and said, "This is great. You guys are terrific. Let's go for pizza."

"They won't let us in," the blond girl whined.

"Fine," Dan said. "Then we'll have it delivered."

Brose kept playing while Dan found a pay phone and ordered pizza. The crust was so tough Brose thought maybe they'd just slathered the thin tomato sauce and greasy cheese on top of the cardboard disk, but nobody else complained. Of course Dan didn't notice. But then, Dan's favorite breakfast was day-old cold oatmeal.

They made a lot more money that day, all of them, and Brose decided that for supper maybe he'd go pick up hamburgers and shakes someplace. By now Dan was showing the blond's two-year-old how to bang on the dulcimer in between troops of onlookers. Brose hoped he didn't invite them all back to the house of Bob and Shirley Kelly, the old folkies who were good enough to house Dan and Terry. On his way back with the burgers and fries sending nice hot greasy smells to his nostrils, Brose stopped at a phone booth to try to find state health and social services numbers, but none were listed. There was not even a Salvation Army shelter listed anymore.

He knew something was wrong the minute he pulled up to the corner of the street they'd been playing on. He didn't have to be psychic to figure it out. The whirling red and blue lights on top of the cop cars were a dead giveaway.

They were loading everybody into the van, and Dan, who was not exactly resisting, was talking as fast as Brose's teeth were chattering. As Brose got closer, he understood that Dan was insisting that they all be arrested.

"Just move along, buddy, and there won't be any problem," one cop said tiredly.

"There's no problem now, officer. We were just standing here talking and singing a little."

"Creating a public nuisance," another cop said.

"No way," said one of the teenagers. "Look at this loot. They wouldn't be givin' us money if we were a nuisance, would they?"

"Shut the fuck *up,*" said the other teenager.

"Panhandling, huh? That's illegal."

"So like I said, arrest us," Dan said. "We have our rights."

This time Brose did not rush to the rescue. He did wait for the paddy wagon, however, and followed it two blocks to the police station, where he handed over the burgers and shakes to the perpetrators waiting to be booked.

▲▲▲

To save jail space, small misdemeanors were tried on the spot, and after several hours Dan and the members of the group who hadn't managed to slink away when the cops arrived were sitting on the hard metal chairs in the little room while the judge listened to what the cops had to say.

"Panhandling, yeah, that's an offense okay," the judge, a petite black woman with a puffy straightened hairdo, said. She had started the night tired and didn't expect to get any more awake. Night after night street people, prostitutes, domestic disputes, and random violence paraded past her. She hardly saw the daylight any more, and the nights she saw weren't pretty. At least she had a job. Her husband had left her for one of his college students two years before, and her children were now themselves college students. She had a hard time sleeping during the day with the new mall going in across the street from her house. "Vagrancy," she said, trying not to mutter.

"Your honor, I'm not a vagrant," Dan said. "I'm a musician." And he hoisted his somewhat battered-looking dulcimer with cuffed hands. "We were playing music."

"Is that so?" she asked.

"Yes, ma'am," he said. "I'll prove it if you like."

"Her honor does not have time for that kinda crap," the cop growled, but her honor was looking hard at the gray-haired man, who was slightly better put together than the group accompanying him. The instrument looked like something that might have cost some money at one time. He could have stolen it. There was something about him that didn't make her think so. Despite his clothes and general dishevelment, he seemed . . . fresher, somehow, than the people she usually saw. Of course, she'd been on the bench way too long to be taken in by appearances, but she couldn't help hoping, in spite of every scrap of experience telling her she was being silly, that this one case might be a little less tedious and boring and depressing than usual. Oh, well. One sure way to find out.

"Very well. Submit your evidence," she said.

"Could you ask the officer to give me that thing that looks like a table leg back, ma'am?" Dan asked. "I guess he thought I'd use it as a club or something. But it's to support the back of the instrument when I lean the front half against my thighs, like this," he said, showing her. She nodded, and one of the policemen, bouncing the wooden leg in his hand, gave it to Dan, and who duly screwed it into the back end of the instrument.

Dan took two thin carved wooden hammers from his pocket—once the police decided they weren't loaded, they'd let him keep them—and began to play a dance tune from Brittany. It took only a bar or so for the judge to understand that he was absolutely telling the truth, but she let him finish anyway for the sheer pleasure of it. The tune was short, and when he finished he paused, hammers still poised in his hands, and grinned up at her expectantly, like a kid who expected to be congratulated on spelling his name correctly.

She said nothing but deliberately maintained a cool and aloof expression, raised her brows, put on a pair of half glasses, and thumbed through a book of statutes. She seemed to recall an applicable one from a test case she'd read about that happened ten years before. Ah, there it was. Definition of vagrancy and statute pertaining thereto. She slammed the book shut and said to the cop, "He's okay. A musician playing on the street is not a panhandler or a vagrant but a street performer practicing his trade. I don't know about the rest of these people." Funny. There was nothing really out of the ordinary about them as far as street people went—they all looked hungry and blitzed out and ill clothed and dirty, but they were as appealing somehow as children with their noses pressed against the window of a bakery. Or the Little Match Girl. Or something. In spite of the stench she could smell from twenty feet away.

▲▲▲

"Hmph," Barbara said. "So much for the great liberal. He got free on charm and let the rest of them get thrown in the slammer, huh?"

"No wonder Brose was so skeptical about him," Shayla said. "But I guess he probably figured a night in jail was better for them than a night on the streets."

"Will you ladies just pipe down and let me finish?" Ute said. "If you'd known Dan, you'd know he did no such thing."

"Seems to me if street music was still allowed, the devils slipped up someplace," Mary Armstrong said.

"Well, a lot of what they did was on the sly, not out-and-out law changing. Besides, they said all along they didn't want musicians in jail. And I guess they didn't figure it would ever come up, especially in Kansas City. Ol' Dan kinda fooled 'em."

▲▲▲

Because while that verdict might have been fine with other people, Dan wasn't the kind of man to let down friends, no matter how newly minted. As Dan would have explained it, he was a Cancer, which made him caring and protective, had his moon in Libra, which made him fierce about fairness, and had his rising sign in Aquarius, which made him into weird causes. He was also Norwegian by ancestry, which made him stubborn. "Excuse me, ma'am. These people are my students," he said. "We were in the process of forming a band—"

"Street Pizza," suggested the Hispanic kid.

"Yeah, Street Pizza," he said. "My friends were just waiting to complete the finishing touches on their instruments."

"Oh, come off it, buddy," one of the cops said. "We've been movin' some of these folks from one corner to the next for three years."

"We don't mind moving," Dan said. "But you did interrupt us in the process of getting ready for our outdoor concert."

"I've heard enough," the judge said. "Dismissed. But the next time the officers find your students, young man, they'd better all be playing instruments too."

"No a cappella?" he asked.

"Don't press your luck with me, son," she said, and banged her gavel on the bench. "Next case."

Because Dan didn't like to lie, a little while later Brose found himself sitting on yet another curbside outside a flea market, kept company by his guitar case and Dan's student body, waiting for Dan to return from shopping.

"Excuse me, am I to assume that dumpster back there is taken?" someone asked. Brose turned to find an unfamiliar derelict being glared at by the rest of the Street Pizza ensemble. "Help yourself," he said indifferently. What was one mouth to feed, more or less?

Dan returned with a handful of bright-colored unopened cardboard and plastic-bubbled packages. "These were really cheap. You wouldn't believe it. Perfectly good kazoos and tambourines."

"What? No Mickey Mouse ukuleles?" Brose asked.

Dan shook his head sadly. "Those all went long ago. The guy said somebody found these in an old warehouse, and he was able to get the whole lot of them for next to nothing. They don't teach kids music anymore, Brose. The guy who sold me this stuff used to be a band teacher. Isn't that the saddest thing you ever heard of? Anyway, folks, if you want pizza on a regular basis . . ."

The newcomer, who seemed a little grubby but otherwise very well groomed for one of these people, shambled back from the dumpster. "Pizza?" he asked. "I musht shay I alwaysh think itsh a good idea to broaden yer cul'tral horishons."

He accepted a kazoo from Dan, lifted it to his lips, and blew through it, producing a farting sound.

"That's the way," Dan said encouragingly. But the man handed it back to him.

"I'm not mush for blowing type inshtrumentsh," he said. "But a mushical shaw, now. I ushed to be able to play a tune on my daddy'sh old shaw."

He didn't mention that the saw was a chain saw, and what he considered the musical part was the shrill vocalizations it inspired.

CHAPTER XXI

▲▲▲

Tom George dreamed of drums that night, and a sharp sting on the back of his hand woke him. He awoke all at once, both feet on the floor, arms swinging, fighting. Even now, so many years after Nam, if he woke up too suddenly, he came to ready to kill.

The porcupine on the windowsill of his sister's mobile home was not impressed. It sat there swearing at him under its breath.

The sky outside was just turning the yellow of an old bruise. He didn't have to get up for hours yet to open that run-down store. His sister would be in her own bed now, and she always got her own kids ready for school in the morning, leaving him to sleep until time for work.

"You dumb critter, I'll use you for jewelry!" he said to the animal. It grumbled back at him and hopped down from the window. He went to the sill and watched it waddle off into the shadows. A quill quivered on the back of his hand. That's what had stung him. Angrily he pulled it out and started to throw it out the window, then realized the window was closed.

He set the quill on the windowsill while he dressed, then tucked it into his shirt pocket.

▲▲▲

Anna Mae crawled out of the tepee and stretched, the bracelet pinching her wrist a little as she twisted her arms skyward. Whatever she was supposed to do, she didn't think it involved sleeping all day, and she felt strangely awake and alert.

Beyond the fence, tires bumped across the gravel and swiss-cheese pits of the parking lot and stopped. Tom George was back then. Good. She was afraid he wouldn't return till later in the morning. She stuck her foot through the opening in the fence and crawled back out.

And stepped right into a scene straight out of the last days of the other Anna Mae.

Two guns pointed at her from the cover of a green-and-brown patrol car. "Hold it right there, lady," said the man behind the left door. "Federal Bureau of Narcotics and Liquor Control."

"So?" Anna Mae asked, her hands raised.

"So move real slow and set down that knapsack. We'll have to ask you to come with us."

"That's stupid," she said, realizing that this was not the best way to handle law-enforcement officers of any kind. "I haven't done anything wrong. I haven't got any booze or narcotics, and even if I did, what's with the guns? Are you afraid I'd try to brain you with a beer bottle, or what?"

Something metallic clicked on one of the guns, and despite her disparaging tone, she felt her unemptied morning bladder give way a little, a trickle of urine run down her leg. Oh, shit, she had thought the bracelet was a sort of initiation gift, but maybe it was just bad luck.

The words to a Hoyt Axton song full of funny curses for overly officious policemen ran through her head suddenly. It gave her a little courage. "Look, I'll take a breathalyzer and we can call my lawyer when the store opens, but I need to see some ID. I was just minding my own business. . . ."

"You were trespassing on federal reservation lands," the cop on the left said. "When you people do that, it usually means you've been drinking, and there's a stiff penalty for that."

Her eyes were trained very firmly on the little metal holes, and her ears were trained on the voice of the cop. She didn't know how these men had known she was here, but their orders were probably coming from higher up—or lower down—than even they suspected. She knew if she went with them, no one would ever hear from her again.

▲▲▲

Tom George parked in the back as he always did, but a little farther down the road. He'd seen the fresh tire tracks headed for the store, and he didn't know who would be coming out here so early. He had a feeling it had to do with that woman, the woman he half suspected had sent the porcupine after him this morning. He had a college education, he had two tours in Vietnam; he had a younger sister dead from injuries in Desert Storm, his sister he'd stayed with last night was a doctor, and another sister practiced law in Oklahoma City—but he still didn't discount the possibility of magic. Or evidence, he thought, touching the quill in his pocket. In fact, the longer he lived, the more he believed the ancestors had been right about a lot of things.

He entered quietly through the back of his store and unbolted the front door. There were two of the firewater fuzz, Harl Ingersoll and Cal Perry. Cal had served in Nam at the same time as George and they had been state cops for years before switching over to the new federal substances division. He and Harl had their guns trained on the porcupine woman, she looking bristly, wary, and desperate, as if she would spring back over the fence or make herself disappear, which somehow wouldn't have greatly surprised George.

Harl was saying something to her about trespassing, which she was, of course, but George felt pretty sure he could have discussed that with her without resort to firearms. " 'Scuse me, boys," he said, taking his cue from Harl, "but what are you doin' harassin' my new security officer?"

"You harborin' drunks, Tom?" Cal asked him, but George knew that, despite his challenging tone, Cal was thrown a little off balance.

"You drunk?" George asked the porcupine woman, trying to remember her name. She shook her head. "She says she's not drunk, Cal. Told me she never touches the stuff. You can test her if you like, but I don't think the guns are necessary."

"We'll be the judge of that," Harl said, but Cal was already disgustedly holstering his weapon, and Harl followed suit. The woman walked slowly to stand beside George.

"You should inform us if there are other authorized people on the premises, George," Cal said.

"I'm informing you. I hired her yesterday."

Cal gave him a disgusted look, but they got back into the car and left without further question.

Porcupine Woman looked George in the eye. "Thanks," she said. "Where's the ladies' room?"

▲▲▲

There had been quite a few health clubs before Willie and the others went to Britain, but nothing quite on this scale. This Temple thing had taken over an old building formerly devoted to the Department of Social Services. It had been redecorated and replumbed, and now a procession of people in bright-colored, formfitting suits that covered their whole bodies pumped weights and moved stuff around with their thighs, soaked in Jacuzzi-like swimming pools that smelled like rotten eggs.

The atmosphere was both hushed and noisy at the same time. Thick carpets covered the floors but did not absorb the noise from the six TV sets featuring other dancing, pumping, bodysuited people. About twenty young folks, pretty and healthy enough to suit the sacrificial taste of even the pickiest Aztec god, bounced around the room bossing other people he assumed were the customers. Some of them looked bewildered, some of them looked grimly determined, and a few just looked as if they were in pain. A bunch of people were busily scaling all the walls, which were designed to look like something out of an ancient ruin from an old Harrison Ford movie.

"Hi, I'm Mindy," said a blond cheerleader type with a physique straight out of one of them old-fashioned macho exploitative men's magazines, or maybe, Willie thought when he looked a little closer at her and saw that she was not quite as young as she looked, a plastic surgeon's office. She gave him a smile with enough sparkling white teeth to pave Congress Avenue in downtown Austin.

"Well, hi there, Mindy darlin'. I'm Willie MacKai." He hefted his guitar and said, by way of explanation, "I'm the band."

"Nice to meet you," she said, and ran her eye down his body. "But, oh dear, Willie, I'm afraid you're overdressed. Wouldn't want to make the clients feel uncomfortable. Aubergine, I think, is just the perfect color for you." She plucked a reddish-brown-purple package from a shelf behind her and handed it to him, then pointed out the locker room.

He undressed and tugged the suit on. It was surprisingly comfortable, but he felt a little ridiculous. He sprinkled a dab of fairy dust over his head to go with the aubergine Peter Pan outfit. He'd need all the help he could get. He'd played stranger gigs than this, but not *much* stranger.

"Where do you want me to play, darlin'?" he asked Mindy.

"Well, I think for the therapeutic dance workshop. I was told you do heart-strengthening songs, and that sounds like just what we need."

Willie stood in front of the class behind the instructor, a hulking young fella with biceps as big as Willie's thighs and a lot of curly blond hair.

"This is experimental, people," the instructor said. "We're going to have live music here, and we'll improvise our moves to go with it." The class looked at Willie with a mixture of expectation and profound doubt.

Trying to pretend he thought he was starting a trend, but feeling as if he were making a fool of himself, he asked, "Well, what would you like to hear first?" But they all looked at him blankly because, of course, they still didn't know any songs at all.

The instructor said, "We got to warm up."

"Then you want somethin' kind of slow," Willie said. He knew slow songs—lots of long, slow, gruesome ones he'd learned in Scotland, but ballads with a hundred verses would take up all the time these folks had paid for and then some. The kind of songs he liked best, the ones he had mentioned, were maybe a little complicated for people who were huffing and puffing so hard they might have trouble hearing him. But work songs, hell, they were designed for singing through noise and exertion. So he said, "Okay, how about a sea chantey? I'll play you a halyard chantey called 'Lowlands Low.' Unless I miss my guess, it'll be extra aerobic if you sing on the chorus while you do your moves, okay?"

To his amazement, it actually worked. This kind of music went even better than he hoped with the exercises. Pumping chanteys like "Strike the Bell" were good for knee bends and push-ups, capstan chanteys like "General Taylor" with its steady, *"walk* him along, John, *car*ry him along" were good for repetitive, smoother moves.

Willie was getting into it. His old buddy Jim Hawkins, the sailing chanteyman he'd met at Anna Mae's festival, might worry about tradition getting a little stretched out of shape— Hawkins was one of those guys who cared a lot about tradition—but what the hell, there was a pool here, that ought to make it wet enough for sea chanteys.

People were singing along too. Willie felt his excitement growing. It was beginning to feel as if this totally ridiculous gig was going to work—some woman was even coming up with a pretty good harmony. Willie found himself doing little dance steps with them as he played and sang and sweated along.

He started something a little livelier, a Caribbean chantey conducive to more rhythmic movement—"Packing Sugar in the Hold Below." The leader had the group doing sets of leg raises followed by trunk circles, followed by hand clapping.

"Now we need something with a steady, even beat," the instructor told him at last. "Like chukachukachukachuka."

"Then what?"

"Then nothing. Just that."

Willie tried "Wimoweh," and the class liked it, but the instructor, who Willie began to see was a little put out that the focus of the class had shifted from himself to Willie, beckoned to Mindy.

"He won't cooperate with the program," Hulk said.

Mindy looked superficially disappointed and deep-down mean as a snake. "Is that true, Willie?"

"Well, hell, ma'am, chukachukachukachuka ain't no kinda *human bein'* type song—that's machine noise. You want that, you'll have to stick with a machine. But we been havin' a pretty good time here, and I think we should keep it up. This guy here said he'd change his routine to go along with me."

"I couldn't hear him all the way back here, Mindy," some guy called out.

"I just don't think this is what we're looking for, Willie," Mindy said.

"Fine."

"Come and pay me for your leotog and leave, please."

"Pay *you*?"

"That's what I said. We can't resell these once they're used, you know." And she sauntered out.

He changed back into his own clothes and started to stalk past without paying the hundred and twenty-five dollars she wanted for the outfit, but the hulk was standing around the desk, glaring at him. Willie didn't figure he was as fast or as strong, and he had the money and he needed his hands and arms unbroken if he was going to play anything, so he paid up and left, hot all over from anger and exertion.

▲▲▲

The ghost-woman just kind of hovered there, above Lucien Santos's skylight. Julianne opened her mind and tried to encourage the ghost to communicate, but all the woman did was stare down at Juli where she lay soaking in Santos's big whirlpool tub. The water grew cooler, and Julianne's skin started getting pruney and puckery from being so waterlogged, and still the ghost said nothing. Juli opened her eyes and glared up at the spirit. She had to admit she was feeling a little peeved. She was used to forthright ghosts who saw right away that she was a receptive sort of person, tuned into her frequency, and came right out with whatever it was they had to communicate. She hadn't encountered such a reticent spook in years.

"Do you maybe have a message from George?" she asked, but the ghost just hovered. Juli could see the moon clean through her face now. Not the man in the moon, she thought, the moon in the woman.

Then she thought, Of course, it's Lucien's house. She probably is waiting for Lucien. "I gotcha now," she told the ghost. "You wanted to see Lucien, huh? I'll go get him." But as soon as she spoke, before she could grab her towel and step from the tub, the ghost had vanished. Juli thought of calling for Lucien, but then decided it could wait until morning. She was much too tired at the moment.

She retired to the pretty room, too preoccupied to notice the black-and-red calico quilt with the bear-claw pattern, the painted animal-skull sculptures on her walls. The crystals lining her windows looked dull and faded. Just outside her window hung a wind chime made of old forks, but she was already in bed and on her way to sleep when something bumped the chimes violently and they tinkled the first few notes of "Banks of the Ohio" over and over again all through the night.

Lucien was already gone by the time she emerged from her room the next morning. She put on her clothes, picked up her new used banjo, grabbed some orange juice from the refrigerator in the cavernous kitchen, and walked out to the deck. The day was just pleasant, not cold or windy at all. The morning sun warmed the wood, and she sat and played "Banks of the Ohio" until she'd worked out some new progressions. When she got tired, she decided to go explore down by the little stream that ran near the house. A few lodgepole pines grew alongside it, but most of the deciduous trees were already stripped to skeletal bareness, and the stones shone through water burdened with dead leaves. She liked the music of the stream, though. It relaxed her, helped her meditate. She found it hard to truly meditate nearer to the house, though, which was funny, since Lucien's whole setup was so obviously designed for that sort of thing.

She really had thought she'd find George here, and instead all she had found was that one reticent ghost.

She sat on the edge of the stream and pulled her banjo into her lap and started playing again. It was chilly, though, when she'd been quiet for a moment, and she started back for the house to see if she could find a jacket of Lucien's to borrow.

That was when she saw the shimmeriest, palest outline of the ghost from the night before, standing there looking at her out of deep sad eye sockets.

Sir Walter Scott's ghost had told them how hard it was for him to amount to much in the daytime, even though he was still around. He said he was sort of like the moon in sunlight during the times when there were lots of vital, living people around. Juli figured that must be pretty universal with ghosts, and she said gently to the woman, "Hi there. Can you talk now?" But the woman put her head in her hands and rocked. Juli got up to go comfort her. "Why didn't you come on in last night?"

The ghost did the sort of thing ghosts were always doing in songs—she pointed, this time at the house. For the first time Juli noticed the tastefully executed hex signs, charms to ward off the supernatural executed in natural wood that matched the rest of the house. The ghost led her onward, and she saw that the signs were prominent on each side of the house and over every door and window. At the window to her room, the chimes hung out a little ways, and the ghost stopped, stood on tiptoe, pursed her lips, and blew.

The chimes played the first few notes of "Banks of the Ohio." Juli stared first at them and then back at the ghost, but by now the ghost was disappearing into a thicket pressed up against the hillside.

Who *was* this spirit? She really wanted to talk to Lucien about her. But when noon came, then one o'clock, Lucien did not appear. Juli decided to walk toward town in hopes of meeting him on the way. If not, maybe she could make a trip to the library and see if she could research this site. The ghost's silhouette was not Indian, nor was it old-fashioned. She looked as if she were wearing trousers and some kind of sweater. Who could she be?

Juli popped back into the house and started hunting for a sweater. Lucien's room was upstairs, and she thought he probably wouldn't care if she just nabbed something out of his closet. She had been living more or less communally with the other musicians for so long that it really didn't occur to her that he might mind an invasion of privacy.

His room overlooked the creek and featured a big cano-pied bed. The walls were uniformly paneled in oak, and she didn't see drawers or closet. A door opened into his bath-room, however, and she thought maybe he might have hung a sweater on a hook in there. No luck, however. The bathroom was just about sterile, looking as if it had been recently wiped down and smelling of chemicals. She wrinkled her nose. She wondered if he had a cleaning lady. If so, she wanted to talk to both of them about maybe using products that were a little better for the environment than what she smelled in there now. The bathroom had a connecting door, and it hung a little ajar.

Bingo! That door opened onto a study, the kind with wonderful floor-to-ceiling bookshelves, Oriental carpeting, and huge arched windows, these with stained-glass panels in them that she realized at once were hex signs too. A rolltop computer desk was open, and a wooly sweater hung on the back of the upholstered office chair. She swooped down on the sweater and plucked it up, noticing as she did that there was a shelf of computer programs held between gargoyle bookends on the top of the desk. One title that leapt out at her was "Voodoo for Power and Profit." Maybe Lucien was doing some kind of reviewing for computer or metaphysical magazines, she thought, though the program didn't appear to be a prepackaged manufactured kind.

She slipped on the sweater and headed for town, carrying the banjo in its padded case over her shoulder.

▲▲▲

When the two federal cops had gone, Tom George turned to Anna Mae. "Now then, who are you and what do you want?"

"I told you. I'm Anna Mae Gunn. I used to be called Mabel Charley, I'm Chickasaw and Comanche, and I need to see the elders about a medicine ceremony."

"You're absolutely sure a simple appointment with me won't do the trick, huh?"

"Absolutely," she said.

"Okay, then, come on."

"Where are we going?"

"To find the elders. That's what you had your friend get me up for this morning, isn't it, Porcupine Woman?"

She looked at him oddly but didn't question him. The drive to the home of the most senior elder in the tribe took a long time. On the way, Tom told her about the porcupine.

She seemed relieved—even grinned at him, and then he noticed again how attractive she could be.

"You just made it a lot easier for me to tell you what happened last night," she said. "I think I can also explain about your porcupine." She told him about the animals, and how their visit was followed by the original Anna Mae's. She showed him the bracelet.

"So what kind of medicine do you think we have that can top that? Sounds like you've been involved in some pretty heavy magic already."

"Well, yeah, I have. But it's been white-man stuff, mostly, and for one thing, I need to be sure I'm purified before I start in on my own journey."

The psychologist nodded as if that were a perfectly reasonable thing to say. "We could manage a sweat lodge, I suppose. Can you supply a feast?"

"Yeah. What about songs?"

"Songs?"

"You know, for the ritual."

"Well, we could have somebody express the general idea maybe, in English. We had one guy who was learning some of the old songs from his grandfather, but the grandfather died. The father just dried out not too long ago and says the old man taught him some stuff when he was a kid, but he doesn't remember any of it."

Anna Mae shifted from one hip to the other, feeling itchy. "Well, maybe, since it's not going to be real traditional and it is *my* purification and *my* feast, I could do some songs that might—remind some people of ones they knew."

"Like what?"

She threw back her head and sang him the two songs about Anna Mae she had sung to the ghost the night before. The hairs rose on the back of his neck, but he sort of liked the way it felt.

"You don't happen to speak any of the old languages, do you?"

"Only a little I tried to teach myself in college. Not much. And these songs aren't our songs, but—well, I think it will work out." She sang him "The Ballad of Ira Hayes" then, and he nodded.

"Where'd you find these songs?" he asked her later, when they stopped off for gas and a Coke. He was dragging the journey out longer than he needed to, he realized, getting to know her better. He would never have described her as beautiful when he first met her, but now he was fascinated by this quality she had, especially when she sang and added the rich timbre of her voice to her particular brand of beauty. It was the kind that seemed to come from the way the light reflected off the skin where it folded close over her bones, or the way it glinted from her eyes and sparked red glints in her hair. It came from the way she held herself, from the quiet passion she had for her songs and stories, so that the psychologist thought to himself, "Well, I bet *her* great-grandma was a god-damn Cherokee princess if anybody's great-grandma ever was." She had presence. She looked as if she were somebody, and he didn't wonder for a moment why the ghost of the original Anna Mae would choose to communicate with her, to adopt her.

Later, when they located the elders one by one, he discovered that she was as good a listener as he was. Better maybe, even though he considered himself a *professional* listener, and often kidded his clients about being a surrogate bartender except that he didn't need a ball bat to finish his conversations.

He took her to meet people to ask them for something and saw that instead of seeming to ask, by her attention and interest in them, she seemed to be giving something. Soon she was talking to and listening to a lot more people than she had ever asked to meet. People, relatives of the elders who were visiting, neighbors and friends, just decided to tell her about how the oil royalties didn't amount to enough to buy a day's groceries this time, or how the developers were swarming around the area, or how it was good that it was finally raining again. Then, eventually, they stopped talking to listen to her. At first they'd just steal a glance now and then, not understanding why they did. She was just a skinny middle-aged Indian woman, the sharp-faced kind, not the round-faced kind, and her shoes looked almost worn out and her jeans were baggy and worn through in a couple of places, her sweatshirt soaked from the rain. But they'd look again pretty soon, and she'd still be there, talking and using her hands in a kind of graceful way, a little like sign language. The way she used her body reminded Tom George of the old days at powwow dances when all the women, no matter what they were wearing—shorts, skirts, jeans, sweatpants, anything—would put on their embroidered dance shawls with the foot-long silk fringe and stand close together in a circle and move, a foot pat at a time, and all you could see was their bright-shawled backs with those fringes softly undulating with their moccasin-soft steps.

Anna Mae said to one of the elders, "There was a woman who told me she was responsible for all the drunkenness, all the bad times our people have had."

"It wasn't a woman. It was a government and a culture," the psychologist said. He sounded exactly the way he used to sound when he'd been drinking, adamant and unhappy, except now he could do it over a cup of coffee and not have a hangover later and could drive his truck without getting arrested for DWI.

"Yeah, I know all that. But it was this woman too. She's sort of a supernatural—"

"Must be related to coyote," the elder chimed in. Anna Mae turned to look at him. He was missing his front teeth, and his face was deeply seamed. One eye had a bandage over it. "I always thought he had something to do with it."

"Maybe she is," Anna Mae said. "It doesn't take much of a stretch of the imagination to see Torchy as a coyote bitch, laughing her head off as somebody stumbles out of a bar and into the path of a truck. She's the kind who would get a kick out of watching someone get drunk enough to stab a relative he'd gone hunting with the week before. But this woman says that the other bad ones—the other evil spirits—made her stop inciting drunkenness for now. They have a new plan."

Tom George grunted. "And I thought it was my therapeutic technique."

Her stories were wild and improbable, the stuff of legend or myth, but not one of the elders expressed any hesitation in granting her a feast and a purification rite. Maybe she just convinced them that she was crazy enough to need one, George thought, but he had seen tears rolling down old man Atoka's face when she sang him the song about Ira Hayes. Atoka's great-grandson, Charles, had been one of the first casualties of the war in the Gulf.

▲▲▲

The ceremonial grounds were beside the river, and they found a good place to build the sweat lodge from sticks and red clay, where people could cleanse themselves in the river before and after if they wished. The sweat lodge was coed and slightly interracial, since a lot of the people had intermarried. There was one Cherokee among them who was so blond and fair she looked less like an Indian than Julianne Martin, Anna Mae thought. Old man Atoka said he sure liked these new ways, but he was having difficulty trying to remember the names of all of his relatives. It didn't matter, since he was hard to understand without his teeth anyway, and he'd forgotten and left them at home.

One or two of the people Anna Mae thought were probably just new-agers, who would have been hippies if they were old enough. One woman she hadn't met with the rest of the elders was introduced to her as a former tribal leader.

A little Indian-owned cafe in Cement catered the feast for a quite reasonable bite out of Anna Mae's expense money. Brown rice and pinto beans with a little chicken for the meat eaters compliments of the cafe owner's Salish husband, who was used to an Oregon diet, and canned corn and a lemon meringue pie from the woman herself, who had a better understanding of how a feast ought to go.

When they finally got down to business, old man Atoka stopped his good-natured attempts at buffoonery and drummed like the beat of eagles' wings, ushering all of the participants into the sweat lodge, where they settled down to live through the heat and let it cleanse them from the inside out.

Tom George said that up until a few years ago at some of these ceremonies, in some places, peyote buttons had once been used, or mushrooms, but now with everybody trying so hard to be straight, the visions and the cleansing were to come from the heat, the lack of oxygen and the mingling of spirits.

Anna Mae felt her heartbeat synchronize to the drum, and her mind cleared of everything she had been meaning to talk about, everything she had been meaning to think. She was not glamorous now. The fairy dust pooled in her sweat on the ground beneath her bare buttocks, under the silver disk in the turquoise bracelet she had not even tried to find out if she could remove. With the others she stared at the glowing rocks and felt herself, mind and body, lighten, until what she essentially was remained.

The drum recalled another drum, and as memories and dreams and fragments of her life from the last few years surfaced to be sweated out, song surged up in her. The first to come was "I Will Go," the one she and Brose had sung at the ruin of his home.

"Is that an Indi'n song?" old man Atoka asked. Anna Mae admitted that it wasn't, but the elder paid no attention. "I learned one like that from my grandfather about going to war." He sang it, his voice high and whispery, with gaps where he stopped to breathe.

With ears trained by listening to Gaelic, French, other languages, Anna Mae listened for the words, grasped them a phrase at a time, and since most of the song was a simple repetition, got into the chant, singing with the old man. The others soon followed. She was not actually singing harmony, but she felt in her blood and bones that this was the real meaning of harmony—tuning human beings to each other so that they all flowed as one. The voices blended into an almost indistinguishable union. Inside the song you came together not just with other people, but with the earth, the world, the universe.

It went like that throughout. She'd sing one, and sometimes the new-agers would start singing with her, but mostly it would just be her and the drum, and even if the beat didn't start out right, pretty soon the Scottish music and the tom-tom understood each other. And then one of the others would remember a song or a snatch of a song or something about a song, and they'd all join together and either resurrect the old song or make a new one. Scottish themes and Indian ones seemed to call up the same subjects. Well, why not? Both were essentially tribal systems. Both had been all but wiped from the earth by invaders who considered themselves to have more advanced culture.

When they had all dipped in the river to wash away the sweat, they dressed and settled down to eat and drink the gallons of Gatorade that were also an integral part of the feast. Anna Mae felt weaker and stronger at the same time. When she finished dressing, she sprinkled herself again with a pinch of dust that looked as if she were doing a ceremony of her own and joined the others at the feast.

"I know who you are now," said the man a little older than she was. "You were three grades behind me in school, but I remember you because you beat me up once when I tried to take a book away from you."

"What a thing to remember," she said, and grinned at him.

"Where'd you get those songs?" he asked. "Off an old Joan Baez album?"

"You won't believe me if I tell you," she said.

But he said, "Oh, yes, I will. I learned my lesson when we were kids." So she told them. She didn't mean to make a speech, but she felt closer to all of these people now—all of whom had been strangers twenty-four hours ago—than she ever would again, she thought. Also in her light-headed, dreamy state, she felt less as if she had to make sense. Still, when she finished, she apologized. "I don't like to think of white man's songs being the magic that brings back our ways. It doesn't seem right, but—"

"That ain't it," the old man said. "Don't you see, girl? You went into the coyote woman's dream and stole those songs back from her, and from what you said, she's the one who brought the drunkenness that stole our songs from us to begin with. You're like fox—you outsmarted her and got back our songs."

"There were a lot of us," she said. "And two of the others were white people, one a black man."

He shook his open hand dismissively. "Don't matter. You're the one that counts. Since you stole her white songs, you ran her off from guarding ours, and now we've got 'em."

Acutely embarrassed, Anna Mae drained her third paper cup full of Gatorade and cut a bigger piece of pie than she intended.

Tom George, watching her, prodded, "There's something more. Are you going to tell them?" She shrugged and he said, "The animals came to her to learn a song too and built her a fire. Then a spirit woman came to hear songs that had been made for her and gave Anna Mae that bracelet for her songs."

"Sing us these songs," old man Atoka said. "We will learn them."

▲▲▲

Usually Brose and Dan drove the van to some parking place, but on the day James Francis Farnham had been patiently waiting for, Gussie kept the van to prepare for the lingerie party she and Terry were using to introduce more songs. In honor of this particular gig, Terry had searched her memory for racy love songs. Street Pizza was so successful that it was getting trendy for Kansas City businesspeople to take their lunch hours and breaks walking down streets formerly frequented by panhandlers but now filled with rustic music that reflected their pioneer history. Dan and Brose piled into the van talking about whether or not to add the street people who hung out on Main Street and where they would find instruments for them.

▲▲▲

Willie tried playing in all manner of public places after that—parks, campgrounds, bus stops, and the airport. But every time he tried to play someplace indoors, he got through a song or two and someone ran him off. Outdoors the weather was getting rawer and colder all the time. He stayed with old friends about so long, and he had to move on. He didn't even get to share the music with them too much—most of them had day jobs and he was a night owl by nature, so when he woke up, they'd be gone to work and he wouldn't get in from trying to find work until they had already gone to bed.

He was playing the unemployment line in Austin, and a big security guard was bearing down on him when Torchy Burns tapped him on the shoulder.

"Come on, sugar. You look like you need a drink."

Naturally she knew where the last of the bars were, but even these had greatly changed. They were allowed to serve only wine and light beer, and nobody was allowed to become anything approaching drunk. The state laws that held the bar and the bartender as well as the owners personally libel for any accidents or injuries incurred by patrons had shut down a great many places. Most places had twenty-four-hour sports, news, or other informational programs playing, which discouraged singing.

Willie was glad Torchy was there with him, bringing with her the comfortable air of unwholesomeness that always surrounded her. They sat in a booth, and she bent low so that he had a great view of her décolletage. Her face was so close to his that her red hair kept tickling his nose.

"Poor Willie," she said, stroking his thigh. "So those bastards at the Temple fired you, did they? I could make them hire you back."

"Oh, no, darlin', I sure wouldn't want you to do anything like that," Willie said. He found he was breaking out in a cold sweat at the very idea—or maybe it was Torchy's hand that was causing the cold sweat. "Damn. I just need the kind of places I *used* to play in. I ain't played enough since settin' foot back on Texas soil to break a damn guitar string yet."

"Well, you can always play in here," she said. "There's not much drinking, true, but there's always a poker game going, and Lady Luck, that's me, sugar, is always welcome. So are her friends."

He took her at her word, but when he tried to find the level of this particular audience, it backfired on him. With gambling as the only one unadulterated vice left to them, people were dead serious about it, and they didn't want any distraction.

So a few nights later, when Willie wandered in, sat down, bought a light wine, and picked up his guitar to play an old Pat Garvey song, "The Lovin' of the Game," which he had suddenly remembered, the reaction was not quite what he'd hoped for.

Even though he had powdered himself with fairy dust real well after his shower, the poker players paid him little attention. Playing for audiences that had no intention of being played for when they came into a bar was not a new experience for him. Sometimes you just had to get rowdy enough to attract their attention, while at the same time appealing to their interest. So he played "Jack of Diamonds," which began, "I'm a rambler, / I'm a gambler, / I'm a long way from home. / And if you don't like me / then leave me alone. / I'll eat when I'm hungry / and drink when I'm dry. / If rye whiskey don't kill me / I'll live till I die."

To his chagrin the prettiest woman said, "If you want to sing that sort of thing, you should be going to SAD meetings instead of bothering people in controlled establishments like this one."

"And just what are SAD meetin's?" he asked. "Anything like funerals?"

"Only if you don't go in time. It's a branch of SA—Stop Addictions. Stop Addictive Drinking has programs all over the country and has been very effective for many people."

"Thank you for your concern, darlin'. I believe I'll do that very thing," he said. What the hell. It was an audience. "Where might a fella find such a group?"

"*Anyone* can find out the location of the group nearest them by calling the number in the book," the woman said. "Or you can ask the bartender. They're all supposed to know. Half of them go themselves. Alcohol Ingestion Management is much too serious to try to do while drinking yourself."

"Nothin' that a ball bat or a shotgun couldn't fix," Willie growled under his breath, but he asked the bartender, and the bartender pointed him to the Baptist church down the street.

"Next meetin's at midnight," the bartender said.

"That's convenient," Willie said.

"Well, just because you stop drinkin' doesn't mean you

have to be so extreme as to keep reg'lar hours," the man said. "Besides, the night's the hardest time. You tell 'em Joe sent you, buddy."

So, at about twenty-five past midnight, there stood Willie, guitar in hand, saying, "Evenin', brothers. My name's Willie MacKai. I'm understand I got me a drinkin' problem, and Joe sent me. By way of tellin' my story, I'd like to sing you a little song."

He sang *them* "Jack of Diamonds" and got much better response than he had in the bar. After the regular business meeting was over, while the group leaders were hunting for the disk containing the informational film for the night, he played three other songs to enthusiastic applause. One was Stan Rogers's "The Mary Ellen Carter," one was "We Shall Overcome," which he lead as a chant and deemed to be as appropriate for an audience of people trying to overcome some*thing,* as it was for an audience of people trying to over-come the oppression of some*one.* And then he sang the "Temperance Union" song, thinking that it would be funny to the people he was singing to. A tactical mistake.

The counselor asked, "Brother, how long did you say it had been since you had your last drink?"

"We're doin' serious work here, MacKai," another man said. "When you're serious about it too, come back."

▲▲▲

"Well, shit," Willie said to Torchy when she showed up later. "I had no damned idea you had to give up a sense of humor when you give up drinkin'."

Torchy didn't find it to her benefit to remind him that a lot of people never had a sense of humor to begin with and definitely didn't have one when they were drinking. What was to her benefit was to sympathize and soothe and hand Willie another bourbon.

"Had it all leeched out of 'em, Willie," she said, swirling the liquid in her glass. "It's terrible. That's why I stuck with you folks so long. You're the only ones left who pretty much haven't been cleaned and scoured into hominy, with no color, no taste, no nourishment, and sure as hell no magic. I don't know how I ever let my bosses talk me into this. I guess just 'cause they're so much more powerful than me. I shoulda fought 'em, Willie. I should never have given up my kingdom. All them poor goddamn little fairies runnin' around over there with no queen. Just because some mortal bitch had the hots for my sacrifice."

Willie shook his head. "The bastards are all the same, Torchy. They'll screw you every time."

"Yeah," she said. "Fuck 'em."

"Damn straight," he agreed, though he wasn't real clear what he was agreeing to right then. It just felt good to have somebody to talk to that he knew, and who wasn't expecting him to solve everything. He felt like Rip Fucking Van Winkle. While he'd been gone seven years, something inconceivable had happened. *Texas* had changed. *Texans* had changed. Well, it seemed that way, anyhow. Maybe it was like Torchy said, and it was the lack of magic in the world, but he privately suspected the Yankees. If they hadn't infiltrated Texas, the devils would never have gotten such a stranglehold. Them with their gun-control laws and their Perrier water and their clippy way of talking. But of course he knew that wasn't it either, not really. Because he had sung for a lot of Yankees, and when they were having a good time, they were as good a people as any. So it probably was the devils, damn 'em, he thought, and then realized how redundant *that* thought was.

"It's a hell of a thing," he told Torchy, "to be home and still be homesick."

"I'll drink to that," she said.

Willie wasn't stupid, and he wasn't really drunk. He knew she was manipulating him, but he had sort of gotten used to the idea that women manipulated men, and his experiences in the ballads had even shown him that maybe sometimes they had good reason. He hated all of this. He thought he would be bringing music back to the United States, and instead he was practically having to beg people to pay attention to him. He was a musician and a good one, and he was tired of being shut up pretty near every time he started a song.

Torchy watched all this in his face as she twirled her drink and smiled to herself. "I've had reports on your friends. *They* all seem to be doing rather well. In fact, the boss is cooking something up to interfere with them again, but I doubt he'll succeed. The music is growing very strong around them, what with the luck I gave them and the fairy dust and all."

"Well, it sure as hell isn't growing very strong around me," he said. "I can't find anybody to *listen.*" He knew in his heart it was because he didn't know how to manage a career—even one he didn't get paid for. He needed help and could certainly understand where it would be a conflict of interest for her to help him any more than she was already.

She, on the other hand, knew in what passed for *her* heart that a major part of his problem was that she had switched his fairy dust for a bag of powdered fool's gold, and he was no more magical or charming than he really was. That suited her purposes down the line.

"Well," she said brightly, "why don't you return to work with the others? I'm sure they'd be delighted to see you again."

"Can't do it," he said. "I'll make my own way. None of them are gonna do any more for the music than me, darlin', and you can bet your little ol' pitchfork on that."

"I'm real pleased to hear it," she said sweetly. "But in the event that things don't work out quite as you *planned,* you know, sugar, there *is* somethin' you could do that would help more than everything the others are doing," she said. "That is, if you can't get this music thing goin' down here, of course."

"I'll do it," he said.

"I only meant if you couldn't."

"Well, what is it?"

"I was thinking that if you couldn't do it the regular way, help bring the music and the magic back, that you might be able to do more by joinin' up with me and—er—helpin' *me.*"

"I thought I was already helping you."

"Well, like you pointed out, despite your best efforts you aren't having a lot of success, are you? And I just thought, if you got too desperate, I mean I wanted you to know that you could still—well, count for something, in the end."

"End?" he asked.

"You aren't exactly young anymore, sweetie. And unless I miss my guess, you're the type who would like to go out with some sort of grand finale. Am I right?"

"Possibly. If it was a good cause."

"The very one we've been discussin', actually."

"What would I need to do, if I should feel like it, that is?"

"I'm in pretty good graces with the bosses now, and they don't seem to need my services as a Debauchery Devil anymore for obvious reasons. I believe I can strike a deal with them—my freedom and the reinstatement of my kingdom right here—well, there are already former subjects scattered throughout Canada, among other places. I'm sure they've been wondering where I am. I only need one teeny little itsy bitsy thing to close the deal."

"And that's where I come in?"

"Well, yes."

"As what?"

"A sacrifice, actually. I need you to replace Tam Lin as my tithe to hell. Still have to pay the mortgage, you know."

▲ ▲ ▲

Juli only had to walk past the first turnoff when a woman picked her up. "Where you staying?" she asked.

"I'm a houseguest of Lucien Santos," Juli said.

"Lucky you," the woman said. She looked to be in her early fifties, her hair reddish blond rather than gray, her clothing neat and functional, a wool skirt, pale blue silk blouse, and a white cardigan sweater. Her shoes were flats. "He travels all over the country, you know, giving lectures. We tried to get him to give one at the library, and he promises he will, but he's always just so busy. Then too, I'm sure he must be as stricken as the rest of us over Marley Bethune's disappearance."

"Who's Marley Bethune?"

"Oh, she was one of his staunchest supporters, as well as the library's and the arts committee's."

"Maybe she just got to where she didn't like groups," Juli said, thinking of Willie. "It can happen."

"Oh, no, honey, she *loved* her life. Her late husband had left her *well* fixed, and she really enjoyed life. In fact, I s'pect that's partly why she enjoyed Lucien Santos so much—he was the only person as worldly as she was. Oh, I do hope she hasn't fallen prey to the Black Widower."

"What's that?" Juli asked.

"Why, girl, where have you been anyhow? Haven't you read the news? All over this part of the country, widow women have turned up missing—they've only found a few of the bodies, and the police think the women were all killed by the same person. The press has dubbed him—or *her*—the Black Widower."

"They should ask Lucien to help them," Juli said. "He's a super medium, really. He helped me keep in contact with my husband George until I left the country. I'm sure he could locate these troubled spirits for the police and help them learn who's responsible. Where is your library anyway? I've been wanting to look up some stuff on local history."

"Oh, it's just down the street from Lucien's office. You can't miss it. Say, I notice you're carrying a musical instrument. I don't suppose you'd be interested in playing for our story hour sometime, would you? It's been years since anyone did that, but we used to have music all the time."

"I'd *love* to," Juli said. "When?"

"Why don't I drop you at Lucien's, and you can let him know you'll be at the library with me. We can talk it over then."

▲▲▲

Ute handed out the plates and sat down to eat with the women.

"You make it sound as if you don't approve of Juli's association with Santos," Heather-Jon said.

"No, ma'am, I don't. Not to use too strong a term but that low-down son-of-a-mother-dog was an evil wizard."

"Now, now. Witchcraft is an accepted religion in these enlightened days," Shayla told him.

"I don't mean he was a Wiccan, ma'am, or any other kind of nature-loving religion. Man was an out-and-out minion of the board of directors of the devil company, and I'd stake a claim he was half devil himself and a major stockholder to boot. It just shows you what a powerful hoodoo artist he was when you think that in a town the size of Joplin, with moral turpitude makin' a comeback, here was a single man engaged in a very—shall we say—interestin' occupation, where he gave intimate advice to large groups of adorin' women and told normal hardworkin' people what to do with their lives and how to contact the dead, and nobody in town had a bad word for him, much less wild speculation or out-and-out gossip.

▲▲▲

When Lucien opened the door of his shop and Juli saw all the nicely dressed people sitting around in a circle, she wished she had washed her clothes before coming to town. She was pretty grubby looking, though thanks to the bath she'd had before being haunted, she didn't stink.

Reflective crystals dangling at various lengths from the tops of the windows sent rainbows flying around the room, flashing incongruously across the sorrowful and pained faces of the people in the circle.

Julianne sank down into her lotus position on the hooked rug carpet protecting Lucien's hardwood floors.

Across from her a woman was crying into a Kleenex, a little dash of blue, pink, and green glinting off tear-wet fingers. "I am so *angry* at that bastard."

And another woman, a timid-looking body whose shoeless feet were still neatly encased in nylons, said, "Now, Charla, he was your *father.*"

"I'd like to continue this in a moment, Charla, Wilma, but right now I want you all to meet a new member of our group —this is Julianna Martin."

"Hi," said Charla with barely a pause for breath before continuing. "You don't understand at all, Wilma. The man wasn't right in the head. He beat my mother and he raped my brothers and me, and then he taught my brothers to beat up on mother *and* me, and when I was sixteen I had a baby by one of them—I'm not sure if it was Daddy's or one of my brothers'—that I gave up for adoption. I just hope it isn't feeble-minded. It was after that I quit school and—"

"And stole a bus and moved to Lawton, Oklahoma, where you met Tom and he was just like your daddy and then you met Jim and he brought you back here and he was as bad as any of them and now you're looking to head on out again. What good's that going to do?"

Julianne shifted uncomfortably. She didn't like the way Wilma was going after poor Charla, though the remarks she was making might have been appropriate if they'd come from a therapist instead, which Lucien was supposed to be.

He took Charla's sudden tight-lipped silence for an opportunity to speak. "Now, then, what we need to do here is insert our knowledge of our past lives into this situation to search for patterns and solutions."

"Well, I am sick to death of hearin' about *her* past life," Wilma said. The others murmured and hushed and now-nowed, but Wilma was defiant. "She just *does* the same stupid things over and over again. She says how much she hates her daddy, but she goes out and marries men just like him. And I'd like to know what good she thinks moving to Topeka, Kansas, is going to do if she just takes her same crappy old taste along with her."

"Wilma Sinclair, you are certainly not bein' very support-ive," another woman said. "You'd think you blamed Charla for what her old man did to her. Can't you see how upset she is? You act like you hate her."

Charla turned on the speaker. "You hush up. Wilma is the best friend I've ever had. It just upsets her to hear me talk about what trash I come from. She's from a nice family, not low-class scum like mine."

Julianne had picked up her banjo out of discomfort, for something to do with her fidgeting hands. She was used to hearing Lazarus comment on whatever was going on around her and her companions, and she found that she now was picking out a tune—what was it?—"Tifty's Annie," about the girl who loved the wrong man and was beaten to death by a committee composed of her nearest and dearest.

"What's that you're playin'?" Wilma demanded. "We're here to talk about our lives, not to go foolin' around while other folks are speakin'."

"I'm sorry," Juli apologized. "I was thinking about Charla's feeling that her family were low-class and scum because of the way they acted, and how somehow or other abusiveness still gets associated with economic status, even though it isn't and never has been."

"You know that from *your* past lives, I suppose," Wilma said.

"Yes, I do. Although actually the songs that relate to Charla's situation are more often the ones that a friend of mine lived through in *his* past lives. But they weren't about peasants or low-class people at all. And most often the lady ended up dead and never got to find out if her true love was as bad as her family or not, because one of her family would kill her or him or both of them."

"Oh, no, I don't think I could bear that," Charla said. "Not so soon after poor Marley died." She shot a significant look in Lucien's direction, but Lucien merely smiled, though Juli caught an unexpected flash of hostility from him.

"Nonsense, my dear. Marley would have wanted us to be as clear about this as possible. And perhaps a song is the most comfortable way for Julianna to express herself just now—later, when she comes to know us better, she may be more open with us."

Now, in times past Juli would have just considered that Lucien was being magnanimous about her poor little frailties, but now she said, with a great deal of dignity, "Lucien, I know that you've never particularly approved of my calling, but it so happens that I am a musician, and sometimes music is the most *eloquent* expression I have of my feelings or of my empathy for the feelings of any other human being."

"Julianna, dear girl, I do apologize if I've put you on the defensive," he said.

"Not at all," she said, standing up and packing her banjo back in its case. "It's I who should apologize for threatening your authority." She glanced around at the thunderstruck faces of the others. "I am so sorry for busting in like this and maybe being inappropriate in the face of your grief over the loss of your friend. Maybe I'll see you around."

She was shaking as she walked down the street, shaking from a mixture of emotions—anger, shock at her own temerity, and suppressed laughter at the look on Lucien's face at the admittedly great exit line she'd come up with. When she'd known him before, confrontation hadn't been exactly her style. She'd been a lot like some of those other women in his group. But going through ballads where she shared a body with some hero or the other who was always having to slay or marry monsters had given her more confidence than she used to have. She felt a little bad about abusing his hospitality.

Her librarian friend was working the reference desk. "Hi," she whispered when Juli came over. "I didn't expect to see you so soon."

Juli told her a polite social lie. Just because she'd made a scene in front of what appeared to be half the town was no reason to spread her personal differences with Lucien any farther. "I think I came at a bad time. Lucien and the others are still so upset about that lady—what did you say her name was, the one who disappeared?"

"Marley Bethune. Yes, I'm sure they would be. Lucien especially. Everybody kind of thought he and Marley might . . ." She looked at Juli, sized her up as a possible love interest for Lucien, smiled brightly, and changed the subject. "So, what kind of research did you want to do?"

"I wanted to find out more about the site where Lucien's house is. It's very interesting."

"Yes, he's written some articles on it himself for the *Joplin Weekly,* and a while back they did a spread on his place for the *Kansas City Star*'s Sunday magazine."

"I'd like to see that," Juli said.

"I can dig it up for you," her new friend said, leading her back through rows of half-empty bookshelves that made the library seem as empty as an abandoned church. The library wasn't large—basically two big rooms with long windows overlooking the street, a fireplace at each end, the rows of shelves, and a couple of long tables with folding chairs around them. One older man was reading a newspaper at the table. On the far side of the table, a row of wooden slanted shelves held magazines, and beside it something that looked like a clothes-drying rack had newspapers draped over it.

The librarian fished underneath the shelf where another stack of newspapers were and opened a wooden compartment, pulling a sheaf of papers from it and laying them on the table. "It's not hard to find anything anymore—this place is so bare. We used to have a big staff, but now there's only the two of us and a couple of volunteers. The last administrator completely gutted the fiction section. Sold everything at the fundraiser for twenty-five cents a book. Can you believe it?"

"You wouldn't believe what I could believe," Juli said fervently. "If I stick around, I'll tell you about it sometime."

"I sure hope you do. I'd love to hear you play that thing. What's your name anyway?"

"Julianne Martin. My husband George and I used to be a duo until—well, the bottom sort of fell out of the music business, which is a long story. George was killed, and since then I've been out of circulation. I met Lucien while I was trying to cope with George's death."

"Gee, that's tough. Well, maybe you came at the right time to help him with Marley's death." She stopped flipping through papers, keeping her finger in her place, and stuck out her other hand. "I'm Flora Harmon. Good to meet you." A moment later she crowed—quietly—"Here it is!"

Lucien's house, in full color, graced the cover. "Rest for the Spirit," the title said. Juli opened it, and on pages five and six another full-color spread with a tiny bit of text showed Lucien in his glass-walled living room. On the next page he was pictured handing a book to a slender, attractive woman of about forty wearing slacks and a sweater. The woman's hair was loose on her shoulders. Juli stared at it hard. There was something very familiar about that woman.

Flora, looking over Juli's shoulder, pointed. "That's Marley."

Lucien came in the front door just then, looked around, then headed toward them.

"Hello, Lucien. I've just been learning from Flora how famous your house is," Juli said pleasantly, to let him know there were no hard feelings.

"Julianna, I cannot tell you how sorry I am to have upset you. Of *course* I know that you were sharing with us your very best when you sang your song. I just felt that, with the recent loss of our friend, perhaps—"

"I understand, Lucien. Perhaps it's time for me to move on."

"No, no, no. I won't hear of it. You must come back home with me and let me make it up to you. I sent the others home early and canceled my afternoon appointments. We have much to tell each other, and I have not been a good host, I fear."

"I'll get in touch with you about playing for the library, Juli," Flora said. Juli waved good-bye, half-absently. Her mind was still on the picture of Marley Bethune.

On the way back to Lucien's, he said, "My Scottish sweater looks good on you. I like to see a beautiful woman wearing my things."

"I'm sorry," she said. "It was just so cold, and I—"

"No, no, keep it. You came with very little. Really, if you are to play for the library—I did hear Flora Harmon mention that, did I not? We must get you some more clothing."

She said nothing. With so many trees around the house, the yard and the creek were already in shadow by the time they arrived back at his place. She helped him unload groceries, and he fixed them delicious omelets with some sort of herbs, a tossed salad, and a lovely, soothing tea.

"Now, my dear, you must tell me all about your sojourn abroad," he said, reclining on his white sofa and patting the place next to him. She was much less enthused about telling him of her adventures now, however.

"I borrowed the sweater from your study. I was noticing the computer programs above your console. Did you write them?"

"Oh, yes. I've been doing the *most* interesting studies on the parameters of the trance state. You were always a wonderful subject. You seem tense."

"I am," she said.

"Let me help you relax."

"No, really, I think I want to go for a walk around the house before it gets too dark."

"Oh, now that's an excellent idea. I'll go with you. Let me get a jacket."

He was gone a long time, and she slipped out the French door onto the deck. The wind was blowing the bare branches together with a clacking, creaking sound, and the little stream seemed agitated. She started humming under her breath "Banks of the Ohio."

A movement caught her eye down by the stream, and she opened the door and shouted, "Hey, Lucien, I'm going to start now. Catch up, okay?"

Her hands were shoved deep in her pockets as she skipped down the paving stone walkway leading from the deck to the creek bank. "And only say that you'll be mine / In no other arms you'll twine," she sang the words to the song she'd been humming as she wound her way as quickly as possible into the trees. "He took her by the lily white hand / and threw her into the river strand. / She cried, Oh Willie, don't murder me / for I am not prepared for eternity."

Just in front of her, where two trees had stood with space between them a moment before, the space filled suddenly with the form of a woman. It wavered.

From the house Lucien called, "Where are you, Julianna?"

Juli heard her words echoed by the stream and thrown back to her. ". . . murder me . . . eternity . . ."

The hair of the apparition was long and wild, the legs separate, as if encased in pants. "Is that you, Marley Bethune?" Juli asked.

"Murder me . . . ," the creek continued to echo, the branches clicking out the rhythm.

The shape moved quickly forward, and Juli followed as quickly, wishing for underbrush, wishing for cover. Behind her Lucien's footsteps stirred the dead leaves. The sharp wind bit her nose and cheeks.

The ghost moved to the place where she had disappeared the night before, but this time she stayed and pointed into the hillside.

Juli excused herself and walked into the apparition, pulling the little spare spruce boughs aside. Beneath them was a hand, moldering and green, with bones poking through at the knuckles.

Another hand, hard and crushing, grasped her shoulder. She turned to face Lucien, whose face was impassive in the moonlight.

"That's why you put wards all around the house isn't it, Lucien?" she asked. "To keep the ghost from bothering you. But there must have been others before Marley. Tell me, are you the Black Widower or just a copycat killer?"

"You wound me, dear girl, to think me capable of anything short of originality. Marley and the others had their uses—as you would have had yours had you restrained your curiosity long enough. Now, I think, you should return with me to the house and write a note to Flora regretting that you will be unable to play at the library because your friends elsewhere need you."

"This kind of thing is really bad karma, Lucien. You know that don't you? You're going to come back as a cockroach for sure."

"No, dear girl, I shall come back even more powerful than I have been in all previous lives, and you and the others will be reborn as my servants."

He'd been herding her to the house as he said this, a dagger in his hand. Between the wind and the trees, the night was far from still. The front of the house was darkened, but suddenly a light dazzled their eyes.

Juli, who had been a hero often enough in the ballads to know a break when she saw one, leapt sideways and back, slamming her head into Lucien's chin and knocking his hand away from her before twisting back toward the stream.

"Mr. Santos," a voice called from the deck. "It's Sheriff Snider. I've come to talk to you about the disappearance of Marley Bethune."

▲▲▲

"Well, my, wasn't that convenient?" Barbara asked.

Ute shrugged. "Just made sense, really. Flora got to thinkin' about Juli's suggestion that Lucien be called in as a psychic to contact the Black Widower's victims, and the sheriff was following up on that. Just happened that ol' Lucien knew a damn sight more than the sheriff figured. He probably would have gone on foolin' everybody even longer if Julianne hadn't showed up. See, her bein' a real psychic and able to communicate with the ghost made things a lot easier for poor Marley."

"I suppose she had to testify and all that?"

"Yeah, but she wasn't real necessary once they found Marley's body and started puttin' together all the evidence Lucien had magically obscured before. Meanwhile, Juli did her gig at the

library, and when she went to explain to Lucien's old therapy group, she ended up singin' songs to them to comfort them for their problems, and they asked her if she'd keep on meetin' with them.

"She got a little famous then, as a witness in a murder trial, but the papers mentioned her connection with Lucien's old group, and pretty soon therapy groups all over Missouri invited her to come and play for them.

"Real music therapists who had degrees and knew how music worked but had somehow or other forgotten any actual pieces of music asked her over for dinner or to lunch or to parties and by the way, bring her instruments. They were very pleased when instead of resenting their transparent ruses to acquire her expertise without recognition or payment, she actually seemed eager to teach them the songs she knew.

"She sometimes had as many as four gigs in one day, like the morning she spent at the special-ed class for children with learning disabilities in a Little Rock school, lunch at a hospice for AIDS patients, spent the afternoon helping a group of therapists learn a group of ballads that did not involve unrequited love, sudden violent death, or dismemberment, and spent the evening leading a veterans group in antiwar songs. She had become quite the therapeutic flavor-of-the-month.

" 'I hate do-gooders,' the Plague and Pestilence Devil said. 'Next thing you know, she'll be doing a benefit for research.'

" 'Not on my station, she won't,' said the Disinformation Devil, who always wore shiny brown shoes and sunglasses and kept his hair mowed short.

" 'I got her, though,' the Plague and Pestilence Devil said. 'After all that singing, I'm sending a little strep virus to get her— she'll have such a case of laryngitis, she won't even be able to whimper.'

"Well, the Plague and Pestilence Devil, or Peepee as he was sometimes called by his associates, knew his business, and the next time he caught Julianne singing to some of his victims, he had a sick kid give her a big smooch that left her sounding about as loud as that one hand the Zen people were always talking about clapping.

"Unfortunately for him, Peepee set up exactly the wrong response in Julianne Martin. Now, it is true that some devils are as insightful as a good mother, able to guess the moods and motives, the layers of need beneath each emotional response, and

that's what helps them manipulate people so well. The Debauchery Devil, for instance, was pretty good at that sort of thing.

"Not the Plague and Pestilence Devil, however. For one thing, he did his most effective work with large groups and depended on the germs and viruses and in some cases evil spirits that were his minions to spread whatever his current poison was. Rats and bugs, pollens and air droplets, the blood cells and secretions of his victims, were a lot more important to him than psychology, though he had been employing it with some success to cause stress-related diseases, but that was almost too easy since music and fiction and a lot of the other escape routes people used to use against their troubles had been cut off. But he never had to actually try to cause the stress, so he didn't worry about it a lot— he was a little like a maggot—just waited until people started to decay, then moved in to feed.

"So he didn't figure that when Julianne Martin lost her voice, it was going to remind her so much of the period during which she was deaf and cut off from all music except that which danced around inside of her. It did, however, and after her first panic attack was over, she caught a number eighteen bus to the deaf school and, using American sign language, set up a concert for that afternoon. It was a big success. She didn't sing a word, but she tapped her foot to the music and signed so that it looked more like an elaborate kind of hula dance than it did like singing. She played her spoons and entertained the kids with her limberjack and had the audience sign and tap along with her, and those who could still speak or who had learned to speak sang the words after she mouthed the chorus to them.

"The Plague and Pestilence Devil was so disgusted he gave up, and Julianne Martin has never had so much as a cold from that day to this, and that's the truth."

▲▲▲

"Our campaign is *not* windin' up the way it should be now, fellow devils," the Chairdevil said to his board. "Even without that, that *instrument*, those blessed warblers are a pain in the tail. Every time they open their mouths, another passel of undead songs start lumberin' out of their graves and havin' baby songs. Pretty soon it's gonna be worse than it was when we started all of this. I tell you, those songs are worse than blackberry brambles for springing up out of nothin' no matter how you kill 'em. By the time we're able to locate the perps from the noise they're making, they've spread songs to another group of people who go away whistlin' and singin' like they didn't have better sense. We never had trouble trackin' them before. What's goin' on here?"

"Maybe you're just used to it being too easy," the Expediency Devil said. "That banjo acted like an antenna so we could find them anyplace. Now you just have to pick them out from all the other cattle out there."

"Some of my best trackers are hot on the trail, sir," the Doom and Destruction Devil said. "The mole I planted in that Martin girl's life almost had her, but there was a little interference from another one of those maverick dead people who keep popping up."

"Hmph," the Chairdevil said. "I want your trackers to see to it that the Martin girl and all her friends *join* their dead buddies soon, Threedee. Without Hawthorne's magic twanger, there's nothin' to stop our people from finishin' them off."

"I've still got the all-points bulletin out on them among my people," Threedee answered soothingly. "And one of my worst has a group of them pinpointed someplace in Kansas City."

The Chairdevil nodded absently and turned to the Debauchery Devil, who as usual hid her red eyes behind high-tech sunglasses and smoked like—well, like a fiend—throughout the meeting. "You're awfully quiet, DD."

"Well, boss," DD said, "I was just thinkin'. I wonder how much of your problem was the banjo and how much of it was the personality that guided it."

"You mean Hawthorne?"

"Nope. I mean Willie MacKai. It seems to me that whether he's doing music or not, MacKai manages to gum up the works. You know, I did us all a big favor back in Scotland when I messed up the songs the singers could go back and live through. Because even though they learned about ballad lives, none of them learned about their own, and of them all, MacKai is the most archetypal minstrel. If I'd let him connect with his true stength and then he'd come back here with the banjo, there'd have been no stopping him. But I've controlled him right along, though y'all have made it pretty blessed hard for me sometimes, and I've disarmed him now too. Still, I think I could suggest a little swap that might be to our mutual benefit."

"DD, do I have to remind you that for a devil to try to

make a deal with the devil is just a little—unorthodox?" the Chairdevil said.

"I made this deal a long time ago," she reminded him. "And I'm a teeny bit late keeping my end, it's true. But then, it was never a fair deal anyway, not like I had any choice. What I propose is fair enough, though. I can tell you that in this whole mess, MacKai is the biggest thorn in your side. With him gone the others will be easy to pick off. Especially if he comes over to our side."

"We tried to get him before," the Chairdevil said. "The man picks the strangest times to sprout principles."

"Well, like I said. I can control him. I can get him to volunteer to come to you—as my tithe, somewhat belated. If you forget the interest on my mortgage, I guarantee MacKai will more than make up the difference in quantity with the quality of service he'll provide in his presence with us and his absence elsewhere. He's a catalytic type of man. He may not do much himself sometimes, but wherever he goes, things start poppin', and those things are usually the kind you don't want to happen. People discover their talent, discover their own drama, when Willie's around. They want to be what they think he is, though he never quite becomes that himself. He could be even more dangerous to you—us—than he is, but like a lot of important people, he isn't real happy with the world, isn't real connected to it. I could get him to defect without much problem, but in exchange I want my freedom."

"Your kingdom doesn't exist anymore, queenie-pie," the Stupidity and Ignorance Devil pointed out nastily.

"Gee whiz, Stu, I hadn't noticed," she drawled in a Lubbock accent. "I really do thank you so much for pointin' that out to me."

"He's right for a change," the Chairdevil said. "If I give you your freedom, what will you do with it? A few of your people are still hanging out in the old country, a few in Canada, but by and large I don't think they'd take to you again. They've gone in for a bit more democracy than in the old days. What would you do?"

"I don't know. I'll think of something. Start a new religion maybe. You'd like that, wouldn't you? Throw in a little more chaos."

"I'll think it over. But if you do make the rent, the sacrifice must be done in the traditional manner, you know. Company protocol demands the Ride with attendants, the whole bit.

And I'd like to remind you, DD, that this particular tithe is long overdue, so I'm afraid I can't give you until Halloween, as is traditional. MacKai has to be delivered at midnight on Summer Solstice, in the usual way—"

"But there's not much darkness to make the Ride in," Torchy protested, playing for time.

"You're a clever little devil. Figure something out. Otherwise, not only no deal, sweetcakes, but no more executive position. You'll have to work your way back up from the bottom, and I'm sure you have a little insight into how painful entry-level positions can be for someone as overqualified as yourself. You've made a few enemies, DD. There's a lot of our people who would be willing to make things hot for you."

She snapped her fingers, and from her fingertips she popped a red silk Chinese fan with a gilt dragon that moved slowly across the spokes of the fan. She fanned herself rapidly, a breath of ammonia cutting through the sulfur-perfumed air as she slumped in her chair with her eyes closed and her mouth half-open. "Mercy me, boss, but ah declare ah feel quite *faint* from fright." Opening one eye so that she was winking at him, she smirked and said in a throaty voice, "Don't you worry 'bout a thing, hotshot. I tell you I'll deliver MacKai, and you can bet your ass I'll deliver him. Trust me."

The Chairdevil couldn't help smiling back. She was so attractive when she sneered at him.

"Now then, Threedee. You need to get somebody else into Oklahoma, particularly Tulsa. There's an epicenter of cheery, merry music radiating from there like bleeding rays of sunshine, and I want it stopped."

"I'll get my people on it," Threedee promised. "I'll pull some of my mercenaries from the West African conflict."

"Oh, goody," the Debauchery Devil yawned. "How original. We just use psychotic killers for everything."

"You think the police are going to notice?" the Chairdevil asked. "We have our people there."

"No," she said. "I'm sure you can pull it off. It just doesn't seem to me as if it's a very interesting solution. Not really in the spirit of things. What I'd prefer to see happen is something with a little more inventiveness."

"Some of my boys can kill in very inventive ways," Threedee said defensively.

"I'm sure," she said.

"We've about exhausted our options in our initial onslaught," the Chairdevil reminded her. "Our opponents have no press, except for that publicity-hound Martin bitch and her girl ghost-detective antics, no distribution, no powerful allies, and now, thanks to you, no banjo. We can use the police, Threedee's boys, or something from the Plague and Pestilence Department. What's your pleasure?"

"It all sounds boring, boring, boring," she said. "I want to see something with more pizzazz. Something dramatic with fire and explosions and walls of water."

The Chairdevil's little red eyes grew misty. "Ah, yes," he sighed. His penchant for loud explosions and large, flamboyant disasters was well-known to his subordinates.

"See what you can dream up in the Acts of Us Department," he said to what we might call the Weather Devil, but who was actually a recycled Norse god and came fully equipped with hammer and many runic names, among which were God of Thunder, Lord of Lightning, the Destroyer who Dispenses Draught, Warden of the Winds and Waters, Earl of Earthquakes, Vizier of Volcanoes, and Purge of Picnics.

Before the Weather Devil could reply in the affirmative, however, the new Pollution and Waste Devil, also known as Peewee, spoke up. "We'll get right on it, CD." He was rewarded by a baleful stare from His Multiply Tempestuous Lordship. "Heh heh, sorry if I spoke out of turn. No need to get thore about it," Peewee said, polluting the atmosphere with his pun and then laughing so hard at his own joke that he had to wipe his running nose and eyes on a mile of nonbiodegradable pink toilet tissue patterned with anemic little blue flowers.

"Well, whichever of you do this, I want the plan to include the Curtises and the Randolphs and as many of those scribblers and music-mongers as we can hit," the Chairdevil said.

"Right, boss."

"And, Accounting?"

The Accounting Devil looked up from his notes and graphs. "Boss?"

"Don't forget to cancel their insurance policies before all of this comes up. I don't care how you do it, but if they survive this, make sure they've lost everything."

"Sure, boss," the Accounting Devil grinned, with teeth like a mouth full of cash-register keys. "I think I know how I can lose their payments in the mail. I'll get my inefficiency experts on it right away."

"Thor, you and Peewee make sure you include the hospitals and the banks in your swath of destruction. Also any charitable agencies that might help."

"No need for that, boss," the Accounting Devil said. "Hospitals won't admit anyone with no insurance, we've closed the charitable institutions down a long time ago, and I can get my embezzlers going on the banks so that any possible funds will be missing or tied up in litigation for the next hundred years. The Inefficiency Department has been in charge of the FDIC for the last seven years as well, and the head of the Tulsa department is due for a nervous breakdown any minute now."

CHAPTER XXII

▲▲▲

The metamorphosis of the banjo's remains into a new instrument was not a short or an easy process. It took a lot of thought, a lot of time, a lot of inspiration, and no little pain to even decide what the remains were to become in their next life.

There were certain compensations, however, if a person was superstitious enough to connect certain facts. The first thing the luthiers noticed was that they had no more car trouble of any kind all the way home from the convention. The second thing—and this could have been attributed to hearing the tail end of a couple of the songs Faron and Ellie and the others were singing at the convention—was that for the first time in years, long-forgotten tunes and song lyrics started wisping across their minds at odd hours or poking through their dreams.

They let the pieces linger in their bag on the shelf above Callie's table saw for several weeks, while they went to work and came home again, ate, drank, slept, and read. Finally the time came, and Aldin took the pieces up one evening and spread them on what was left of the kitchen table aside from the part where freshly sealed, newly hewn bits of instruments-in-progress were drying.

"The obvious thing," Aldin said, spreading out the skin from the head of the banjo, "is to make another banjo. But this piece is cracked around the edges and split."

Callie touched it. "It's gotten stiff and hard too—leathery, and it's curling around the edges. Seems to me it's a lot darker than it was when we picked it up."

Aldin smiled. "Maybe it got a suntan sitting near the window on your table saw.

"Yeah, well, I think we need to do something with these things soon."

She uncurled the strings from the bracelet Ellie had twined of them. They unwound, and unwound, and unwound. And unwound. They stretched across the table and draped over both sides and across the floor.

Callie was silent for a long time. Aldin was silent too.

"They grew," Callie said finally.

"Ellie did say they were from a *magic* banjo," Aldin reminded her.

Callie stroked them with a fingertip. "This is the strangest stuff I ever tried to work with. It's like hair, only each one is stronger. I hope it will work in my string-winding machine. Whatever we make, we're going to have to change the tuning of each string."

"Faron said these strings were always in tune," Aldin remembered, fingering one himself. "And Ellie mentioned dreaming the story of the 'Two Sisters' ballad. Do you suppose this really is what remains of the harp the minstrel made from that dead girl's body?"

"Ooh, gross," Callie said. "But intriguing. If it wasn't for this stuff, I'd wonder a little if the trip abroad wasn't—you know—a little hard on Faron and Ellie. I mean, I know they're creative, but this stuff is all a little—"

"I know what you mean. Beyond the ken of those of us who are stuck in the States with regular jobs and can only be weekend weirdos. Speaking of which—"

They went to bed. Aldin read for a while before going to sleep, but Callie was exhausted and drifted off. "Cal?" he asked, waking her.

"Hmm?"

"You remember Homer Brooks?"

"Oh yeah, good ol' Homer. Duck Soul. Uh-huh. How could I forget? *Used* to come have rock 'n' roll parties with *our* stuff, and we were all gonna be stars till *he* took over music single-handed. What about him?"

"Nothing. I was just thinking he might be kind of excited about something like this. He always was fascinated by that supernatural stuff."

"Uh-huh. G'night."

When she awoke, Callie yawned and stretched. Their waterbed was a good five feet off the floor, with storage underneath and no windows in the room, the bathroom closet carved out to make room for two chests of drawers Aldin had inherited. Only a narrow path ran around the bed, and now Callie hopped down onto it. Aldin stretched and looked down at her. "I dreamed of a song," they said to each other at the same time.

"You first," Aldin said.

"Well, it's kind of funny, because I know I never learned this song. It has a pretty, easygoing melody that's the kind that's so soothing you just find yourself da-da-deeing along and don't pay much attention to the words. But last night I heard the words—loud and clear."

"So? Bet it's not the same song. Sing."

She stood by the side of the bed and began:

"This here mandolin is carved out of pine,
   It was willed to me by a hobo down the line.
   He donated this mandolin with these last words,
   'Before I pass over I'll show you some chords. . . .' "

At this point Aldin joined in without missing a beat and with added emphasis on the end of the first line:

"This here mandolin is made out of *earth and stone*.
   If the sound of the railroad makes you feel all alone
   This here mandolin takes a hobo back home."

"So it was the same song?" she asked.

"Sure was. I never learned it either, though I knew it was written by Michael Smith and he wrote 'The Dutchman,' which was also a hell of a song. I'd never really listened to the words to this one until last night—then something or other made sure that I did."

"Well, Ellie did say that when the banjo was still together, it would play them songs to communicate with them, and sometimes they'd sort of learn the words through it. I think we've been haunted."

"I think so. Let's see what we can get out of the rest of the song, other than that the banjo pieces obviously want to be a mandolin when they grow up."

"This here mandolin is sure full of sand
   It only plays out of tune when there's a cop on the train.
   It can play you the rhythm of the Super Chief
   Out of St. Paul."

Callie had found a harmony now,

"That ain't all.
   This here mandolin'll make a young girl open up her window

Like a warm bed on a rainy night.
Like a hex sign on a barn
This here mandolin keeps a hobo from harm."

"Protective powers," Callie said. "Very spooky. I wonder
how Michael *knew* this was going to happen."
"Come on, let's keep going—" Aldin urged.

"This here mandolin can play the hard times
 Play the booze and the breadlines and the men killed for
   dimes.
 It can play you the cry in the night
 Of a jungle fire band
 Deep in the heart of this land.
 This here mandolin is made out of *old barns and water tanks.*
 If the jukebox is busted and you need an old song,
 This here mandolin takes a hobo back home."

Aldin had a literal kind of mind, since he was a computer
type. So it took a while longer for them to find just the right
decrepit pine barn and steal just the right planks for the
banjo's body. The water tank wasn't too hard—stock tanks
were easy to find. Machining the metal parts of tuners and the
frets from the stock-tank metal took a while, though. Callie
suggested that the banjo already had enough magical ele-
ments to it, but Aldin said, "It gave us a very clear message
what we were to use, and we can do it. Now then, we have five
tuning-peg heads from the original—if we have your potter
friend in Mountain Home do us three more, that will be
something made out of earth, but as for stone?"
"Hey, I've been sanding those barn planks, and let me tell
you, there's enough teensy grains of sand in that wood now to
qualify."
Callie liked the work, though—it was an exciting secret to
come home to. All the time she worked, her mind kept singing
the mandolin song, so that the wood came out smooth and
surprisingly beautiful. The pegs her friend made matched the
bone ones so well it was hard to tell the difference. At last the
body was finished, smooth and lustrous, with the skin head
shaped into veneer patches for the trim and the pegs in place.
All that remained was the strings.
Callie noticed when she put the first one in her string-
winder that though the strings were longer, only the cores

remained. She cut the first length and was trying to find a wire fine enough to wind it with for the first string, bending over the machine, glancing from the incredible hairlike core back to her stock again. Her hair was down on her neck for warmth, and it swung forward as she worked, its long buttery strands pooling on the table of the string-winder. She knew enough to tie it back while she was working, but the machine wasn't on. She would regulate it with a foot pedal like an old treadle sewing machine, so she wasn't too worried about it.

But then the core string started whirling on its own, and a lock of her hair fell into the center of the machine, jerking her head down. "Ouch, dammit!" she said. "Hold it!" The machine stopped. She jerked her hair loose, all but a single strand, which wound around the core of the string. "Just hold your horses," she said to the string. "I'm not dead yet. But I get the idea."

Aldin came running from the bathroom. "What's the matter, Cal?"

"This thing tried to scalp me. Remember the Two Sisters song about how he made the strings of her long golden hair? Well, our mandolin isn't picky about whose long golden hair it is, and mine's been drafted."

Aldin walked over to her sewing center, picked up her scissors, and handed them to her.

"You said you'd kill me if I cut it. You said you'd leave me for a tall brunette."

Aldin shrugged. "I think you'd look great in short hair. And we can't have you getting hurt around the machinery, can we?" He waited, and when she hesitated, he said, "Go on, Cal. It's the last thing. The final touch. Your hair will grow back, and I really want to hear strings that will always stay in tune."

▲▲▲

Some nights, especially when it had been stormy and nobody in their right minds would go out, Molly Curtis had a special urge to go for a run, checking everything out, patrolling her neighborhood, making sure the wet streets were just wet streets filled with nothing more sinister than broken tree limbs and water.

She pounded along the side of the streets, her shoes splashing her through puddles she didn't manage to dodge, her feet beating the rhythm on the pavement beneath her.

The song spreading was going well. Morgan Richards's computer virus had songs being sung at high speed all over the country now, and he was always finding applications. Writers and musicians who traveled were taking their new repertoires with them from city to city, infecting new audiences all the time.

LeeAnn Richards, Morgan's wife, had complained. "It's almost too easy, Molly. Easier even than it was before. Now you don't even have to pay to hear the songs or have any talent or anything—they *give* them to you, and you're supposed to sing all the time, and even if you play an instrument real badly, they make you keep playing. Except for having to learn something new, there's nothing to it, and you don't even have to learn it right. I heard one boy mess up the lyrics something fierce, and Mark Simmons just told him it was part of the folk process and complimented him on the lyrics he got right."

Molly had pooh-poohed her at the time. Although LeeAnn was usually sunny and optimistic, like most human beings she was suspicious when everything was going too smoothly. Molly knew exactly what she meant. If it was going to be this easy to reinstate the songs, why had the devils ever thought they could eradicate them? Molly had been in the world long enough to know that while there were many beings who were hateful and mean because they had been deprived of basic needs at an early age, there were others who were just plain rotten clear through, and the devils the kids had told her about were responsible for the rottenness.

Molly considered herself pretty tolerant. As a social worker she mostly dealt with people others would cross the street to avoid, and she liked them. Of course, it had become fashionable in recent years to patronize the homeless, but the prostitutes, even the occasional prostitutes, had been hard-hit by both the new diseases and the new morality. And while there was less in the way of drugs and booze on the street because of more rigid law enforcement, there was no less poverty and no less misery. And the people who weren't Molly's clients seemed to her to be if anything even more unhappy than their poorer neighbors—maybe because they still had something to lose.

Of course, it was good that people were trying to stay healthy and improve the environment, but sometimes getting through the day seemed like a grim round of spending half the morning asleep because you weren't drinking caffeine, not pausing for a smoke to think, not having lunch because you were on your run or going to exercise in some other way, not eating much of anything because you were watching it, not having a drink to relax in the evening just before not having sex with your partner because you were both too tired from a long day of virtue. Fortunately, she and Barry had retained some deviant degenerate impulses. Even after the music had disappeared, they spent evenings reading and talking about books with friends, trading and reading old books that contained very little solid factual information or helpful hints on the right way to live.

She liked to think that they were marginally happier than her colleagues at work, who, despite incredibly healthful and serious regimes, including massage therapy and other acceptable forms of relaxing from stress, still never allowed themselves to escape from their daily concerns and the problems of the world around them. They had as many responsibilities as the others, worried about Ellie and Faron, the cats, jobs, bills, an old house, and a yard, but because those things were not the only excitement they had or the only lives they knew about, they didn't take it quite as *seriously* as her co-workers did. Or so she thought. Her hypothesis was about to be tested.

The wind picked up, and the sky, despite the darkness, seemed to boil, as if suffering from indigestion. The day had been warm, but the breeze was cool. Molly rounded the corner to run back toward her house.

Darkness against darkness, columns spun crazily down from the sky, clearly lit by the lightning strafing the churning clouds. She had never seen so many twisters at once—six or seven of the whirling columns, drilling the earth. They still looked distant, but Molly picked up her feet and flew back to her house. She felt like Dorothy from Kansas as she banged open the screen door, unlocked the front door, and started yelling at Barry before she burst through the bedroom door.

The sirens started as the two of them grabbed the cellular phone, a flashlight, a bag of cat food, and all of the cats, who were sleeping in the house and therefore were drowsy enough to be cooperative, as well as the portable computer. They got everything to the cellar in three quick trips. Molly was still wearing the portable radio–cassette player she wore when she ran, even though she hadn't had tapes for the cassette player in years. She thanked God she and Barry lived in an old farmhouse that still had a cellar, and not a high-rise condo. Faron and Ellie's little house didn't even have a basement.

The cellar smelled like rain and mold and slightly damp earth. They tripped over jars washed and set aside for reuse, cardboard boxes from equipment that might have to be returned to the factory but that had, in fact, broken down or been sold several years ago. Somewhere in the mess was a pile of blankets, no doubt flea ridden, shelves of canned goods, mostly jelly and green beans, and a black snake who liked to hibernate down there.

The cats found the blankets immediately, and Barry's flashlight bounced off the walls, the dirt floor, and the ceiling as he began shoving boxes aside. Molly heard a smash as he knocked over one of the jars. The light quavered, and she knew his hands were shaking. She resolutely punched in numbers on the phone, dialing Faron and Ellie's number.

She heard two rings, and then the sirens and the roar filled the cellar, followed by a crashing, grinding, smashing noise overhead.

▲▲▲

The answering machine at Faron and Ellie's house received no message except the din created when the twister picked up the Curtis house, tore it from its foundations, and carried it into the sky to whirl it to pieces, some of which smashed into adjacent houses, some of which would be found miles from the original site. By the time the phone was on its fourth ring, the Randolph house was also torn from its roots, and a great part of it ended up as the second story of a house across the street before both homes crumbled into the back of the next house over, which was otherwise unharmed.

Faron and Ellie, fortunately, were not home. The call they had been waiting for had come: Callie and Aldin had finished the instrument that was heir to the banjo's magic parts. They had been very secretive about the nature of the object but sounded tickled with themselves. So while their house was being smashed to smithereens, Faron and Ellie were on their way to the Arkansas border.

Just ten miles from the turnoff to Callie and Aldin's house, the Randolphs heard the tornado reports on the car radio and pulled off at a minimart to use the phone. When there was no answer, they got back into the car, turned it around, and headed back to Tulsa. Ellie told herself things were okay, she was a fool to worry, she was just being overly dramatic. She pictured her mom and dad out eating someplace, laughing it up with the Richardses.

The picture exploded when they hit the roadblock on the highway just before they got to their exit. Policemen in raincoats and boots splashed around near the roadblock, and people got out of their cars and dived back and forth in the rain trying to find out what was happening. Spotting a woman and child walking back toward them, Ellie rolled down the window and asked her, "What's going on?"

"Cyclones," the woman said. "More than anyone has ever seen before in one storm. Whole neighborhoods just blew away, I heard, and half the town is flooded. We're going to be stuck here until they get rescue areas set up for the evacuees. The streets are choked right now, I guess. Probably the best thing is to turn around and go back."

"Home," the kid said, pulling on its mother's coat.

"Can't go home now, baby," the mother said, but the kid kept repeating, whining, demanding, "Home, home, *home.*"

The mother shrugged, picked up the kid, and headed back for her car again, and Ellie heard the kid crying to go home after she could no longer see either one of them.

Wet leaves picked up in the wind and whirled high over the car so that Ellie felt as if she were a figurine in one of those snow domes you bought for children, the kind you turn upside down so that the snow swirls and drifts down on a house or a Santa or a reindeer. The leaves plastered themselves to the windshield while the trees beckoned and bobbed, mocking like dirty old men, "Come on, little girl, come over here. Whatcha afraid of? Come on, I got something to show you."

▲▲▲

"Sold my flax, sold my wheel
To buy my love a sword of steel
So it in battle he might wield.
Johnny's gone for a soldier.
Shool shool shoolaroo—"

Julie sang in time to the stitching at the meeting of the local quilters' guild.

One lady looked up and asked, "What's all those funny words for?"

"They probably used to be Gaelic," Julie explained, "but

when the song got translated into English, they got left out. Other people say they're some kind of magic words, but of course, later on people might have thought some old language had magical abilities. Or maybe they really were magic, I don't know. Sometimes too, when they held dances in poor places where there are no instruments, or like in Scotland once the bagpipes were banned or in Ireland after the harps were burned, or in Nova Scotia in the old days when the ships came in and sailors wanted to dance but had no instruments, some people knew how to make mouth music—just imitating the sounds of instruments with their voices. Maybe some of the nonsense words came from that."

The lady nodded. "How does that go again?"

"Shool shool—" Juli began. But all at once her hands stopped sewing and her mouth stopped moving. Her face felt suddenly wet, and her ears were filled with a roar of wind and thunder. Her eyes turned inward, and she saw only darkness and felt only dampness and cold. And the husband of the woman who was hosting the quilting bee stepped into the doorway from the living room, where he'd been watching TV.

"Beryl-Bee," he said, "do you suppose we ought to call up the Bible college and make sure Lucy Dawn is safe?"

"Now, Henry, why would we do something like that?" the hostess asked, and Juli could almost hear past arguments about him wanting Beryl-Bee's attention while she was busy with her ladies' groups, even though he probably ignored her for months at a time when it was football or baseball season.

"They just now interrupted the game to tell about the terrible storms they're havin' down in Tulsa. Floods and cyclones. Lots of 'em."

"Lord have mercy!"

And Julianne was rocking back and forth, singing under her breath, "Wasn't that a mighty time?" about the Johnstown flood. Her hair was blowing and wet around her face, and big drops of water fell onto the quilt. Tears ran down her face to mingle with what looked like rain water, and Beryl-Bee looked sharply at her husband and back up at her ceiling, which she was sure from the looks of her guest he'd forgotten to fix. It was dry and white and plastery-textured like always.

▲▲▲

Tom George had asked Anna Mae if she could speak to the health workers' union at his sister's hospital. His sister and two RNs were the only professional medical staff. LPNs were not exactly considered professional or management, but neither were they welcome in the union. Tom thought maybe if Anna Mae talked to some of the members of the health-care workers' union, she might encourage some of the more talented Indian aides and orderlies to seek further training, better incomes, and maybe encourage the union to include the LPNs in their structure.

Anna Mae Gunn thought she would rather have put up with old-time company thugs than with the union stewards of the present day.

"If our workers want something, lady, they get it by negotiating. We don't have to have a lot of show-business types coming in to lead them in a singsong. These are serious working people you're dealing with here. They *need* their jobs."

"Look, yourself, *lady*," Anna Mae said. "Music helped organize unions to begin with. Men and women singing of their struggles were part of what got other men and women to band together for better treatment. I think your workers would really like to know these songs—it would help give them some pride in their jobs, put them in touch with what it is they're achieving, help morale."

"You saying maybe they don't have pride in their jobs or know what they're doing? I keep morale pretty high already, you know." The fact was, the woman was worried that Anna Mae was going to convince her membership to do something that wasn't in the settlement the woman had already negotiated with the bosses. You couldn't trust workers to know what was good for them, and this Indian broad had a way about her —she had star quality, the woman figured you'd call it. She wasn't beautiful, but she moved a certain way and her voice rang with authority and her face and body seemed to be just what they should be—a person would trust her. And she'd sung a couple of the songs for the steward and told her the background. Oh, no. This gal wasn't getting anywhere near the union's workers. She was a troublemaker.

The phone on the steward's desk rang and she picked it up.

"I'd like to speak with Ms. Gunn, please," said a man's voice, as ringing and important sounding as Gunn's voice. In the background was a faint babble of voices and what sounded like music.

"Who did you tell you were coming here?" the steward demanded.

"Nobody," Anna Mae said. "Why, should I have?"

"Here, dammit. But keep it short. This is a business phone."

Anna Mae took the receiver.

"Mae? Sam Hawthorne here. Look, I hate to bother you with another one of these phone calls from the dead again, but there's work for you down Tulsa way. They're going to need a good organizer down there, and you're the best we've got. Go stand at the corner of Twentieth and Garfield and I'll have the ghost of the last run of the Atchison, Topeka and the Santa Fe pick you up in twenty minutes, okay?"

"Okay, Sam," she said. But the line, of course, was dead.

CHAPTER XXIII

▲▲▲

James Francis Farnham had been ingratiating himself with the singers—mostly the men—for the last couple of months. One problem was, the women moved around. He saw the young one occasionally, but the old biddy hardly ever showed up. He also sort of liked the black guy. There was something about him that soothed Farnham and shut up his voices for a while and reminded Farnham a little of a teacher he used to have, though all Brose wanted him to learn was songs. Farnham proved to be good at them, and the voices were quiet when he sang them.

But they wouldn't stay quiet all the time and had to be obeyed, so one night when the old gal came to pick up Brose and Dan, Farnham hid in the back while they were talking. She would lead him to the other women, he thought. When he got her alone, he'd do her and then go find the others.

Except that on this night, Dan took the wheel and the woman scooted outside. Farnham had to risk peeking out the window at a dreary-looking little ranch-style home among a bunch of others. He noted the house number and that it was pink, which he naturally hated.

As soon as the van stopped and Dan and Brose emerged and walked away, leaving the van parked, Farnham started to leave the vehicle, brushing Brose's coat hanging from the back of the seat. The coat jingled, and Farnham, on sudden inspiration, fished in the pocket until he found a duplicate set of keys.

He drove back there, though it took him some time to find the address again, since he hadn't been watching where Dan drove. Cars crowded the double driveway and lined the street on both sides, so he had no difficulty looking natural as he pulled up in front of a red Pinto and walked toward the house, keeping close to the shrubbery. He peered in the side window to get the house's general layout. The women were all sitting in the living room, except for a few who were back in the kitchen fixing eats. He might get them first. He took the antique switchblade out of his pocket and fingered it. He still hadn't been able to get a gun. That was all right. Maybe there was one in the house. Besides, a bunch of women like this, he could pick off one at a time, or by taking a hostage. That was half the fun of it. Knowing the odds were really against you, but the dumb bitches were too scared to turn on you. He felt like a fox in a henhouse and smiled a foxy smile.

▲▲▲

The new group of music-party women were very skeptical about the benefits of the party, but between Gussie's story and Terry's songs, they soon relaxed and were singing along. Terry had a new planxty all composed for the hostess, a woman who in her time had hosted coffee houses and even strummed a little guitar herself. Many of the people who came to these parties had past connections with the music, severed when their lives grew more demanding or because the music was no longer popular.

"Oh, God, I hope they don't sing 'Kumbaya,' " said one woman the hostess had known since her hippie days. She had bright red hair and rolled her eyes and spoke in a world-weary manner. "I'll just puke if I have to hear it one more time."

"Was it that bad a song?" asked a younger woman.

"Well, no, but honey, over*done,* let me tell you."

"How did it go?"

"I—" the woman hadn't tried to remember it, naturally, since before the songs had been erased from memory, and she wrinkled her forehead trying to remember. "I dunno—say, Terry, honey?"

"Yes—the woman in the lime-and-teal sweatshirt in the back. What's your name?"

"Bev. Look, this gal beside me doesn't know 'Kumbaya.' Could you sing it?"

"If you help me, sure."

"I—uh—I don't remember. Mostly it's 'Kumbaya' over and over again isn't it?"

"That and other vastly more complex concepts," Terry said. "Such as—someone's sleepin', prayin', laughin', cryin'—pretty easy, huh? It's the melody that makes it—and harmony."

"I used to do harmony in church," another lady said. "Before they decided choirs weren't cost effective and the money could be better spent on retreats to Vail, Colorado, and such."

"Church harmony is really appropriate for this song," Terry told her. "It's a lullaby, but it was once used in church work by missionaries to Angola. These songs have a lot of power, you know. This one, as some of you remember, gained power in the sixties—like a lot of African-inspired songs, it chants well, can be sung for hours, and you can feel its spirit building until you know it can move mountains."

At that point a sharp scream split the air, and the floor moved beneath their feet as the house rattled and shook all the collector's plates down from the wall.

▲▲▲

James Francis Farnham had his hand on the door when a new voice spoke to him inside his head.

"You'll need to give this one a miss, Jimbo," the voice said in an accent that was half Southern drawl and half like some detective on the PBS programs Farnham used to enjoy in the old days. Perhaps the mystery shows weren't exactly factual, but Farnham found them inspiring.

"Wha—you're new, aren't you?" He didn't like the ambiguous tone of the voice. The other voices had been deep and commanding—reassuringly male. This was somewhere between a tenor and an alto, and he wasn't sure. He didn't want to take any more orders from female voices.

"Bright boy."

"I want to finish up this mission first. The other voices told me to get Terry and the old broad."

"We changed our mind, Jimbo. Here's what you're to do instead—"

James Francis Farnham listened, and grinned, and ran his fingers up and down the flat of the blade as the voices spoke to him. He nodded and smiled and laughed with growing excitement, his lips leaking a little drool, which he licked happily from his chin. The voices put a finishing touch on their message, and he laughed ecstatically. The earth moved.

▲▲▲

When the roaring died down, Barry and Molly switched on the portable radio they kept in the cellar, along with the kerosene lantern Barry lit to save the flashlight batteries. He also needed it to find the can opener. He kept canned peaches down here for emergencies, and it wouldn't be any fun at all to have an emergency if he didn't eat some of them.

The dial was set on the university station and had to be

wiggled a bit to get something other than static, though the broadcasting station was less than three miles away.

"We have a late bulletin on the tornado damage in the west end," a familiar baritone voice said.

"That's Mark," Molly said.

"What's he doin' announcin' news?" Barry asked. "He's s'posed to be general manager. Honestly, that boy. He's always letting people take advantage of his good nat—"

"Shush!" Molly said.

". . . and flood waters are rising," Mark's voice continued. "The west end, completely cut off by the collapse of the bridge, is being evacuated by boat and helicopter. A temporary refugee camp is being erected in the park, and listeners who are in need of temporary shelter or who have shelter, blankets, or foodstuffs to offer may call this number—"

"Oh, shit," Molly said. "We gotta get out of here."

"I'm sure it must still be a little windy out there," Barry said. The truth was, he was pretty sure he knew the sound of his house blowing away when he heard it, and he didn't think he was quite ready to look yet.

"Yeah, I bet it is," Molly said grimly. With resignation Barry set down his peaches. There was no arguing with Molly when she was determined.

"I guess it *could* be we ought to get ourselves above ground before the flood waters get this far," he allowed.

"Oh, that," she said. "Maybe so. But way before *that* I need to be at work. There'll be all kinds of clients applyin' for emergency assistance, and the department will be swamped."

▲▲▲

The New Madrid Fault was the dubious pride of New Madrid, Missouri. It ran from somewhere around Little Tree, Arkansas, up through New Madrid in the boot heel of Missouri, up to Cairo, Illinois, and the Kentucky-Tennessee border. There had been only a few minor tremors in recent years, but in the 1800s, legend and history had it, the fault had provided the entire area with the biggest earthquake recorded in the United States. Lots bigger than anything they'd ever had before or since in Los Angeles or San Francisco. So big, it was said, that the Mississippi River backed up and flowed backward for four hours, causing humongous floods. Why, for weeks afterward citizens walked around carrying board planks to throw across the crevices, just to get from one place to another. Of course, the only reason it wasn't world famous was because the area was sparsely populated back then. Still, seismologists were very interested, and so were the citizens of New Madrid, some of whom sported the T-shirts found in the hopeful New Madrid tourist trap, saying "It's Our Fault."

The area was far more heavily populated on that late spring night when the Earl of the Earthquakes busted loose with his tornadoes and jiggled the fault, which provided a quake so bad it was felt from New Madrid clear across Missouri to Kansas, Illinois, Kentucky, Tennessee, Arkansas, and into Oklahoma. There it caused a tidal wave from the rush of the Arkansas River into the gap left by the Mississippi just before the Mississippi came gushing back down its bed in a huge wall of water that sent the Arkansas curling right up on itself, wreaking devastation all across Arkansas and up into Oklahoma to far northwest of Tulsa.

Where the Canadian River ran into the Arkansas, it too backed up to cause flooding all over Texas. The Weather Devil was ably assisted by the Flimflam and Misinformation Department, who had been in charge of the media for some time now. Despite a national emergency in several states, no state of National Emergency was declared, and the regions were left to struggle through on their own.

▲▲▲

Julianne hitched a ride from one of the ladies at the quilting bee and borrowed the woman's phone. The phone at the Curtis's house beeped the continual out-of-order beep in her ear, as did the Randolphs'. She burrowed in her knapsack and emerged with the other contact number, that of Morgan and LeeAnn Richards. LeeAnn answered the phone, and Juli, who realized suddenly she had been holding her breath, exhaled.

"Are you okay?" she asked LeeAnn. "I couldn't get ahold of the Curtises or Randolphs."

"Well, Ellie told me she and Faron were going up to see their instrument-maker friends. But I don't know where Molly and Barry could be. They have to work tomorrow and—oh, my lord!" Juli heard the TV blaring in the background. "Oh, Juli, I can't talk now. I just saw—I'm sure it was the Curtises' street—" There was a catch in her voice, and to one side her voice said urgently, "Morgan, Morgan, wake up! I think Molly and Barry's street was hit by the tornadoes—I can't talk now, Juli honey."

"No, LeeAnn, wait! Where are these friends Faron and Ellie went to see? I want to see if they're okay."

"They live up in Arkansas someplace—"

Morgan mumbled into the phone, "Mountain Home. Callie and Aldin—don't know the last names, in Mountain Home, Arkansas. Call us when you hear from them, okay? Leave a message."

"I will," Juli promised, and hung up.

"I've got to make one more call," she told her hostess, who stood in the doorway looking anxious and a little bit shocky. "I'll give you some money for the bill."

"Never mind that," the woman said.

She dialed again and asked for Mountain Home information. "May I help you?" a real person, the man on the other end, asked.

"I hope so. It's an emergency."

"Right now everything is," the man said ruefully. "I hope we can help you before lines go down here too."

"I need to find a couple named Callie and Aldin. They're instrument makers. I know I should have the last name and the street, but please try—"

"No problem. Aldin used to work here on the computerized equipment before he got on with the new GTE lab. Nice guy. Here's the number."

"Wait! Listen, can you give me the address too? In case the phone lines go down before I can reach them? It really is an emergency."

"Sure. Four-point-six Mile County Highway. Look for the mileposts. Mailbox shaped like an accordion."

"Did you find them, honey?" asked Juli's hostess, a regal, gray-haired woman with beautiful green eyes. Juli thought her friends had called her Helen.

"Yes, ma'am. Now I just need to figure out how to get there—they're in Mountain Home, Arkansas. I guess I'll hitch."

"Don't do that, honey. It's dangerous out there now. Look, why don't you take the truck? My husband drove it before he died, and now my son just uses it once in a while when he comes in from St. Louis and needs it to help me haul stuff."

Juli hugged her and accepted the keys. "You are a doll. I promise to get it back to you as soon as possible."

She drove kitty-corner across the lower eastern corner of Missouri, detouring for flooded banks, her hands clutching the wheel as tornado warnings and reports of damage blared over the radio. All the way she sang. No particular song, just everything she could think of. Gospel songs figured prominently in her repertoire, particularly ones with reference to the River Jordan and waters parting, that sort of thing. She was a Universalist Mystic by affiliation, if she was anything, but childhood training was very comforting in this kind of situation.

The ground bucked and quaked beneath her like a believer in a fervor of religious ecstasy at a tent revival. Finally she found Mountain Home. The town was completely dark. No stoplights or streetlights lit the way, but County Highway ran right through town, and she followed it until her lights picked up the accordion-shaped mailbox. She had to leave the truck beside the mailbox and stumble through the yard to the house. Dim light emerged from within. Behind the house were pastures, and horses and cows were charging back and forth across the pasture, mooing and neighing with alarm.

Juli was scared too. She could scarcely think for the noise in her head, psychic alarms clanging all around her in a world gone wrong and besieged by disaster.

Eyes peered out from under the peeling white board that skirted the porch, and as Juli knocked on the front door, she heard a plaintive meow from under her feet.

She fell to one side as the earth bucked under her feet and the front porch flipped from side to side like a tilt-a-whirl. From the back of the house came the sound of shattering glass, and the screen door twisted on its hinges as Juli opened it, the frame crunching against the rest of the porch and splintering into an S-curve.

"Anybody home?" Juli called out, and presently heard what sounded like a human voice; then with another tip of the porch a front window split, and a woman peeked out of it.

"Callie?" Juli asked. "I'm Julianne Martin. My friends the Randolphs were going to see you about making an instrument. Have you seen them?"

"No," said the little round woman, plucking glass and plaster from her short blond bob. She came to the front door. A tambourine was in one hand. "But I've just been cowering beneath the table saw, mentally designing new instruments. It's all I can do with the power out. Come on in and pull up a blanket. Aldin's still gone. This was his night for volunteer fireman. I do it on Thursdays."

"You mean the Randolphs didn't make it here yet? Their friends said they left hours ago."

"Sorry," Callie said. "They probably stopped off somewhere—I hope. It's dangerous out on the roads now. You shouldn't have been driving around either."

"I know," Juli said. "But—well, we've been through a lot together, and I needed to make sure they were okay."

"As soon as Aldin gets home, we'll go try to find them, okay?"

"I guess."

"Come on in and have a cup of tea or coffee or something. I've turned off the gas, and the power went out about nine-thirty tonight, but I set up our camp stove."

Juli followed Callie through the workshop, which had once been the living room. The table saw, ban saw, router, sander, and string-winder filled a room otherwise appointed with built-in cabinets full of china and crystal and an ornamental fireplace with a wood stove hooked up to it.

The biggest quake, according to the papers, lasted only seconds, but the aftershocks, including several almost as severe, went on for hours. Julianne and Callie sat on the floor in Callie's kitchen feeling a little like grease on a griddle, ready to hop up and move around if it got too hot where they were sitting, or if the floor suddenly split beneath them. Callie had a big battery-operated lantern, and some of the light bounced off the window.

When the ground finally stilled, Juli felt as if she were still moving with it, the way she felt when she took off roller skates after skating for an hour or two. Rain splattered on the windows that remained, or sprinkled cold against her skin as it came in through the broken panes in the kitchen. Callie turned around and opened a drawer, sorting through it till she pulled out a dish towel, which she handed to Juli. Later Callie brought sleeping bags into the kitchen too, and each woman lay with the bag cuddled around her, though neither wanted to use the zipper.

Finally at dawn, twenty-four hours after the quake, the door rattled, someone swore, and then it sounded as if someone might be climbing through the broken window. Callie roused as a voice said, "Shit, I cut myself."

"In here, babe," Callie called, and scrambled to her feet. A red-eyed man wearing a rumpled plaid flannel shirt over his T-shirt appeared in the kitchen. The sound of mandolin music accompanied him, coming from the case he carried into the kitchen. The song was a Scottish one, sounding funny on mandolin, "The Highland Roll Call," a call to battle whose lyrics, the names of different clans, had the sound of rumbling thunder. It wasn't exactly a mandolin piece. "We have company," Calli added unnecessarily. "This is Julianne Martin, Aldin."

Aldin's red eyes took a minute to focus, and then he raised a weary hand and said, "Hi—here," and handed her the mandolin, then collapsed on the floor beside them, burrowing onto one of the vacated sleeping bags, and fell immediately asleep.

"Is that—is it Lazarus? Did Aldin bring Lazarus home with him?" Juli asked, staring at the mandolin case.

"Well, sort of. It's the mandolin we made out of the pieces, and it seems to work about the same."

"Why a mandolin?" Juli asked. Callie explained. "Faron and Ellie were coming for it tonight and then were going to stay over. We didn't want to leave it home alone, so Aldin took it to work with him. Usually you don't have to stay at the fire-department meetings, just get a briefing. We thought he'd be home with the mandolin by the time they got here."

Juli cradled it on her lap and let it play through her fingers. When it switched from general disaster songs to train songs, she decided it was just playing for enjoyment, and reluctantly recalled why she had come, and packed it back into its case.

"I need to go find Ellie and Faron now."

"Let's let Aldin sleep a little longer, then we can all go look," Callie said.

"I can't wait," Juli told her. "Something could have happened to Faron and Ellie—I know something *has* happened. I mean, I can feel it. I just don't know what."

The mandolin busily doodled "Way Out There," an old Cisco Houston song about a hobo, a moon, and a train.

CHAPTER XXIV

▲▲▲

Brose Fairchild was humming "I Ain't Got No Home" under his breath and restringing his guitar with his Sunday-best strings, the ones he didn't regularly beat to death on the street. He was fed up with the streets. Oh, sure, he and the others were doing good work and all that, but as soon as they left, he felt pretty sure the people they'd been working with would go back to their old routine. He didn't much like the streets, having spent plenty of time on them when he was growing up, at which time he switched to the road for many years. Then he settled down with the humane society and the little farm that was now full of rows of identical houses—which was just exactly what the world needed more of, of course.

He didn't much like some of the people he'd been associating with lately, either. That new guy gave him the creeps, and he knew that when you were dealing with any crowd of people, maybe particularly a transient crowd, there would be a few mean ones. He didn't like Jimbo's eyes, especially the way he stopped looking at Terry or Gussie if he caught Brose watching him.

He was just tuning the last string when someone pounded at the door. Dan was on the phone, talking to Lettie and Mic Chaves in Tacoma. They'd called to talk to Gussie, but since she was gone, Dan was filling them in, and when the quake came, he added, "Oh, wow, and we just had an earthquake. How big? I don't know, let me see," he said, and switched on a television set.

Brose could hear him talking as the room shimmied, giving him the feeling that he was aboard a ship in rough seas. The pounding at the door grew more intense. Brose carefully set down the guitar, lumbered to his feet, and opened the door. There stood Jimbo himself, all afroth with excitement.

"We gotta go and you gotta take me with you," he said.

"What you talkin' about, man?"

"Disaster. Didn't you feel the quake?"

"Well, yeah."

"It's caused floods all over. And there were twisters wiped out half of Tulsa."

"Holy shit," Brose said. Then to Dan he said, "Better tell the Chaveses we need to pack up Lettie's mama and Terry and head south."

"Jeez, will you look at that!" Dan said, pointing to the TV. "Look, you guys, I got to go," he told Lettie and Mic. "That quake I just told you about? It's causing all kinds of problems —tornadoes and floods and stuff. We got to try to find the others. Yeah, Anna Mae and Juli are out there on their own."

"I just know with so much bad luck happenin', there's bound to be some of our people smack dab in the middle," Brose said.

"You got to take me along," Jimbo insisted, and Brose looked at him like he was crazy, which he was, of course.

▲▲▲

Now, the Debauchery Devil was no fool. She knew that Willie MacKai had the ability to lift the spirits of those flood and tornado victims, and she also knew it would have cheered him up to do so. It would have solidified the whole effort of reintroducing the music to the States to have had all of the singers together with Willie in the lead, which was exactly what Torchy could not allow to happen. If Willie could do a thing like that, he might start to get the idea he had better things to do than to sacrifice himself for her sake.

So she took him as far from the flooding rivers and earthquakes as she could get him, and as far from people as possible, back to his old stomping grounds at the ranch. Roundup was over, the cattle sold off, and the cowboy poets were all away at writers' conferences, where they were learning that poetry was impractical, unless it was used to write advertising jingles, advice which, them being cowboy poets, they paid no attention to whatsoever.

But Willie was no fool either, and he was not as completely under her influence as she thought, nor was he as easy to manipulate as she hoped. He noticed a whole lot more than she thought. He had always been a tad psychic, and messing around with ghosts, astral travel, magic banjos, and such hadn't exactly blunted his natural psychic talents.

So maybe it was the same mental alarms Julianne had sensed, or maybe it was the just-fresh infusion of ozone in the air, but even though he had no contact with other people or the media, when the storms commenced elsewhere, Willie started feeling a little agitated, kind of more energetic than usual. The wind from the storms picked up heat as it drove down through Texas, until all Willie could scent was a hint of rain on it and see the dust kicking up its heels in the acres of nothing all around him.

He decided to do a little target practice for recreation and picked up a rifle and walked away from the house. He couldn't find any beer cans or nothin', though, because the boss was into recycling along with the rest of the state, and all the beer cans had been duly packed off before the boss left for his meeting. Willie hoped the boss and the cowboy poets would be back soon. He had finally gotten his fill of bein' alone. The ranch hands were a colorful bunch to talk to. In absentia, however, they were as damned dull as everybody else.

Finally Willie spotted an old truck hubcap that had been discarded out by the barn, and he squeezed off a few potshots at it.

He was serious about his shooting, more serious maybe than he'd ever been about his music, up until he went to Scotland with Sam's banjo, and he was concentrating so hard that if the intruder who walked toward him from the prairie on the right had been ill intended, he could have shot Willie dead while Willie was murdering the hubcap.

But the stranger had no such intentions. And the stranger was only ten years old. *"Señor, señor, por favor—"* the boy called out, and Willie whirled at the sound of the voice, but lowered the barrel of the pistol to the ground. He knew enough not to point guns at anything you weren't sure you wanted to kill.

"Que pasa?" Willie asked, and the boy in rapid-fire Mexican Spanish told him his folks got in trouble trying to ford the Rio Grande the night before, and in spite of his mother's protests he had come for help. There were many in their party, and if the *señor* wanted to report them to the federales, that was as it might be, but without help many in their party would die, as several already had of drowning.

In many a barroom conversation, Willie had sometimes been heard to talk against the wetbacks and other illegal immigrants. The fact was, these were the people he was brought up among, and he was used to them and thought of them as neighbors, even if they were from as far away as Monterrey or Mexico City.

He took the kid with him to the house and called the number of one of the workers who didn't live right on the main part of the ranch, but up in the little town the boss provided for his workers with families.

The worker, Juanito Sanchez, was the stepson of the cook, who was the second ex-wife of Dally Morales, and he quickly brought around his pickup truck and some blankets and a couple of extra half-grown boys in case anything funny was going on. He also brought a big bowl of cold refried beans and a covered pan full of fresh tortillas.

"That's mighty nice of Carmencita," Willie said.

"She does it mostly because she will annoy Dally," Juanito shrugged. "She don't like them Mexicans from Mexico any more than we do, but she knows he's s'posed to keep 'em off the place, so of course she's ready to help."

He said it in English, so the boy couldn't understand.

Now, this was all handled within a few hours, everybody was saved, and as a matter of fact, no federales were called. Willie, wetbacks, and all went back to Carmencita Morales's place to eat and bed down. There was a guitar belonging to Carmencita's first husband, Rosario, and one of the newly rescued men, as easy as if he were saying "Thank you kindly," made up a song for Willie and Carmencita and them and sang it on the spot, which made Willie trot out his repertoire, and even though the Mexicans could understand only his Tex-Mex border ballads, everybody had a very good time and seemed to appreciate all the music. Willie felt a whole lot better than he had at any time since before he returned to the United States.

▲▲▲

"Well, goodness, that's a lot of disasters for a short period of time," Heather-Jon said.

"Where have you been? Didn't you hear about it?" Shayla St. Michael asked.

"No. I was in Germany, actually."

"Well, I was in St. Louis for a Green convention, and I remember it vividly. Silly me, I thought it was caused by shifts in tectonic plates. I should have known it was diabolical supernatural forces," she said with an archly lifted eyebrow in Dally's direction.

*And Mary Armstrong looked up at Ute with an expression
that was both grave and startled. "You don't mean the storms
this year? The ones a few weeks ago?"*

"The very ones."

*"Why do I get the feeling this is leading somewhere?"
Heather-Jon asked.*

*"I'll be glad to answer that in just a little bit, but I got some
finishin' up to do on this yarn first."*

▲ ▲ ▲

Anna Mae Gunn's ghost train looked the same as a real one
to her, a really old one, beat up and disused, with mice in the
upholstery and rust all over the metal parts. She knew it was
what Sam said it was, however, when it pulled up right at the
corner he told her to wait by. There weren't any ghost conduc-
tors or ghost engineers or other ghost passengers she could
see, so she swung herself and her instruments aboard and
took her pick of the least ratty seats. They were the old long
seats, not all divided up like they are nowadays, and since she
was tired, she stretched out on one and went to sleep while
the train bumped silently over weed-grown ground scarred
with torn-up tracks and the ghosts of tracks that ran through
deserted shopping malls and darkened apartment houses and
through the panicked traffic that was packing partially
washed-out or collapsed six-lane highways. It was a good thing
Anna Mae didn't know she was riding through all of that, or it
might have given her a bad turn . . . but probably not. She
was a tough sort of woman, and she had learned by now to
take things on faith.

The best thing about her ghost train was that it paid no
heed to the earthly weather. Oh yes, it was just as well that
Anna Mae slept through most of that night with the wind
howling around her and the flood waters roaring over the
long-gone tracks, the branches whipping through the cars but
never touching so much as a lash of her sleeping eye.

The little medicine bag between her pointy breasts rose
and fell, rose and fell. You could almost hear a chanting in the
wind sometimes, or in the silent clicking that the train wheels
should have been making rolling down the nonexistent tracks.

Along about morning Anna Mae woke and found the
worn-out moth-eaten carpet soaked and the metal all beaded
with moisture, but the seats beneath her and her sleeping bag

and her instruments were still dusty enough to make you cough. The train had stopped moving.

Looking out the window, she saw that the train had parked itself in somebody's side yard. She sat facing the window of someone's kitchen and through that window, she heard a mandolin playing "This Train Is Bound for Glory."

A man lay snoring in a sleeping bag on the kitchen floor. Another woman sat up looking apprehensively around her. Then a second woman entered the room, and to her relief Anna Mae saw that it was Julianne. Juli turned around, saw her, and waved, as unconcerned as if she caught trains parked outside people's kitchens every day.

Anna Mae suddenly heard a voice very like Sam Hawthorne's sing out, " 'Board! All aboard!" and Julianne beckoned to the other woman, the two of them helping the man to his feet. "No problem, Callie," she said. "It's okay. It's Anna Mae and she's come for us."

They clacked on throughout the stormy day as if they were ghosts themselves until they reached the outskirts of Tulsa. In the midst of lines and lines of cars, the train chuffed silently to a halt beside a beat-up car, and the train passengers looked down into the drawn faces of Ellie and Faron. At first the Randolphs didn't see them any more than the cops at the blockade did, or any of the rest of the people in the cars, but Julianne leaned out the window and hollered, "Hey, guys! It's us! Get on board."

Then Faron and Ellie saw the train just fine and climbed into the same car as the others and off they went, through the blockade, across the bridge that was now under repair, and over the flood waters of the angry Arkansas River. They picked up two cows, a horse, and a yellow-striped kitty-cat who was clinging to a mostly submerged roof on the way.

Ellie bounced up and down on the seat like a little girl on her first ride. "I know where it's taking us! I know! There's abandoned tracks in the lot across the street from Mama and Daddy's house. I know it's taking us there."

And sure enough, that's where it took them, right across from the yard Ellie had played in as a girl. Ellie gasped and started crying, Faron groaned, and the others just tried to hope for the best when they saw that there was nothing left of the Curtis house but foundation and splintered floorboards and what used to be a chimney left from the days when the old farmhouse had had a fireplace. The flood waters covered the yard. The water was shallow enough you could still see the tallest blades of grass poking up through it along with snakes and frogs and backed-up sewage and all kinds of other stuff that had floated in with the water.

Ellie jumped down from the train and splashed across the street and up to the side of the house, calling back, "Come on you guys and help me! There's boards blocking the cellar door!"

Anna Mae was about to ask if the Curtises were down there for sure, but then she, like everybody else, heard the happy, somewhat wobbly voices, tenor and alto, of the two people who had found the supply of plum cordial Barry had put up three years ago and then forgotten about, wailing, in Oklahomese, the refrain from "The Wildwood Flower": "You've gone and neglected yer frail waldwood florrer."

CHAPTER XXV

▲▲▲

The refugee and relief camp was set up on high ground in the middle of the beautiful park where Faron and Ellie had gotten married. The garden center was right in the middle, and all around it tents and shelters were set up with Christmas bulbs strung around the entrances so people could see where they were going in the darkness and the rain. The churches donated food, and people kept calling the emergency phone operators and the radio and TV stations to say, "We have an extra bedroom and could maybe care for a family of three for a few days."

Molly went back to work with almost no rest, handing out emergency checks to hard-hit families, though it was going to take some time for any aid to come to her and Barry or to the Randolphs.

Aldin managed to patch a call through to his office to tell them he'd been dragged by a family emergency—absolutely unavoidable—to Tulsa and wouldn't be able to get back to Arkansas for days. The office there talked to the office in Tulsa, which drafted him to work on emergency communications there.

The Weather Devil had blown himself out for the time being, and there were no more twisters. He could only generate puny little piddling twenty- and thirty-mile-an-hour winds and drizzly rain that kept the tents from ever being warm or dry. Flood waters just kept rising instead of falling, so nobody could move permanently back into their houses, and emergency efforts had to continue.

▲▲▲

If anybody had asked Brose, he would have said he was absolutely opposed to having James Francis Farnham ride with them, but Dan swept them both along. Among Dan's best qualities were his friendliness and overwhelming belief in the goodness of all people and the triumph of brotherly love over mere human considerations such as greed, power lust, other kinds of lust, and just plain craziness. His worst qualities included his indiscriminate friendliness and overwhelming and unfounded trust in the ultimate triumph of good over evil in his fellow man.

If anybody had asked Gussie about allowing the man they knew as Jimbo to ride with them, she would have backed Brose up. So would Terry. But what with the quakes and the floods and being worried about all of their other companions of the last seven years, neither woman was feeling particularly like quibbling over the roster of people to go on the trip. Farnham made another driver and another person to push the van out of trouble if it got stuck.

They headed for Tulsa to find the Randolphs and the Curtises first, thinking that those families might help them locate Julianne, Anna Mae, and Willie.

Gussie, sleeping in the seat behind the driver while Farnham drove and Brose nodded in the passenger seat beside him with Terry and Dan in the back, heard Farnham giggling to himself and felt a chill pierce her nightmares. She had felt all along, especially when she watched him move—which had not been often, since she hadn't been involved in the street-singing project—that there was something familiar about him. In the rearview mirror she saw him glance back and lick his lips, and she didn't sleep another wink until he was sound asleep in the back with everybody else awake and she was in the passenger seat next to Brose.

But they detoured around the worst-hit spots by driving down on the Kansas side into Oklahoma, so except for some detours in areas where roads were flooded around Tulsa, their trip was without significant incident. Their windshield wipers were all but shredded from the pouring rain and the sleet and hail, and they rapidly learned they could not reach the place where the Curtis house used to stand.

Gussie remembered where Molly worked and called her there. Barry was spending part of every day in a rowboat with a policeman, looking for people stranded by the flood and offering help.

At the improvised refugee camp, Gussie and the others shared soup from a local church and bread from several area bakeries and grocery stores. First the Randolphs, then Barry, then Anna Mae, and finally Julianne told what had happened to them. Gussie completely forgot about Farnham, the rain, or any other depressing subjects when, with a dramatic flourish, Callie and Aldin hauled out the mandolin.

"Lazarus!" Gussie cried as the mandolin played the Michael Smith song it had played in the dream of its resurrectionists, and soon everyone was singing along, heedless of the wind and rain.

Later Faron played the mandolin while Brose plunked away on the guitar Gussie had found for him at the second-hand store. He was playing "The Brown Girl Blues," which had become his signature tune, and all the others knew it and joined in, then went on to "In the Pines," which was particularly appropriate as the wind picked up, since the chorus was, "In the pines, in the pines where the sun never shines, and you shiver when the cold wind moans."

The rain started again, and they crowded into a lean-to made of milk cartons lashed together with string and canopied with plastic tarp. Right in front of it somebody had lit a fire in an oil barrel, one of several around the park, and people in nearby tents and standing under the trees watched it as if hypnotized.

Julianne stared into the fire and thought of all the floods and storms there had ever been and all the displaced people who had no place in the world anymore. The mandolin in Faron's hands started playing, and she sang the words. People quickly joined in—it was not a song only people who went to folk-music clubs knew. Just an old Stephen Foster song that seemed to fit the times:

"'Tis the song, the sigh of the weary,
 Hard times, hard times, come again no more.
 Many days you have lingered around my cabin door,
 O, Hard times come again no more."

That felt so good that for a long time they comforted themselves and everyone who was listening, which seemed to be most of the camp, with songs that had easy choruses: "Darling Clementine," "You Are My Sunshine," "She'll be Coming around the Mountain," and "Red River Valley." Camp songs, childhood songs for most of the people, although many of the children looked baffled, having grown up without hearing those songs.

Faron wondered aloud if singing a dust-bowl ballad or two wouldn't make the weather seem drier. Although the author of many of the songs—Woody Guthrie—had been an Oklahoma native, Faron had to wait while the kids asked what a dust bowl was, and the older adults explained. He sang "Dust Bowl Refugee" for three verses, then changed it to "Mud Hole Refugee," at which the crowd, including the kids, joined in.

Brose played "Deep River Blues," with a chorus unfamiliar to most of the people gathered around. But they were in the mood to listen now, and Anna Mae sang a song called "Here Comes the Water," one of the "singer-songwriter" brand of folk songs so popular through the late eighties and early nineties, written by Colorado songwriter Chuck Pyle about the flood in Big Thompson Canyon.

Gussie watched fondly as the mandolin whittled away at the various melodies, suggesting songs and harmonizing with the other instruments. It was so good to have Lazarus among them again.

The gold-striped cat Anna Mae had rescued from the flood and pulled onto the ghost train yawned and fell asleep across Brose's broad shoulders, purring a little, until the board of devils yanked her back to do a little explaining.

▲▲▲

"You took my murderer!" Doom and Destruction thundered at Torchy, who cowered, hissed, and spat at him before remembering herself and turning back into a two-legged cat with long red hair.

"Oh, lighten up. I just borrowed him for a little bit. I was doing you a favor. He was going to screw up in Kansas City. Those women weren't going to sit still for some maniac with a bread knife while there was an earthquake going on. Besides, the party Gussie and Terry were playing that night was a ladies' self-defense class. Your boy would have been dog meat. I saved him for you so he can do some real harm."

"You're getting way too nice, DD," snarled the Stupidity and Ignorance Devil, who actually believed what the redhead said.

"I think we can work up a little something together in that camp that will top a mere killer," said the Pestilence Devil.

"I'm already working on a mutant form of combined cholera and diphtheria," said Peewee.

"That's *my* department."

"I'm culturing it from sewage effluvia," Peewee countered, "so I guess that makes it *my* department."

"I think if you play your cards right," Chairdevil said

thoughtfully, "we can have our murders *and* a plague. Maybe even make people kill off all surviving household pets in the meantime, which should add to the misery."

"You sure you don't want me to show up with some drugs or booze or something to help those people kind of ease their pain?" DD asked, not because she especially wanted to, just to test the waters, as it were, and see if they were changing their minds about her effectiveness.

"I don't want their pain eased," the Chairdevil said. "While there is a certain value in having drunk or stoned people abusing those around them, I think we can let human nature stand on its own merits these days. Put enough pressure on sober people, and they'll say and do things someone who's had too much to drink wouldn't have the imagination to think of. I already have a few of the more dedicated obsessive types going into work and shopping withdrawal. All that fear and anger was bubbling along real good till those damned noisemakers started that group-singing shit and calmed everybody down. I think DD was right and your killer is just where we want him. And, Pestilence?" He turned his attention to the Plague and Pestilence devil.

"Yes, boss?"

"While Peewee is working on the new disease that you should have thought of, can't you stir yourself to start spreading the common cold, at least, or really stretch your imagination and go for laryngitis and pneumonia?"

"I'll get right on it, boss."

▲▲▲

Willie hitched a ride into San Antonio with Juanito, discreetly leaving the matter of the illegal aliens to the current ranch workers, and from there rented a car with what was left of his expense money.

He stopped in at a convenience store in San Marcos for munchies and on impulse dialed the operator.

"I want to make a collect call from Willie MacKai to this number, please," he said to the operator.

After a few seconds the operator replied, "I'm sorry, sir, that number is no longer in service."

"The hell it's not! I was just there a couple of months ago."

"I can't help you, sir." The operator, a young-sounding man, seemed to be gritting his teeth. Willie, who had been alone so much recently and suddenly felt as if he had no place to go, relented.

"Look, buddy, I'm sorry if I sound a little testy, but I had good friends I was supposed to be able to reach at that number—"

The operator relented slightly too and broke a few rules. He'd been doing that pretty often lately, with everything in a state of crisis. "That's okay, sir. I can understand how you'd be a little upset, what with all the trouble they've been having up there. It may be just that some of the lines are still down after the tornadoes, or that repairmen are unable to reach them to repair them because of the floods they've been having."

"Is there any way to find out about that?"

"We have emergency information at this number. I'll try to transfer you, but if we become disconnected, the number is—"

▲▲▲

When Torchy popped back into the world, she popped onto the ranch, but nobody was there but a bunch of word-drunk cowboy poets just back from their writer's conferences and a boss who had heard way too much bullshit at the Cattlemen's Association meeting.

She ascertained this by looking around, and when Nobby Watanabe spotted her, she managed to look like a very pretty academic and explained that she was an editor for Bull-Pen Press and she was looking for her old friend Willie MacKai, who had told her he might be staying at the ranch off and on.

The cowboys all had varying theories, which they offered in jest and verse, vying with one another to impress her, especially after she explained to a very interested query that Bull-Pen Press was the publisher of *Bull-Pen,* the magazine of contemporary western literature.

With no banjo and no fairy dust to track Willie by—she didn't have a clear fix on exactly where to find him. Even Gussie had left a trail with her storytelling. There were a lot of mortals out there in the world, and perseverance and industry were not among the limited number of Torchy's virtues.

The problem was, each of the ranch hands had a different theory about where Willie was. Her only idea was that he might have gone back to Tulsa, but her outfit had done their dirty work so well that she couldn't just call. And meanwhile,

Dally Morales was writing a poem about her, and she wanted to stick around for a while. Besides, she had a few plans to make for Summer Solstice. She was sure she'd be able to round up Willie from someplace, and the ranch was beginning to fit into her plans. While Dally was waxing poetic about the reflection of her hair in the stock tank, she was eyeing the horses.

"Is that—" she asked Dally hesitantly, and he looked up from his scribbling.

"Huh?"

"That horse out there—that elfin gray. I thought they'd died out—"

"You mean the Appaloosa? Well, ma'am, they purty nearly did when the Nez Percé had their horses massacred by the cavalry—there's a real good song about it Willie sang for us when he was here before. Fellow named Fred Small wrote it. It's called 'The Heart of the Appaloosa.' I got it wrote down. I could sing it for you if you like."

"Thanks," she said. "I'll pass."

▲▲▲

The devils did a real number on those poor people from Tulsa. Everybody came down sick, including the medical people—even Brose, who occupied himself with the human animal instead of the other kind for a change.

Julianne and Anna Mae kept singing, though Gussie succumbed to a sore throat. Anna Mae wore a little medicine bag around her neck. Now, for you or me maybe the medicine in that bag might not have been anything much at all—it was just a little old amethyst rock like they used to sell in metaphysical bookstores in the late eighties, plus a crow's feather and some other stuff that mostly it's only Indian people who care about. But the medicine man who made it for her was none other than old man Atoka, and she was real attached to it. So now, thanks to the little bag, she felt strong in body as well as spirit, and she didn't catch anything any more than Julianne, who, as has been mentioned, defied any germs the worst devils could throw at her.

The music was medicine too, and they all knew it. Lazarus the Mandolin began playing not just at danger or for a joke, but every time they cooked food or accepted food. They sang when they washed clothes or took a bath, and they sang when they put up new tents or filled sandbags to shore up the riverbanks. They taught anybody who was willing to learn every song they could think of, old ones and new ones.

In the evenings Molly and Barry joined them, and so did Faron, Ellie, Callie, and Aldin. But later in the evening, when most of the music had stopped and lots of people had gone to bed, you could still hear Lazarus playing away in its case, making a spritely song sound sadder and lonesomer than it had ever sounded before as the strings played "Rattlin' Roarin' Willie."

The first time that the murderer struck—and we all know it was Farnham—everybody thought that maybe the crime was committed by one of the refugees who had cracked under the strain. Except for the music and the kindness they showed to one another, people were feeling pretty low and short-tempered.

But it was hard to believe that anybody could have ever been more than mildly irritated at the first victim, a childless, unmarried retired children's librarian. The cops insisted she might have been selling drugs to kids at the library or something, you never knew. She wrote furiously across a page of paper that she most certainly had not, but she couldn't speak up for herself because she had laryngitis.

She wrote that she had not seen her assailant because he was plagiarizing the old slasher movies by wearing a hockey mask, and it was dark, so she couldn't make out the details of his clothing. Really, if she had not fallen asleep with the five-book hardbound collection of Agatha Christie under her sleeping bag, where she read with her flashlight as she had when she was a little girl, the horrible deed might have done more than make a point. When she felt the knife strike, the pages of the book crushed themselves against her chest as if imploring protection, and she sat bolt upright, banging heads with the hockey mask and automatically spewing the speech she had given children for the last forty years about how damaging books was a shame and a crime, and only good-for-nothing low-down no-account little video-games-for-brains brats would do such a loathsome and despicable deed.

When it occurred to her, after the assailant had fled without his knife, that he had meant to damage her instead of the book, she screamed and shook and cried, which was partly how her laryngitis came to be such a problem.

Farnham was a sorry sight now. He had to steal another knife, not nearly as good as the first one, and his hockey mask had a crack in it, besides which, his voices would not let him alone a second and they told him that he should be preaching against the singers by day while trying to kill them secretly by night and reminded him that he had a score to settle with Gussie.

He tried preaching. He really did. And since he was crazy, he didn't sound much worse than your average TV evangelist, though he did forget to ask for money often enough. A few malcontents listened and tried to get a disturbing-the-peace order enforced against the little group of singers, but mostly everybody was too sick or too busy to pay him much mind, so he went on with his killing plans.

Gussie was his target of choice. For one thing, she looked more fragile than the younger women. For another, she was the right age to remind him of the figure in his life that he kept trying to kill over and over.

Actually, if he had asked her permission, she might have agreed, because she was in that state where she was so sick that even though she knew she wasn't going to die, she sort of wished she would.

▲▲▲

It was a dark and stormy night. It hadn't been much of anything else for weeks. Some days it *was* just cold and the wind blew and there was actually a little sunshine, and other days it was fairly warm and it rained all the time. But basically you didn't get away without one or the other—rain, or wind, or dark of night when it should have been getting light outside.

Little streamlets seeped inside the single musicians' tent. Although it was a big enough tent as tents went (when the center crosspieces didn't collapse its dome shape into more of a squashed melon shape), it was pretty small for four people. The floor was a mire of muddy footprints. Gussie was wrapped up in all of her blankets and all of Brose's and all of Molly's, since Molly was working late. Gussie had taken three aspirin and a tot of cough syrup that was mostly alcohol, but she still hurt too bad to sleep. Her throat burned and her ears burned and her eyes ached and she kept coughing.

Furthermore, she had heard about the attack and it confirmed her fears about Farnham, but the others had been steering clear of her cough, so she hadn't had a chance to tell them about it.

The Doom and Destruction Devil was determined to do

his bit so that Farnham should have all of the coincidence his patron devil could manufacture. To that end, at nine o'clock that evening a careless and soon-deceased soul smoked his last cigarette too near the flood-battered gasworks across town, while at the same time an oil tank truck crashed into a munitions factory. Nobody needed a flashlight to see that night, which was the only thing that was unfortunate for Farnham. Every able-bodied person from the refugee camp had gone to help the new evacuations under the direction of every national guardsman, policeman, army reserve soldier, and fireman for miles around. Faron, Brose, Dan, Terry, Anna Mae, and Ellie, the Curtises and Aldin and Callie, all went, leaving the re-resurrected Lazarus in Gussie's care. The mandolin lured Threedee's henchman to Gussie's tent as if she had hung out a big neon sign that said, "Victim Available: Inquire Within" outside her tent flap.

She woke up about to cough again and heard Lazarus screeching away at "Silver Dagger" so loud and fast it sounded as if the mandolin were trying to play its way out of the case. The music startled her, and she began one of those long spasmodic coughs even before she opened her eyes.

She jerked into a sitting position with the violence of her cough and felt something make a cool breeze past her feverish neck before digging into her shoulder with burning intensity. Her eyes flew open. She saw the masked figure and screamed like a banshee.

Just about then Julianne Martin, who had decided that maybe the mandolin could be useful in calming the refugees, returned to the camp, heard the mandolin screeching away at "Silver Dagger," and started running.

She saw right off that Gussie was engaged in hand-to-hand combat with a man. At first she didn't see the man's masked face or the knife and mistook the activity for something more intimate and almost said, "Excuse me," and backed out. Then she saw his knife gleam as he tried to wrench it out of Gussie's two-handed grip while her feet were pummeling his midsection like an angry cat's. Juli decided she was not intruding after all.

She had her trusty set of spoons stuck in the pocket of her zip-fronted sweatshirt, and she pulled one out and stuck its handle in the man's back, saying "Drop it, buster," and took the assailant's knife away from him and held that on him too.

"Good—ahuh ahuh—work, kiddo," Gussie said between

coughs as she ripped off her attacker's hockey mask, whipped
the shoelaces out of her sopping wet running shoes and bound
the man's wrists behind him with a trick she had learned from
her early girlhood as a barrel-racing and calf-roping cowgirl.
To Farnham she said, "You're the same bozo who attacked
that Miz Galbraith and tried to kill me down in the Big Bend,
aren't you?"

"You recognized me!" he said with pleasure, and her tying
him up did not seem to bother him none except that he
looked as if he expected her to ask for his autograph.

"I certainly do, you awful man."

"I'm not so awful," he said. "The prison therapist will tell
you—I've had a terrible past."

"Hmph," said Juli. "We'll be glad to give you the opportunity to go back and talk with him about it some more, if you
don't make us incur a lot of negative karma by having to kill
your sorry ass first." She was very angry, and starting to be
very scared, as scared as she had been back at Lucien's. She
felt like the tiger rider of folkloric fame who had managed to
ride the tiger, then realized it wasn't too healthy to try to get
off.

"Oh, you haven't seen anything yet," he said. "I've left
bodies from Nevada to Kansas City, just practicing—and I'll
be out in three to eight years for good behavior, so don't
forget to write and include a forwarding address while I'm in
the pen. I plan to remember you."

He started to toy with them then, because he realized Julianne didn't have a gun, just his knife. Gussie tried to tie his
feet with his own shoelaces, but he kicked his feet around, not
even trying to hurt her, just harassing her.

She smacked his face good for him. "You cut that out,
degenerate," she said, and to Juli, "Give me that knife, honey.
I'll see that he holds still while you gift wrap him."

But he dodged her knife and kept playing with them. Juli
grabbed a foot and Gussie waited for her to start tying, but
suddenly she froze and the killer froze too.

Julianne, touching him, felt the monster in him raging to
get at her and Gussie, bragging about the foul murders it had
done of other women and all that it intended to do. Farnham
looked like a vicious giant-size weasel, wiry, mean, and strong.
The orange glow of the disastrous oil fires cast flickers of
shadow over his face and turned his teeth and eyes red.

He rammed into Juli, knocking her down and dragging her.

Struggling with him, Juli heard the voice of his inner dragon raging, muttering, whispering, shrilling at her as it twisted from her hands, broke her arms free, kicked her with all its might. It gloated inside itself, muttering, "watched her as she floated down." Juli snatched at that clue, and others came tumbling out of the monster's inner workings, "stabbed her with my knife," "took my razor blade and laid him in the shade and started me a graveyard of my own," "been diggin' on your grave the best part of the night."

The knife was lost, but Farnham's fingers were digging into Juli's neck, and her eyes were turned up in their sockets, going back and forth like a typewriter carriage across her partially closed upper lids.

Farnham hunched his shoulder up and knocked the knife from Gussie's hand, getting only a little gash for his trouble, and kicked Juli over backward at the same time that he struggled to his feet and dived out the flap.

Just in time to face the business end of the gun Willie had carried with him from the ranch. " 'Scuse me, mister. I can see you're all tied up. But Mr. Smith and Mr. Wesson and I would like you to join us inside a while longer whilst we figure out what it was you were so anxious to get away from."

After a while, the other refugees, who were mostly in the way of the rescue efforts, came straggling back to camp, and so did a few tired cops. They were able to get a make on Farnham's fingerprints and take him off to jail.

But not before Julianne had changed him forever.

"He's a what?" Willie asked indignantly when she made her pronouncement. "Other than a scurvy-assed, snake-bellied, lizard-tongued etc. etc. puke-faced murderin' bastard."

"A channel," Julianne said. "He sort of goes through in this life what we went through in Scotland with the wizard's magic, except that he's not living through the ballad people—they're living through him. And where you got victimized girls and I got monster-taming heroes, he got murderers. All this stuff he's been saying about his childhood may be unfortunate, but the fact is that every ballad murderer in the history of the U.S. has taken over some part of his personality. Furthermore, I think it's pretty certain that our adversaries are exploiting his misfortune by goading him to kill—"

"Misfortune! Good lord, woman, this character was ready to fillet you and Gussie both, and you sound like you're ready to be a character witness for him."

"Oh, no," she said. "I think he should be put away for the rest of his life. But not before he brings all those occupying souls forward." To Farnham she said, "Now then, we're going to take off your gag in a moment. But first I'm going to sing you some songs, and I want you to listen carefully so you can sing with me when we remove the gag."

And she sang "Pretty Polly" and "The Banks of the Ohio" and "Love Henry" (about a murder*ess* who Farnham, given his prejudice against the female sex, was appalled to find had taken up residence in his skull) and "The Ballad of Omie Wise" and "Tom Dooley" and "Old Reuben" and all the other songs that had spat out at her when she came in contact with the murdering force inside him.

Willie sang with her on some of them, the choruses and such, and when Farnham was ungagged, even though part of him kept thinking how silly this was, he knew these were his songs, and in a way he was perversely pleased so that he hissed them back at her. But something funny happened. With every verse and chorus that he sang, he felt lighter and easier and less as if he had to cut something or explode. It was the most rest he'd gotten since those few times singing on the street blocked out the voices. When he sang his songs, he didn't hear voices and he didn't feel like killing anybody, even women. He released those entities into the air, and they had to fly around out there being songs for a while before they could come back and roost in his head.

As the police hauled him away, he was still singing, and gentle as a lamb, even though the arresting officer was a woman.

Juli grunted with satisfaction the others didn't quite understand, but she knew that she had once more transformed a monster. The man would never be safe to let out of jail, but inside a jail full of other men, instead of a raving murderer, he would be a jailhouse bard and spread a certain kind of very powerful song throughout the penal system and beyond. She dusted her hands and said aloud, "Take that, you devils."

Willie gave her a sideways hug and told her she done good, and she explained to him and to Gussie about how Farnham would carry on the songs now.

Willie nodded gravely. "Well, that's just fine, darlin'."

"Willie, I'm so glad you're, like, getting into believing in spiritual things after our time in Scotland. I've always considered you to be a sensitive," Juli said gravely, taking both of his hands in hers.

"Oh, I am. *High*ly sensitive. And I know that what you say is more than likely true. Either that ol' boy will become a jailhouse bard, just like you say, and have all the other prisoners singin' too in self-defense, or more likely, what with his lack of pitch and him havin' to sing acapulco and all, he ain't gonna be there very long singin' away the way you say he needs to if he's going to feel good, 'cause the rest of the boys'll give him what's comin' to him just to shut him up."

CHAPTER XXVI

▲▲▲

"It sounds to me," Heather-Jon said disdainfully, "as if those women were doing just fine until that guy came swaggering in brandishing his steel-barreled manhood."

"Excuse me, ma'am," Ute said, pulling out a notepad. "You wouldn't happen to be a poet, would you?"

"No, I'm not," she said.

"Could I use that phrase then? Steel-barreled manhood? It goes with a composition I'm working on right now."

"Be my guest."

"Thank you. And as for your remark, well, I imagine Gussie and Juli could have kept Farnham in his place until the cops got back, but he was a dangerous man, and Willie had been feeling useless for a long time. Both of the women knew Willie pretty well, remember, so what's a little steel-barreled manhood among friends?" Only Heather-Jon looked even mildly outraged. Mary Armstrong snickered.

▲▲▲

When the others got back, they were all glad to see Willie, and he was powerfully happy to see them too. He held Lazarus as if it were the Holy Grail and played as he had never played before, he was so glad to feel that magic again. And to have an audience. He borrowed some of Brose's fairy dust and put on just the kind of shows that everybody needed. It pulled some people right out of their sleeping bags where they'd gone to be sick and heartsore. Even Gussie and the others with laryngitis lip-synced the choruses—they were that good. He sang the songs he was best at—his "strong-heart songs," full of hope and courage. "The Mary Ellen Carter" with its chorus exhorting people to "rise again," "Gone, Gonna Rise Again," by John McCutcheon, and so many others, plus all the ballads he could think of that made wonderful stories. Nothing depressing or sad. He put people through their paces, laughing, crying—but only so they could laugh in the next breath—dancing right there in the mud and rain to the songs he and the others played. Brose, Juli, Anna Mae, and the others were all glad for the infusion of energy because theirs was plain tuckered out.

And Gussie thought to herself, "Willie's finally found his real niche. I never saw him so happy. He's being useful. He's treating his music like he's a doctor healin' the sick."

Everybody else felt it too. He was kind and patient with everybody there, and an inspiration to boot. By the time the camp started breakin' up as the rain stopped and people started digging out their homes again, he looked tired and very peaceful.

He handed Lazarus back to Faron saying, "Here, son, you're the mandolin player."

Faron ducked his head and tried to give the mandolin back. "Nah, Willie, Lazarus was given to you, and you're the one who played it. You should have Lazarus Two too."

But Willie declined.

"A deal's a deal. Torchy's kept her end of it, and now, I'm afraid, it's time to keep mine."

▲▲▲

You better believe Torchy appreciated Willie's integrity right about then, because she was on the hot seat.

"I thought you were going to shut him up!" the Chairdevil howled. "The others have been doing enough damage without him, and those blessed songs are spreading like, like—"

"Like me," Plague and Pestilence said in a pleased sort of way.

"Like him," the Chairdevil agreed. "These damned civilians got no sense of decorum either. They sing the songs on their jobs or in the bathroom, and they sing them at home. Lullabies and play-party songs to quiet children are starting to replace child abuse, and instead of firing the incompetent fools like they're supposed to, the bosses are reporting that whistling while they work is actually increasing worker efficiency, particularly with proper soundproofing. Where one of the infected parties goes, there's always someone who used to sing this kind of thing who knows a billion other songs he or she gets 'reminded' of after hearing some amateur yodel his stupid lips off."

"I thought you wiped the songs from memory," Torchy said. "So I don't really see how they can be coming back to people who used to know them without direct contact from my—the vector group."

The Chairdevil looked sly and sneaky. He did it well. It was one of his best looks. "I didn't exactly wipe them—just blocked them, you see. Little mental block. Okay, *big* mental block. Something like, 'look what happens to idiots who sing this kind of stuff. It's bad for your health,' and now there are people wandering around singing at the top of their lungs with apparently complete impunity, and the block dissolves and all that stuff comes pouring out. We messed up on the Turner woman's get and their friends at Triumph music. They've been making home recordings over the telephone with the Curtis and Randolph people and smuggling computer disks. They've been passing these things on to children, to people like this woman who runs a shelter in Seattle. *She* used to know way too many songs, even wrote some, and she infected three-quarters of the city before we knew it.

"That Street Pizza business has caught on too, so now beggars beg by singing. The new Arts and Entertainment section in the Kansas City paper says the new leader of the Street Pizza people, a fellow named Todd, says street singing is a venerable and old Seattle tradition. It's caught on in New York, L.A., San Francisco, Philly, Boston, all the big places, even Washington, D.C. Even the politicians have started re-membering songs from their activist days and are getting principles on us again! Some uppity senator sassed Threedee the other day when he told him to vote against more disaster relief for Tulsa."

"Well, I never!" the Expediency Devil said.

"That senator will never again either, since Threedee of course sicced a crazed assassin on him that very afternoon. But he was singing "Which Side Are You On," with his last breath and his fellow congressmen voted for the bill anyway. Then there's that hit-and-run chanteyman on the coast—Hawkins. He's infected the whole shipping industry again, longshoremen, net menders, fishermen, tourists, cruise directors, anything that floats. I've had Thor too busy in the Midwest to chase him down. With all the music in the air these days, it's hard to track down one fellow anyway. Except for your little friends, DD. Especially MacKai. You promised him to me—"

"I recall our deal," Torchy said. "But you didn't really commit to much. What was it you were going to give me in exchange? Besides freedom from devildom and immunity from persecution in the future?"

"So long as you pay your tithe," the Chairdevil reminded her.

"What tithe?" she wanted to know. "Before, I was paying mortgage on my kingdom, but that's long gone. I want to be free and clear with MacKai gone."

"Fine."

"And I want a place to go—"

"Why, DD, you've had that all along," the Chairdevil said warmly. "I'm afraid there's not much work in your line anymore. Even with these songs back, people are still much too logical and literal and scientific to believe in your kind of nonsense."

"Give me my luck function then," she said. "I'll be Lady Luck."

"Better choice than Mother Nature, dearie-o," said Peewee with a greasy smile.

"You can be Lady Macbeth for all I care," said the Chairdevil. "But not until you produce MacKai. You have until Summer Solstice, and then *your* luck runs out."

▲▲▲

"Summer Solstice," said Mary Armstrong. "Why, that's tomorrow."

"Right you are," Ute said. "And we need your help on a little matter. I want to teach you a song, and then we're going to meet at the stock tank under the cottonwoods at the south fork in the road. There's some people I think you women will want to meet, including a tour group of animal-rights activists."

▲▲▲

"There's something going on with Willie," Julianne told Brose and Gussie the day they were set to leave the Tulsa refugee camp.

"Like what?" Gussie asked.

"Somethin' like indigestion or somethin' like a problem with a woman?" Brose asked.

"I don't know," Juli said. "But haven't you noticed how he's just sort of resigned, and even though everybody loves his music and people have been learning more songs than ever and there have even been some professional offers cropping up—just for him, mind you, not the rest of us—he sort of shrugs it off with a vague smile. I'd think he was happy except . . . well, he's not. And the way he goes around wringing your hand when he talks to you and getting a little teary or hugging a person for no reason at all—"

"Yeah," said Brose. "I did notice that. At first I thought he was just glad to see me, but it's been gettin' embarrassing, to tell you the truth."

"And he's pacing more than ever too. Why, all the grass is completely worn out on the perimeter of the park just from Willie tramping back and forth at all hours," Gussie said. "I wonder what's eating him."

"I wish I knew," Juli said. "I sense that it's something serious—something he's—sparing—us."

Brose shook his head. "It ain't like Willie to spare others. He's a spiller not a sparer."

"Then see if you can get him to spill to you," Juli said earnestly. "And mention it to the others."

But it wasn't to Brose or Gussie that Willie spilled, or even to Juli, the Curtises, or the Randolphs, of whom he was fond. No, when he finally let loose with what was bothering him, it was to Anna Mae Gunn, who aggravated him.

She was packing up and singing under her breath "I Will Go," and that reminded Willie of where he was going, and he began singing louder than she was "Don't Think Twice, It's All Right," and she, being tired and half-mildewed and not the most tractable of women at the best of times, snapped, "I wish I wouldn't sing that. You've been hinting away that you're leaving for some mysterious reason like you think you're better than the rest of us. Well, we did good work without you. And can continue to do so if you just want to keep pissing your life away."

"I never said I was better than you," he said. "And I'm not pissing my life away. But maybe I've found something worth spending it for. Maybe I'll leave you to carry things on and just sort of clear the way for you," he said, and told her the whole deal, finishing with, "Maybe I'll be doomed forever to be a ghost rider in the sky. I'd like that."

"What kind of weird bullshit is that, anyway?" asked Anna Mae. She had a lot of nerve calling anybody else's strange ideas weird bullshit, since as soon as he told her and strolled off into the sunset, she left the compound and picked up the nearest out-of-order—and therefore dead—phone. When she didn't get a dial tone, she said into the receiver, "This is Mae Gunn calling Sam Hawthorne. Sam, you out there?"

And pretty soon there was a click on the other end, and a

sleepy voice said, "Mae. What a surprise. Nice to hear from you. What's up?"

"Sam, I think we're going to need that ghost train again." She briefly explained the situation.

Finally, after hearing her out, Sam said, "Okay, Mae. Here's how to summon it. I think you'd better gather your forces while you're gathering information. As Willie told you, this will take place at Summer Solstice, which is the next magical window. What he didn't tell you is where, so when you figure that out, here's how to create a whistle stop," and he told her.

Anna Mae told the others immediately and finished, "But I'm afraid I ran Willie off, and now we don't know where this sacrifice thing is supposed to take place. I don't even know where he's gone, do you?"

Brose scratched his chin a minute and said, "Well, from a few things he's let drop, I think he's been back to the ranch. Maybe he's gone back there again to say good-bye to the boss and the boys. I'd start my phone callin' there if I was you."

Dally Morales answered and said that no, he hadn't seen Willie, but he hoped he would show up because Dally had a message for him from a fancy redheaded lady from *Bull-Pen* magazine.

Anna Mae said in a soft, grim voice, "Hold it, Dally. This is very important. I want you to tell me everything the woman said and did." He told her about the woman looking at the Appaloosa and calling it an elfin gray and about her lack of interest in their poetry, and Anna Mae said, "If she comes back, try to keep her there. Willie too."

"I'll try to. I might miss 'em. The boys are doin' dude tours right now—activist groups of one kind or another. It's the boss's new profit-making scheme."

"Are your men teaching the dudes any songs?"

"Do buzzards eat dead stuff?" he asked. "Of course they're teaching songs. And telling that story Ms. Turner told us too."

"I'm going to put Gussie on with some more of the story then. It's vital that your men pass this part onto the other people there too. We'll be meeting you at the boss's house on Summer Solstice, and when you hear the story, you'll know why."

Dally heard all Gussie had to say and said, *"Chi*huahua,

Miz Turner, you got us all beat for tellin' a yarn. But sure, we can pass this along."

Anna Mae got back on the phone and sang him one more long song, which he promised he was recording as he listened. She was about to ring off when he said, "I sure want to thank Faron Randolph for invitin' me up to that convention of theirs in Tulsa. I found me a fine golden thread I braided into the new riata I was makin', and it works like a charm."

▲▲▲

Lettie and Mic drove down to Tulsa to meet Gussie and the others, as did some of the contacts from Kansas City and a good quarter of the south-central Native American population. The writer-musicians were there too, but Morgan Richards was staying at a friend's house, where he was dispatching a new virus with the one song that would help Willie's situation.

Finally, the lot of them stood on the corner outside the park, lining the street for a half mile in each direction. "Now what?" Gussie asked.

"Now we sing. And play whatever instruments are handy."

"Sing what?" Faron asked.

"Train songs," she said. "The Wreck of the Old Ninety-seven," "Casey Jones," "Wabash Cannonball," "Rock Island Line," "Freight Train." We just keeping singing and playing all the train songs we know until it shows up. I didn't have to do it the first time, but San Hawthorne says the train would *like* it if we did. Especially now that we've got Lazarus back."

So they sang train songs, three or four of them as the traffic splashed by.

Soon they heard the tires on the pavement take on a new sound. Instead of the squishing and rumbling of individual sets of four soft tires against cement, the sound began to co-alesce into a hard iron noise. The stench of steam and coal filled the moisture-laden air too, and the smell of hot steel. As the crowd sang, "Clickety clack, clickety clack—" on the chorus of one song, their words were echoed by a real clickety clack on the highway in front of them. Then suddenly, from a brief shimmer in the heat waves on the road, a solid steam engine and a line of cars took shape in front of them, and a ghostly voice cried, " 'Bo—oard! All Aboard!"

▲▲▲

The sacrifice was to take place during the darkest part of the night of the longest day of the year. Torchy had already picked out a geomantically correct place for the event to happen— the southwest fork, which had a road to ride in on, one fork symbolizing the way to heaven, the other to hell, and, for old times' sake, a well, symbolized by the stock tank. Except this time there would be no pesky Bird Janet to foul things up. This time there would be no maidens for some song to warn:

> "O, I forbid you, maidens a',
> That wear gold in your hair,
> To come or go by Carterhaugh,
> For young Tam Lin is there."

Willie wasn't all that young, of course. He was on the downhill side of middle age, in fact, though he didn't seem to know it. And maidens didn't last around him very long. But Tam Lin hadn't been real respectful of virgin womanhood either.

> "There's nane that goes by Carterhaugh
> But they leave him a wad,
> Either their rings, or green mantles,
> Or else their maidenhead."

Charming guy, Tam Lin, as well Torchy remembered. The song made him seem like a mugger and a rapist in places, but the truth was, he was like Willie in that he could weasel the birds out of the trees—even birds he would just as soon had stayed perched. Like Janet.

> "Janet has kilted her green kirtle
> A little aboon her knee,
> And she has braided her yellow hair
> A little aboon her bree,
> And she's awa to Carterhaugh
> As fast as she can hie."

Couldn't mind her own damn business, little kingdom wrecker. There were a lot of other verses about her meeting Tam and him telling her to go away and her saying Carterhaugh, which was clearly fairy domain, was hers and her la-di-daddie-da gave it to her. And she plucked her a highly symbolic rose, and then he did what any guy living in ballad times would do and:

> "He's taen her by the milk-white hand
>   And by the grass-green sleeve
>   And laid her low on gude green wood,
>   At her he spierd nae leave.

> "When he had got his wills of her
>   His wills as he had taen"
>   . . . *and his wills weren't the only ones served* . . .
> "He's taen her by the middle sma
>   Set her to feet again."

Well, yes, and she took her own sweet time about it too. Torchy had tried to confound the girl with magicks, but the former fairy queen had reckoned without the mortal contrariness which she now knew so well.

She had also reckoned without an indulgent daddy who didn't immediately kill his baby girl for getting knocked up, and a pragmatic brother who suggested an herb to terminate the pregnancy. That's when the girl went back to Carterhaugh and plucked another rose. Tam Lin could never resist the plucking of a rose, and out he came again to see this blossom about to burst the bud she carried.

An early advocate of Father's Rights, Tam asked Janet,

> "O why pou ye the pile, Janet
>   The pile o the gravil green,
>   For to destroy the bonny bairn
>   That we got us between?

> "O why pou ye the pile, Janet
>   The pile o the gravil gray,
>   For to destroy the bonny bairn
>   That we got in our play?

> "For if it be a knave-bairn
>   He's heir o a' my land
>   But if it be a lass-bairn
>   In red gold she shall gang."

And Janet, the little twit, used emotional blackmail, indicating that it was his affiliation with Faerie that was to blame, not Janet's own round heels.

> "If my love were an earthly man,
>   As he's an elfin rae,
>   I could gang bound, love, for your sake,
>   A twelvemonth and a day."

And Tam had told her how he wasn't an elf knight at all but a man, and then, of course, Janet wanted to know what his lineage was. When Janet got wind that Tam was an earl, *well,* she sympathized with Tam when he told her about the bargain he had made and why. She convinced him to tell her the way to abduct him out of it.

But no, Willie had more reason for keeping his word than Tam, and he was a volunteer, after all.

He came out of the bunkhouse after talking to Dally Morales, ostensibly to buy the horse she meant to send him to hell on but probably also to say good-bye. He strode toward her nodding, and she took his arm and smiled up at him. *"You* won't go and desert me like that last ol' boy, will you now, Willie?"

"Perish the thought, darlin'," Willie said, patting her hand. "I'm a man of my word. I told you I'd help you out, and I will."

And her thoughts turned to their retinue, the creatures who would join them on the ride. And to what she would wear, of course.

▲▲▲

Early in the long bright evening of the longest day of the year, about fifty people milled around the stock tank at the southwest fork, small groups shepherded by cowboy poets. Nobby Watanabe herded a cadre of Amerasian teenagers who had been born in Asia and were now looking for their *other* roots. Then there were the animal-rights activists led by the Swede and glaring at the leather in the boots and saddles, petting the horses, and feeding them freeze-dried carrot chips and apple slices. All current illegal aliens and former illegal aliens and American citizens of Mexican descent currently residing on the ranch formed another group. Finally, trailed by his contingent of ecofeminists, came Ute, formerly known as Steve Guttenberg, rechristened because of his association with the University of Texas, or UT, to something that sounded more poetically cowboyish than merely "Steve."

"I reckon we can start now," Dally Morales said, his voice cutting through a multilingual chatter that could have been literally called Babel. "I'm hopin' you've all been briefed on your songs—"

"Oh, *I* get it," Barbara Harrington-Smith said. "This is a pageant of some sort for our last night. How quaint. What a colossal waste of time."

"Don't be such a spoilsport," Shayla St. Michael hissed. "It might be fun."

"If it's a pageant, I hope somebody brought Cokes and hot dogs," Heather-Jon complained. "I'm so sick of freeze-dried I could puke."

About then the chuck truck drove up with corn bread and chili, and people milled around spooning chili from tin cups and sopping it in the corn bread. The sun finally went down and the moon came up over the stock tank, its reflection yellow and round as a Hi-Ho cracker and growing a little beard of light as its rays skipped across wavelets and the breeze rippled in the scummy water. Across the prairie a steer looked longingly at the tank but didn't want anything to do with all those humans.

The night cooled off, and when almost everyone was finished eating, Dally suggested they start on the song again. He didn't have trouble making himself heard, but the people were harder to herd than stampeding cattle because they were used to the blare of the city. He winked at Ute and Nobby, and they joined him on the tailgate of the truck and said, "Okay, take it from when he tells her what's wrong—"

"You start, Dally," Ute said.

Dally grimaced. His Tex-Mex made the Scottish accent in the song sound kind of funny.

> "Then up she rode, that Elfin Queen
>   And laid her hand on me;
>   And ever since she did I've been
>   Part of her company.
>
> "An' Elfland's such a purty place
>   A darn good place to dwell,
>   But at the end of seven years

> They pay a tithe to hell;
> And I'm so full of flesh and blood
> I'm afraid they'll use myself."

Ute, unwilling to hear the song's lyrics butchered that way, broke in, singing Janet's lines;

> "O tell me, tell me, Tam-a-Line
> O tell me, an' tell me true,
> Tell me this night and make no lie
> What way I'll borrow you?"

Everyone had suddenly turned toward them, and they heard a clickety clack clickety clack, and rising over that, the cry of a mandolin and the words Tam Lin used to tell Janet how to break the spell.

> "On Halloween night
> The elfin court will ride,
> Through England and through all Scotland
> And through the world wide.

> "O they begin at sky setting
> Rides all the evening tide;
> And she that will her true-love borrow
> At Miles-corse will him bide."

The ghost train, at first a noisy speck way off in the distance, grew and grew until they could see the smokestack, but though they could smell the smoke, they saw none. The cattle stared at the train, impervious to it, and walked right through it, though it seemed solid enough when its shining wheels screamed to a halt and the whistle blew and people unloaded from two of the passenger cars.

"I think we better revise some of it," Faron was saying. "How about: This is the Summer Solstice night / And the fairy queen will ride / Through Texas to the Rio Grande / And all the world wide. / O, they begin at sky setting / Ride through the evening tide—"

"Damn!" said Dally. "Is that right?"

"What?" Faron asked.

"That they started at sunset. If so, they're on their way, and we better get this sucker learned and get into position." He whistled a sharp shrill blast and beckoned to Faron, who revised as he went, singing the lyrics:

> "You'll take you to the stock tank
> Between midnight and one
> And fill your hands with holy water
> And cast your compass round."

"We didn't bring any holy water," Ute said.

"All water is holy," Heather-Jon reminded him piously. "It's the blood of the earth."

"So it is," Anna Mae said. "Besides, it's probably a pre-Christian song anyway, and they just added that to please the priests. The compass bit is probably a pentagram drawn for Janet's protection."

"We're s'posed to draw one around *all* of us?" Brose asked. "Hell, Torchy and Willie won't be able to ride within a mile of us if we draw one big enough to cover all of us."

"What does the rest of the song say?" Dally asked.

"Well, it goes on about the fairy court—how there'll be first kings and queens, though I don't know where Torchy's going to find any of those around here, then many maidens, then there'll be grooms and knights and then—"

He sang the appropriate verses. Then Faron and Brose and the others revised them where it seemed absolutely necessary. People grew restless, and Anna Mae sprinkled more fairy dust over Dally and everyone who had been on the train. She wasn't sure that was the thing to do, because somehow it might negate their ability to fight Torchy, but the dust made the rest of the people more attentive, and they muttered lines to themselves and took notes.

Clouds scudded across the moon, ringing it, halving it, flirting like veils across the belly of a Middle Eastern dancer. People looked away every few minutes, down each fork of the road every few minutes.

Dally hushed everyone and lay down with his ear to the ground, then jumped up, brushed his hands on his thighs, and palms down gestured everyone to prostrate themselves and be quiet.

The chuck truck and the other vehicles had been driven a distance away and parked.

The ghost train, one moment seemingly solid iron that had transported a hundred people over several hundred miles, the next moment had faded away like a dollar the day after pay-day.

All the people except Julianne, Brose, Anna Mae, Gussie, Faron, and Dally lay huddled together on the ground. The other six hunkered down against the still-warm side of the water tank, sweat rolling off them as Juli scratched a penta-gram with the toe of her laceless shoe, and they all stepped forward into it and waited.

The first horses to clop by the stock tank were painted pinto ponies, ridden by a feather-and-leather-bedecked In-dian chieftain and his woman, Indians and ponies both trans-parent as the white man's treaty promises. The black tails of the Indian mounts flicked the steam blowing out the noses of the proud arch-necked horses ridden by a black-and-silver-clad grandee with an arrow in his back, and his lady, whose skirts all but covered the horse's body and swept the ground on both sides. None of these people looked to the right or the left, not even when a gasp or two came from the shadows around the stock tank.

Behind them, however, came the rumble of wagon wheels and a team of handsome matched black horses responded with a trot to the whistle and crack of a whip over their heads. A fancy decorated wagon carried a group of laughing, drink-ing, waving wanton women that, if Willie had been paying attention to such things—which for the first time in his life he was too preoccupied to do—he would have recognized as em-ployees of Lulubelle Baker's Petroleum Puncher's Paradise. Not exactly maidens, but definitely female women and most likely unmarried, which was what maiden once meant anyway.

Faron began to play Lazarus II softly and sing. In a whisper other voices joined his. "The next in court that comes to you / Are footmen, grooms, and squires"—he sang as a motley col-lection of cowboys, Indians, and soldiers both Mexican and Texan, some wearing remnants of rebel uniforms from the Civil War, filed solemnly past—"The next in court that comes to you / Are knights, and I'll be there."

And so he was. Willie MacKai rode the boss's finest white thoroughbred and wore a white Stetson hat with a band that held one fine golden star in the front, like something you'd find on a famous actor's dressing-room door.

Faron stood and so did the others, Julianne at the fore-front, Dally nodding to his poets to keep their groups on the right verse.

"I, MacKai, on a milk white steed
  A gold star at my crown
  Because I was a singin' star
  They gave me that renown."

Julianne rose up as the next verse began. She was not in love with Willie, but Janet was the single *female* monster-changer she had been while she inhabited the ballads, and so Julianne figured she was the best woman for the job. Besides, she looked the part.

The singing was quite loud now but was noticed by neither Willie nor Torchy, who wore a Spanish lady's riding habit in glowing green with tinkling bells comprising the silver trim on the bolero and skirt hem and forming a band around the brim of her flat-crowned Spanish riding hat. Like the grandee's lady before her, her skirts swept the ground around her Appaloosa's feet.

"Look," Brose whispered, and Juli spared a look away from Willie. Down the left fork a business-suited man and what looked like a crew of gangsters stood waiting. If they'd been wearing trench coats and the scene had been on a bridge, it would have been something like a spy movie where they changed prisoners at the border. Her head swiveled back to Willie, and while everyone else sang the traditional verse, Faron sang:

"You'll take my horse then by the head
  And let the bridle fall;
  The queen of Elfin she'll cry out
  Willie's gone awa' "

One of the animal-rights activists cried out when Juli touched the horse and scuttled forward to soothe it while Juli pulled Willie—who seemed stoned or something—down from the horse and into her arms. He was a little big for her to handle, so Gussie and Anna Mae and Brose helped her pull him into the pentagram. All of them were sweating rivers, but Willie's skin was as cool as if he'd just stepped out of a freezer, and his eyes stared over their heads.

But though Willie didn't snap out of his trance, Torchy snapped out of hers with a whoop and a holler. "Wait just a blessed minute!" she yelled, not to the people who held Willie but to the dark figures waiting beyond the left-hand fork.

"Are you settin' me up or what? You going to let mortals rob you of your sacrifice? He's a *volunteer,* for heaven sakes. The song says now that I'll turn him into a wolf and a fire, a snake, a deer, and a silken string, and these people are ready for that. Help me out, can't you? This deal is going to do more for you than it will for me."

"Very well," the Chairdevil said. "And no matter what the others do, if the little blond lets go, the deal's off. Come on, team. We'll show her something to really scare her."

CHAPTER XXVII
▲▲▲

The devils didn't even need to consult among themselves to
know what to do. The singers had brought all those people
together, figuring that the more voices they had to raise the
song, the more thwarted the devils would be. But the devils
were smart and were wearing earplugs that night, though
Torchy wasn't, of course.

The magical force generated by the song was greater because it came from more throats. Still, there was no safety in
numbers of mere mortals against that crew of devils. They
concentrated all their power on Julianne Martin and loosed
upon her their most terrible weapon: a projection of literal
reality.

She looked into Willie's staring eyes as the others sang the
verse:

> "Then I'll appear in your arms
> Like a wolf that ne'er would tame."

And suddenly she and he were together after he did a big
concert—she didn't seem to have been singing. And there
were crowds of other women around, and he had eyes and
hands for every single one but her—

> "You hold me fast, don't let me go
> Or we'll never meet again."

Listening to them sing, she could only barely remember
that this was someone she cared about, not some worthless
womanizing chauvinistic macho—

> "Then I'll appear in your arms
> Like the fire that burns saw bold—"

And she was still holding him, but he was burning with
fever, was so thin she found it hard to believe even his bones
could be so small, and stank to high heaven. More horrible,

when she looked at her own strong arms, she saw them shrinking to the bone too, and knew that he had caught some terrible disease and was giving it to her. But if she already caught it, there was no hope for her, was there, and she couldn't abandon him like this no matter—

> "You'll hold me fast, not let me go
> I'll be as cold as iron."

And his face filled out and reddened, and his eyes seemed to bulge with pointless anger, his arms to tighten around her and his hands into bruising fists. She felt her body ache with past blows and her heart break with the lash of humiliating, sarcastic insults he'd just hurled at her.

> "Then I'll appear in your arms
> Like the adder and the snake."

And she would have let go of him then, but Brose and Gussie's grip held her arms fast as they felt her trying to let go, and she remembered it was just her friend, Willie, as the words changed again—

> "You'll hold me fast, not let me go
> I am your own soul's mate."

And he was, of course, just Willie.

> "Then I'll appear in your arms
> Like to the deer so wild"

And he was wild—out drinking and partying and driving fast and being a dear, if not a deer, to everybody in the world but her, and she home and pregnant and having given up her career. Again Brose and Anna Mae and Gussie had to hold her arms around him even after the verse continued:

> "You'll hold me fast, not let me go
> And I'll father your child."

And Juli stared at her swollen belly, thinking, "as if he hasn't already done enough of *that*."

> "And I'll appear in your arms
> Like to a silken string."

And he did—except it was silken threads and him so elegant and dandified while she was barefoot and pregnant at home. With every little favor she wanted, there was a string attached of one more pleasure or privilege she had to give up for him to help her.

> "You hold me fast, don't let me go
> Till you see the fair morning."

Time didn't pass quickly for anyone. Juli suffered through every transformation, and the people on the ground had cramps and mouths full of dust. Gussie's arms had gone to sleep and so had Anna Mae's when Brose said, with relief, "Sky's lighter. That's close enough for me."

And Willie suddenly was just Willie, attired appropriately for skinny-dipping and the chorus in the cacti sang,

> "And I'll appear in your arms
> Like to a naked man
> Dip me into a water strand
> And take me out again."

And they did, and according to another version of the song and for decency's sake, Juli and the others wrapped him up in a blanket. He seemed to see them for the first time and said, "Water's fine. Aren't any of y'all gonna join me?"

But Torchy was having a redheaded fit. She threw down her riding crop and snarled, "Curse you, Willie MacKai. You're no better than that other sorry scamp, and after you volunteered and *promised* to help me! Those devils will take me for sure now, and I'll be lost for good."

Willie shook his head and looked down the road where the devils were catcalling to Torchy, making her horse leap forward while she hung on for dear life.

Willie grabbed for the reins and missed, and Dally Morales shoved something into his hand.

Dropping the blanket and all sense of decorum—which he was never big on anyway—Willie whirled a loop of Dally's riata up in the air and over Torchy's shoulders and lassoed her off her horse just as it cantered down the left fork, pursued by eighteen animal-rights activists who weren't about to let the devils hurt that pretty Appaloosa horse.

Willie reeled Torchy in and hollered, "Keep singin'," and Brose and the others helped him hold fast to the Debauchery Devil as she changed from a quite literal wolf to a fire to a snake the size of an anaconda, to a deer and a silken string, and finally was ready for a dunking, which Anna Mae, Gussie, and Julianne were quite ready to help with.

But they pulled as big a surprise out of the pond as any that had preceded her final transformation. She still had red hair, but it was not the hard-looking fire-engine red it had been, more a shade somewhere between a sunrise and a fox coat. Her teeth were white, her eyes were hazel green with flecks as gold as autumn leaves, and her young white body was covered all over with rusty-looking freckles.

Gussie put it best. "Who the devil are you?" she asked.

CHAPTER XXVIII
▲▲▲

They never exactly found out who she was. She wasn't a devil anymore—all the devils at the left-hand fork disappeared sometime during the dunking, leaving behind the only mortal among them—Hughie Graham, the Man from SWALLOW, busily recording every illegal word of that unlicensed song in his little notebook.

Nobody remembered seeing Torchy leave, though everybody sort of remembered her, and some saw her in their dreams for a long time after.

Willie MacKai, for one. He saw her every once in a while but most often when he felt blue and lonesome. Then he would see that freckled face in his mind for an instant and feel loving arms all around him. He'd smile and learn a new song or tell another story or, sometimes, try to write a song that would bring a smile to that easy-smiling pretty face.

Barbara Harrington-Smith thought she saw something of that face again when she met a younger man, a marine biologist with a sense of humor who told her jokes he claimed dolphins had told him.

And Mary Armstrong had never noticed the girl at all, but she still saw an elvish grin on the face of Ute Guttenberg. Some of the other cowboy poets saw that flash of mystical beauty and quicksilver fun in Mary's face, sometimes, as she wrote humorous cowgirl-poet lyrics there at the ranch and worked on a western novel.

The Amerasian kids left the ranch knowing that the fox woman in the States was a kinder, gentler fox woman than the one in Chinese myth. Her memory helped them excel not only academically, but as singers and storytellers of new and remembered stories and songs from both cultures.

The animal-rights activists who were there that day began winning people over with songs and published stories true and fictional about animals who were friends and individuals and the stories won many more people to their cause.

The Native American people who had come to help Anna Mae remembered the spirits they had seen and particularly the last one—though they remembered her as black-haired and golden-skinned, with snapping black eyes. All of them carried the memory of her laughter back with them and sang to pass it on to the others they knew. This spirit told them and kept telling them inside their heads that they were as good and strong a people as their ancestors even though they lived differently, and they were winning honor in the battle to survive despite great odds. Anna Mae saw in the elfin figure the spirits of her sisters, martyrs, happy and free and no longer bound down by pain, showing her that if she did not let pain make her a slave, she was better equipped to lead others to freedom.

Brose saw those gold-flecked eyes look out of the eyes of the countless kittens and puppies, horses, wolves, deer, and other animals he helped the animal-rights activists save and shelter. He no longer needed one home himself. He was too busy singing animal songs and dance songs and telling stories to children's groups and donors all over the country.

The insurance agent who had been about to stiff the Curtises and the Randolphs only saw what lovely people they were. He not only covered their losses, but paid them several thousand dollars to appear on a television commercial (much to the dismay of the devils, who no longer had such a tight grip on the media with all the new whimsy and the popular demand for the lovely, mystical meaning people were beginning to glimpse flitting from literal truth to literal truth).

And the refugees from the Tulsa camp, they saw the spirit in their mirrors as they remembered pioneer ancestors who had come across the prairie and fought illness and exhaustion and hostility. They recollected how some of those people were descended from the people in the old songs they had heard, who had another kind of strength, and how all that strength had been passed onto them with all those songs and how they could most certainly begin again.

And the Curtises and the Randolphs began to find more people who were like them or wanted to be, and all of their writer friends suddenly had hundreds of good ideas for books and some left over for songs.

Gussie saw a reflection of that spirit—which for all she knew was mostly just part of her very longest story—in the eyes of Lettie and Mic, who were canvassing publishers and recording companies to reproduce lost books and records, leaving traditional material free to public domain.

Julianne, for all her psychic powers, never saw that red-head straight-on again except in dreams she couldn't quite remember. Although the fairy dust had turned to dime-store glitter—pretty and fun but absolutely without power to do anything except reflect light—Juli still felt that new spirit possessing her hands as she played and her voice as she sang. On her pillow in the morning, she found little gifts of observations the spirit had gathered while Juli slept, so that Juli could make songs of them.

The only kind of people the spirit didn't touch and leave a little better were those like the SWALLOW agent, Graham. People say that elfin figure drove him nuts. He would spot a glimpse of her hair or catch the lilt of her voice from some office-building window and chase after her as she tossed the inspirations for one uncontrolled unlicensed song after another like confetti to hungry pickers everywhere. He tried to catch her for her beauty, her voice, her songs that acted on him like a drug. After all, he had once been a lover of music. He followed her all over, tracked down every mention of her, ran so fast after her he finally ended up throwing away his tape recorder and his notebook to lighten his load. One day some kind person told him that she was easy to find if he just went away by himself and sat still for a spell. Last anybody heard, he's still sittin'.

ABOUT THE AUTHOR

ELIZABETH ANN SCARBOROUGH, who won the 1989 Nebula award for *The Healer's War,* a fantasy novel of Vietnam, is not a musician. Though at one time she played guitar and mountain dulcimer in a mediocre fashion, she now confines herself to tapping the keys of her computer to process words. In her spare time, however, she is an avid listener and collector of folk music and an enthusiastic volunteer roadie.

A Special 16-page Preview of
LAST REFUGE, the stunning new
novel by Nebula Award-winning author
Elizabeth Ann Scarborough

---

*Both Mike and Chime have lived their entire lives
in the sacred city of Shambala. Though he is
three years older than she, Chime has always
treated Mike as if he were the younger of the two.
Now Chime, barely eighteen, has decided to em-
bark on a dangerous journey. While everyone else
in Shambala tries to prevent her from leaving,
Mike is the only one who seeks to protect her.*

That's what the meeting had been all about. That's what she was trying to do. She wanted to go investigate those voices. She *knew* they were out there and she had been trying to convince the elders to help her launch an expedition to go find them. Mike suddenly felt extremely ill at ease that she had disappeared from the meeting like that. He didn't suppose for a minute she was lying on her bed crying. In fact, he was very relieved not to spot her in her winter clothing heading for the mountain pass.

His relief faded when he recalled her interest in the new passage under excavation, the passage with the mysterious noises. He remembered suddenly her interest in the stories of tunnels connecting the outside world to Shambala.

He didn't know *what* he was so worried about. She couldn't just take off. Any journey, by any route, would need a little practical preparation. She'd need food, winter clothing, blankets, a flashlight. A flashlight? He clearly remembered leaving his, its solar battery-powered beam gleaming off some object inside the hole. Like a beacon. A beacon for determined but very impractical girls. She could be badly hurt in those passages, alone, with no one to hear her in the dark, and Mike was suddenly convinced that's where she was, winding her way down to the new hole.

He had to catch up with her. He sprinted to the entrance of the old underground compound, grabbed and lit one of the oil lamps kept by the entrance for those who had to go below after the generator was shut down for the day.

He half-ran, half-walked through the twisting corridors, protecting the lamp flame with his cupped hand, past the old offices and the library, past the storerooms and through hallways that were barely navigable paths through piles of junk, down toward the new hole.

He knew the passages well, maze-like as they were, the doors to the library, the old dining room, formerly the reception room for the high lama, the room that was once headquarters for Nyima Wu during the time when Kalapa Compound had been disguised by Wu and the Terton as a prison camp.

His parents had personally uncovered, reinforced, and reclaimed most of the rooms on the lower level and he felt in some ways as if he now moved like a blood corpuscle through the veins and arteries of some larger sibling of his.

He had only been down here once or twice at night, after the chug of the generator stilled for the day. He thought of his mother's journals, how it must have been for her, kept alone in a cell here during the first part of her stay, not knowing she was pregnant and losing a baby, seeing the walls breathe, hearing voices in the generator during the day, voices from the walls at night, chanting.

He listened closely but all he could hear was the fall of his own sandals on the stone-tiled floor, the settling of the earth, the scurry of a rat, his own breathing, very loud.

And then his breathing was offset just a half a beat by other, deeper breathing that emerged in a half-pant, half groan—more than one breath, more than one person. And his own hurried footsteps were counterpointed, as he turned the corner, by the rapid slap of other sandals on the tiles up ahead of him. He knew it was Chime Cincinnati. He knew it was.

She was coming back to the hole because somehow she thought it had something to do with the voices she heard, the babies she said had no souls and the sudden compulsion she had to leave Shambala.

He quickened his steps, half running down the long twisting corridors leading downward and ever more downward. How could she so unerringly be heading for the place he and his father had just discovered?

His lamp illuminated only a small circle of light, within which his shadow jigged, grew and shrank, but in less time than he would have believed possible, he saw another light ahead of him.

Chime, her back to him, poked her front half through the ragged hole which was now two feet wide by three feet wide.

"Chime Cincinnati!" he shouted to her. "Stop! Don't go in there. It's very dangerous."

His shout delayed her while she twisted and smiled at him, her smile unearthly in the combined glow of her lamp and the beam of his flashlight. He closed the distance between them. He had never seen her this way before. She practically vibrated with excitement, the veins pulsing in her small dark throat beneath the wild black ringlets.

"It's not dangerous," she argued, not bothering to offer any logical support for her words but turning away from him to hitch herself up into the opening. He grabbed for her but before he could get a grip on her, she had hoisted her hips through the hole, slipped her legs in after, and walked over to the glittering object the flashlight illuminated. Her own oil lamp she had left behind on the outside of the hole when she climbed in and now he retrieved his flashlight from the place where it was wedged and switched it off.

"Meekay, please turn it back on," she said.

"Come out of there, Chime. I have an idea what you're up to and you're crazy. It's very dangerous in there and I won't be a party to it. Come out. You'll hurt yourself there in the dark."

"Meekay, stop being difficult and trying to sound like my father," she said then wheedled, "Please, let me have the flashlight for a moment. Oh! Look there! I think I've found a golden prayer wheel. It's a guide of some kind. I remember this now."

She was just trying to tempt him with something she knew he would love to find and show to his father. He knew that, but he shone the light inside the hole anyway. Maybe she'd come out once she had a chance to look. Anyway, he'd have to carry her back up to the top if she fell and hurt herself in the dark.

He waited a few moments while she poked and prodded, investigated everything within the range of the oil lamp he extended into the hole. His breathing had quieted now and the roar he had heard from the hole before was louder than it had been during the day. It came from far off inside the hole. This was no single room or short abandoned passageway, judging from the roar and its echos.

He couldn't see much but she seemed delighted with what she saw inside the hole. "Chime, it's time to go now," he said after a while.

She turned around grinning affectionately at him, but he saw that she was trembling with some strong emotion and her black eyes were wet, the tears leaving shining tracks on her dark cheeks.

"I'm sorry but I can't come back with you, Meekay," she said. "I always knew you would be the key somehow and you were. You found this place, this portal and it's time to go now."

And with that, she left the hole and disappeared into the darkness.

What could he do? No one would hear him if he yelled and if he ran for help, she would go further forward. She had no supplies with her, no protective gear, not even a coat, and whatever powers she thought she had, she was just one girl. She wasn't even very good at martial arts, to the disappointment of her father. Too spiritual, too cerebral, too inwardly focused, her mother said. Her father said she had her head up her ass a lot.

Mike could have kicked himself. He should have turned on the generator, he should have gone for help, but he had only suspected, he hadn't really known. And now she was retreating deeper into the hole.

She was going to do it. She was going to defy everybody and leave Shambala. Maybe she was right about this hole because her former selves told her, as she claimed they could, or maybe she'd just found old blueprints or something. But she was nuts enough to try it. Damn her. What a dumb idea. Shambala was safe and warm, even in the winter, with friends and family and food and shelter. He definitely didn't want to leave all that. He wasn't afraid of what was in the hole, not really. Fear wasn't what he was feeling at all. He was just angry at her for forcing him to leave when he didn't want to.

But he knew he had to follow her. Without even a flashlight, she'd be lost down here. His father said these lower tunnels had so many twists and turns you could stay down here for months and never cross the same path twice. If he left her now, no matter what she *intended* to do, she'd be hopelessly lost. He pocketed his flashlight and set his oil lamp down. There was no time to go back for food or even a sweater, but maybe he could catch up with her, maybe he could bring her back and get her to at least wait until she was better prepared.

"Chime! Chime Cincinnati, you stop right there and wait for me!" he cried, climbing through the hole. "Wait, Chime, I'm bringing the light! Wait for me!"

*   *   *

Chime Cincinnati plunged ahead of Mike, her upper half groping in darkness as absolute as if a bag had been thrust over her head, her hands stretching out in front of her so she wouldn't accidentally walk into anything. Her faith that this was the right course of action was justified not by her head, but by her feet, which walked resolutely forward as if they were possessed of knowledge the rest of her was not privy to. That was the trouble with having so many former incarnations. The former selves tended to get overzealous at times and start directing parts of her body to do things without consulting with her current personality first.

The part of her that was a girl just turned eighteen leaving behind everything and everyone she knew had many trepidations about this path she now followed, but the bodhisattva she had been for several past generations exalted.

To that part, the portion of her being that had been and was becoming again the Terton, her current life to date had been rather like a tedious extended holiday where she was always tolerated as a guest but had no useful work to do. Her work was just beginning again and she knew that however frightening it was, however hazardous, it would be absolute necessary for the sake of the world.

Lobsang Taring knew what she must do but he had not been able to help her this time. No, that was wrong. He and his son had found this portal for her, so once more Taring had enabled her in her role as the Terton as he had when she was Ama-La and several incarnations prior to that one.

Meanwhile she had worked and studied even though no one but Taring, who had forgotten much of his early training, had ever been learned enough to instruct her in even the most elementary skills necessary to the fulfillment of her own dharma. She could only use the books of her past incarnation and hope that she was learning the things she needed to know.

Sometimes, when she slept or her mind drifted, she became aware that she was visualizing herself performing tasks and rituals with which she was totally unfamiliar. She knew at those times that such dreams were manifestations of her former selves trying to instruct her present body, but as soon as she tried to pay attention, the lesson dissolved. Meditation had always been difficult for this present restless young body, which would have preferred to be admired by young men, to dance, to plan the names and faces of children she doubted she would ever find time to bear. Lobsand Taring said she was no less learned or earnest than she had been in former lives, and he ought to know.

But only sometimes did she gain access to a piece of the secret that was her inner self. Like now, when her feet carried her as surely as if they knew what she was doing, though all of her other senses were useless.

The old soul within her told her young mind to stop dwelling on its past concerns, which were behind her, to be quiet now and follow where her feet led her. Her shoulders straightened and fell somewhat, letting her hands dangle by her sides and her neck relax as her knees, ankles, and feet carried her down the maze of corridors. A sense of calm, even of happiness, flowed like honey over the knives of her fears.

*   *   *

Mike, larger than Chime, stumbled over objects in his path, almost sprawling headlong as he tried to race after her, hollering to her, listening for replies, and clutching his flashlight in one hand. He scrambled, climbed up and over and down obstacles until he totally lost track of how long he had been away or how far he had come. Once he had looked behind him briefly and felt a jolt of panic when he found he could no longer see the light of his oil lamp shining through the entrance hole.

Maybe he should start unraveling his clothes and leaving a trail for himself of the threads, except that he'd never be able to see well enought to pick out the thread. Even if he did, thread was so fine it would break and he would never find it with only his flashlight beam.

He called to Chime over and over, cringing a little at the sound of his own voice being swallowed by the roaring darkness, thinking of the stories of the great mining disasters his father liked to tell. But if the tunnels hadn't already collapsed from the noise pounding through them already, they certainly wouldn't succumb to his puny little human raised voice and maybe, if he was close enough, Chime would hear him and wait.

At first the footing was made difficult by fallen debris, collapsed timbers, articles of furniture strewn across the passage but after awhile, he entered corridors which were less damaged and the walking was easier. He could see by his flashlight that these passages were merely the continuation of all of the other long, downward sloping hallways he and his parents had already excavated. Those passages were honeycombed with rooms, many of them storage rooms for useful things, so perhaps these were too. Sure enough, as he shone the thin pale beam to one side and then the other, he saw the darkened holes on either side of the hallway, and, telling himself Chime could be hiding in one of them, allowed himself a few seconds to explore each one. He found another room like the one on the upper levels which bulged with seed packets, but the other rooms were empty.

He imagined starving to death though so far he wasn't even hungry. Had it really been such a short time ago that he sat in warm and well-lit dining hall digesting his dinner while listening to the elders argue?

The farther down the corridor he traveled, the more pervasive grew the roaring until it became a barrier against which he must push, its sound overpowering every other sensation so that he almost did not feel his feet hit the floor or his hand hold the flashlight. His voice had stopped crying Chime's name of its own volition and only his eyes kept staring at the darkness unwinding before him until suddenly he found that the darkness was a solid wall in front of him and he had reached the end of the corridor.

For just a moment, he felt trapped and then it was the roaring that saved him. He had yet to reach its source, so he knew he could not have reached the end of his journey. Besides, Chime had to be ahead of him somewhere. He moved his light a little to the left and saw that he had been standing too one side of a pair of huge doors. He leaned against them and they swung open with surprising ease, responding to his first touch.

On the other side of the doors, his eyes and nose discovered the source of the roaring noise. His nose filled with the heavy smell of wetness that suddenly dewed his skin and dampened the tip of his tongue with a sweet familiar mineral taste. His flashlight beam struck sparks of purple, ruby, green and another irridescence to which he could put no name from geode-inlaid tile and crystalline walls along which flowed a surging underground river. Just as it reached the wall with the double doors, the river bent into sheer rock and vanished. This, he realized, must be the source of "the jewel in the eye of the lotus" that was the sacred lake of Shambala.

The cavern was so immense that Mike's flashlight beam could not find the ceiling. He was inspecting the walls, gazing around him, and did not see the piece of golden statuary until he banged into it with his shins and let out a yelp, the noise instantly swallowed by the river's voice. He bent to examine the object, his flashlight picking up the valleys and brazen highlights of the design. It bore no dust, no doubt thanks to the humidity from the river water, but more amazingly, neither was it tarnished or moldy. The design was of a circle on a pedestal, and in the center of the pedestal the Rin-chen gDugs, the Precious Parasol—his father had dug up several other examples of this first of the Eight Auspicious Symbols once used as altar bronzes throughout Shambala. This one was knee high, the parasol in the middle looking something like a chafing dish with ornamental carving and a knob on the top of the lid, with ribbons twirling around the base. Mike forgot about Chime for a moment, thinking how pleased his father would be at this discovery. His father had taught him the meaning of the symbols too. The parasol was supposed to give protection from evil.

He gave it a pat and walked on more carefully, watching the path ahead of him, and thus avoided more bruises when he came upon gSer-gyi Nya, the Two Golden Fish, in outer design similar to the parasol but within the circle two fish bumped noses. The fish were supposed to be symbolic of beings saved from the ocean of earthly suffering, his father said. That sounded good too, which Mike supposed was why these were called the *auspicious* symboles.

They were Buddhist symbols, as Mike's father had at one time been a Buddhist lama or teacher, though Buddhism was practiced by very few of the residents of Kalapa. Too many people had lived too long under the materialism of the PRC.

Why had the ancients placed these symbols along the river, so far from the main part of the city? He shone his light across the water and noticed for the first time that the wall on the other side of the river was lined with alcoves. Holding his arm straight in front of him, he probed the alcove with the flashlight beam. He almost dropped his light into the water when he saw the form of someone seated in lotus position just above the water level. He decided that's what the auspicious symbols were for, to mark the area containing these statues.

On the other side of this alcove was another, and another statue, but this one slumped a little, the head tilted forward and slightly away from the direction Mike had come. Mike banged into the third altar bronze, the gTer-chen-phoi Bum-pa or Vase of Golden Treasures, said to contain spiritual jewels, as he walked upstream to view the third alcove and the third statue.

This statue slumped too, and his flashlight beam picked up the gleam of an eye. Mike realized suddenly that the figures in the alcoves weren't statues at all, but life-sized human bodies wrapped with gilded bandages. Mummies, then such as the Egyptians once made. His father had told him that sometimes the great lamas were mummified too. Why were they kept in here, where it was so damp? Maybe the mummies were too holy to rot.

Mike's eyes began playing tricks on him, the little penlight bounding off the tumbling waters sending shadows dancing across the face of the mummy, so that the bandages seemed to part in a grin.

Mike walked on so quickly that he barely dodged the Padma bZang-po, the Excellent Lotus Flower, emblem of original purity.

He crossed the corridor away from the statuary. He had to find Chime and although the auspicious symbols and the statues were interesting, the wet from the river was soaking through his clothing, the statues gave him the creeps, and it wouldn't be the least bit auspicious if he fell over one of the symbols and broke his leg or his neck.

"Chime!" he hollered with more force than ever before. He did not see the ceiling lower, but he felt its pressure against his head. Eventually he had to turn his face to take the last breath before the water closed chillingly over his scalp and swallowed him whole.

Gagging as he sucked water into his lungs, he couldn't even scream as the whirling waters dragged him, not further down, but up into a luminous blue vortex.

Elizabeth Ann Scarborough's novel *Nothing Sacred*, is a moving tale set in a sacred Tibetan city disguised as a prison camp. In the sequel, *Last Refuge*, it is twenty years after the nuclear explosions which wracked the world. The children of the camp's one-time prisoners decide it is time to explore what has survived outside. By the Nebula Award-winning author of *The Healer's War*, this new novel plumbs the depths of the human soul as it examines the spirituality in us all.

Read *Last Refuge* on sale in August 1992, wherever Bantam Spectra Books are sold.

The Masterworks of
Elizabeth Ann Scarborough

Nothing Sacred

Shot down over the Tibetan Himalayas during a war
that neither side can win, Viveka Jeng Vanachek is a
prisoner lost in the no-man's land between battle-
fields. Captured, she survives cruel treatment only
to arrive at a hidden prisoner-of-war camp where she
is faced not only with torture but with ancient ruins,
weirdly beautiful dreams, and mysteries that only
the heat of nuclear fire can burn away.
"A powerful story."
—Minneapolis Star-Tribune

The Healer's War
Winner of the Nebula Award

Kitty McCulley's hopes as an Army nurse in Vietnam
were dashed by the realities of war. In a warzone,
there's little time for real compassion or true healing.
It all changes, however, when Kitty is given a
magical amulet by one of her patients, a dying
Vietnamese holy man. Now she sees things no one
else around her perceives, and can heal even the
near-dead. The question is, when faced with the
ultimate threat to her own survival, can she use
these powers to save herself?
"Scarborough writes powerfully and
convincingly of the war."
—Kirkus

Look for the works of Elizabeth Ann
Scarborough on sale now wherever
Bantam Spectra Books are sold.

AN 372 12/91

ABOUT THE AUTHOR

DAVID EDDINGS was born in Spokane, Washington, in 1931 and was raised in the Puget Sound area north of Seattle. He received a Bachelor of Arts degree from Reed College in Portland, Oregon, in 1954 and a Master of Arts degree from the University of Washington in 1961. He has served in the United States Army, worked as a buyer for the Boeing Company, has been a grocery clerk, and has taught English. He has lived in many parts of the United States.

His first novel, *High Hunt* (published by Putnam in 1973), was a contemporary adventure story. The field of fantasy has always been of interest to him, however, and he turned to *The Belgariad* in an effort to develop certain technical and philosophical ideas concerning that genre.

Eddings currently resides with his wife, Leigh, in the Southwest.